HOWARD STREET

NATHAN C. HEARD

D1313339

First published in Great Britain in 1998 by Payback Press,
an imprint of Canongate Books Ltd,
14 High Street, Edinburgh EH1 1TE

10 9 8 7 6 5 4 3 2 1

British Library Cataloguing in Publication Data

A catalogue record for this book is available on
request from the British Library

ISBN 0 86241 764 3

Typeset in Minion and Serif Modular by
Palimpsest Book Production Limited,
Polmont, Stirlingshire
Printed and bound in Great Britain by
Caledonian International Book Manufacturing Ltd,
Bishopbriggs, Scotland

HOWARD STREET

Part One

A man can't fool with the Golden Rule
in a crowd that don't play fair . . .

'The Tropics,' *a doggerel hip poem*
(AUTHOR UNKNOWN)

One

She pulled his head down and pressed their cheeks together so she wouldn't have to look at him. His time was up. He was lasting longer than most. Now she quickened the grinding motion of her body, catching him off-stroke and making him speed up his own motion in an attempt to keep the rhythm smooth. The maneuver worked; he grunted, his breath wheezed past her ear and into it with tense harshness. His whole body stiffened, frenetically aquiver. He pushed down hard upon her, as if to drive her through the bed. His forearms were braced under her armpits, his hands gripped her shoulders like two steel traps.

Again he grunted and murmured something incoherent as his thick lips slobbered greedily at her neck.

'Yeah, baby,' she cooed softly but without any real feeling. 'Come, honey, come to momma.'

Her eyes roamed over the drab ceiling. She meditated absently for a few moments upon the broken-lined veins of cracked plaster and old peeling paint, wondering why Sue didn't at least give the place a cheap paint job. It certainly wasn't because she couldn't afford it; no, Sue had the money all right. But what the hell, she thought, she didn't come here for decoration anyway. It had a bed, that was all she needed.

The man finally lay still, his breathing subsided to almost normal. She pushed at his shoulders and he began to raise himself slowly, reluctantly. Then, suddenly, he jumped up very quickly and stood beside the bed looking down at her. She forced a smile of what she hoped was dreamy satisfaction and crossed her legs at the thighs. He didn't seem the type to go for a terse, businesslike attitude, she'd guessed.

In the dim light of the room his tree-trunk of a body glistened with a slight film of sweat. He was very black, one of the blackest men she'd ever seen. His head was clean-shaven, and an ugly scar, beginning at his temple, zipped its way down the left side of his face to lose itself under the curve of his jutted chin. She could tell that it was an old scar, but it still looked raw: a reddish-brown stripe in his negritude. He stared down at her until she began to feel uneasy, a little afraid even. He was so big! His look seemed to become a glare and her stomach knotted with anxiety. The saliva glands in her mouth became overactive and she had a hard time swallowing. She thought that he must surely be able to hear the gulp that sounded so loud in her own ears. What was the matter with him? she wondered, but she couldn't figure it out.

Bigger and blacker he seemed to loom above her. She could smell his odor drying on her now. The pungent smell of years of sex activity seemed to take this opportunity to restir itself within the room. The residue of hundreds, perhaps thousands, of couples, triples, and quintuples came extravagantly alive: lost and unlamented orgasms: and many of them due directly to her.

She wanted to go and wash away his odor, to wash away all the odors of a long year of prostitution. The stink felt as stuck to her as a barrel of feathers poured over molasses. And still he stood over her menacingly, held her captive without a word to indicate such. She thought of Hip with a fleeting moment of relief. He knew how long it usually took her to turn a trick – and he needed a fix, so he'd be along directly.

The big john finally moved – quickly to put on his work cover-alls – then promptly took up his silent vigil again. The dim light and his darkness made it extremely hard for her to make out his features. The whites of his eyes and the lividity of the scar stood out more than anything else, except the impressive hugeness of him.

His large lips were moving now, or shaking; she couldn't make out words; his breathing, a low, animal growling, was the only sound in the room. She wondered if he were insane and going to kill her. She offered up a quick, silent prayer and waited, all her senses keenly alert. Then the growl carried his harsh words, which, strangely enough, released the tension in her a little.

'Bitch, gimme my money back,' he demanded. Though his voice seemed normal enough to him, to her it was extremely loud, and she flinched. She almost reached into her brassiere to give him his ten dollars back. But long months of mud-stomping prostitution caused her to hesitate. Hustled money was harder to let go of than money legitimately earned.

She thought of trying to run past him, but there were three locks on the door and she couldn't possibly unlock them all before he caught her. And even if she could somehow manage it she still would have to leave her skirt and shoes behind. The other whores would ridicule her up and down Howard Street if she let a trick run her bare-assed out into the night. The only underclothing she'd worn tonight was her bra. The same thing had happened to Sadie Tucker about ten years ago, she'd heard, and the bitches still laughed about it. No . . . she couldn't take that humiliation.

The man shifted impatiently. She asked soothingly, 'What's the matter, big daddy, didn't you dig it?' She tried to smile and was glad of the dim light, because she knew that her smile looked more like a begging plea than a pleasant compromise.

'Whore' – he pronounced it 'Ho' – 'I said gimme my money back, and that's what I meant!'

'Look, honey, now be nice. Don't make trouble, huh? Like, I don't want no trouble. I'm tired, y'know?' Where was that dopefiend bastard, Hip! She cursed him mutely.

Then, before she realized what had happened, the man moved with incredible speed. His big hand shot out, clamped on her ankle like a vise, and she was suspended upside down with just her shoulders, the back of her head, and her neck touching the bed. Her free leg thrashed wildly around; she gave a little cry and tried to kick him. A close-mouthed laugh rumbled deep in his throat, his free hand groped roughly at her vaginal area.

She was too surprised to scream, and when she thought to do so she was checked by the fear of death from the man, who might panic; of the cops, who, if they came, would lock her up; and of Sue, who maintained that her house would be orderly and quiet. Sadie Tucker couldn't get a room because she'd brought the cops down on Sue ten years ago by trying to get the john who'd run her out into the street naked arrested for assault. Instead, Sue had been arrested for running a disorderly house, and Sadie, for prostitution. The john had gone free with a boot in the behind. Sue never let Sadie have another room – to pay her money out finished their relationship. Now most of Sadie's tricks were car tricks.

The big paw fumbled at her. If she cried out he might kill her. His hand finally snatched away from between her thighs, and she barely stifled the acute agony her vocal cords strained to release. Then he flung her disdainfully back on the bed. A terrible smile played around his yellow teeth.

'There, you stinkin' whore!' he roared. Triumphantly he held up a spongy object designed to look and function like a real female genital. He held it delicately between thumb and forefinger. 'You musta thought I was a real lame, pullin' some cold shit like this on me, huh?'

She sat up on the side of the bed looking comically disheveled and gently rubbing her fingers over her crotch. Pain had made tears spring into her eyes, but her fear, in spite of herself, was turning to defiance.

'What's the difference, man?' she said. 'You got a nut, didn't you? Ain't that what you paid for?' She was angry at herself for getting caught, but she hated him for catching her. She attempted to get up, and he pushed her violently back on the bed and threw the contraption at her. It smacked against her forehead and stuck there. Her eyes widened in astonishment, her mouth dropped open. Then she shook her head fiercely until the thing fell off, leaving a viscid splotch. She grabbed a handful of sheet and rubbed furiously at it.

He took a step toward her and warned, 'Now woman, I'm askin' you nice one more time to gimme my money back – else I'm gon' break both yo' legs right goddamn here and now.' Indignantly he added: 'Man work hard all week long, he don't dig nobody beatin' him.'

She looked up at him. 'I'm makin' a livin' too, you know. You gon' blame a girl for trying to make it easy as she can? Don't you try to make your work easier for you?' Her voice changed tones, it became pleading, with lady-in-distress signals oozing sensuality. But she knew the attempt would be futile, because few men were sympathetic after orgasm, and especially if it was a dupe.

'Don't take my money, mister. I got five kids and no man . . .' She cursed Hip vehemently, then immediately felt her body tremble with elation as his shrill whistle came from three flights below. It meant he would be waiting in the hallway for her.

To the big man it was just another sound among the myriad sounds of a transit house. Rooms were constantly being filled and vacated; anything might be heard at any time.

'Yeah,' he said, 'I try t'make my work easy, but goddammit, I give people what they pay for, too. When I pays for pussy I don't feature doin' it to no sponge. And I don't believe you got no five kids, neither, but if you do that's your red wagon, you fucked for 'em. Now git my money up!'

She sighed: 'Okay, baby, be cool.' He let her up to put her skirt and shoes on while he finished lacing his brogans.

Along with her money, she also kept her switchblade in her brassiere – and he was half-turned away from her. Her fingers played over the handle, her pinkie touched the button. She never opened her blade by pressing the button with her thumb, but rather with her pinkie, so that it opened in stab position. No time would have to be wasted in turning it around. Speed was the thing.

Watching the man's tremendously broad back, however, his Herculean shoulders, and what must have been a twenty-inch neck, she faltered, unsure whether her blade along with her suddenly inadequate one hundred and twenty pounds could really hurt this huge piece of granite – two hundred and fifty, at least – which she'd felt lying on top of her.

Then he stood, and it seemed that he'd never stop going up, with his hand outstretched toward her; fingers splayed, slightly curled. His thumb looked as big as her wrist.

'What kinda work you do, honey?' she asked, still fingering inside the bra. Should she try him? He was standing pretty close; she could hit him before he knew it.

'Handle scrap iron,' he boomed at her with gruff pride.

Her hand arched gracefully out of her bra and she put a ten-dollar bill into his waiting paw. Almost by way of apology she said, 'You can't get the two back, I had to pay for the room.'

He smiled his yellow smile again, took out a large roll of bills, and tenderly wrapped the ten onto it. She grew a little less tense as she unlocked the locks. 'Listen, how'd you know?' she asked. 'I been spongin' tricks for six months now, and you was the first one to dig.' She wanted to know her mistake so as not to make it again.

His smile was full of mystery and pride; and he wasn't about to tell her the truth: that it was the habitual look he'd taken, for the extra thrill of seeing himself emerge from a woman's body, which had tipped him. Actually, all the while he'd been thinking that she was one of the best he'd ever had. But she hadn't counted on him looking down to see what he'd been doing it to. He said, boastfully, 'Woman, I ain't no stranger to buyin' pussy. I been in enough of 'em to know. I been all over the world, 'cross seas, too. I been to Europe, Asia, Africa, and I know when a pussy's real and when it ain't.'

She didn't believe him. No man could tell just by feeling. All the old-time whores said that. She came to the conclusion that he somehow must've seen it, that she wasn't as careful as she should have been. But there was one sure remedy for that: she'd ask Sue to get her one of the kind that goes inside.

Downstairs in the hallway Hip waited impatiently for Gypsy Pearl to finish with the trick. He'd be needing another fix soon. She seemed to be taking longer with that big john than she usually did. He'd give her ten minutes more; Sue would raise holy hell if he whistled again. Her and her damned 'orderly house' business were a pain in the ass. Few more minutes and he'd go and see what was taking Gypsy Pearl so long . . .

Five minutes. That woman knew he hadn't got off since six this evening, and it was close to eleven now. She'd better hurry up with that money – if he had to go get that bitch he'd stomp a mudhole in her – probably up there getting her kicks along with that john; probably even took her sponge off for him. She'd always been partial to big guys, anyway. A cat had to watch these Howard Street whores carefully; they pulled some funny money now and then.

Hip felt himself beginning to sweat, just a little bit, not enough to stain the thin short-sleeved white shirt he wore. But this, along with the slight pinch of nausea circulating in his stomach, told him that he'd have to cop some stuff soon, or almost die.

He was a big man, or rather, he had been a big man once, before he started using dope. Now he was a six-foot-three-inch frame, gaunt and asthenic-looking. Someone had jokingly observed recently that he had to put apples in his mouth to fill out his cheeks enough for him to shave.

His appearance notwithstanding, he wasn't a physically weak man; not as strong as he'd been when he first ventured onto Howard Street, and drugs, but still, no weakling. This he proved by his ability to take money from the johns who came to Howard Street. A lot of them were very strong men, workhorses of industry and day labor; but there had been only one time when he'd failed to relieve one of them of the paycheck intended for partying – and that was because the man had carried a gun along with his money. Usually Hip knocked them out easily, many times with one punch; and he seldom had to pull his blade. Robbing by fist was more fun anyway. Sometimes he got a damned good fight. It felt so fine afterwards when he'd won and the paper was in his pocket.

His fistic prowess had helped him to pull Gypsy Pearl away from Red Shirt Charlie. That had been one *mean* battle. That fight was one of the most memorable events of his twenty-six years. Red Shirt had been good – but he had been better. And he'd been a mild sensation even before that, too, before they'd gotten used to him. The chicks had dug him because he had been so handsome, a prerequisite of a pimp for many of the whores. He'd had an enticing nut-brown complexion, with coal black eyes that seemed to pierce whatever he looked at. Now his skin was sallow, its sheen completely gone, and his eyes were evasive rather than bold. His hair had been stiff and close-cut but now was nappy and unattended; he sometimes went for months without getting a haircut. His nose was still the same:

not too big or flat. And it set above full lips that were very nicely molded. His teeth were still pearly, but now one of the front ones was missing, and in the back decay was very evident. He'd been through hell since coming to Howard Street, and he looked it. Now he was the same as any of the rest of its people and was looked upon with the same indifference they showed toward everything else.

If Gypsy Pearl didn't hurry up he'd be too weak to off that big trick. He had to take a leak, too. If he asked Sue to use her bathroom she'd want to charge him. He could go into one of the bars, but then he might miss Gypsy Pearl and the john when they came down. He cursed; he had to go badly. He began to sway rhythmically from side to side like a small child, and finally said, 'To hell with this!' He walked to the back of the hallway, cursing dope for his plight. Sometimes he could hardly go two hours without his bladder threatening to burst wide open.

Under the stairwell he gratefully relieved himself. Some of it splashed through his mesh-top shoes. A whore and a trick came into the hallway just as he finished. He didn't want them to see him because the whore would most certainly tell Sue, who'd have a fit on him. The bitches went to extremes to stay tight with Sue.

He stepped further back under the stairwell and was immediately sorry for it – he'd forgotten about the hole in his right sole.

As the couple went upstairs he heard them greet someone and recognized Gypsy Pearl's voice. The women spoke to each other with the prostitute's classic show of affection and gaiety; the men mumbled softly, in the demure manner of the universal, eternal trick.

Hip went quickly to his post outside, beside the five-stepped stoop, and lit a cigarette. The game he and Gypsy Pearl used was probably as old as the profession itself: he would play the jealous lover or husband, then, faking anger at her infidelity, he'd pick a fight with the man – usually by throwing a Sunday punch. A real good punch most of the time takes all of the fight out of a man even if it doesn't knock him out. The tricks, not wanting trouble anyway, gave up their money willingly most of the time, and, knowing Howard Street's reputation, were glad to get away with their lives. Assault and murder on Howard Street was seldom prosecuted except by the unwritten law of the lye can, switchblade, and sometimes, the gun. There were, of course, teenage gangs who roamed about mugging and rolling drunks, and it was they who painted on the side of buildings: *Tricks and Lames, Beware* in glaring white letters. But the real threat lay with the adults.

Gypsy Pearl and the john stepped out onto the stoop, and before Hip could go into his act she said, quite phlegmatically, 'He took his money back, daddy.'

Surprise flitted across Hip's face for a moment, but he was immediately gladdened by the now legitimate excuse he had to take the man's money. He put one hand in his pocket and said, 'Why you go there on my woman, man? You don't be takin' advantage of her like that. Gimme the bread back. And just 'cause you's a wise guy, gimme yours, too.'

He made a vague attempt to move in closer and met with a smashing right hand. It caught him in the center of the forehead and sent him skidding on his back to the curb, knocking over garbage cans and landing halfway under a parked car. The man had literally dived from the stoop, and all of his two hundred and fifty pounds was behind the blow.

Gypsy Pearl screamed, 'Oh! You black bastard! Don't hit my man!'

The man paid no attention to her and grabbed Hip by the belt, pulling him from under the car. People, hearing the loud rattle of the garbage cans and Gypsy Pearl's screams, came out of the bars to see what was going on.

A bleeding crucifix marked Hip's forehead. He wasn't completely out, but his eyes were glazed, and it was easy to see that he didn't know up from down at that moment. Gypsy Pearl's hand blurred to her bosom and flashed out again. The blade of her knife was like a smooth streak of lightning. She ran up behind the man, shouting, 'Leave him alone, you mothafucka!'

More people spilled out of the Howard Bar, the M&M Bar,

and Mann's Manor to pin the action, as always. 'Man, dig this!' somebody yelled. 'Hip's gittin' done up! Baby, that big stud's puttin' somethin' on his back!'

But by this time Gypsy Pearl was putting something in the man's back. Her hand just gave out quick short flicks, and the knife sank deep into his back every time.

The man finally felt the pain; he screamed and wheeled about, dropping Hip, who, fully conscious now, screamed as his head banged against the car fender. A heavy back-arm blow sent Gypsy Pearl falling up the steps of the stoop. Her knife clattered to the ground, but she quickly recovered it.

The man saw the knife. He put his hand on his back and brought it away bloody; for a moment he stared incredulously at his own blood. Then, as if realization were a hammer, it hit him, and he rocked back against the overturned cans, bellowing in pain, 'Oh, Lawd, call the cops! That bitch done stabbed me!' He had thought that she'd been hitting him with her fists; now he knew better and was deathly afraid. 'Great Godamighty,' he pleaded, 'one of y'all folks call the cops! Git me to a hospital, *please*!'

They all looked at him as if he were insane, and began to disperse, going back into the various bars. One said, 'Man, I ain't got nuthin' t'do wit'it.' Another said, 'I don' know dat chump – where he come from?'

Meanwhile Hip had rummaged through the debris of the spilled garbage and come up with a mason brick, chipped and jagged, and a beer bottle with its bottom broken out. He flung the brick at the man with all his might. It hit him on the side of the face where the scar was. He grabbed at his face and yowled loudly, sinking to his knees in a slow, undulating sort of dance.

Gypsy Pearl was on her feet shouting, 'Kill that nigga, baby, kill 'im!'

Lights flashed yellow in the surrounding buildings; heads peeped out, saw what was all too usual, went back in, and the lights went out once again.

Hip stepped quickly over to where the man knelt in a caricature of the Muslim prayer. Hip gripped the bottle by its neck, his teeth bared, his face one of total triumph. Straddling the man, he brought the bottle down hard on the back of the bald head, and blood gushed out, running down the sides and back of the head. The man groaned and rolled over – out, or dead.

'Git the money, bitch,' Hip gasped, pulling out his handkerchief to wipe his bloody forehead. The bottle had cut his hand. He licked the wound and wrapped the handkerchief around it.

Gypsy Pearl went through the prostrate hulk's pockets, found the roll of bills, and handed it to Hip. 'That's all, honey, he ain't got no more.'

Sweating hard and breathing heavily, Hip said, 'Awright, let's go.' He turned away toward Broome Street.

She started to follow him, then said, 'Wait, Hip, wait a minute.' She went over to the body on the ground.

Hip looked around nervously and said, 'C'mon, woman, we ain't got no time to be messin' 'round here.'

'Okay, I just wanna get even for what he did to me upstairs.'

She bent down and opened his legs, measured carefully, and then kicked as hard as she could into his groin. A deep groan issued from the man, his body rose a little, shivered, and settled back down to a rock stillness. Gypsy Pearl's laughter was a chilling, piercing sound that made Hip wince. She walked to him and tenderly took his arm.

'What was that for?' he asked.

'That baldheaded bastard threw my sponge at me.'

'So?' He looked down at her, puzzled.

'Well, dammit, it was full of his come!' she retorted with an indignant toss of her head.

Hip let out a roar of mirth. 'Baby, you too much,' he said, shaking his head.

A wave of nausea swept over Hip as they were walking. He reached into his pocket, pulled out the roll of bills, and nervously separated three five-dollar bills from the rest. Handing them to Gypsy Pearl, he said, 'Here, go cop me three things off Cowboy – I'm goin' on to the room and git my works ready. And hurry up.' He went in the direction of

Court Street, where they had their room, and she went in the opposite direction, toward Springfield Avenue.

Two blocks bisected by Howard Street are bordered by Court, Broome, and West Streets, and Springfield Avenue. Dark little Mercer Street crosses Howard between Court Street and Springfield Avenue. From Court to Mercer is a long block with two trees (birch) fighting valiantly but vainly to stay alive; two taverns – small, dark places with a small, regular clientele – one in the middle of the block and the other on the corner of Mercer; a service station on the corner of Court; a masseur's bathhouse next to the tavern in the middle of the block. And ten apartment buildings, none rising higher than four stories. There is also a greasy-spoon restaurant, a small grocery store, an ice-house, and a fairly large plumbing supplies business.

The short block between Mercer Street and Springfield Avenue is something so different as to be classed almost as another world. While laborers and domestics – poor but respectable people – live on the long block, the short one is as wild and as rowdy as Dodge City or Tombstone ever was, with no Hickock or Earp in evidence. It also has the strange, but familiar and inevitable, combination of religion mixed in with every conceivable vice.

Beginning at Mercer and looking toward Springfield, on the left side of the street is Mann's Manor; then comes an apartment building, about three stories high; a restaurant specializing in fried fish; an empty storefront; an alley which serves as a shooting gallery for addicts, a place to turn tricks for whores like Sadie Tucker, a cover for muggers to mug or rapists to knock off a quick piece, a place to cop a fast blow job from a fag, and an escape route for everybody – leading to Springfield Avenue or Broome Street – when the cops are out to make a bust.

Then comes the Howard Bar, in a four-story red brick building which covers a quarter of the whole block from the alley to the corner. The only time the doors of its two entrances stop swinging for any length of time is from three to nine in the morning, when the place is closed.

One entrance faces obliquely out toward Springfield Avenue.

Upon entering here one can either go into the package store, small and separated from the bar, or walk the narrow passage-way which is between the package store and the outer wall of the building. It leads directly into the barroom.

The big oval bar inside fills the whole room, which is about fifty feet long and thirty feet wide. There is so little space between the bar and the walls that two people cannot pass abreast behind those sitting at the bar, and even one passer is likely to knock a customer off a stool if he's not well glued to it.

The place stinks. Especially over near the 'Gents' and 'Ladies' rooms. Urine odors assail the nostrils each time a gent or a lady enters or leaves the rest rooms – and few leave without frowns on their faces. No one thinks of complaining to the owner, though. Next to the rest rooms is the jukebox, which blares almost as raucously as the customers. At the end of the bar, away from Springfield Avenue, is the other entrance, the one most often used . . .

This is where Gypsy Pearl entered looking for Cowboy. She saw his wide-brimmed white hat above the crowd. In the center of the bar was a small bandstand. The musicians – an organ trio with saxophone added – were trying to keep out of the way of the three busy bartenders without losing the spirit of their brand of rock'n'roll jazz. Cowboy sat near the dead jukebox, snapping his fingers in time to the heavy back-beat of the drummer's left hand.

Gypsy Pearl started around to him, but it was hard going because the joint was jumping tonight. She must have said 'Excuse me' at least forty times as she squeezed between those standing along the wall and those sitting at the bar. One man moving around the bar behind her seemed to rub against her more than was necessary. The front of his body pressed the back of her in an all too familiar manner. She wheeled angrily and snapped, 'Get off me, you goddamn freak!' He laughed and backed off.

Angry, and breathing heavily from her exertions, she finally made it around to Cowboy and tapped him on the shoulder. He turned. 'You doin'?' she asked.

He had been so engrossed in the music that he didn't even recognize her at first. 'Hey now, chick! How's tricks?' He laughed at his pun. She repeated her question. Suddenly he was all business: 'Yeah, baby, What's up?'

'I want three things, for Hip.'

'Cool. Meet me outside.' He took the three bills from her and slipped them into his pocket.

Outside again, the early June night felt delicious to her, especially after the oppressive heat inside the bar. Her silk blouse, wet here and there with sweat, stuck to her, but the wonderful night air turned them cool, so that she felt goosebumps rise on her back and arms. She stood by the door of the bar and looked toward Mercer Street, where they'd left the big man lying. An ambulance from Martland Medical Center was there along with a police car, its red light revolving menacingly. She felt a sudden fear about what she'd done and hoped that the man wasn't dead.

Cowboy came out of the Howard Street entrance and walked past her into the alley. She waited about a minute and then followed him. It was pitch dark. She had to feel her way along the sides of the walls, which were so close together that she didn't have to stretch her arms out to their fullest length in order to touch both of them. She stumbled over a garbage can; the lid fell off and clang-a-langed along the ground; a tomcat screeched loudly and scared her senseless for a moment as it brushed her leg in a mad dash out of the alley. She regained herself in time to keep from falling.

'Bitch, shut up that noise!' Cowboy hissed hotly from somewhere in the darkness ahead of her. 'You wanna bring the man down on me or somethin'? You jus' wait right there an' don' move, hear?'

She leaned her back against the rough bricks. They felt good through the thin blouse, and she scratched her itching back against them.

'Awright,' he said as he went by her, back to the mouth of the alley. He looked to his right, then to his left. She watched his silhouette guardedly – Cowboy had been known to take the money without coming across with the stuff. She saw him light a cigarette, crumple the package slightly, and throw it down at the alley's entrance. Then he turned to his right and quickly walked away toward Mann's Manor.

Gypsy Pearl picked up the package, emptied its contents into her hand, and threw it down again. She felt the three little glassine stamp bags in her palm; they were folded rectangularly and fastened with Scotch tape. She hurried down Springfield Avenue, turned in Broome, and crossed Mercer – looking furtively again at the police car. The ambulance was gone, but the cops were standing on the corner questioning people, who shrugged their shoulders and shook their heads, their palms turned upward. Her high heels beat a sharp tattoo toward Court Street.

Two

When Franchot Ritchwood was growing up on Broome Street, everyone predicted that he would wind up in jail for life, or die by the hand of a policeman or the executioner at state prison. Hip, who was his brother, and whose real name was Lonnie, had been predicted to go far, which, in the Third Ward of Newark – 'the Hill,' as they called it – could mean that he would wind up being a pimp, or opening a tavern, or making it big in the numbers racket, fronting for a syndicate. Since very few had dreams of becoming something in the professions or business – like Eddie Garrett, who became a doctor – making it big illegitimately was really big; any alternative success was just something they watched on television.

Yet the people in the neighborhood saw something special in Hip. The women could actually picture him as their personal doctor attending their sickbeds, because he was so good-looking and spoke to them so politely. The men could see him as an eloquent power in the courtroom, winning their compensation suits, because he was, by their standards, an articulate extrovert. Franchot was the only one who suspected that he would be nothing.

The main reason for the neighborhood's thinking that Franchot was criminally inclined was his sullen attitude and his persistent – often insulting – silence. For in a black slum if one is not loudmouthed and aggressive, then one is mean, a square or a punk; and Franchot was not a punk in any sense of the word.

There had been one incident in his life which seemed to bear out the general opinion of him, though: when he was fourteen he almost killed another boy of the same age who had beaten Hip terribly with a leather whip. And he had almost been sent to the State Home for Boys; however, because he'd never been in trouble before, his parents had prevailed upon the judge to give him a break, so he got off with two years probation.

After that he taught Hip how to box, and Hip became very good with his hands under his tutelage, so good in fact that he won the Golden Gloves Middleweight Championship of New Jersey when he was fifteen. On his eighteenth birthday he also knocked out Franchot – who was five years older – when they'd had a fight because Franchot wanted to keep him out of trouble – a promise he'd made to their parents, who, by this time, were dead . . .

Tonight, when Franchot came in from work, he fell across his bed without even removing his work clothes, dog-tired. He was a brick mason – the fastest on his job. He could build a seven-foot wall, twenty feet long, in forty-five minutes, and it would be almost perfectly plumb. Usually he felt pretty good after a hard day's work, but today the man who was supposed to show up for work as a hod carrier hadn't shown at all – he was a replacement for their regular carrier, who was sick – so the masons had to mix their own mortar and carry their own bricks. And Franchot had still tried to lay his usual quota; he hadn't made it and was sorry now that he'd even tried. The pain in his back bespoke the heavy tax for his efforts. Yet maybe it was worth it. He hoped to make foreman next year, after the present man's retirement.

Lying on the bed he thought of how nice it would be to have his wife rub him down with alcohol or wintergreen – if he had a wife. He reached for a cigarette from the pack on his table, then sat up smoking solemnly. Some of the guys on the job got on his nerves, always talking about their wives: the way they would rub them down when the working day was over, give them a good, hot supper and equally hot loving at night. They were so goddamned satisfied that it took them all of a second to cheat on their heaven-producing wives with the first woman who'd climb into bed with them. They'd talk about that, too, with the same degree of reverence, he thought. It made him sick to hear them sometimes. Whiskey, women, and cars, or their damned brats. They didn't talk about anything else. Sometimes . . . sometimes he was a damned fool.

What was he getting mad at them for? He was honest enough with himself to admit that perhaps jealousy played a part in his anger, and he was tired. In fact, he knew that he really enjoyed listening to them. He was tired, and felt a little left out of their conversations, a little lonely.

He stood up. What he needed was a little fun. He hadn't been anywhere in a long time; he hadn't done anything more exciting than to take Rosemary to the movies a couple of times. He'd get cleaned up and go around to Howard Street. If anything could pull him out of the slump he was in, Howard Street could, and especially Howard Street on a Friday night. He might even see his brother – and in that case it would be well to take a few extra dollars with him, because his little brother would be sure to hit him for a 'loan' to buy some of that junk.

He put water into the great washtub that he used for bathing and set it on the stove to heat. There were fifteen apartments of four rooms apiece in the building, and not a bathtub among them, and no hot water. The stoves were never free of kettles and pots cooking nothing but water. But he loved the place, perhaps because he and his brother had been born and raised there. After their parents died – of heart attacks one month apart – he'd supported his brother, and never really considered moving, even after Hip left.

Franchot had never ceased to believe that Hip's winning the Golden Gloves had ruined him, because Hip quit school and began to hang around the gym on Market Street. He roamed the streets with his cronies, talking slick, and his bouncy, one-shoulder-hunched walk soon earned him the name Hippy-dip, which was shortened to Hippy, and finally to Hip. The sad thing about it was that he tried to live up to the name in every way.

Franchot had been working in a toy factory then and attending night classes at the Boys' Vocational and Technical High School on Sussex Avenue. He stood for his brother's idleness for a year, hoping that he would get interested in something constructive without being pushed, hoping that he'd work all the wildness out of his system. But it became apparent that

Hip was not going to change on his own; he would accept no responsibility for anything. If Franchot gave him money to pay a bill he'd squander it drinking cheap wine with his friends and tell Franchot that he'd lost it. When Franchot came home from work he would find Hip drunk, standing on the corner with his equally drunk hangout partners, harmonizing rock 'n' roll songs.

The final break came when he got Hip a job at the factory with him. Hip worked through the winter months, but at the first hint of spring in the air he quit to draw unemployment checks. Franchot was disgusted by this, especially because it was apparent that the head of the factory had been interested in Hip, who could be lively, bright, and winning when he felt like turning it on. The genuine interest of the boss had made Franchot think that he might even send Hip to business school, as he'd already done with a number of other young men whom he considered good potential salesmen, ambitious and personable. Hip showed these qualities only when the boss was around, even after Franchot had told him what the boss seemed to be thinking. He explained that the manager of this very factory was a product of the boss's benevolence. But Franchot's hopes were shattered by Hip's 'resignation,' as he called it.

They argued fiercely at home about it and soon were fighting. They fought with the fury that only brothers can seem to muster against each other. Though Hip had gotten to be too good a fighter for his brother, it wasn't an easy win. Franchot wouldn't give up, and Hip had to beat him senseless before the fight ended. Later Franchot told him that if he didn't intend to change his ways he would have to leave the apartment. He gave him a choice of going back to school or going to work. Hip chose to leave . . .

Franchot was tying his tie when a knock came at the door. He opened it, and Rosemary Baker walked in, giving him a small peck on the lips. She and Irene Smith shared the apartment above his. Rosemary considered herself as Franchot's woman, since they had made love any number of times, but, to him, they were more like friends who enjoyed giving each other the pleasure of their bodies. It was like borrowing a neighborly cup of sugar.

She sat down at the kitchen table. Like all the apartments in the building, this one, too, was entered by the kitchen door. The kitchen was the largest room, with the other rooms – two bedrooms, a living room, and a very small toilet – on three sides of it. As one entered there was a bedroom on the right, then the toilet, then the kitchen sink overlooking the filthy backyard, and the stove, and the other bedroom, and the living room on the left. The kitchens in all but name were the real living rooms of the building's occupants; even close friends seldom went past the kitchens. But the way many of the women cooked made some visitors glad of it. Many times when Franchot went upstairs it was because Rosemary and Irene had the pots on.

With the exception of a new refrigerator, Franchot hadn't changed the furniture or its arrangement since his parents' deaths. The wallpaper, a Dutch girl-and-windmill design, was turning yellow where it was supposed to be white. The linoleum was still holding up well, and the dish cabinet only needed a whitewash to look almost new. He had always liked the yellow, blue, and white colors of the kitchen. Sometimes, when he sat alone there, he could imagine his mother fussing around the stove, and the kitchen would become alive with her presence and the delicious smells that she used to fill it with.

He went into the bedroom and came out a moment later wearing a light brown Italian silk suit, white shirt, cocoa-brown hat, and brown alligator shoes which matched perfectly the tie he wore. Rosemary gave a low wolf-whistle. 'Hey, baby,' she approved, 'you look like you into a little somethin'.'

He fingered his lapels, grinning bashfully. 'Yeah, I bought it last week. Figured it was about time, my other three's just about shot. Wanna drink?'

'No,' she answered as he sat down. 'I just came down to find out if you heard the news yet.'

'News? No. What news?' He looked disapprovingly down at his right shoelace, then bent to carefully retie it.

Blandly she watched him primping. 'Hip and some woman he go with liked to killed a man last night on Howard Street.'

He straightened and looked at her anxiously. 'Where you hear that?'

'Well, Irene told me about it. That new boyfriend she got, Tal Murphy, told her he saw the whole thing.' She took the cigarette he offered, adding: 'The man's up in Martland now, on the critical list, they say. Say that woman stabbed him a half a dozen times.'

Franchot said nothing for a while. He puffed on his cigarette, wondering if he should call Meyers the lawyer now, or wait until his brother got arrested – if he got arrested. Chances for an arrest were slim, since it had happened on Howard Street, but it might just happen. He decided to wait. If he went to Meyers now and told him to stand by in case of an arrest and nothing came of it, Meyers was liable to call the cops and tell who to arrest just so he could keep the retainer and obtain more money for the case. He seldom won a case in court, but, because of his connections, he seldom had to go into court in the first place. Five hundred dollars paid to Meyers would take care of just about anything short of treason. He allowed his clients to pay him in weekly installments since few people in the Ward ever had five hundred dollars at one time, unless they hit the numbers, stole it, or inherited it via some insurance firm. Usually, though, insurance money was just enough to pay for the showy funeral which relatives believed that their dead couldn't rest in peace without.

'I wondered how long it would take before he got in some bad trouble,' Franchot said finally. 'Momma used to tell us all the time that a hard head makes a soft ass, but that boy wouldn't listen.' He suddenly became very angry, so much so that Rosemary saw a tremor shake him. 'No siree, not that boy! He the slickest thing that ever let out a turd!'

'What you gon' do about it, Franchot?'

'Nothin'. I ain't gon' do a damn thing; not unless he git locked up, and then I might not do nothin'. He so goddamn slick, let him do somethin'.' But he spoke without conviction, and Rosemary knew it.

She smiled, 'Aw, Franchot, who you think you juggin', tryin' to be so hard? I know how you love Hip, and I can just picture him gettin' in some bad trouble and you not being right there to help him get out. Hah!'

Feigning displeasure, he asked, 'Listen, woman, what you come down here for, to git on my nerves?'

With mock indignation, she said, 'To tell you about Hip. What's the matter, can't nobody pay you a friendly visit no more? I bet you ain't gotta tell me what you come upstairs for.' She smiled impishly, looking up at the ceiling where her bedroom was located in the apartment above.

'Well, I ain't up there now, so make it and let me go give some other chicks a treat for a change.'

She stood up. 'Yeah, you might treat them, but it's mighty funny you keep comin' back here when you want to be treated.' She swayed her behind at him and gave it an exaggerated, slowmotion pat, then jerked her hand away quickly. 'Oowee, hot!' she exclaimed.

They laughed together, and he followed her to the door. Placing his hand on her hip, he agreed, and approved, 'Hummm, girl, it sure is hot.'

'Baby, you better know it. The hottest thing in town.' She laughed, opening the door.

'Hey,' he called before she'd gone two steps.

'What?' she answered.

'C'mere.'

'What you want?'

'You ain't kissed me.'

'You ain't kissed me, neither.'

'C'mere.'

She stepped back. He grabbed her tightly in his arms, and they kissed long and hungrily. She had the softest lips that he'd ever touched, as soft and as sweet as cotton candy, with an underlying resilience that tempted him to gobble them up at times and feel their firmness bloom again to fullness under his own lips. Her tongue was always sweet with a hint of the mint candy she liked so much. He enjoyed kissing her so much that sometimes he'd sit with her on the sofa or on the bed for hours and they'd neck like two kids in a car. There had been times when he had actually hated to begin the sex act itself because it seemed to break the spell which her kisses put him under. He laughed to remember that he used to feel kissing was overrated – before he met her.

She felt a serious stir in him; his kisses were taking on a familiar kind of greed, and she realized that they were standing in the hallway. When his hands gripped her buttocks she broke her lips from under his, but reluctantly: it was her time of the month. Breathing very heavily, she said, 'No.'

'No what?' he asked innocently. 'I ain't even said nothin'.'

'No for what you about to say. No, no.'

'Awright now,' he warned. 'Them girls on Howard Street'll cut it off and take it home with 'em. What'll you do then?'

'Buy you another one.'

'Won't be as good as this one, though.'

'Might be better – no, Franchot, really I can't.' She wriggled out of his embrace.

'You wanna go out with me?' he asked.

'I can't tonight. Irene wants me to do her hair. Tal Murphy – did I tell you about him?'

He nodded. 'Her new boyfriend, right?'

'Uh-huh. Well, he takin' her to a fashion show at the Terrace Ballroom tomorrow afternoon. Real siditty affair, you know, all them stuck-up Montclair bitches and everything.'

'Yeah, well the Howard Street chicks can thank you for the blessin' they's about to receive tonight. I'll tell 'em you sent me with your best regards.'

'You can also tell 'em to leave some of the white in my peppermint stick, too. When it's all red it's all dead.' She laughed and ran upstairs.

Franchot went back inside to turn off the lights. His fatigue had completely left him; he felt kind of good, damn near happy, he had to admit to himself. A few drinks would top it off in a boss way.

Three

In the same block as Mann's Manor and the Howard Bar, but on the opposite side of the street, are a few of the establishments belonging to Father Divine and his followers. Besides the main building, which houses among other things a banquet room and a swimming pool, is a barber shop, featuring several pictures of Divine and a sign reading: 'Peace. Haircuts gratis. You are free to give what you can afford.' The shop is seldom empty of customers. Kids whose parents give them a dollar for a haircut break the bill and rush to the Divine shop, where they rarely pay more than a dime for a cutting. Most grown-ups seem embarrassed to give less than a dollar, but not all of them. In fact, some climb into the chair and when the barber is done say, 'Peace, brother,' without paying at all. This doesn't seem to disturb the barbers; they return the peace and continue to give out good haircuts.

In the banquet room of the main building one can get a full-course meal for a quarter. The many characters who live or hang out on Howard Street have been virtually saved from starvation because of Divine, especially in tough times when money is low and the cops are feeling mean. The other Divine business is a small grocer's run by a little old lady who is always in good humor; and the products in the store are dirt cheap.

The streeters don't bother the Divine followers. They don't steal from them or try to con them out of anything. The followers in turn don't try to beat their religion over anyone's head or even attempt to proselytize. It seems a mutual agreement, a tacit understanding with toleration on the part of the followers and respect on the part of even the most disrespectful of the fast-lifers. The streeters show more respect for the Divine people than they do for their own families' various religions.

The M&M Bar is on the same side of the street as the Divine establishments and caters mostly to homosexual trade, mostly females. However, everyone goes there as much as to the other two bars. But men looking for women are extremely careful. Jealous reaction to a dance with one of the women has caused some men to be cut, shot, and beaten up by a gang of 'studbroads,' and robbed in the process.

Franchot decided on Mann's Manor as his first stop. The horseshoe bar was filled with people when he walked in, from the entrance, which was on the corner of Mercer Street, all the way around to the unused and boarded-up other entrance closer to Springfield Avenue. There was a gallery running along both of the long walls back to the rear, where the rest rooms were. It took two high steps to get up into the gallery, and once seated, one was offered a view of the whole room because of the mirrors that covered every wall. A person could enjoy the sight of himself sipping a drink. The posing that went on among those was a sight to behold. Many were too self-conscious to outrightly watch themselves in the mirrors, so they wore dark glasses and assumed an air of casual unconcern.

A small jazz combo was up on the little stage behind the bar, playing 'Cherokee' at a furious tempo. Franchot looked around for a seat at the bar but found none. Glancing over the gallery, he saw a man who seemed to be waving at him, though he couldn't remember ever having seen him before. The man smiled and waved to him again, so he went over, climbed up, and sat next to him.

'Say, my man, ain't you Hip's brother?' he asked. A gold tooth flashed in front of his mouth.

Franchot was immediately on the defensive. 'Yeah, what about it?'

'Ain't nothin', jack. I seen you around, an' Irene Smith, the chick I go with, told me about you. I'm Tal Murphy.'

'Oh, yeah,' Franchot replied, relieved. For a minute he thought this was a cop. 'Rosemary said that you seen what went down with my brother last night.' The bartender was looking their way. Franchot ordered White Horse and a refill for Tal.

'Yeah, I dug it,' Tal said. 'Man, him and his chick did a boss job on that stud; he was a great big cat, too.' He got down and went to pick up their drinks. Franchot was surprised to see that he was so short. Tal was very dark brown, with an almost invisible scar on the outer corner of his right eye. He'd looked like a big man while he was seated, and Franchot could tell that he was something of a dandy by the meticulous manner of his movements, his carefully manicured nails, the neatness of everything about him. Then he remembered where he'd seen Tal before: at the Red Tower restaurant, an after-hours hangout for the pimps and their women, turning their last tricks before calling it a night. Tal was a pimp. Franchot wondered if Irene was selling herself. He knew that Howard Street pimps rarely had a woman who didn't and didn't want one who wouldn't.

Tal set the drinks down, with a conscious display of his diamond pinkie ring. Franchot had to smile at the pure vanity of the man's every move, which seemed as calculated as any woman's. Tal's snap-brim hat, turned up all the way around, sat neatly cocked to one side on his head, and he pulled an imaginary piece of lint from his blue iridescent suit. His face was rodent-like, with a high-bridged nose and big eyes above puckered lips. His teeth looked false, but Franchot couldn't definitely tell whether or not they were.

After taking a sip from his glass, Franchot asked, 'Do the cops know who did it?'

'I don't think so; at least I didn't hear nobody say nothin'. But you know how that goes – the minute some of these stool-pigeon niggas know somethin', you can bet that they go tell the man about it. I ain't never seen so many stool pigeons in one block before in all my life. Drop a dime on you 'fore God can git the news. They trade each other worse than the white slave-masters did, and for a lot less profit, too.'

Franchot said nothing. He continued to sip his drink and waved to the bartender for refills.

'Yeah,' Tal went on: 'I don't think Hip got no enemies except maybe Red Shirt Charlie; but he ain't no pigeon. It's the ones who supposed to be your friends that you gotta watch, though. These chumps blow the whistle on each other an' still stay tight, like ain't nothin' happened.

That shit don't happen in New York, though – you can bet on that.'

'I know where you at,' Franchot said. 'I tried to tell him a long time ago that these so-called slickers and thoroughbreds don't mean him no good. Ain't none of 'em got nothin'; just livin' from day to day, and they don't wanna see nobody else doin' halfway good. But he don't listen. He ain't never listened to nobody.'

The band came down for intermission, but the voices, humming and laughing, still seemed to carry the tempo and rhythm created by the musicians, and the volume too. The heat was oppressive, but no one seemed to mind. They wiped the sweat from their foreheads, drank some more, and dug each other.

'You seen him tonight?' Franchot asked.

Before Tal could answer a bottle crashed to the floor back near the rest rooms. The place quieted down as all eyes turned in the direction of a new noise.

Big Frieda stood with both hands on her huge hips glaring menacingly at a man and woman seated at the bar. The woman was facing her but the man kept his back to her, calmly drinking beer. Franchot knew them all. It was Bill Grumsley and Bunny Scotia whom Big Frieda menaced.

Bill had been a creeper at one time, who made his living by breaking into homes and apartments. After a particularly big sting, he bought a Cadillac and began pimping. Bunny and Big Frieda both turned tricks for him, but Big Frieda wouldn't recognize Bunny as one of Bill's whores. The two women hated each other and had had a couple of fights which were famous in the neighborhood. Bill usually stopped them before one of them got really hurt. They argued or fought only when he was around; at other times they left each other alone.

'Bitch,' Bunny said, 'why you knock that bottle outta my hand? Is you crazy?'

'Cause I done tol' you t'stay away from my man, tha's why, bitch!'

'*Yo' man!* Now I *know* you crazy. Where you git that junk from?'

'I done tol' you about messin' with him when my back's turned. Git your yaller ass outta that seat!' Someone turned the jukebox down, and Big Frieda's voice boomed throughout the bar.

'I ain't gittin' nowhere, but you better git outta my face, that's what you better do,' Bunny warned. 'Who the hell is you, anyway? Why don't you tell him t'stay away from me if you so such-a-much? You oughta run along an' turn a trick 'steada standin' here runnin' off at the mouth. If you bring him back a good piece of money I might let you have him a little while.' Bunny reached into her bosom and pulled out a fifty-dollar bill. 'Can you do that, bitch?' she asked contemptuously, placing the money in Bill's hand. 'How much *you* give him tonight, you triflin' two-dollar whore?' She shouted just as loud as Frieda.

The crowd in the bar roared with laughter as the banter and wisecracks flew between the two women. Both weighed close to one hundred and fifty pounds and were near six feet tall, solidly built from head to toe. Bunny Scotia was light-skinned, but ugly beside Big Frieda, who was dark and smooth with a cute girlish face. But both could make good money from the johns who came to Howard Street.

Just as Bunny started to speak again, Big Frieda reached and grabbed her, throwing her from the barstool onto the floor. Bunny's dress flew up around her waist and the crowd again roared. Bunny wore no underwear, and her big thighs shook as she scrambled to her feet. Big Frieda started for her, but at that moment Bill turned and grabbed her by the hair. Her wig came off in his hands. The crowd loved it.

Frieda was flabbergasted, standing there with her own hair shooting straight up from her head. She snatched the wig out of Bill's hands and put it quickly back on her head. It was lopsided.

'Awright now,' Bill commanded, 'y'all bitches knock it off.' Tears streamed down Big Frieda's face, but he paid them no mind. Her breasts were heaving as though she were an asthma victim or a long-distance runner, and her eye make-up was all over her face. Bunny was convulsed with laughter.

'Shut up, bitch!' Bill spat. With difficulty she managed to

do so, and climbed back onto her stool. 'Y'all chicks jus' cool down. I don't want no more of this shit tonight.' He was in his glory: the unquestionable lord and master. The last time the two women had fought he'd smacked them both, asserting his masculine sovereignty. Now he was playing cool, posing for the crowd.

He spoke loudly to Big Frieda. 'You got any bread, woman?'

'I ain't turned but two so far, Bill.' Her voice was a classic example of female supplication. Even she didn't realize how much she enjoyed the humiliation.

'Gimme,' Bill ordered, holding out his hand, which sported his expensive watch and ring. Frieda took two ten-dollar bills from the top of her stocking and handed them to him. Bill turned to a man sitting next to him: 'Mind givin' my woman yo' seat, champ?' The man shook his head and got up. Bill told the bartender to give him a drink, then made Frieda sit down.

'I done told that yaller bitch to stay 'way from you, Bill,' she whined, but her eyes threw hateful looks at Bunny. 'She don't mean you no good in the world. You wait, one day she gon git you sent t'jail – just mark my words.'

Bunny screamed, 'You lyin' black bitch! Who you puttin' bad mouth on—'

'You just stay 'way from him, that's all!' Frieda yelled back at her across Bill.

A malicious glint came into Bunny's eyes as she said, 'Girl, it look like we just gon' have to have a battle of pussies 'bout this thing here; and I'm bankin' I win. What you bet?'

'You worn-out, half-white bitch,' Frieda countered, 'that well you call a pussy is big enough *for* a battle. You was trickin' with mules 'fore they run your ass from down south!'

Bill made them shut up, not so much because he really wanted to, but because he had already ordered them to be quiet, and disobedience by a whore is something no decent pimp would tolerate. With finality he said, 'I ain't go' tell y'all but one more time to shut up this fuss.'

The musicians were going back up on the stand. Frieda got up. 'Where you think you goin'?' Bill asked.

'To straighten my goddamn hair what you done messed up for that *other* party. Does you mind?' she said resentfully, putting on her version of airs.

'Go 'head then,' he snapped. 'You look like what the cat buried.'

The crowd turned immediately back to their conversations, drinking, and propositionings as the band swung into 'Sister Sadie.'

Tal saw Gypsy Pearl enter. 'That's your brother's old lady there, man,' he told Franchot.

Franchot watched her. He'd seen her around before, but he'd had no idea that she was mixed up with his brother. And he'd certainly heard about her, as had everyone else on the Hill. Not just because she was one of the best moneymakers to hit Howard Street since the mid-forties, but because her beauty was almost legendary. She was one of the most beautiful women he'd seen. He couldn't imagine her doing the things that he'd heard she'd done. He knew she was a whore, but he couldn't picture her as one. From all that he'd heard of her she should have been like Bunny Scotia or Big Frieda, or even Sadie Tucker – any of the women who made their livings on their backs: stout, loud, and probably scarred up. That was the usual description of a Howard Street whore. But by Gypsy Pearl's very appearance, she became an immediate contradiction, an enigma which caused him to stare at her in fascination. She looked like a model for teenage clothes, yet she was just a whore.

She had hazel eyes, and her hair hung down her back in a long, silky ponytail; a spit curl, directly opposed to her tightly pulled-back hair, fell softly over her high fore-head. She moved like a graceful dancer, and a tight green skirt showed the full and ungirdled curve of her hips. Her legs were as shapely as a ballerina's, without the bulge of muscle to jar the delicate symmetry of them; they tapered down into slim ankles and small feet, which hid within green spike-heeled pumps. From under a white silk blouse her breasts jutted pertly, the kind that weren't too big and felt so comfortable in the hand of a lover. The blouse was sleeveless, and her arms, the color of burnished copper, looked firm and soft.

Down in front of Franchot and Tal, a trick got up to follow one of the women out into the humid night. Gypsy Pearl sat on the vacated stool. Both men watched her hips gently hug it; she ordered gin and orange and lit a cigarette.

In the mirror Franchot got a very good look at her face. It was the same color as her arms, and smooth and flawless. Whenever she had occasion to smile at a familiar face among the crowd a dimple came subtly into her left cheek. Her nose, he saw, was small, sloping like a pyramid to a wide base above full lips, which held the only make-up that he could discern. The only jewelry she wore was large, golden earrings, which went well with her name and enhanced her resemblance to a gypsy – as she no doubt knew. Franchot couldn't take his eyes from her, and his imagination was running wild between images of violence and unadulterated sex.

He'd completely forgotten Tal was at his side until Tal nudged him and said, 'She was the biggest moneymaker 'round here, next to Big Louise, man. The only reason Lou's so good, though, is 'cause she don't turn down no money; that bitch is a real mudkicker.' He spoke with the reverence peculiar to pimps for a good whore; reverence, however, which lacked any real respect. Franchot had noticed this attitude before, and couldn't understand it; like many people, he had a distaste for pimps while admiring and patronizing them. Tal went on: 'But Hip don't know what to do with a woman like that Gypsy Pearl. If I had her, baby, I'd be rich by next year.'

Franchot didn't answer him. Tal kept talking, but Franchot wasn't listening. Gypsy Pearl totally occupied his mind; he was digesting her. Every once in a while a phrase of Tal's gossip would reach him, bragging, but envious of Hip. Franchot was tired of him and wanted to tell him to shut up, but he said nothing. He just nodded dutifully from time to time.

If Franchot had noticed her, she, in turn, had noticed him, the way she noticed all men at first: as potential money. But her eyes kept coming back to him in the mirror. There was something about him, something that she couldn't quite put her finger on. In her business it wasn't easy to remember all the faces and names that one ran across unless there was a particular reason, like a big spender, or an easy hit, or someone she'd robbed. She could find no connection to fit the face of the man behind her, but she knew Tal Murphy. Later on she'd ask him who his drinking partner was.

She was glad that Hip didn't want to show his swollen face in public and had let her come out alone tonight. With the money they'd taken from that big john last night, she didn't have to work tonight . . . Hip! Her eyes shot back to Franchot. That was it! He looked like Hip! That was what she saw in him; that's why her mind wouldn't relinquish the toehold of familiarity it had taken upon him. He was darker, and bigger, and he wore a moustache, but the features were very definitely those of Hip, a healthy Hip. She knew that he had a brother somewhere on Broome Street – 'a real square,' Hip said – she wondered if this was him.

Franchot had caught her eye and felt warmed by her look. Tal saw them both, and said, 'Dig, man, why don't you ask her about your brother. I gotta go check on Big Louise, anyway. She been gone too long.' He smiled, showing the gold tooth in his dark countenance. 'You know how these bitches is – you don't keep a foot in their behinds, they git outta hand.'

He called to Gypsy Pearl, and when she looked up, he said, 'C'mon up here an' meet yo' brother-in-common-law, woman.'

She picked up her drink and waited for Tal to vacate his seat. He stepped down and stood next to her, automatically straightening to make himself seem taller: she still had a couple of inches on him. He formally introduced them. 'This here's Gypsy Pearl, Franchot. This is Hip's brother, girl, I don't know his last name.' He doffed his hat to them, enjoying his role. 'I'll dig y'all later,' he said. He started toward the door, hat cocked jauntily to the side. His diamond ring glittered as he waved to people among the crowd.

Gypsy Pearl watched him weave his way to the door and, with a sudden vehemence that startled Franchot, said, 'That little bastard think he so cute.' Then, just as suddenly, in a voice that warmed his insides, she said, 'So you my guy's brother, huh? I thought you looked familiar, but you better-lookin' than him.'

Franchot sipped his drink, feeling self-conscious and slightly irritable because he could think of nothing to say. Finally, he lit a cigarette to gain a little composure. 'How's that boy doin'?' he asked. A weight seemed to be lifted from his tongue.

'Oh, he all right,' she answered. 'But right now he hurtin' a little. Guess you heard about what happened last night . . .'

'Yeah, I heard, and it's a wonder y'all ain't in jail right now, too. Suppose that man dies, y'all gon' be in a helluva fix.' He was angry. Last night's actions seemed so out of place, something he just couldn't imagine her doing – and she didn't even appear upset about it.

'If he dies,' she said coldly, 'that's his tough luck. He ain't had no business doin' what he done.'

'What'd he do?' Franchot asked.

'Somethin' he shouldn't've.' She smiled at him.

'Like what?' he persisted.

She looked momentarily embarrassed, then replied curtly, 'That's personal, man.' Abruptly, her voice changed to a musical quality as she asked, 'Is you goin' 'round to see Hip?'

He didn't even notice that his own voice became softer. 'Well, I hadn't planned to. Thought I'd see 'im around here. But it might be a good idea if I did. He still on Court Street?'

'Yeah. I stay there, too.'

'Both of y'all in that same little dingy room?' He raised his eyebrows in surprise. 'I thought you was suppose to be such a good moneymaker?'

She bristled. 'I am. I can't help it if his damn habit take almost every cent I can hustle. I tried to git him to move a long time ago, but he don't care where he live as long as the dope don't run out—' She stopped and watched the door. A white man had just walked in. 'Look, baby, one of my regulars just came in. I gotta go git him before one of these other bitches do. They steal like hell on Fridays. I'll see you later, hear?' Without waiting for a reply she climbed down.

'Yeah, later,' he said as sarcastically as he could.

She looked up at him with a quizzical wrinkle of her brow. It seemed as though she were going to speak; however, she turned and walked away.

Franchot watched as she went over to the man, who gave her his seat and stood next to her, smiling and talking. Franchot hated him in that moment, not because he was white, but because of jealousy; yet he was not aware of any sensation except loss, which he mistook for bitterness at the injury she happily inflicted upon herself, her total waste of beauty.

As she was leaving with the trick she called up to him and casually said that if he were around later on, she'd go with him to see Hip. He had intended to go now, but he knew without even thinking about it that he'd wait for her. Still, he didn't want to sit in Mann's; he paid for his last drink and started down the street to the Howard Bar.

In bed, with the trick humping fast and furiously on top of her, Gypsy Pearl thought of Franchot. She could even imagine him in the place of this man now who was pecking at her like a dog; and she could feel a strange stir in her body somewhere, a slight tingle that made her wiggle her toes. She'd never had an orgasm before, not even with Hip or Red Shirt Charlie. This john didn't know how to do it, and she was angry at herself for reacting to his bumbling. She was also angry because she half-wished he did know how to move his body and touch her in order to make her really feel it. Everybody was always talking about how frigid white women were; if this was an example of what they had to go through, she could certainly see why they'd be frigid. Any woman who had to put up with this dry humping couldn't help but turn cold.

She couldn't make Franchot's image go away. The harder she tried the clearer it got. It was him here with her now, taking it slow and easy, the way it was supposed to be done. She bit down hard on her bottom lip, hoping the pain would disperse the pleasure that would surely come if the trick stayed on her much longer. She whispered her usual love-phrases into his ear while her mind ran over various incidents and faces. The thought of the big man last night helped her most to elude

Franchot's face. She thought about the broad back facing her, and her knife digging into it, until she wanted to cry out. But then she felt the trick coming, his body trembling out of control.

'Oh, you black bitch,' he hissed into her ear. 'You black bitch!' He repeated it again and again, until his body was once again his subject; then he lay on her, crying, as he always did at the end. It was the same every time he was with her. She had been insulted the first time it happened, but he'd convinced her that he meant no harm, he just couldn't help it. She found it extremely funny when he confessed that he did the same thing with his wife; this placated Gypsy Pearl more than his apology.

She was glad that he came quickly. That was one good thing about most of the white tricks she'd known: they didn't last very long, and they paid much better for their pleasures. The damned niggers wanted to jew the price down and then stay on all night, too. They were too long-winded. She was glad, too, because she didn't know how much longer she could've held out against him, with the thoughts of Franchot bugging her. She'd have to remind Sue to get her another sponge. The internal kind were hard to get, so Sue claimed, but that only meant, she knew, that Sue would charge hell out of her for it . . .

She found it hard to keep from thinking about Franchot as she took on four other tricks during the night. And in between them her mind was totally filled with him. She wondered what he thought about her life, and was slightly irritated by what she thought she read in his eyes when he looked at her: the same censure, though not quite as apparent, as she'd seen in countless other eyes, which only increased her stubborn arrogance. She hadn't felt shamed since the initial shame of her first couple of weeks as a whore. She believed with her heart and soul that she was immune to what people thought of her – even her mother's 'disowning' of her hadn't really touched her, or, at least, had not caused her any loss of sleep. After all, she had only taken her mother's advice: 'Whatever you be, honey, be a good one.' She'd been told it so many times that the statement had lost its real meaning for her; she followed it unconsciously. Her consolation was that she was not like the other Howard Street whores; she was very good.

But now she found herself wondering what Franchot thought, and if he looked down on her; and she was suddenly aware of a deep need to prove to him that she was good, and who the hell was he to look down on her, on excellence? He had no business to look down on her, especially when his own brother was responsible for whatever she was.

When she saw him sitting in the Howard Bar talking to a woman, a square chick, she felt a pang of jealousy and swore mutely at him. His head was turned away, and she caught the woman's eye, fixing her with a glare of cold hatred that made the woman turn away self-consciously.

Gypsy Pearl watched Franchot over her drink. He looked married, but not happy. She liked his fiery black eyes even though they appeared to reproach her. His thick, evenly trimmed moustache made his teeth seem whiter than they were, and so big and even. She liked his powerful shoulders, which seemed as capable of holding up the world as Atlas's. His hands were rugged and strong; she would like to feel them touching her. He was about an inch taller than Hip and looked a lot younger. She couldn't remember which was the oldest, if she'd ever known, but Hip looked like he was forty.

A trick approached her. She started to tell him no, but she looked over at Franchot and the woman – they were laughing. She said, pointing over at them, 'He's out for the same thing, but to get it free is all right, huh.'

The man grunted quizzically, 'Huh?'

'Nothin', baby.' She grabbed his hand. 'C'mon, it's goodies time.' She led him out without looking back.

An hour later she was back at the Howard Bar. Franchot was gone. Her heart fell when she didn't see him; she'd half-expected him to wait for her. 'Like a cheap pimp?' her mind questioned. He probably got disgusted watching her run to rooms with any man who asked her.

She walked to Mann's Manor: he wasn't there, either. By the time she decided to go over to the M&M Bar, she'd succeeded in convincing herself that she wasn't looking for him. But when she walked in and saw him sitting at the bar she felt tremendous relief flood throughout her body. He didn't see her as she went past him; he was staring down into his drink. She sat down near the rear of the room, a little deflated that he hadn't called her.

The barroom of the M&M is smaller than either of the other two bars in the block; it has a back room with tables, which, however, is rarely used. It smells even worse than the other two bars. At one time it had been a very nice place indeed.

The bar itself is situated along the left wall. The inevitable blasting jukebox guards the entrance to the rear. Like the other two bars, the M&M is extremely well lighted; so much so that the dark glasses worn by some customers seem quite appropriate.

The place was fairly crowded, mostly with women sitting together, and others dancing. About five male couples were in the place – queens with their 'husbands' – talking in high, shrill tones, and laughing loudly in lavish efforts to attract attention. There were only two mixed couples among the customers.

When Franchot finally saw Gypsy Pearl he felt his pulse rate go up; he took a big swallow of whiskey to calm himself. She was sitting and talking with a female couple. He hesitated to go to her, though – it wasn't cool to hang around a whore, because a potential trick might get the impression that she wasn't available, and she would lose money.

Next to Franchot were a fag and a Puerto Rican, who obviously thought the fag was a real woman. Franchot was amused at the small hand-wrestling match they were having. The man's hand would rest on the fag's thigh, but when it tried to work itself upward, a more effeminate hand would grasp it and push it away, gently but definitely.

After suffering repeated defeats, the Puerto Rican laughed in a piercing tone and said, '*Qué pasa, mujer, no me quieres a sentir la chocha?*'

'*Dah*ling,' the fag drawled, in the ubiquitous imitation of Tallulah Bankhead, 'I don't *comprende* La Spanish. If you want mother to understand, you'll just *have* to declare your love in English – *Si?*'

It wasn't hard for Franchot to see why the man had mistaken the fag for a woman: he looked very female indeed. He looked about twenty years old, with a fragile, girlish face, smooth and unmarked by the inconvenience of having to shave. If he hadn't had such exaggerated vocal inflections, Franchot would've been fooled into thinking he was a woman, too – especially in this bar – and he'd been sitting next to him for a half hour.

'Don't *do* that, *dahling!*' he admonished the Puerto Rican again. 'Not in public. Too Loo . . .' he called to another fag sitting at the far end of the bar. 'Sister, how *does* one say "later" to this dear boy? I'm simply *exasperated* to communicate with him.'

Too Loo waved a nonchalant hand adorned with two-inch nails. 'Oh, Miss *One*, you only have to say "*después*" with one of your sultry smiles, and he'll be in the palm of your hand.' He turned back to his date.

'He's *that* already, Miss *Thing*,' the fag said as he once more grasped at the Puerto Rican's explorative hand. He smiled, '*Después*, lover, *después*.' They both laughed. The man ordered drinks for them in such broken English that the bartender finally had to take the order from the fag – though he knew, undoubtedly, what the other was trying to say – and the look that he gave the fag bespoke pure jealousy.

When Franchot decided there was nothing going on for Gypsy Pearl, he got up and went over to where she sat. She feigned a mild surprise at seeing him. The people with whom she was talking excused themselves and left, not even bothering to look twice at him.

'Had a good time tonight?' she asked as he sat down.

'Oh, I didn't do nothin' but wander from bar to bar, drinkin',' he replied. 'Really wasn't much to do anyway, except listen to the music and watch the people.'

'If you watched these people, then you had plenty to do,' she said, rather caustically. Again, her voice changed to a sweetness which made Franchot wonder why she chose to be a whore, of all things, and a Howard Street one at that. 'Well, I'm finished work for tonight,' she said, smiling at him. 'Wanna go see Hip now?'

He looked at his watch. 'It's only a little after twelve; I thought y'all chicks worked till the wee hours.'

'I usually do, but me and Hip made a pretty good sting last night, so I don't have to break my back for a while. In fact, I didn't have to do nothin' tonight if I didn't wanna.'

Franchot smiled wryly: 'Keepin' in practice, huh?'

'No – makin' that bread.' She was beginning to bristle again. 'You see somethin' wrong with that?'

'No, no. I didn't say anything was wrong with it.'

'Well, don't sound so much like some kinda puritan or somethin', then,' she rejoined. She looked up and saw Cowboy come in. ''Scuse me. I gotta go take care some business for your brother.' She got up and walked away.

'Monkey business,' Franchot muttered angrily under his breath. But she didn't hear him.

'I ain't in no shape, girl,' Cowboy said when she approached him. 'I jus' downed my last two things to Cotton Alice. You shoulda hit on me sooner; I'da stashed some for ya – can't cop till I see the wops tomorrow.'

'Ain't nobody else doin' nothin'?' she asked.

'I see Big-feet Roland standin' over by Mann's with his hands in his pockets – you know what that means.'

'Yeah, awright. Thanks.' She went back to where Franchot waited.

'Listen, honey,' she spoke without sitting down. 'I gotta go 'cross the street a minute. Be right back, hear? Then we can split.'

He nodded. 'I'll be here.' He watched her hips gently rolling as she moved away from him. She was so beautiful that the sight of her was a physical shock to him.

'*Oyé, niña!*' the Puerto Rican called out as she walked past him. '*Qué manera andar en la calle!*'

The fag slapped him very softly on the cheek. 'I don't know what you said, lover, but I don't approve – especially when you have the *real thing* right here!'

The Puerto Rican laughed his high laugh and patted the fag's thigh.

Fifteen minutes later Gypsy Pearl came back, stuck her head inside, and waved Franchot out. They walked down Howard Street toward Court; past the bathhouse, down to the service station on the corner, where they turned right and stopped in front of a rooming house in the middle of the block. Gypsy Pearl took out her key as they started up the six steps leading to the door.

She led him into a narrow hall that had a staircase on the right – which he almost stumbled on – leading up into total darkness. A door to a room on the left was slightly open, allowing a little light to sneak out into the gloomy surroundings. Gypsy Pearl looked in and spoke to a little black woman with steel-rimmed glasses perched delicately on a button of a nose. She was drinking gin straight from the bottle.

'Winnie,' Gypsy Pearl scolded gently, 'you know the doctor told you you ain't s'poze to drink. You got sugar, girl.'

'First today, chile, first today,' Winnie said. If she drank a pint, she'd still claim it was the first.

Gypsy Pearl shook her head and turned away. She led Franchot back through the kitchen to the first-floor room that she and Hip lived in.

When she knocked and called, 'It's me, Hip. I got a surprise for you,' a voice, muffled by the door, which Franchot hardly recognized, said in biting tones: 'Well, come the fuck on in and quit that damn yellin'!'

Four

It was with a dubious pride and a cynical despair that Jackie Brown displayed the distinction of having been the only Streeter to have attended a university. Few of the Streeters had ever even been to high school, but he'd had one year at Rutgers – on a basketball scholarship.

With only a few weeks remaining in his freshman year he'd been expelled for smoking reefers, or, as he now said, for taking 'the weight' for a bunch of chumps who couldn't care less about him. All he did now was drink cheap wine and flunky for anyone who'd give a dime to help him along toward the forty-nine cents it cost to buy a pint.

If asked, he could expound for hours on the psychological, economic, and social reasons that made Howard Street what it was. He'd taken freshman sociology at Rutgers and he knew the reasons behind everyone's vice. He told the whores, addicts, and small-time pimps just why they did the things they did – it didn't matter that they never listened to him anymore. He knew it was because they were stymied by the complexity of the white power structure, and because they were also stupid.

It hadn't been so long ago, when he first showed on the scene, that they'd made a point of listening to him; most, he knew, simply wanted a handout, but they'd listened. They'd sought his opinion on anything from Ivy League dress to abortion. He'd had an intellectualism of sorts – being fresh from his little year at Rutgers – and an attitude so vastly different from their own that he was actually, to many of them, an awesome embodiment of success.

Jackie had come to Howard with the intention of trying to do something to help the Streeters find a path into the mainstream of American life; to try and instill in them the growing pride that was being evidenced by the southern Afro-Americans. He'd organized demonstrations and pickets against the Springfield Avenue merchants who didn't hire black help in their businesses. And he'd had mild success – with the merchants. Those with businesses large enough to afford it agreed that since they depended upon black trade for their livelihood they would hire black help. However, when it came to persuading the fast-lifers of Howard Street to take jobs, Jackie ran into a little difficulty: they didn't want to work.

'But,' he would cry when a Streeter either quit after drawing the first pay, or failed to show up for the job in the first place, 'you said you wanted to get out of this rut, man. You said you was tired of jail. You said you wanted a purpose to your life. How you expect t'make a better life for your kids and yourself if you don't make a start?'

To which would come the imperturbable, and almost universal, reply: 'Yeah, man. I know where you at – but that gig ain't sayin' nuthin'. Like, it's a drag, man. That white man don't wanna git up off no bread at all. I c'n make more'n that in a good day's hustlin', man. Dig . . . like, if you cop me a good job, man, I'll work.' An answer Jackie got just as often was: 'Take it on the hop, man. I don't wanna hear that shit.'

His project had failed miserably, and it hadn't helped his morale any to realize that the merchants were happy about it. Disheartened but resolute, he'd kept at the Streeters until they would hide from him like he was the cops.

Meanwhile, he'd been working in the Boys' Club on Morton Street as an athletic instructor. It was a probationary job. They knew that he'd been kicked out of school, and why. But he was an excellent all-around athlete, and had been a member of the Boys' Club since the age of eight, so they'd decided to give him a chance to prove himself. Most of the personnel, including the director, Mr Anderson, had watched him grow from a lanky, awkward boy into the graceful young man for whom they wildly cheered during all his school years. They took credit for making him the athlete he was. He was a bright feather in the Boys' Club's many-feathered cap. The Club had been a second home for him, and he was treated with genuine affection, and even respect.

But the Club wasn't enough. He was obsessed with his

inability to make any headway on Howard Street. He couldn't, or wouldn't, understand why, with the knowledge of a better way of life, the Streeters chose the life they did. Mr Anderson had talked to him, told him he couldn't move mountains with a spoon, but Jackie was inconsolable. In his apartment, crushed by failures and frustrations, he literally cried; and he began to drink.

On a few occasions he got drunk on Howard Street, and to the Streeters, this brought him down to their level, and who the hell was he to tell them they were wrong, who the hell was he to moralize when he got drunk as a jaybird? Now their consciences were clear: further reason not to listen to him.

He wasn't an alcoholic then – not by a long shot – but he did drink more than was his custom, and eventually it cost him his job.

He'd gotten high on the day that the Club invited parents and civic leaders to tour the facilities and get a firsthand look at the progress of the kids. He had been in his office, thinking that they were downstairs in the boxing gym, and had just poured himself a nip and raised it to his lips when the door of his office opened. Twenty-eight mothers and fathers, plus an assortment of local politicos – with an eye to coming elections – oh'ed and ah'ed and sputtered at the sight of him drinking Scotch. Despite the protestations of a few of the fathers, Jackie was fired on the spot.

Now, when he got a chance to tell the story of his decline, Jackie would often say: 'That job could've been my redemption after what happened at school. I could've probably risen to be director, you know? But that day, baby, I was too pissy-pukey to give a damn about anything. When Mr Anderson fired me, I just smiled, finished my drink, put my bottle in my pocket, and walked out. I didn't give a damn.'

The next time he came to Howard Street he came to stay. Its way of talking, walking, and acting became his with little difficulty; and he still didn't give a damn . . .

Last Saturday night, for instance, when Jackie saw little Jimmy Johnson and his gang drag a woman off the street into a hallway and come running out an hour later, he demonstrated that he didn't give a damn. He could've stopped them, even if he'd gotten beaten up in the process. He didn't.

Jimmy had looked up to him when he worked in the Boys' Club. The youngster was a natural athlete who seemed destined to eventually make the pros. But he'd been so attached to Jackie that he'd quit the Club and sports when Jackie was fired. He'd taken to the streets just as his hero had; but Jackie didn't give a damn. So he'd done nothing to keep them from raping that woman.

And tonight – he could've warned that Puerto Rican who came out of the M&M with the fag, Lillie, that he was in for a hell of a surprise, and might get robbed to boot. But, what the hell, he'd thought, hadn't he tried his damnedest to help these characters? None of them appreciated the sacrifices he'd made. Hadn't he messed up his own chances at life by boogy-joogying with them? Fuck them! They're down because they want to be down. That's why they resisted all help. If he ever raised a finger to help another no-good black bastard again, it would be a cold day in hell, no more wine would be made, and Skippy would be a punk.

He saw Cowboy coming out of the M&M. 'Hey, Cowboy. Can y'do a little somethin' for me tonight, man? Please, I need a taste bad.' His servile act never bothered him anymore; he was used to it, and he knew he needed it. If he didn't play on the egos of the Streeters he couldn't get anything from them.

'Man,' Cowboy said, 'didn't I just see you with a bottle 'bout an hour ago? What you think I am? – a good thing or somethin'?' He feigned more disgust for Jackie than he really had.

'No, no, Cowboy. I don't think that 'bout you, you do me better'n anybody I know. I had t'share that other bottle with Stanley White. I didn't hardly get none at all, he so greedy. Please, Cowboy ...? I swear I won't bother you no more tonight. And I'ma see you straight, too – soon's my ship comes in ...' He was so busy pleading that he didn't even notice that Cowboy had reached into his pocket and brought out a package of fifty wrapped pennies, which he'd gotten from an addict. He threw them at Jackie.

'Here, man,' Cowboy snarled. 'Now git the hell outta here an' lea' me alone!'

'Thanks, Cowboy baby! I ain't never gon' forgit you. I mean it, man, you one in a million. Soon's I git on my feet . . .'

'Yeah, yeah, man,' Cowboy interrupted. 'Make it, willya?'

Jackie did. He was anxious to get a bottle that he could drink all by himself for a change. But he cursed Cowboy savagely when he was out of earshot. As always, his attitude changed abruptly when his sense of security returned – and money for a bottle always brought it back – and all of his hate for the Streeters came crashing into his mind, bulldozing all other thoughts out of its way until the next time he was forced to beg from one of them.

Upon obtaining the bottle, he became occupied with escaping the sharp eyes of Stanley, Beeks, or any of the other mulligans of the street. If they saw him he'd be forced to share it with them, just as they were when he caught one of them with the groovy grape.

Lillie and the Puerto Rican, Jorge, were in one of Sue's rooms, lying across the bed, but, as yet, fully dressed, and kissing with a frenzy. Jorge had his hand on Lillie's false breast, while Lillie played around inside his pants. Lillie still, however, wouldn't let Jorge touch below the waist, except to feel his buttocks. Whenever the hand moved to the front their wrestling match would begin again. '*Después*, sugar, *después*,' Lillie whispered. 'Mother wants you good and hot.'

'*Qué pasa?*' Jorge asked breathlessly. 'For why we wait? *Quiero chingar, mujer.* Poosy – I wan poosy, *ahora*!'

His mixed Spanish and broken English presented no problem for Lillie now. He knew well what Jorge wanted, and that he was as ready as he'd ever be. After a final, lingering kiss, Lillie indicated the string which hung from the light: 'Now, sweetie. Turn out the light.'

They undressed in the dark, but Lillie kept on his bra and panties. Even while he toyed with Jorge's genitals he still wouldn't allow Jorge's hand to touch any place but on his back and his falsies. They continued to kiss for a few more minutes.

'How do you say "I love you" in Spanish, darling thing?' Lillie asked.

When Jorge finally understood he answered, 'Yo te amo.'

'Ooooh, that's so pretty, lover!' Lillie gushed. 'Tell me you love and I'll tell you. Oh, we'll be so exotic in Spanish!' He giggled and gave a tender squeeze to Jorge's tumid flesh; and when Jorge said, 'Yo te amo,' his voice trembled so with thick passion that he hardly understood himself.

'Yes, oh yes, you delightful animal! Yo te amo – Yo te amo, too.' They kissed and felt, and panted and kissed again. Jorge was whispering in rapid-fire Spanish now.

Moments passed, with just their breathing and soft moans to testify to any presence in the room. It was completely dark. There was no window and no light in the hall to peek in under the door.

The bedsprings squeaked feebly for a moment, then suddenly began to squeal like a boxful of frightened mice. A mad kind of scuffling and frenzied breathing followed the dull thud of a pillow hitting the floor. 'Ai yi yi!' Jorge bellowed. 'Un bicho. Tiene un bicho grande!' He scrambled around trying to get out of the bed. 'Wooman, fron where you getta deek?'

He jumped out of bed, frantically searching for the light string in the darkness. His hand hit it several times, but he was too excited to feel its lightness.

When he did finally grasp and jerk it, he saw that Lillie had reclined upon the bed in a seductive pose, looking quite calm. 'Now really, dear,' Lillie said, his expression turning to pained tolerance, 'there's no need to carry on so. After all, mother's loving is as good as any – and better than most. Don't look so upset.'

But Jorge couldn't take his eyes from the jockstrap which Lillie's organ was threatening to tear asunder. 'Maricón!' he spat. 'For why you no tella me what you are? I breaka you neck, good!' He was quivering with rage and frustration.

'Now, now, sweetie,' Lillie said soothingly. 'Don't get violent. Your mother's not exactly a weakling, you know. She can take care of herself very well.'

And he could. Lillie had dumped more than one guy who'd

made the stupid mistake of thinking that homosexuality and the ability to fight were mutually exclusive.

'*Cabrón!*' Jorge cried, still staring bug-eyed. 'You tricka me – you no a wooman. For why you no tella me what you are?'

Lillie turned over on his stomach. Looking over his shoulder and patting his behind, he said, '*Here* is what I am, baby. It's *all* that I am – and if you'll turn out that damned light, I'll guarantee you won't care, nor be able to tell the difference *what* I am.'

But he saw Jorge's pride demanded that he do something to soothe it. Lillie had been through this any number of times with men who hadn't known that he was a man himself. To assuage their petty little egos he usually had to take a punch or a slap; but when this was done he almost as often was treated to the sexual exhilaration he sought, as well as the enjoyment of seeing that he wasn't the real phony at all. The he-men huffed and puffed, and left the bed like lambs. Many came back for more.

He only hoped that Jorge wouldn't get too violent or pull a knife; otherwise he'd take a beating in silence: it was a fair enough price for the thrills he anticipated later on. He watched as Jorge slowly advanced upon him, he watched very carefully. If Jorge reached for his pants it would just be too bad.

The smack surprised him, it came so fast. With a perfunctory scream – not too loud – he fell back on the bed: 'Don't hurt mother, darling! *Yo te amo, yo te amo!*' In truth he wanted to laugh joyously for his victory. '*Yo te amo, yo te amo*, baby,' he repeated over and over again.

He succeeded in tying up Jorge's hands so that the blows became almost totally ineffective, and finally Jorge stopped fighting altogether; but he snatched away and stood by the bed, out of breath. Lillie sat up, making a good pretense at crying. Jorge stood over him, his chest heaving, and stared down at his head.

With a quick movement Lillie grabbed him around the waist, pulled him close, opened his mouth to Jorge's advancing organ, and closed his lips around it. In spite of his surprise, Jorge felt himself being filled by little leaps and bounds. And he didn't try to snatch away again.

'That's mother's delight, honey. That's it,' Lillie said softly against his abdomen. 'You're *so* sweet. *Yo te amo.*'

Within a few seconds, though, Jorge abruptly pushed Lillie's head away. Now it was Lillie's turn to get angry: he wasn't going to spend all night playing scapegoat to an ego. It was best to get someone more compatible than to put up with too much resistance. A little resistance was intriguing, but too much disgusted him.

But Jorge only went to the door to make sure that it was securely locked. He came back to Lillie, pulled out the light, and said with a shrug, '*Por Dios*, I try everyt'ing wan tine – but you remember: I no lika you, *maricón*!' He spoke with enough force to convince himself.

'Oh, I under*stand*, lover,' Lillie replied with sarcasm which escaped Jorge. 'Yes, your mother understands *per*fectly. She's had you *so* many times before; believe me, she has in*deed.*'

Jorge climbed into bed.

'Come on now, sweetie,' Lillie said tenderly, 'mother's steaming, simply *raging* . . . Uh-huh, that's it, lover, that's the way . . . Oooh! not so *hard*, darling – you'll *ruin* mother! Delightful, de*light*ful . . . Oh, you brute . . . You *hombre*!'

Jorge began to pant.

Lillie chuckled.

Five

Jimmy Johnson had known many disappointments in his sixteen years of life, but the greatest came when he saw Jackie Brown join the growing number of Howard Street derelicts.

Jackie had been everything that he himself wanted to be. People even said that they looked alike – because they both had very distinct Asiatic features – though Jimmy was smaller and darker. Jackie had been the older brother he'd never had and almost a replacement for his now-you-see-him-now-you-don't father. Outside of his mother, Jackie had been the only person he'd ever felt love for, and with it, respect. When Jackie had lost the job at the Boys' Club Jimmy had gone to the director and pleaded with him to take Jackie back. But Mr Anderson told him that the matter was out of his hands. Jimmy left the Club in tears and never returned.

He began to hang around Jackie as much as the man would allow. Jackie 'borrowed' Jimmy's allowance to buy drinks – he was still drinking whiskey then – and wouldn't even look for a job because, he explained, he had been 'blackballed.' Jimmy helped him move out of his apartment and into one room in the building where Hip and Gypsy Pearl had their room. Jimmy would go there every morning before school and leave Jackie most, and sometimes all, of his lunch money so that he could buy something to eat. Jackie bought whiskey; then he began to drink wine in order to get drunk quicker and more often.

No matter what Jimmy said to him he wouldn't even try to straighten out the mess he was making of his life. Jackie began to get sick, and Jimmy would stay from school to be with him. He even began to steal canned foods and wine for Jackie. He missed so many of South Side High's basketball practices that the coach, thinking that city and statewide stardom was swelling his head, benched him in games that were important, and, without him, certain to be losses. But this had no effect upon Jimmy; he missed practices and games, whenever Jackie wanted him to stay with him. Jimmy was finally kicked off the team. The school, which had been accustomed to finishing the season in first or second place, went into a string of losses that put it out of the running for the championship.

When Jimmy wasn't with Jackie, he was with a gang of young toughs who hung around the neighborhood, stole, and sneaked into movies. Mr Anderson found this out, and knew about Jimmy's connection with Jackie too. So one day he went to Jimmy's mother's house on Broome Street to try and talk him into going back to the Club and to school. Caught between the two grown-ups, one he liked and one he loved, Jimmy made a halfhearted promise to think it over and 'be good,' as his mother had pleaded. But once away from them, he didn't give their ideas a second thought; he felt too free now. He began to attend school, at most, only three or four times a month.

Yet something was happening to the feelings he'd had for Jackie. He was almost always in a state of morose depression, and everything seemed to disgust him, including Jackie, and many times, especially Jackie. The guidance counselor at school tried to talk to him on several occasions, but Jimmy was uncommunicative and even called the woman a 'drag' – at which, misunderstanding, she lost her temper – but everything was a drag these days. Finally he was suspended until his mother would come to school with him to talk with the principal.

He didn't tell his mother that he'd been suspended; he told her that he'd quit school and had a job. His mother, a low-paid factory worker who was finding it hard enough to be dunned each week for 'a little something' on the regular bills without owing for such extras as a sweatsuit she'd bought for Jimmy, was not as sorry as she pretended to be. Jimmy's father was worse than useless; he only turned up now and then, usually drunk and truculent. At first she asked Jimmy some embarrassing questions about his job – which he evaded by starting an argument about something else – but a week later, when he brought home seventy-five dollars and gave it to her, she stopped bothering him.

After that, Jimmy gave her money regularly. He worked one night a week, Saturday, when he and his gang went out mugging.

The Boys' Club and the school were far back in his past now, and his turnabout on Jackie was so total that he hated him with the intensity of a passion. One night he got his gang to hold Jackie while he beat him, smashed his wine bottle, and left him lying in the street, hoping that a passing car would complete the job. The beating was a relief to him, but it didn't stop the hating. Once Jackie could have taken on the whole gang; now he was pleading, abject, destroyed. Jimmy saw his face on every wino he met, and he hated them too.

Jackie knew that it was Jimmy who'd beaten him, yet, once the physical pain of it had gone, the emptiness inside of him remained. He faced this realization as he now faced everything else: he didn't give a damn . . .

As he lay on the hard oakwood bench in Police Headquarters, Jimmy Johnson cried without realizing it, until he felt the tears run down the sides of his face and into his ears. He wiped them away. There was no bravado about him now; he was afraid and he knew it. It had been a long time since he'd been afraid of anything; and, for the first time, he began to feel remorse about the rape. All the guys had admitted their parts in it – they couldn't very well deny it from the way everything turned on them. Sy had told everything, and the cops would soon get around to questioning them about some robberies, too, before they were finished. But he really couldn't blame Sy; under the same circumstances he probably would have done the same thing himself.

He wondered what Sy felt about the gang; it would be damned hard to look at each other now. He wouldn't admit to any robberies, though, no matter what Sy told the cops. Having a rape charge was bad enough; he wasn't going to put himself under the jail. He lit a cigarette, reminding himself that he'd have to stub it for later; there were only two left in the pack. Thinking again about the trouble he was in, and the probability of getting his head busted by the cops, he let out a curse.

A wino, sleeping on the floor, stirred and woke from the drunken stupor he'd been in ever since Jimmy had been put into the cell with him. In a voice as croaked and as brittle as burnt paper, he said, 'Hey, Sonny – sa'me on that butt, willya.'

Jimmy reached down calmly and punched the man in the face. 'My name ain't Sonny, and go fuck yourself, you wine-head bastard.' He stubbed out the cigarette on the bars of the cell, took off his sweater to use as a pillow, and lay back on the bench thinking about last Saturday night. It seemed to be far in the past, and as if it had happened to someone else, not to him. The whole scene was replayed for him. He might have been sitting in some movie watching it.

Jimmy, Butch, and Brother were huddled in the doorway of a closed storefront on Broome Street. It was raining very hard, the drops falling like so many beats of an endless drum roll, threatening to drown the world, it seemed, in rat-ta-tats. And while waiting for the rain to stop, and for Sy, they played a game called 'Mine,' in which each would pick a year and the closest to that of the next passing auto could claim it for his. The first one to reach five 'Mines' was the winner and got to punch the others once on each arm.

They had been playing the game for over an hour. Butch was ahead by a car. But then Jimmy decided that there weren't enough cars passing to make the game interesting, so they quit playing and just stood looking out at the rain, waiting.

'Man!' Brother complained, 'this weather is somethin' else! Damn rain ain't go' never stop fallin'. I should go home an' watch TV or somethin'.'

Jimmy listened to him without taking his eyes from the direction from which Sy was to come. He had both hands jammed deep into his pockets; his shoulders were hunched as if he were cold, though it was a warm night, and he only wore khaki pants and a pullover sweatershirt. He had a cigarette in his mouth with an extraordinary long ash drooping from it.

Butch, a short, very dark and stocky seventeen-year-old, said to Brother, 'Aw, man, take it easy. It ain't gon' rain all night –

'sides, Sy'll be here soon anyways.' He was irritated by Brother's reluctance to go out, which seemed to get greater with each passing week. To him, it smacked of fear. Turning to Jimmy, he said, 'Save me on that butt, Jim.'

Jimmy still didn't speak, but turned his head so that Butch could remove it from his lips; then he swung back around to his vigil.

'I damn sure oughta go home, boy,' Brother repeated. 'Ain't too many people comin' out tonight. We ain't go' make nuthin'. Hey, Jimmy, whyn't we cool it for tonight? Sy don't look like he comin' nohow.' It was true that he was becoming afraid, but he was even more afraid of being called 'chicken' if he refused to go with them. They'd spread it around the neighborhood that he was afraid and he'd have to fight every day – he'd probably have to fight Butch, too, before it was over. But he didn't want to; he'd seen what Butch would do to people, he was crazy. No, he didn't want to fight Butch, but he didn't want anybody looking down on him, either.

Butch responded to his last statement with a look of contempt, but before he could speak, Jimmy said, 'Here come Sy now.'

The three of them watched down the street as a figure approached, running from the direction of Morton Street School. Sy reached the comparative shelter of the doorway, breathing hard.

'Hey now,' he greeted as he burrowed his way to the back of the doorway. Steam rose from his forehead. 'What's to it, kinda dry tonight, ain't it?' He was smiling broadly.

Butch sneered, 'What took you so long, man? We thought you wasn't comin'.' He felt that he and Jimmy were the only ones who weren't afraid.

'Ahhh, you know how my mother is, man. She didn't want me to go outta the house, so I had to sneak.' He lit a cigarette.

Brother laughed. 'Yeah – *we* a bad influence on *you*! Boy, ain't *that* a bitch? She don't know you very good, do she?'

'She keep yellin' 'bout that time we got caught in ol' man Solomon's store,' Sy replied. 'She even searched my room, lookin' for that gun we took outta there.'

'Betcha she don't believe you really had somethin' to do with it,' Butch said. ''Member how she kept sayin' you was framed? An' it was your tip from the jump – hah!'

Brother said, 'Shit, you know how mothers is.' Then he mimicked: '"*My* son wouldn't *think* of doing something like that if it wasn't for those hoodlums, he's a *good* boy!"' Jimmy was the only one who didn't join in the laughter.

Butch bummed another cigarette, from Sy this time – but not before Sy complained, 'Man, don't you never buy none?' He handed him one, adding: 'You gon' smoke us all outta house an' home.' Butch paid no attention to him, but lit the cigarette. He looked at Jimmy, who was still watching the rain making small rivers in the gutter.

Butch asked, 'What's on your mind, Jim-Jam? Thinkin' 'bout that new cake you pulled from Baxter Terrace, huh?'

'What new cake?' asked Brother.

'You don't know her, man,' Butch rejoined. 'Name's Dee-Dee. She a fox, too. I think Jimmy strung out behind her. His nose is wide open.' He gave a lewd laugh.

Jimmy reached over and took the cigarette from Butch's lips, inhaled deeply, and let out a thick stream of smoke from his nostrils, but he said nothing. The streetlamp halfway down the block lighted his oriental features with an eerie glow; his nostrils flared and a strange smile played around his mouth. When he looked this way most people didn't know how to take him; sometimes he was being serious and sometimes he felt like joking.

He glanced at them, finally saying, 'I ain't thinkin' about that tramp. Don't no broad hook me.' The force of his words was all out of proportion to his expression. Sy and Butch knew that he really liked the girl, but they also believed that he meant what he'd said. 'I was thinkin' about cars,' Jimmy added softly. The others looked at each other, then at him quizzically.

'But we ain't playin' "Mine" now, Jimmy,' Brother said.

'No goddamn kiddin'!' Jimmy snapped at him. 'Don't you think I know that, Stupe? ... I mean, look at 'em. In this stinkin' weather you know what they remind me of?'

'What?' came the unison reply.

Jimmy's nostrils flared, the eyes chinked still more. 'They remind me of big, black man-eatin' bugs. From a distance that's just what they look like comin' toward you; those big, bright eyes all bugged out and devourin' everything in sight. And when they pass—' he grunted what could have been a laugh '—then those other eyes, the bloodshot ones, remind me of a little drunken papoose hangin' on a' Indian's back, winkin' and blinkin' its eyes, full and satisfied.'

They looked at him. The smile wavered on his lips for a moment before he burst out into the soft laughter which was one of his characteristics. Slowly, and then more certainly, they joined in with him.

Sy said, 'Man, you sure is somethin' else. Where you git them weird ideas you come up with?'

'Damn, Jimmy,' Butch chimed in. 'Sometimes I think you been usin' dope or somethin'.'

Jimmy stopped laughing abruptly. 'The rain's stoppin', let's go make some bread before we blow the whole night.'

'Yeah!' Butch seconded enthusiastically. He took out his sandbag, made from three pairs of socks and filled with sand packed around a wooden ball about the size of a regulation baseball. 'C'mon, le's go.' He whacked Brother on the leg with it.

Brother yelped, 'Oow, you bastard, knock it off!' and missed with a punch aimed at Butch's arm.

'What time was it when you left home, Sy?' Jimmy asked.

''Bout ten-thirty. I can't stay out too late, neither. My mother'll have a goddamn fit on me if she finds out I split.'

Butch, in an impatient and accusing tone, said, 'So quit beefin', man. You must be gittin' scared or somethin'.'

Sy flew hot: 'You little black mothafucka! Who you talkin' 'bout scared?' He lunged at Butch, but Jimmy and Brother got between them. Brother grabbed Butch's arm just as he was about to bring the sandbag down on Sy's head.

'I'ma show you who scared!' Sy shouted at Butch.

'Yeah, punk – show me!' Butch yelled right back.

Sy started for him again, but Jimmy, struggling with him, said, 'Lay off, Sy. He didn't mean nothin'. He only kiddin', man, be cool.' He gave Butch a look which told him that he'd better agree.

Without showing any reluctance Butch said, 'Yeah, man, I was just kiddin'. Since when you can't take a joke? Jesus fuckin' Christ!'

'Since you started that scared shit – that's since when,' Sy retorted in a calmer voice. 'I don't play that junk, man, and you better know.'

'Aw*right*, like, I'm *sorry*, okay?' Butch said in an exaggerated display of deference, with palms up, shoulders hunched, and an indefinable smile on his face.

'Okay,' Sy answered, forcing himself to be satisfied with the apology which didn't really apologize.

Jimmy said, 'We gon' git enough fightin' tryin' to take off some of these chumps' money tonight, so let's save it for them.' Brother seconded that, and the four boys left the storefront.

Jimmy, it seemed, had an almost uncanny knack for spotting a loaded chump. He wasn't wrong often, and the others had come to rely upon his judgment. He'd told them that, in their neighborhood, when a chump had money you could tell it by the way he walked. One night he picked two hundred-dollar chumps in succession; the other boys were amazed and from then on would pounce on anyone he indicated.

They walked around for an hour without seeing anything likely. Butch became impatient and let Jimmy know it. They were going up Fifteenth Avenue toward Bergen Street, but Jimmy abruptly reversed direction. He'd decided to try the sop joint – the bathhouse and masseur's salon on Howard Street – even though they'd been working Howard Street much too regularly, along with a couple of other gangs.

As they walked no one spoke, but Butch whistled a tuneless song between his teeth. He and Brother were behind Jimmy and Sy. All of them had their hands in their pockets. Jimmy was the only one with a cap, perched jauntily upon his woolly head. They passed few people, and those they did meet almost invariably crossed to the other side of the street. Butch would yell at one occasionally: 'Ain't nobody thinkin' 'bout you, mothafucka!' Or, if it was a woman: 'Don't nobody want you, you worn-out bitch!'

The others seldom bothered to look unless the person spoken to made a reply. If the boys were feeling good they would chase the person for a little ways, not really trying to catch up, but getting a little excitement out of their otherwise boring life.

When they finally reached Howard Street, it was just beginning to be peopled again after the rain. A few doors from the bathhouse was an alley between two buildings, which always served as their escape route. They would go through the backyards, over fences, and, in some cases, over rooftops, and come out anywhere in the square-block area. Without such a good escape route Jimmy wouldn't have picked out the bathhouse: there were far too many plainclothes cops on Howard Street, and it was easy to get caught if one didn't know the way out. Of course, the cops knew about the alley, but it wasn't the only way out. Many of the buildings had protection for escapists, and there weren't enough cops to cover them all.

The boys waited in a darkened hallway near the bathhouse, waiting and watching the bathhouse and the street. They let two men leave the bathhouse, but as the third left Jimmy said in a whisper, 'This one.'

He whistled as he walked toward them. They heard his foot-steps coming closer and closer.

'Yeah,' Jimmy whispered. 'He's happy. He done had a bath and a rubdown, and he got money in his slide. You git low, Brother. Butch, git that bag ready – and don't miss! Me and Sy'll hit when he falls.'

The man came even with the hallway. 'Now!' Jimmy said.

The man turned, surprised. Reflex made him throw up his hands for defense, and when he did, Brother hit him hard in the groin; the hundred and sixty pounds behind the punch was heavy and accurate. A half-second later the sandbag landed against the man's head with a deep thud. He crumpled, trying to clutch at both spots at the same time. His knees hit the pavement with a thump and he pitched forward on his face – out.

Jimmy and Sy wasted no time in going through his pockets. They searched for a money belt and ripped his shoes from his feet while Butch and Brother played chickie. In two minutes or less the man was naked except for his undershorts.

Someone came out of the bathhouse, saw them, and ran back inside after realizing what was happening and yelling to them to stop. They heard him shouting for someone inside to call the police.

'Awright, let's make it!' Jimmy ordered. They ran through the alley. After climbing two fences they reached Broome Street and from there proceeded quickly to their hideout: an old, condemned house which served as a retreat for winos and junkies in bad weather.

When they'd placed all of their loot on top of a steel footlocker which they kept on the top floor of the building, they found that they had an expensive-looking watch, a ring, and one hundred and forty-seven dollars and some odd change.

'Hot damn!' Brother shouted joyously. 'Boy, you sure hit the number tonight, baby – in both races! Hot damn, Jim-baby, I love you!'

Sy exclaimed, 'Don't know what we'd do without you, man. A big, fat one on the first try!'

And Butch cried, 'Man, we ain't gotta do nuthin' else tonight. This is the most, baby. I mean abso-goddamn-lute most! Know what? I'ma sleep good tonight – then tomorra, after we down the watch and ring to Gus the Fence, I'm goin' downtown and buy me some new duds. Yeah!'

Jimmy hardly even smiled, but he was basking in the praise. Something else was on his mind: 'Let's celebrate with some free cunt,' he said.

'How?' the others said at once.

'What, y'all kiddin' or somethin'?' Jimmy barked derisively. 'We grab one of them whores off Howard Street and take what the squares gotta pay for – that's how!'

'Yeah, yeah!' Sy jumped up. In the semidarkness of the room he tripped and bumped his shin against the footlocker. They laughed at him. He rubbed at the sore spot and continued talking: 'And she can't go to the cops neither, 'cause everybody knows ain't nothin' but whores around there. All of 'em got records for sellin' it. All we gotta say is we bought it and she got mad 'cause we wouldn't give her a tip or somethin', dig it?'

'Man, what the hell we waitin' for then?' Butch cried excitedly. 'Ain't nuthin' like a little bit to make ya feel *so* good. Ooowee! I sure can sleep tight then.' Jimmy was the only one who wasn't up dancing around.

They left the building separately to meet on Howard Street in an hour.

No one was around the bathhouse. The cops were gone and so was the ambulance which had taken the mugging victim to Martland Medical Center. The boys were near Mercer Street now, waiting in the shadows of the icehouse. An old, ragged-looking birch tree provided them with further protection, though it had seen better days and would be dead before much longer.

The long block had only one light that was any good, and it stood down near Court Street. The street was dark and the whores and their tricks preferred it that way.

It was an hour's wait for them before they finally saw an unescorted woman coming in their direction. She seemed to be searching for something or someone. The bars in the short block were full and noisy, but few people came onto the street except to go to Sue's or to one of the other bars.

The boys ducked back into the shadows. There was a hallway next to the icehouse in which they'd busted the light bulb. Their plan was simple: they'd grab the woman and take her in the backyard.

'Look at her,' Butch said. 'She just a-lookin' for a john.'

'Sy,' Jimmy said harshly, 'stop that gigglin'!'

'I can't help it,' Sy said, barely containing himself. 'We gon' give her a workout so she don't git rusty.' He grabbed his mouth to keep from letting uncontrollable laughter escape him.

Jimmy allowed the woman to get a step beyond where they hid themselves, then he jumped out and grabbed her from behind, clasping one hand firmly over her mouth while his other locked on her arm. Butch grabbed her other arm and they dragged her into the dark hallway. She struggled violently, trying to scream and to bite Jimmy's hand.

'Grab her legs, Sy!' Jimmy gasped. The woman struggled even more. She obviously knew what was in store for her.

'I can't hold this bitch much longer. Dammit, Butch, knock her out! Hurry up before she screams!'

Butch brought the bag down. 'Ow, you sonofabitch!' Jimmy yelled out. 'Dumb bastard, *you hit me*!'

'Shit, man, I'm sorry. I can't see in this dark.' He was almost panicky as he felt for her head with his free hand. Taking a deep breath he brought the sandbag down, snatching his hand away just before the familiar thud of the bag reached its target. The woman went limp and Butch sighed in relief.

Jimmy had to catch his breath: 'Goddamn, she was strong,' he said, rubbing gingerly at the sore spot on his shoulder where the sandbag had landed. 'Put a gag on her and take her in the backyard,' he ordered. 'And make sure her hands is tied good, too.'

The others carried her to the back and put her on the ground. They tore down a couple of clotheslines, knotted them around her wrists, and tied the other ends to two of the poles. She lay arms outstretched, legs free.

'Wake her up,' Jimmy said. 'I don't want no knocked-out stuff. She might as well git her kicks, too.'

Brother felt for her face and slapped her awake. She moaned, then realizing what was happening to her, began kicking about in the darkness. But she could move only from the waist down.

'Seconds!' Sy called. No one but Jimmy could get firsts, as they all knew. Butch got thirds and Brother last – which he wasn't too happy about.

After they'd all had their turn on her Sy wanted to go again. 'Goddamn, Sy, let her alone. Let's git outta her,' Brother said. 'Don't be greedy, man, let's make it.'

'You mind your own fuckin' business!' Sy bristled at him. Then, without another word, he again lay down in the darkness with the woman. They had needlessly put a blindfold on her; it, along with the gag, was soaked in tears and the mucus from her running nose.

Jimmy and Butch smoked cigarettes while Brother looked nervously around at the tall buildings which surrounded them. They cast long and deep shadows in the still cloudy and damp night. To himself he vowed solemnly that this was his last Saturday for being with them. No matter what the others said or thought about him, he wasn't going out again. He'd even fight Butch, and Jimmy too, if it came to that, but he wasn't going to do this anymore.

Sy felt the heaving, racking sobs that came from the woman's stomach shake him along with her. He got an acute attack of conscience and got up before he was finished. He felt suddenly weak in his stomach now. Something was wrong and he didn't know what it was.

Butch, seeing him get up, said, 'She sure got hot nookie huh, Sy?' He laughed ribaldly.

'Sure is, bay-bee,' Sy answered gaily. He hesitated: 'I gotta take a leak. Be right back.' He went to the hall entrance which led to the street. He hoped that they wouldn't hear him vomiting.

'I wonder what she look like?' Butch mused apathetically to no one in particular.

'Hell, strick a match and let's see,' Jimmy said.

Interestedly now, Butch said, 'I hope it's Gypsy Pearl, man, she a fine babe!' But his voice dropped: 'Ain't her, though. This bitch's hair is too nappy – Gypsy Pearl got *good* hair.' He was disappointed and a little angry.

Brother struck a match after Jimmy pulled the blindfold from the woman's eyes. It flared bright for a moment and a loud gasp came from each of the boys.

'Sy! Sy!' Jimmy called, not caring who heard now. 'Sy, looka here, man! She musta been lookin' for you!'

Sy came swaggering toward them. 'What the hell you talkin' 'bout, man. Ain't no whores got no business lookin' for me.'

As he stood over the woman, preparing to light a match, the others ran toward the entrance. He smiled. They were trying to play a joke on him. Making like the cops were coming, trying to get him to run blindly.

He struck the match and looked at the woman's face in the first harsh glow of the light.

Tears were streaming profusely down her cheeks. She closed her eyes to keep from looking at him. Sy's breath was pushed violently out of him. He backed away, bug-eyed with astonished disbelief. He staggered and almost fell, whimpering lightly, then louder, until he was screaming at the top of his lungs: 'Oh no! No! My God, NO! *MOMMAAAAA!*'

The bum lying on the floor woke up again. 'Whatcha say, kid?'

Jimmy realized that he'd spoken aloud, but he repeated it automatically to the wino. 'I said, "How the hell was we to know it was his mother?"' But he'd said it softly, almost to himself.

'Whatcha talkin' about, kid. You talkin' about my dead mother? I don't play the dozens, kid. Don't talk about my mother. I'll kill ya right now.' He got up from the floor and staggered to the rear of the cell to the toilet, mumbling to himself. The toilets of the cellblock had the whole place smelling of excrement and urine. This, mixed in with the vomit of junkies and alcoholics and the blood of 'interrogated' suspects, had Jimmy continuously on the edge of nausea. Although he'd been here all day and a good part of the night, he couldn't get his stomach to really settle down. He was sure that he'd never get the scent out of his clothes. He'd have to throw them away.

He lit his last cigarette, hoping that his mother would soon come and bring him some money. It would be tough going in this place without cigarettes.

Suddenly, the bum's presence began to irritate him and he shouted, 'Why don't you stop pissin' so damn much? You got this place stinkin' like hell!' Why they put a bum in with him he'd never know.

The man was perhaps forty years old, but he looked every bit of sixty. He turned his red-rimmed eyes on Jimmy: 'You think you're a pretty hip kid, don't you?' he asked.

'You fuckin' A-right!' Jimmy snapped. 'The hippest thing a bum like you'll ever know.'

Solicitously the man asked, 'Would ya save me on that butt, please?'

'Suck! I ain't supportin' you.' Jimmy threw it into the toilet even though he wasn't nearly finished with it himself. He knew that he'd regret it later on, but, he reasoned, he wasn't going to let this wine-head make him look like a chump.

'You go to school, kid?'

'Non'a your business! Hey, look – why don't you just shut up? Go back to sleep or somethin', huh?' He needed to use the toilet himself now, but he resolved to burst open rather than use the one in this cell.

The man lay back on the floor. 'What makes you think you're so hip, kid?' he asked.

'What makes anybody, lame? It's what you got goin' for ya. What ya got up here,' Jimmy answered in a nasty tone as he tapped his temple.

'How old are you – sixteen? Seventeen? You think talkin' slick and walkin' *hep* makes you hip? You're wrong, kid. That's not where it's at.'

'Aaah, man, what the hell you know? You ain't nothin' but a skid-row stewbum. I seen guys like you before. You can't tell me a damned thing. I got more on the ball right now than you ever had or ever *will* have. You ain't shit!'

The man sat up on the floor and crossed his legs in yoga fashion, and leaned his back against the wall facing Jimmy. His face was a horrible mask of cuts from fighting with knives and bottles – plus the ravages of substituting alcohol for breakfast, lunch, and dinner and in-between-meals snacks. He was of medium height, but his shoulders were terribly stooped. The crown of his head was completely bald, but along the sides, where hair grew, Jimmy saw that he was white-headed. His skin was very light and the part of his face that wasn't covered with a week-old beard had a greenish tinge to it.

He pointed a nicotine-stained finger at Jimmy and said, 'You got a lot to learn, kid, a lot to learn . . . While you're on your high horse lookin' down at me, life's passin' you by. You'll learn that your shit stinks too one day.'

'I know one thing, though,' Jimmy hooted at him. 'It's a lot sweeter than that green junk that comes outta you.'

'That may be true,' the man agreed. 'But it don't stop yours from smellin' just the same. How much you stink don't really matter – the fact is you stink. That's why you think a person is hip from the mind; the mind don't make you hip, kid. People are hip from here.' He pointed at his stomach. 'He's born that way – nobody, no mental attitude can make him hip. If you were really hip then you'd be the first one to admit that you ain't nothin' but people, and stink right along with the rest of us, no better than anybody else. Do you know what a prerequisite is?'

'Hell, yes,' Jimmy lied.

'Well, what I just told you is the prerequisite to hipness. You oughta dig yourself before it's too late. But I realize that you're still young yet. You really don't know where it's at.'

Jimmy sat in silence for a long while, looking at the man, overwhelmed by what he'd said, but determined to make some reply that would be cool and vitiating.

At length he said, 'You wanna know why I look down on a bum like you?' Without waiting for a reply he went on: 'I look down on you to see how high I stand, I can judge better that way. Can you dig that?' His nostrils flared and his sardonic smile caused his eyes almost to close.

The man didn't say anything, however, so Jimmy continued pressing home his point. 'Yeah, that's where it's at for real. All you wash-up cocksuckas think that age and *experience* means so damn much, but how come you ain't got nothin' then? Age don't git you a damn thing if you ain't right in the knowledge-box. I done peeped you old cats' hole card – and you know what I dug?' He smiled again without waiting for an answer: 'I dug that the only thing you ever had on a young, down stud was a longer length of time to make damn fools outta yourselves, that's all. And that's why you ain't got a damn thing, never had a damn thing and ain't gon never git a damn thing! – Now dig your*self*, bum! If you wanna prove what I say, then just look at you – on the goddamn floor of a smelly cell. What the fuck can *you* tell *me*?'

The man farted and Jimmy cursed him. 'I dig myself, kid,' the man said. 'I dig myself now. But it's too late for me, and it's too late for you, too, because you ain't got it in the stomach. I'm like I am because I *was* like you at one time, just like you. Pretty soon you'll be like me, so we're even.' He lay down again with his face to the wall, farting again in the process.

Jimmy merely repeated the first words he'd ever spoken to the man: 'Go fuck yourself, punk.' Then he lay down again on the hard bench, staring up at the ceiling.

He even hoped that the detectives would come to get him soon, just so he could get out of this cell – even though he knew that their 'questioning' would probably take the form of a beating for him; he almost welcomed that. He needed some sleep, too, in order to be alert in case they tried to trick him into admitting any robberies. The way Sy was talking they'd all wind up in jail for a thousand years if he weren't careful.

Again he wondered what Sy was feeling, and he couldn't suppress the giggle that shook him for a moment. He shut his eyes tight, trying to forget the whole thing, hoping that sleep would rob his conscious thoughts. But all he could do was to think about his own mother and what he would have done if it had been her that they'd raped. He could see no other way in which he would have been able to face her, and he saw none for Sy, either. He suddenly felt worn out and exhausted, and before he knew it sleep had captured him.

He only slept for a few minutes before the man on the floor woke him with loud snores. Now he wasn't tired anymore. He sat up and watched him sleeping. Nothing but a tramp, he thought to himself. Like Jackie Brown: educated and stupid. Educated and so what? It didn't mean a damned thing – they were bums in spite of it.

There was an inch-long butt lying in the corner near the toilet, brown with age, or piss, and hard as a pebble. Jimmy reached for it.

Six

Hip was only mildly surprised to see his brother walk into the room with Gypsy Pearl, and he recovered from it very quickly. 'Shots, baby. How you doin'?' he greeted. Without waiting for a reply he turned to Gypsy Pearl. 'You bring any stuff, woman?' When she nodded sullenly he added, 'Well, what the hell you standin' there lookin' stupid for? – give it up!'

She threw four little packets on the bed beside him. He smiled with a painful effort that made him blink his eyes rapidly, like a prelude to crying. But he was far from tears. He grabbed up the stuff possessively, got off the bed, which took almost half of the room's space, and placed them on top of the large TV console that served as a table – it was just a shell, there was no tube in it and no knobs. Hip sat back down on the bed looking at them. He seemed to smile more easily now. Franchot studied him and sadly reflected on how much Hip had physically changed. They looked at each other for a long while.

The room had one large window near the head of the bed, which was fixed with a wire mesh screen; Hip often thought it was to keep him in rather than to keep thieves out. At the foot of the bed was a four-foot aisle, separating the bed from a wardrobe which took up the whole back wall. A small bureau sat there also, and had to be moved in order to open the right side of the wardrobe. This left about five feet for Gypsy Pearl and Franchot to stand in comfortably after entering.

Wallpaper covered two of the walls, but most of the flowers designs were obscured by brownish stains. 'The flowers done pissed on the walls!' Hip had once told Gypsy Pearl. The other two walls were bare and dirty gray. The wooden floor had strips missing so that Gypsy Pearl had to take care where she stepped in her high heels. The bed was extraordinarily large with a big stuffed mattress that hung over the sides and sagged deeply in the middle. The rancid smells of the place almost made Franchot wish that he hadn't come.

He looked at Hip with a pity and contempt that almost overwhelmed him. Hip looked like a bum. Like any of the thousands of bums he'd seen during his life; and the crossed scar on his forehead, scabby and black, would make him look much worse when it healed. Franchot shook his head and finally took his eyes away from his brother.

Hip didn't like the implications of the headshake. 'Have a seat, Shots, have a seat,' he said, slightly miffed. Then, to Gypsy Pearl: 'Git the stool, bitch. Can't you see my brother wanna siddown?' He smiled crookedly at Franchot as she got down on her knees and pulled a short tripod from under the bed. Still on her knees, she pushed it toward Franchot, but he refused it.

'You sit on it,' he said softly, helping her to her feet.

'She can sit on the goddamn TV!' Hip said, but Franchot insistently sat her on the stool anyway. Hip took a crumpled pack of cigarettes from his shirt pocket without offering any. Franchot pushed the dope to the side and sat on the console shell. He took out his own cigarettes, gave Gypsy Pearl one, and lighted them both.

Hip's face was distorted with his crooked smile. 'Still the same ol' Sir Galahad, eh, Shots?'

'No,' Franchot said calmly, 'just still ol' Sir Me.' Then, to try and get his visit off to a more congenial start, he added: 'What you been doin' for yourself, little bro?'

Hip wasn't reluctant to make it pleasanter. 'Oh, I been coolin' it pretty much, man. Ain't nothin' t'me – by the way, I heard somethin' 'bout you s'poze to git married. Congrats.'

'Married!' Franchot's eyes widened in surprise. 'Me? To who!'

'Rosemary Baker – at least that's what Irene Smith told me one night on Howard Street. I think we was in Mann's that night. It ain't true?'

Before Franchot had a chance to answer Hip began to laugh loudly, and even though his laugh rasped and croaked, it nevertheless was contagious. Before long Franchot had joined in with him, laughing just as hard. Gypsy Pearl looked from one to the other, then she began to laugh also, not knowing what was so funny, but unable to resist the spirit of their mood. It was a good laugh and the tension which had been building was now completely gone.

Franchot's laughter slowed, and he looked at Hip. He tried to bring a look of seriousness – without severity – to his own face. He asked, 'When you gon' get yourself together, Lonnie?'

The question hadn't been unexpected by Hip. He knew that it was inevitable from the moment he saw Franchot come through the door of the room – it always came up when they met. They'd both been laughing so hard simply because they knew the question would come. The monotony of thinking about getting 'together' – getting a job and living like Franchot – was merely lightened by the preceding laughter.

However, before Hip had a chance to answer, Gypsy Pearl cut in: 'Lonnie? Is that your real name, Hip? Lonnie? Well I'll be—'

'On your ass if you don't shut up!' Hip snapped.

'Lonnie?' she laughed. 'My goodness, who woulda thought it!'

'Bitch, I done told you . . .' Hip started for her, but he had to go past Franchot, who gently grabbed him by the shoulders and sat him back down on the bed.

'Take it easy, Lonnie,' he soothed. 'She didn't mean no harm. You oughta be proud of your name, not 'shamed of it.'

'It ain't that, Shots. You don't know that whore like I do. I'm fuckin' her and I know where she at.' He glared at her for a moment, and when he finally looked away from her it was as if the small disturbance had never occurred; he immediately went back to the question Franchot had asked: 'I'm gittin' myself together, Shots. Soon's I kick this habit I'm gon' square up and git a job. In fact, just yesterday I was thinkin' about askin' you to see what you can do for me. I mean, like, when I get clean. Think you can git me on with you?'

'You really mean that, Lonnie?' Franchot asked incredulously.

'Yeah, man. 'Co'se I do!' Hip was nodding his head vigorously. 'I'ma really kick, bro; square right on up. I been thinkin' 'bout it a long time now. I'm tired of this grind' – here he gave Gypsy Pearl a hostile look, adding: '—and everything about it.'

She raised one of her eyebrows in uncensored doubt and looked away from him to the wall, then back to him again. She'd heard this before. She also knew that it was normal for almost all junkies to make the very same statement – until it came time to really do it.

Hip knew what she was thinking. He turned on her again. 'You git outta here, woman! Shots, didn't I tell you she bears watchin'? Look at her! Starin' big-eyed at me. What you thinkin', woman? You thinkin' I can't kick if I wanna?'

'Hip, I didn't say nothin',' she answered in a small voice that tore at Franchot's heart. Her beautiful eyes were imploring.

Franchot blurted out, 'Lay off the woman, Lonnie. You act like you got a complex or somethin'.'

'Shit!' Hip exclaimed. 'She enough to gimme more'n a complex – that bitch thinks she slick, man!'

Gypsy Pearl said, 'I'm sorry, Hip,' so innocently that it made Franchot even more sympathetic to her. He was desperately hoping that his brother wouldn't try to beat her while he was here. He didn't want to get into their business, but he couldn't have stood by and watched it without doing anything.

He felt vastly relieved when Hip went into his pocket, pulled out a roll of bills, and handed them to her. 'Take one of them ten-spots off and go get my brother some likker – and bring some smokes back, too. Stay gone for an hour. If you a minute late or early I'm breakin' you neck!' He held out his hand while she put the money, except for the ten dollars, back into it.

Franchot hadn't particularly wanted anything else to drink tonight, but it seemed best to let her get away for a while, even though he hated to see her leave. He was positive that no other woman had ever looked so delicious to him as she.

Once outside of the room Gypsy Pearl began to cry. The tears came steadily and angrily. Usually she didn't mind the way

Hip treated her, but to be humiliated in front of Franchot seemed the height of painful frustration. He was everything that Hip wasn't. How could they have come from the same two people?

She wiped away her tears and headed for Broome Street, where Two-Day Sheik ran an after-hours joint. She walked along wondering how she'd ever got involved with Hip, how she could've allowed herself to get involved in the type of life he made her lead. It all had happened so fast – and so naturally – that she had a hard time trying to piece it together. One minute, it seemed, she was Pearl Dupree, wondering what it was to be a Howard Streeter, and the next thing she was Gypsy Pearl, Howard Street personified, with all of her curiosity about everything gone. Now she knew, but she was sorry for the firsthand knowledge.

Her mother used to hate even to walk past Howard Street. She'd walked on Broome or West, but not Howard, many times going far out of her way to avoid it. Everything her mother hated was on Howard Street: wine-heads, junkies, whores, and a religion that wasn't compatible with her own. Gypsy Pearl hadn't found out until much later that her father was also on Howard Street – living common-law with another woman. Then Gypsy Pearl realized that this was what her mother hated most about Howard Street.

Nevertheless, Gypsy Pearl had loved her father; and she cherished his memory now that he was dead: stabbed in his sleep by his common-law wife.

She'd never known the reason for the breakup of her parents' marriage or understood why her mother tried so hard to turn her against her father. But the more her mother tried, the more she clung to the love she bore him. There was nothing he didn't try to give her, and nothing that she asked for was ever long in coming. He even had two pet names for her: Pete, which he used most of the time, and Pigeon, which was saved for the times when she would cuddle in his lap to be held in the tremendous safety of his secure arms. And there was his teasing name for her: Ol' Ugly; his use of this reflected a jolly mood because, when she was five or six years old, anyone or anything which drew her anger would be treated to her equivalent of cursing – she'd shout: 'You ol'ugly, you!'

He used to take her to Coney Island, the Zoo, movies, and once even to a Broadway show. Many times they'd just spend a whole afternoon riding in his car; and she'd always return home to her mother's apartment loaded down with things he'd bought for her.

No austere mother could compete with this treatment – and Gypsy Pearl's didn't try; her main concerns were Church and discipline.

Gypsy Pearl used to sneak away and visit him on Howard Street whenever she could. She loved being around him, and when it came time to return to her mother's she'd always put up a fight. She even liked his woman, Savannah, as she liked everything connected with her father. She'd pester him with questions about why she couldn't live with him instead of her mother, not knowing that it was a question of law which kept them separated, not love. In fact, his love for her was the very indirect cause of his death.

On her last visit to him she'd cried and argued as usual when he tried to take her home. 'Why can't I stay with you?' she'd asked. 'I don't wanna go home, I wanna stay here!'

'Pete, honey,' he said in his smooth deep voice, 'you know I want you, but the law says your mother has to keep you.'

'I don't care, I don't care! I want you!'

He couldn't make her see why she couldn't live with him, and by the time they'd reached her mother's both of them were in tears. He returned to his apartment and told Savannah that he was going to take his daughter and leave the state, perhaps even the country. Savannah, seeing that he'd been drinking, tried to talk him out of it. Soon they were arguing, and still later, when he was completely drunk, he gave her a terrible beating. That night while he slept she stabbed him to death with a butcher knife.

That had been ten years ago and Gypsy Pearl still sometimes cried about it. Savannah had been sentenced to five years for manslaughter. She did two years and made parole. No one in Newark had seen her since.

After finishing high school, Gypsy Pearl went to work in a restaurant co-owned by Red Shirt Charlie and Fish-Man Floyd. She still lived with her mother, but it was only through a tenuous toleration that was easily broken by insignificant arguments. Many times an argument would involve no more than her mother's concept of 'late hours,' though Gypsy Pearl was supporting herself and had never stayed out past one o'clock in her life.

The chief cause of their dissension, however, was that her mother knew that Red Shirt and Floyd were Howard Streeters – and pimps at that. She didn't like the idea of her daughter working for them, though the restaurant was a very nice place, and inexpensive. Their last argument came to a head when her mother told her to quit either the job or the house. Gypsy Pearl chose the latter. They'd seen each other only twice since.

It wasn't long after she'd moved out of her mother's apartment that she'd started going with Red Shirt Charlie. Although she was dazzled by his flamboyant attitude toward life, his new car, fast friends, and the ease with which he handled money and women, it was more out of defiance for what she knew were her mother's wishes that she went with him than because she really cared for him. But he treated her well; he doubled her salary and paid the rent for the three-room apartment she'd moved into on Belmont Avenue.

Red Shirt Charlie had most of the things that women admired. Besides his Cadillac and business, there was his beautiful apartment, his lavish parties – the wondrous facade of a 'doin' good' pimp and gambler. He was Third Ward successful.

The restaurant wasn't, though. If he and Fish-Man Floyd hadn't poured their hustling and gambling money into it, trying to make it pay off, it would have gone under, because the people seemed to prefer a little greasy-spoon joint down the street from their place. It was the kind of place where the customers could raise all the hell they wanted without danger of being thrown out, and, in the type neighborhood they were in, this meant a lot.

Nevertheless, male patronage increased after Gypsy Pearl

began working in the restaurant – The Fleetwood, named in honor of its owners' cars. She was beautiful and they spent money to watch her walk and hear her talk. It was here that she'd first seen Hip Ritchwood, and he, her.

He had come in with a friend, and, after seeing her, he came often and alone. When he didn't feel like eating he'd sit and drink cup after cup of coffee, making small talk and watching. He knew that she was Red Shirt's woman, and knowing Red Shirt, automatically assumed that she was tricking – probably exclusively for Red Shirt's big shot friends, since he hadn't seen her working Howard Street.

Hip didn't particularly care for her as a woman alone, though he couldn't help but be struck by such a vision, and from looking at her got the same sensual pleasure that any other man would. Aware that she was special, being without a woman at the time, he acted on the premise that if he could put her on Howard Street he'd clean up. She'd easily be a ten-dollar chick and he'd be through worrying about where his next fix was coming from. He could stop throwing so many bricks at the jailhouse and lie back in the shade, cooling it.

She liked him immediately; thought him a little thin for his height, but handsome. And when he talked to her – which was as often as he could – she found him intelligent and refreshing in his hipster way, and a relief during the dull hours when the restaurant was doing slow-walk business. She hadn't known that he was a junkie. But it wouldn't have mattered, since she had the same tolerant attitude toward them as most of the Third Ward people had: 'Mind your business and I'll tend to mine.' Gypsy Pearl liked to have him come, but Red Shirt didn't, though he said nothing to Hip.

One afternoon Hip asked her, 'You like the movies?'

'I like 'em pretty good,' she answered.

'There's a boss one at the Paramount – wanna go with me tomorrow?'

'Oh, I don't know if I can,' she replied coyly. 'Red Shirt is already jealous of me talkin' to you so much – told me about it last night, in fact.'

'He don't have to know about it. You don't tell, I won't. How 'bout it?'

'Well, I'd like to and all, but . . .'

'Then do it! You ain't married to him, you know, and he . . . I mean, like, he probably won't ever marry you—' Hip hesitated, then said, 'But that's you and his business. I just wanna take you to the show.' He'd brought up the impossibility of Red Shirt marrying her because he'd thought that she was a whore. This was the manner in which many of the small-time pimps took up the assault of another's woman. And it was true that holding out the teaser of marriage many times worked wonders.

But Gypsy Pearl was only irritated by his presumptuousness. 'I realize that,' she answered curtly. 'But what you don't seem to know is that maybe *I* don't wanna marry *him*. You don't wanna marry every girl you go with, do you?'

'No,' he rejoined, realizing his mistake.

'Well, then, why should I wanna marry every guy I go with?' The conversation's unfavorable circle was interrupted by a late afternoon customer who came in for a cup of coffee and a piece of custard pie.

After serving him, she came back to the table, sat down, and took up where she'd left off. 'You know, I'd like to know what it is that makes men think every girl who goes with them, or even goes to bed with them, wants to marry them, too. Why do y'all have such stupid egos?'

Her agitation, he saw, was gone. He gave her his most contrite look. 'I'm sorry, really. I took too much for granted.' He smiled slowly. 'But you goin' with me to the show, ain't you?'

She answered his smile with a warming one of her own. 'Yeah, I'll go. Tomorrow?'

'Uh-huh; 'bout five o'clock. Crazy?'

'Crazy,' she said . . .

That had been their beginning. So simple, she recalled, no different than millions of other beginnings. But now, the complexity of it!

There were only four people in Two-Day Sheik's joint: black-jack players. She had been so wrapped up in her thoughts that she couldn't even remember what had so attracted her to Hip. The things he valued, dope – and the almost impossible junkie's dream of 'squaring up' – meant nothing to her. Yet, now that she was with him, she didn't see any way out; any way of living a decent life ... with someone like Franchot. No. There was no need even to think about it. Franchot was a world removed. And Hip was not about to let her go, anyway – she was a damned good meal ticket, and a status symbol with high prestige for him. She knew this all too well.

She pulled herself from her thoughts by taking a large swig of her drink and abstractedly watched the cardplayers. Two-Day Sheik's joint was the first-floor apartment in a four-story building of eighteen units. His place, and all the other after-hours joints, wouldn't begin to swing until the bars closed, then they'd come alive. Part of the fun – since it was Friday – would no doubt include someone getting cut up or shot before dawn broke.

Two-Day Sheik was an unusual man. He had eight women, all living in this same apartment building. He paid their keep and regularly spent two consecutive days with each of them – hence, his name. His clothes were distributed evenly in each apartment, and he didn't mind if the women had other men as long as they weren't around during his two days' occupation. There was one young woman, however, to whom he wouldn't allow such liberties – Selma: she was private stuff, like his private stock of whiskey; and she couldn't leave the building without telling him where she was going, whom she would probably see, and what time she'd be back. Gypsy Pearl hated him.

'The offer is still open, baby. Leave that dope fiend and come live with me. You know I'll do you good.' It was Two-Day. She hadn't seen him standing so close to her chair.

Perhaps she didn't really hate Two-Day – she didn't know him that well – but she just couldn't stand him. His voice, the queer odor that hung like an invisible curtain around him, and his eyes especially, rubbed her wrong. No doubt the rumor in the neighborhood that he was a 'nasty man' who liked to have his women urinate in his face prior to lovemaking had something to do with the way she felt toward him. It was said that he could get an erection without this ritual, but couldn't keep it. Gypsy Pearl didn't know whether the story was true, and she didn't intend to find out, either. Yet, the way he looked at her with his wild bug-eyes inclined her toward believing it. She didn't even take 'nasty men' as customers, much less go with one steady.

She took another drink, to cool her anger, then, fairly calm, she said, 'Two-Day, if I told you once I done told you a hundred times: ain't nothin' in this world you can do for me, man. Now if you don't want the business I bring here, you just keep messin' with me, hear? I'll go across the street to Greyhound's, even if you do sell better stuff. I mean it.'

'Aaw, 'ho', I's jus' kiddin' witcha,' Two-Day said quickly. The loss of revenue was the only way to hurt him other than the loss of his main woman, until he was ready to replace her. 'Whut the hell you gittin' all shook up 'bout?'

She was disgusted by his big stomach which hung over his belt sloppily; his breath smelled awful, engulfing her like hot steam. His light-brown skin was covered with juicy acne, and his too-thick moustache failed to hide his blubbery lips. He had his hair conked, but around his ears and at the nape of his neck were the hard, tight burrs he wanted so much to hide.

'Just leave me alone and everything'll be cool,' Gypsy Pearl said. 'You know what Hip'd do if I told him how you botherin' me all the time.'

He knew. He'd witnessed the fight between Hip and Red Shirt Charlie; but he retorted, 'He ain't go' do nothin' t'me, not long as I got my equalizer.' He patted his stomach, where a small .22 automatic pistol was hidden by the flab that struggled against his belt. 'Anyhow, bitch,' he went on, 'you ain't gotta git snotty. Whut is you? Nuthin' but a 'ho'. Seem like t'me you oughta be glad t'have a man want you fuh his woman 'steada his 'ho'.'

'I would be glad – if a *man* wanted me. Dig it, germ?' She set down her glass. 'Here, gimme a bottle of Canadian Club so I can git the hell outta here – stinks in here.' She handed him the ten-dollar bill.

As she was leaving with the bottle and her change, he followed her to the door. She turned suddenly, and with a spiteful smile, said, 'How'd you like it if I told Hip to pull Selma from you? You know she go for him, and I'd be glad to share my workload.' She laughed in his face and walked out, leaving him sputtering incoherently.

'If you don't mean it, Lonnie,' Franchot said seriously, 'don't make me stick my neck out. I'm hopin' to make foreman next year.'

'I mean it, Shots, I really do. If you git me on with you I swear to God I'll work like a sonofabitch. Man, I coulda kicked this habit any time I wanted to, but I didn't have no good reason. That's the truth.'

'I didn't say you couldn't quit, I just don't want you messin' me around, that's all.' Franchot was really happy that Hip had promised to move back home and go to work, even though he wasn't very confident that Hip could quit drugs as easily as he'd said. Nobody could be as miserable as continually as junkies if quitting was so easy. They couldn't hate themselves that much.

Gypsy Pearl came in while they were talking and handed the whiskey and the change from it to Hip.

'What about her?' he asked Franchot. They'd forgotten all about her in their enthusiasm.

'What about her?' Franchot said. 'She your woman, ain't she?'

'I mean, like, you want her to move in, too? She can stay right here—'

'*Your* woman, Lonnie. What you askin' me for?' Franchot wouldn't look at her. He knew what Hip meant and felt embarrassed without knowing exactly why.

'What I'm tryin' t'say is that she also's a whore, man. I ain't gon' let her stop trickin' till I git myself together. Now you want her livin' with us, too?'

'It'll be your house, too. If you want your woman livin' with you it's your business what she do. But I don't want y'all bringin' no johns there. I don't care what all else y'all do.'

'Awright, then, it's settled,' Hip said. Then, to Gypsy Pearl: 'What the hell you standin' there gawkin' for? Go git him a glass! Man, that's the dumbest woman sometimes.' As she was leaving he called: 'Git yourself one, too! That ignorant oil might clear your head some.'

While she was gone, Franchot said, 'I don't want no fightin' between y'all, either, Lonnie. Ain't but two rules: no johns and no fightin'. Okay?'

'Crazy, bro. I gotcha,' Hip smiled . . .

They sat and talked a long time afterward, recalling old memories of their parents and their childhood, and friends they didn't see anymore. They even got into a good-natured argument concerning a dog they'd had. Hip claimed the dog liked him the best, even though Franchot fed and took care of him.

Gypsy Pearl watched and laughed with them. Franchot was a little high now and he felt all the warmer for it. She found that she liked him more and more; and in listening to the two brothers talk, she could almost remember the things that had attracted her to Hip in the first place. It was confusing; she didn't really know him at all.

It seemed a long, long time ago that she'd thought of herself as in love with him. When she'd finally quit Red Shirt Charlie for him, she'd done it for a great love. She'd known he used dope, but he was going to quit and get a job. There was even the dream of marriage. It was to be happily-ever-after, just like the movies. Without a qualm, she'd given up her job to depend on him. It was after his fight with Red Shirt Charlie that she found out how futile a gesture that was.

She and Hip were in the Howard Bar not long after she'd quit Red Shirt, and the talk among the Streeters concerning the small-time cat who'd pulled a woman from Red Shirt Charlie was still heavy. This was unusual; the process mostly reversed itself and it was the big-timer who did the pulling of others' women.

And Red Shirt had made it big on Howard Street, since coming from Mississippi to Newark in the days when he had only one shirt – a red one – to his name. As the

Streeters got to know him, he'd stopped being 'the guy with the red shirt' and became Red Shirt Charlie. He never wore anything red anymore, but the name had stuck and he was rather proud of it.

His pride couldn't stand being laughed at. He didn't like it that his cronies and the small-time lames were sniggering behind his back. When he saw Gypsy Pearl and Hip in the Howard Bar he sent over a drink to her, knowing that Hip would make her refuse it. When she did, he came around to their side of the bar.

He seldom smiled, and his small black eyes seemed to look holes into people. His hair was carefully processed and his moustache lustrously waxed; two gold teeth lighted his mouth in his dark face above a cleft chin made even darker from shaving. He was good-looking in a slick way.

Standing behind Hip and Gypsy Pearl, he said, 'You so high and mighty you can't take a drink from me, woman?'

'I made her send it back,' Hip said without turning around.

Red Shirt ignored him. To Gypsy Pearl he said, 'You didn't answer me, baby – I'm the same guy who knew you when, dig?'

Hip swung around on the barstool. His knife was open, as it had been ever since he'd seen Red Shirt coming over to them; he had the blade pointed up his sleeve. 'If my woman wanna drink I'll do the buyin', man. Now you better make it and leave us alone.'

Gypsy Pearl looked deep into her glass as Red Shirt, still speaking only to her, said, 'I figger you be tireda messin' 'round with a lame 'fore long, girl. When you do, let me know.' She said nothing. 'Talk, woman!' Red Shirt said with exasperation. 'What you want with this dope fiend? You know how junkies do women, don't you?' When she still said nothing, he leaned closer to her and said loudly, 'Is you bought him any dope yet . . . whore?'

Hip got up, his knife cradled in his palm. In the small aisle they were forced to stand face to face, feeling each other's words brush their skin as well as hearing them. Hip hissed, 'Mothafucka, if you say one more word, it's your ass!'

Red Shirt laughed: 'No harm, man.' Taking a step backward, he looked at Hip for the first time. 'Jus' sorta slipped off my tongue, y'know?'

'You keep fuckin' with my woman and you won't have no tongue, nigga!' Hip was trembling with rage and fear, for he knew Red Shirt carried a gun. The slightest move on Red Shirt's part and Hip would have plunged the knife into him.

Red Shirt just shrugged and said, 'I hear you, baby.' Hip relaxed somewhat at this and started to turn back to the bar. He should have known that few Streeters take low, especially with a woman around to witness it, and Red Shirt wasn't the type to do it at all.

Red Shirt turned as if to leave, and Hip took his eyes off him in order to sit down again, but something made Hip look up again. Red Shirt had wheeled and was sending a terrific punch at Hip, who didn't get his head out of the way fast enough to avoid having the side of his face scraped bloody by Red Shirt's glancing fist, which, because of the ring he wore, left a line from Hip's right eye to his ear.

His momentum carried him into Hip and they fell up against the bar. Hip grabbed him around the neck with his left arm while his right hand flashed up, ready to descend and bury the knife into Red Shirt. But the bartender caught his arm and wrenched the knife away from him. Hip brought his fist down instead.

'Hey! You guys take that stuff outside!' the bartender shouted. But they didn't even hear him. Hip fought with more desperation, because he didn't want Red Shirt to reach his gun. The place became a madhouse of screams and shouting. Too many wanted to see what was going on and the narrow space made that impossible.

Hip wrestled Red Shirt to the floor, punching wildly at his head. He hit the wall and the floor as much as he hit the man. Red Shirt tried to bite him, then, with a mighty heave, he tossed Hip with such force that he landed flat on his back with barstools and glasses falling all around him.

Red Shirt jumped to his feet yelling, 'I'ma kill you, nigga!' He rushed toward the door, and Hip, realizing that he didn't have the gun on him, was momentarily relieved. But then he realized that Red Shirt must have left the gun in his car and was going to get it.

He raced after him, pushing people out of the way, knocking many of them to the floor. There was no time for apologies, he had to get Red Shirt before Red Shirt got the gun. The white Cadillac was parked in the middle of the block, and Hip caught him only because, in his agitated haste, Red Shirt fumbled with his keys.

Hip leaped at him feet first. They flew against the car, putting a deep dent into its side. Red Shirt cried out, 'Oh, you bastid! You dope fiend mothafucka! You done ruined my car!' Tears sprang into his eyes; he scrambled to his feet and blindly rushed at Hip, who was ready and poised like a boxer.

Red Shirt, crouched very low, came head on. Hip side-stepped, swung his fist down like a hammer on the back of the passing head, and made Red Shirt fall flat on his face. Then he jumped on him, but Red Shirt bucked him off. Red Shirt kicked back and landed his foot in the pit of Hip's stomach. The unexpected blow shot the air from Hip and he went down on one knee, gasping for breath.

Red Shirt laughed contemptuously, 'You finished now, punk,' he said, as he kicked again. Hip rolled with the impact, but it still sent sharp pain up and down the right side of his body.

He got up, shuffling toward Red Shirt with his hands high up around his chin, his teeth bared. They both circled around, cautious, each waiting for an opening in the other's defense. Hip weaved under a couple of wild blows, spun Red Shirt around, and landed the point of his shoe in the seat of the other man's pants. The crowd that had gathered yelled their approval, laughing and cheering, shouting encouragement to their favorite. As usual, the windows of the surrounding buildings lighted and filled with people; some even left their apartments for closer looks at the spectacle, and there were quick bets made on the winner.

Fast living was making both fighters extremely tired. Yet Hip knew that he was going to win, because Red Shirt didn't know the first thing about fighting with his hands. He could use a weapon – even with his women – but not his hands. Hip knew that he was on his way to getting a reputation. When Red Shirt rushed him again Hip brought up an uppercut which set Red Shirt's head in perfect position to meet the left hook and right cross which followed. It was a beautiful combination and some of the crowd applauded it. '*Go 'head, Sugar Ray!*' someone yelled.

Hip moved in and dug a right to Red Shirt's stomach, and when Red Shirt doubled up he stepped back and said, 'I got feet, too, nigga.' He kicked the lowered face with the hard grace of a football player. Red Shirt was lifted off his feet to land with a final thud on his back on the hard pavement.

The crowd wasn't satisfied, and neither was Hip. Red Shirt's defeat had to be complete. Hip knew that if he stopped now Red Shirt would undoubtedly return and one of them would wind up dead.

He straddled the supine body, grabbed Red Shirt's head, and began to beat it against the ground, not enough to kill, he hoped, but enough to give all-around satisfaction. He tore one of Red Shirt's ears badly. He punched and beat until someone pulled him from the unconscious man. It was Gypsy Pearl.

Weeks later, when Red Shirt came out of the hospital, he made a pretense of looking for Hip, but it was only a token gesture. Hip stayed clear of him so as not force his hand; and one night, when Red Shirt was riding through Howard Street and saw Hip and Gypsy Pearl standing in front of Mann's Manor, he didn't stop.

Gypsy Pearl's interference with the fight had provided Hip with an excuse to put a plan into action which would have taken longer any other way, and might not have worked even then.

He hadn't been making the kind of stings which netted enough to maintain his habit and for them to live off, too. The habit tolerated no rival. So one night he delayed taking his regular fix, and while he and Gypsy Pearl were lying in bed he felt the first stirrings of the familiar yearning – the prelude to junkie sickness. He had a bag of stuff hidden away in the communal bathroom.

It had been a week since his fight with Red Shirt Charlie. He hadn't said anything to her about stopping him from beating Red Shirt's head on the ground because he knew that she'd done it more for his good than for the other man's. They hadn't even mentioned the fight.

He lay with his hands behind his head while her head lay on his chest. His accusation began: 'I heard you went up to Martland to see Red Shirt. What you go for?' He spoke calmly. She raised her head to look into his eyes.

'I didn't go to see him. I went to find out if he was all right. Who told you that?' They never wore anything in bed together, and as she leaned on one elbow her bare breasts hung lovely, kissing his chest.

'Never mind who told me – I was told. It got me to thinkin' 'bout somethin', too.'

'Thinkin' about what?' she asked.

''Bout how you was so quick to pull me offa that chump, that's what. Didn't wanna see 'im git hurt too bad, huh?'

Her look rapidly changed from uncertainty to irritability and back again. He didn't sound angry. She thought that he was teasing her. Sometimes, before making love to her, he'd fake anger or jealousy until she was on the verge of tears; then he'd burst out laughing and cuddle her in his arms until she too was smiling, relieved that he was just playing. Afterwards their lovemaking was such that there were times when she almost achieved a full climax.

Faintly hoping that this was one of his jokes, but still unsure – when he wasn't joking he was terrible – she said, 'Hip, you know good and well why I pulled you off him.'

'I don't know a goddamn thing!' he said viciously. Then, pushing her slightly: 'And git that damn white folk's hair outta my face!' Her hair had spilled onto the pillow and part of it caressed his face and tickled his arm.

She let herself down onto her pillow and stared at the ceiling, trying to think of the real reason for his acting this way. Finally she repeated, 'Hip, you know good and well why I pulled you off him. What's the matter with you?'

'I said I don't know a goddamn thing – I'm waitin' for you to tell me somethin', bitch.' It was the first time he'd ever called her that. She knew that no laughter would follow now.

'Ain't nothin' to tell, if you don't know already,' she said in a choked voice. She turned away from him, as frustrated tears welled in her eyes. She felt terribly hot; the heat rose up into her head and gave her a headache.

The first anguish of sickness caught Hip fully now and he began to sweat. She heard him retch, felt the bed shake from his trembling. She turned around to him, her face anxious. In a strained voice, he said, 'I'm sick, baby.'

'Where's your stuff?' she asked.

'I ain't got none left,' he whispered.

'You ain't got none?' Her eyes widened in fear. 'You ain't got none at *all?*' Stories of the violence committed by sick junkies filled her mind for a second, but quickly vanished in a flood of compassion for him.

'Dammit, woman, I just *said* I ain't got none,' he snapped. 'What you askin' stupid questions for?'

She watched transfixed as the veins in his forehead, neck, and temple rose and seemed about to erupt. He was wringing wet now.

She jumped out of bed and hurried into her dress. 'Where's the money? I'll go git some from Cowboy for you. I'll hurry, honey. You just take it easy, hear?'

'I ain't go no money, either,' he said.

'Oh, Lord, is the nigga crazy?' she cried softly, turning to him. 'You ain't got no money? What you mean, you ain't got no money?'

'Woman, if you ask me one more dumb question I'm gon' break your neck when I git myself together. You—' He retched again and doubled up, holding his stomach. His face was horribly contorted. He began to root under the covers and rolled from side to side, moaning. It seemed that he would strangle on his own saliva, and the stench which had begun to rise from his open pores was almost inhuman. He looked at her with pleading eyes.

Her hands flew to her mouth to stifle a scream. 'What we gon' do, Hip? What we gon' do? I ain't got no money, neither. Won't Cowboy trust you?'

'You know better than that,' he said softly through clenched, chattering teeth. 'You gotta git me some stuff, baby . . .'

'How, Hip?' she asked desperately. 'Where can I git the money?' She grabbed up his pants and frantically searched the pockets. 'Hip, Hip' – she was crying hard now – 'ain't nothin' in here!'

'Baby, git me some stuff!' he pleaded.

'How can I, if Cowboy don't trust you?' She wrung her hands in helpless despair, looking down at him in anguish.

His eyes seemed to be sweating now, swimming in pools of blood. He was a pitiful caricature of himself, and she was, for a moment, disgusted by him, wondering how she could ever have loved something like him, and, at the same time, she wanted to hold his head against her breast and rock away his torment. She stood in the middle of her indecision, not knowing what to do, staring at him in wide-eyed wonder, in fear.

Finally he said, 'Baby, you know Cowboy goes for you.'

She didn't answer. She didn't seem to understand his words at all. He said, 'He go for you enough to do anything you ask him, if you act right.' She still watched silently. 'Act right,' he said.

She didn't want to believe that he meant what he so obviously did mean, and yet, it was inescapable. There could be but one meaning to what he said. She knew it and now her tears flowed for a different reason. 'You want me to go to bed with him.' It wasn't a question. Her voice was flat. 'You want me to sell myself for dope, be a whore for dope?' She didn't want him to reply, and yet she wanted him to be thoroughly committed to it when he did.

'I just want you to git me straight, that's all,' he said, adding: 'And I don't know nothin' that'd do it quicker'n you playin' up to Cowboy.'

'You want me to be a whore,' she said again. Now that he

had voiced it she could sneer. Red Shirt had been right. 'Was this why you made me quit my job? You said you wanted me with you all the time. You didn't mean that, did you? You knew it would come to this, didn't you? Answer me, goddammit! You didn't want a woman, you just wanted to be a pimp, didn't you?'

'Is you gon' help me, or what, woman? If you got some other way of coppin' the money, then do it. Don't make me no difference. I'm sick, don't you understand – I'm sick!' He retched again, to prove it. 'What would you do if I was Red Shirt Charlie? You helped him by goin' there, but you won't help me – and I'm s'pozed to be your man. Yeah, well I know where you at now, baby. Git the hell outta here and let me be sick by my goddamn self. Go on – git! If I gotta die I don't want no witnesses.'

She continued to look at him. Her tears had stopped and her eyes were glinting. He could see resolution creep over her like a veil. She didn't seem to be breathing at all. He pulled the sheet over his head and lay there trembling.

Gypsy Pearl turned, walked to the closet, put on a thin sweater, and left without another word.

Hip stole a look at her as she left. He couldn't help but marvel at her proud, stiff back. But he was certain that he'd won and that she'd be back with Cowboy and the dope. He'd challenged her loyalty, and he knew that a woman will do anything to prove she's loyal – particularly if she's not, and no matter how much she hates later.

Hip got up and made sure that she was gone before he went to the bathroom to get his works and stuff. With slightly trembling hands he cooked it, and shot half the bag. It was enough to take away immediately the sickness he'd been feeling. If he was wrong and she didn't return, he'd at least have something to start tomorrow off with. He put everything back in its place and went back to bed . . .

Cowboy was only too glad to give her two bags. He walked back to the room with her to collect his payment. Hip waited in the kitchen while they used the bed. In about thirty minutes Cowboy came out smiling; as he passed Hip, he said, 'You make her a little more agreeable, man, and you'll have a gold mine.'

Gypsy Pearl was turned to the wall with the covers up around her chin when Hip returned to the room. She lay stiff and stared defiantly at the wall.

'Now that wasn't so bad, was it?' he asked cheerfully. She didn't answer. He shrugged and got into bed, careful not to touch her. They didn't speak anymore that night.

She'd gone with Cowboy twice more to get drugs for Hip, and Hip beat her each time to make her more agreeable. In truth, she'd been only numb. She'd wrung herself dry of feeling for almost everything. It was because she was able to do this that she started to become the gold mine that Cowboy had predicted she'd be.

She learned to time herself by watching the other whores go in and out of Sue's with their tricks. Whores are usually eager to teach a newcomer their devices, and Gypsy Pearl learned quickly from them. Yet, all the while, she was numb. She didn't believe that she was really a whore – she was only doing it for Hip, until he could start making good stings again. When she went with a man it wasn't for profit, like the other women, it was for Hip. He needed her.

When she'd gone with her first total stranger she'd gotten sick. She wouldn't go with anyone else that night and Hip took her home and beat her. She went out again the next night while Hip watched, waited, and collected the twenty-five dollars she made. She began to make more, especially when she learned how to clip a trick as he concentrated on his kicks, or was drunk. And as she made more, Hip's habit increased.

Her favorite clipping method was to place a chair near enough to the bed so that, as the john humped, she could search through his pockets. Most were too drunk to check their pockets before they left the room. And, if they caught on, there was always Hip waiting downstairs.

It was quite a while before Gypsy Pearl admitted to herself that she was a whore, just like the rest. When she did she began to really hate Hip. She hated him for his weakness that was his strength over her. She hated him because she hadn't been strong enough to walk out and leave him as she'd planned to do. She hadn't planned to come back that day she went to get Cowboy, but she had come back, and she didn't know why. She no longer believed she loved him, yet she couldn't leave him.

'Don't you hear me talkin' to you, woman?' Hip yelled. She was jolted back to the present. She jumped, startled, and spilled whiskey on her skirt.

'I'm sorry,' she said. 'I was daydreamin', I guess.'

'You been smokin' herb at Two-Day's!' Hip accused. 'You got a mighty funny look on your face.'

'Hip, you know damn well I don't mess with none of that junk. You git on my nerves.'

'Ain't no tellin' what one of you dumb bitches liable to do when a man's back is turned. I better not find out you smokin' pot, you hear?'

It wasn't for her that he was so concerned, he just didn't want the money to decrease. If she began smoking pot, it wouldn't hurt her, but it might lead to horse. It was only a miracle that had stayed her curiosity this long. And he knew that a dope-fiend whore didn't know the meaning of loyalty. If they made a hundred dollars they'd tell their man that they only made fifty. They couldn't be trusted.

Before he could speak again, Franchot said, 'Look, Lonnie, I gotta be goin'. But I sure hope you two don't carry on like this all the time . . .'

'We do,' Gypsy Pearl answered, looking boldly at Hip. He gave her a nasty look, but said nothing.

A long silence was finally broken by Franchot's embarrassed cough. 'Well,' he said, 'maybe all that'll change once he gits some hard work in his back.' He smiled at them. 'Be too damn tired to do much arguin' then.'

No one made any reply and he got down from the television shell. 'I see you don't need no money, Lonnie . . .'

'Naw, I'm doin' good, bro,' Hip answered.

'Well, I guess I'll be goin' then. Take it easy.'

Hip told Gypsy Pearl to see him to the door. 'And if she git to lookin' good to you, Shots, ain't no charge. Just throw her on in bed and wail, dig?' He laughed, adding: 'She ain't nothin' but a whore, anyhow – ain't fragile in the least.'

Franchot looked at him, then at her. 'She a woman, Lonnie. A human bein' – and from what I seen tonight, much too good for you. You better be careful before you blow, man, and you know that you don't really miss your water till your well runs dry.'

'Shee-it!' Hip cried. 'Man, I don't need her! That bitch can git her hat any time she feel like it. I don't care.' He lay back on the bed as they walked out.

At the front door Gypsy Pearl said, 'Thanks for comin' to my defense, Franchot. I sure hope we don't cause you no trouble.'

'Yeah, me too.'

She gave him a long, searching look, then asked slowly, 'You really ain't gittin' married to that Rosemary?'

He lit a cigarette, smiled at her, and said, 'Not long as she stay black and pretty – and that's gon' be a mighty long time.' He closed the door. She waited until she no longer heard his footsteps before she went back to Hip. The slight elation she'd begun feeling with Franchot now became as squalid as the room she entered.

Hip was taking a fix. All of his concentration was on the needle that punctured his vein; a belt was tied tightly around his arm and one end of it was in his mouth. After a while he spat the belt out and his face took on the familiar relaxed, contented look. He sat for a long while seeing nothing, saying nothing.

When he did finally speak, his voice was very thick, very lazy, with a little whine. He was almost a different person after a fix, almost likable. But, as she well knew, this never lasted.

'Honey, pack our things,' he said softly. 'We blowin' this rat-trap.'

'Yeah, I know,' she replied evenly.

'I love you, baby. You know that, don't you?'

'Yeah, I know.'

'And I'ma really kick this habit. I'ma do it for you, baby,

and soon's I git myself together I'ma let you stop trickin'. We gon really live then, sugar. Git married and everything.'

'Yeah, I know.'

She watched his chin descend lower and lower until it was resting on his chest. She went to the bathroom and got ready for bed.

Seven

Slim McNair was one of the detectives who interrogated Jimmy Johnson and the other boys. He was an honest enough cop – except for the fact that he had a whore tricking for him on Howard Street and he took money for various other things from the hustlers, including Sue. He was honest enough because he did nothing that wasn't common practice among cops working the Third Ward, or, for that matter, almost any town in any state. Howard Streets could not function so efficiently without the complicity of the authorities.

Few people knew about Slim and Sue – which was one of the reasons he often knew things that happened on the Street even before many of the Streeters themselves did – but everyone knew about him and Emma Dee. The Streeters gave her a wide berth and plenty of respect because of her relationship with Slim. One word from her could land someone in jail quick. Slim had 'found' dope on more than one person whose only crime had been a sarcastic remark to Emma Dee. He was also the kind of cop who carried a knife around with him in case a suspect had to be maimed or killed: it was 'evidence' that he'd had to protect himself as he acted in the line of his duty. All he had to say was that the suspect had threatened him with the knife.

In sharp contrast to his name, Slim was a short, stocky man. Too short, in fact, to be on the police force, but at the time he was hired the city had been in dire need of manpower to combat the escalating crime rate, especially in the Third Ward, where he was put. So his lack of another half-inch was overlooked, and, through the years, he had come to seem very tall to the people who got in his way. Yet he hated the nickname, and because he did, everyone, including his colleagues, used it when referring to him. The only person who didn't make him angry by calling him 'Slim' was Sue.

Jimmy's athletic exploits in school were well known to Slim. South Side High, at one time, *was* Jimmy Johnson, and Slim had followed the game avidly. He had presented Jimmy with a PAL award at the Boys' Club as an outstanding Third Ward youth. The newspapers had played up the all-American boy routine, and the captions under the pictures of Slim handing Jimmy the award had read:

Detective Edward McNair, presenting P.A.L. Outstanding Youth Award to James Johnson, says: 'Boys like Jimmy are a credit to our city and to the Negro.'

His endorsement of Jimmy had come back to haunt him many times since. He'd known that Jimmy was hanging with a gang, and that they were committing crimes, but there were so many gangs in the Ward that he hadn't known which one to tap for them. But he had time obviously on his side.

Slim had come to hate Jimmy – for making a fool of him and for choosing failure when success was being thrown at him. He hated him almost as much as he hated junkies. It was good news when Jimmy was arrested. Slim promised to give the young punk a special reception.

When they came to take Jimmy out of his cell for questioning, Slim gave him a malicious smile, one that told the boy exactly what to expect. Slim and another detective marched him to the 'red room,' so named for the abundance of suspects' blood which had spilled in it. All the way Jimmy looked only at the floor in front of him.

As he stepped into the room Slim smacked him on the back of his head with such force that he flew over the stationary chair which was fixed to the middle of the floor and sprawled beyond it. His head was spinning wildly and began to ache with a throbbing thunder. He couldn't focus his sight for a long while. Finally, he saw the large oak desk melt into a single whole. It only had one drawer, and he knew from the stories he'd heard from others who had been questioned here that it held the dreaded rubber hose, weighted and taped at one end. A filing cabinet was the only other object in the room. One large window faced the street far below.

Slim looked contemptuously down at him. Jimmy sat where he'd fallen; he knew that to get up before he was told would be taken as definite proof of his hostility and defiance. He'd been told so much about this room and the things that went on here that he felt as though he'd been through all of this before.

'Get up, you little bastard,' Slim ordered. He grabbed Jimmy by the shirt, but it ripped and Jimmy fell back to the floor. 'You're a rape artist as well as a mugger, eh, you little chink-eyed punk? Get up and sit in this goddamn chair!' Slim yelled.

Jimmy did as he was told. Two white detectives stood behind him, silent and mean-looking. Jimmy wondered briefly if the other boys had been beaten, and how they took it. Brother had probably cried. Damned if he would though.

Slim parked a hefty buttock on the edge of the desk, which was bare except for a worn green ledger with red-tipped corners. He reached into the drawer and brought out the hose. Dramatically, he let it fall back into the drawer so that Jimmy could hear how heavily weighted it was. He lit a cigarette and, in a conversational tone which startled Jimmy by its marked contrast to the previous barking, said, 'Now, you're gonna tell us all about it – right, little nigger?' He held out the pack to Jimmy.

Reaching for the pack, Jimmy said, 'Y'all already know everything I done. Ain't nothin' else t'tell.' Slim snatched the pack away and sat it on the desk.

'C'mon now, you can't get a smoke by bein' nasty and unco-operative. Tell us about the breaking-and-enterings, armed robberies – stuff like that. We know all about it so you might as well come clean. The other guys have already signed statements on you, y'know. *Now start talkin'!*' He shouted the last words and brought his hand down on the desk with a slap that sounded like a firecracker.

Jimmy stared at the foamy saliva that clung to the corners of Slim's mouth. Every time it opened it looked as adhesive as Scotch tape being pulled slowly from a soft surface. Jimmy couldn't help wondering how any girl could kiss those spitty lips without wanting to throw up afterwards.

'Officer McNair, I ain't done nothin' else,' he said. 'Everything I done you already know about.' He was fighting to stay calm. He wanted to scream until his lungs collapsed; and it was a mild shock to have a black cop call him a nigger in front of white people. He was accustomed to hearing his people call each other that, it was part of his growing up, but it was not the same as when it was said in the presence of the other race. He'd often heard of black cops putting on this nigger show for their white colleagues: calling black suspects niggers as if the name didn't apply to themselves as well. It often shocked more confessions out of suspects than the beatings did. Worse than this, he knew that the black cops tended to take their frustrations out on black suspects only. Seldom would they punch a white man around. Slim never had.

He reached into the drawer again and brought out the hose. Jimmy bit down hard on his bottom lip, prepared not to confess to what he didn't do, and not to cry for what he did.

The hose smacked heavily into Slim's palm. Jimmy watched the hands warily, so that a sudden swing would not catch him by surprise. Slim's hands were babyish: pudgy, short fingers with nails bitten to the quick.

Jimmy's headache seemed to catch the rhythm of the hose pounding against Slim's palm. He glanced anxiously at the man's face, wondering if he really intended to hit him with it. He knew that juveniles weren't supposed to be beaten, but he also knew that many of the cops at Headquarters, as well as in the precincts, didn't give a damn how old a suspect was. They were virtually immune to retaliation, first by the victim's own reluctance to become involved in the mysteries of City Hall – the white power structure, which he'd have to face without money and in fear and ignorance; and second, because the lies of two or more cops in court would overwhelm his simple truth, especially if he had a record, which many in the Third Ward had.

Slim asked, 'You've got nothin' to say, boy?' Jimmy didn't answer, he couldn't. Slim went on: 'You think you're pretty tough, huh? Stickin' to the Code, right? Well, you punks got your code and we got ours!' His arm moved with a speed that Jimmy had believed impossible in one so fat. He got his head out of the way just in time to avoid being solidly sapped on the ear. The blow landed on his collarbone as he leaned away.

The other detectives grabbed him and sat him straight in the chair again. One of them cuffed him, but he was too busy watching the hose to pay much attention. The weight inside it had hurt him enough to make him concentrate on keeping his head out of its path.

Slim got up and stood directly in front of him. 'You're a quick nigger. I forgot you used to be an athlete. Real fast,' he sneered. 'But it won't do you no good here.'

He began to tap repeatedly upon Jimmy's head with the weighted end of the hose while the others held him fast. Then one of them got the green ledger and placed it on Jimmy's head. Slim brought the hose down hard on it and Jimmy's head seemed to explode. His headache became worse as Slim went back to his tapping. 'I'll keep this up until you open your black mouth, boy,' he said, 'and when you lie it'll get harder.'

This was one of Slim's favorite practices; not many men could stand it for long. Jimmy couldn't stand it long either, and Slim seemed to hit the same spot each time. The blows were hard when he denied something, then grew softer until the next question; finally they all felt the same to Jimmy. His head felt soft and gushy, he heard strange sounds, and at any moment he expected the flashing lights, the rainbowed rings that surrounded the polka-dots he saw, to spill and cover him, to blot him out.

'Sit still, punk!' Slim commanded. One of the white cops was pressing hard and steadily into Jimmy's left arm muscle, but it was a distant pain and couldn't compete with the taps. The pain in his head was all one; sound took control of him now, deafening, detonating, thundering sound: *boom, Boom, BOom, BOOm, BOOOOM! BOOOMMMmm!* He was ready to sign anything they put in front of him – sight unseen.

He was about to scream and kick Slim in the groin, in the

hope that they would knock him out and the torture would stop for a while. As he braced himself for it, the door to the red room opened and a voice said: 'If it hits, you're through, McNair!'

Slim's hand halted in midair and the hose bent to within an inch of Jimmy's head, but it didn't touch him. The other two detectives released him and he immediately grabbed his head, grimacing in pain.

The voice belonged to a tall, blond, balding man standing in the doorway with a pipe clenched angrily between his teeth. Jimmy saw him through a blur, though whether it was tears in his eyes or the blows' effect on his vision, he couldn't have said. His head hurt more now that the tapping had stopped. The pains were rolling over him like ripples racing across a lake, like big waves roaring to an ocean shore. He felt nauseous and dizzy.

'Don't you know this is a juvenile, McNair?' the man said coldly. 'I could suspend you men until departmental trial for this.'

Slim said, 'Lieutenant, this punk took a punch at Chirechillo. We were just teachin' him a lesson, he's a wise guy.'

'That's a lie!' Jimmy blurted. 'I didn't take a punch at nobody. You was tryin' t'make me admit stuff I didn't do! I done told y'all what I know . . .'

'Shut up, you!' the lieutenant said tersely, for the first time looking directly at Jimmy. His eyes were light blue, gelid, piercing, and he had a great hawk nose overhanging a light moustache and a tight mouth. Jimmy shut up. 'Get up outta that chair,' the lieutenant commanded. Jimmy rose, holding his head, and made his way to the filing cabinet, where he propped his elbows and leaned. He was still dizzy, but the nausea had gone.

'The fact that you're an officer of the law doesn't give you the right to break it, McNair,' the lieutenant was saying. 'Your hands aren't so clean, and you know it. I'd watch my step if I was you. Next time I catch you wrong, you've had it.'

Gorcey and Chirechillo ambled over toward Jimmy and stood there, watching him hard.

'Listen,' the lieutenant went on. 'I want those kids taken over to the Parental Home tomorrow, and they'd better not have a scratch on them. The one in the hospital, Simon Peele, should be getting out around next week, or whenever he comes out of his shock. I don't want him brought here under any circumstances – straight to the Home, you got that?'

'Yes, sir, Lieutenant O'Brien,' Slim said carefully.

Jimmy had gotten it too. Sy was in a hospital now?

Lieutenant O'Brien turned to leave, and Jimmy raised his head. To his relief, the lieutenant stopped, remembered him, and said, 'Gorcey, you and Chirechillo take the kid back to his cell.'

Jimmy had never thought a jail cell could look good to him. When they put him back in it, he said to Gorcey, who had a cigarette dangling from his lips, 'Can I git a coupla smokes from you, please, sir?'

Chirechillo said, 'The store man'll be around soon – buy some. You got money?' Jimmy shook his head, no.

Just then the turnkey came and brought Jimmy a food package from his mother and handed him three dollars. 'Ya got two more out front, Johnson,' he said, handing Jimmy a receipt.

'Now ya can buy butts, kid,' Chirechillo said.

Jimmy felt a little bolder now that he had food and money; even the headache was letting up. 'I'd like to have one now, if you can spare it.' He looked at Gorcey.

'Gimme one of them dollars,' Gorcey said. 'Ya can buy some.'

Jimmy handed him a dollar, thinking they were going to buy him some. He watched Gorcey reach into his pocket and pull out a crumpled half pack. He threw it at Jimmy and walked away saying, 'Ya just bought some, Sambo.' Chirechillo laughed and followed Gorcey out.

Jimmy sat on the bench, confused, but at least glad of the few smokes he had. Suddenly he jumped up and shouted at them: 'Hey! I ain't got no matches! Hey, officers, gimme some matches, willya please!' He heard their laughter, then, around the corner the iron door slammed shut.

He looked around the cell and in all of his pockets several times. He found no matches. It was only then that he thought of the wino, and realized he had been taken out of the cell. He sat again on the bench, cursing to himself, cursing at the world.

A few hours later a new shift came on duty and he was able to get a whole book of matches from the new turnkey.

All during the night they brought prisoners in and out of the cellblock, but no one was put into the cell with him. He wondered where Butch and Brother were; he hadn't seen them since they'd gotten arrested.

Around four o'clock in the morning the place got as quiet as a funeral parlor. He yelled, but the only answer was his own echo. The cellblock was an excellent echo chamber. He sang some of the current rock'n'roll hits. They sounded good to him, full and resonant. Finally he ate a little of the food, watching anxiously for the roaches and rats, who all seemed, sooner or later, to find their way to his cell. Then he lay back and waded through the countless scratches and scribblings on the walls and ceiling:

Killroy was here ... Sally Ann sucks ... Leroy 1962 1963 196 ... Fuck you ... Cops stink ... Your mother takes it in her ear ... Joe 1945 ... I love Gladys ... Pablo y Fontessa ... If you take time to read this you'll take dick ... Hitler rah rah ... niggers and jews stink ... Shirley Barbara Carole ... Some come here to sit and think but I come to shit and stink ... Hank from the Neck ... Brady from Pusan 15th ave ... Pussy ... Cunt ... asshole ... Your father is a junkie ...

They were all over the cell. Jimmy debated whether to put his name on the wall, but finally decided against it.

He was glad he didn't have to face his mother yet; he didn't want to go through that. He could hear her already: 'Why did

you do it, why did you do it?' How the hell was he supposed
to know!

It seemed that he hadn't been asleep two minutes when he
was startled awake by a roach trying to crawl up his nose. It
was light outside.

Eight

Hip and Gypsy Pearl moved in with Franchot on a Sunday afternoon. They had only two pieces of luggage, and in any other situation the event would have gone unnoticed. But within an hour the block on Broome Street was alive with the news that Hip Ritchwood had come back home and had brought the Howard Street whore Gypsy Pearl with him.

Sundays were usually quiet days, when many slept off their drunks, others made love, and still others spent the day – and a good part of the night – in storefront churches. The kids converged on the movies in wild, screaming masses. At about 6:00 P.M. the last bit of fun preceding *meet-the-man* day commenced. For the younger kids the 'man' was school, and for the older ones, employers; to the hustlers he was a trick or a score.

Gossip about Hip and Gypsy Pearl consisted chiefly of speculation as to whether or not Franchot would allow her to trick from his apartment. Not that anyone cared, but to speculate provided a break in the monotony that permeated most lives on Broome Street. In less than a week, the question of whether she did or didn't would be treated with the same indifference that was shown almost everything else.

Franchot gave them the room next to the toilet. After the unpacking of their things the three of them went into the living room to celebrate. Franchot was agitated and happier about Gypsy Pearl's being here than he'd admit, even to himself. He and she drank bourbon while Hip had ginger ale. Being a junkie, Hip wouldn't touch whiskey; it was about as useless to him as an empty eyedropper.

Gypsy Pearl cooked dinner for them. She was surprised at the cleanliness of the whole apartment. A man living alone in four rooms was unusual in itself, and for him to keep them as clean as this was miraculous. She cast furtive glances around for signs of female occupancy – finally found them in Franchot's bedroom: stockings and some bobby pins. But a tightness that had formed in her chest at seeing them was considerably loosened when she saw nothing to indicate permanent female lodging . . .

When word of the invasion reached Rosemary she wasted no time hurrying downstairs. She didn't care about Hip moving in, but Gypsy Pearl was a different story. In fact, an easy woman wouldn't have bothered her overmuch, but a seasoned whore, a beautiful seasoned whore like Gypsy Pearl, was something else; she knew too many tricks designed to snare a man. She descended upon them just as they were finishing the fried chicken and rice that Gypsy Pearl had cooked.

When the two women were introduced they were excessively cordial, immediately aware that they were enemies. Their competition began at once, each trying to outdo the other in gaiety and wit. Impressed with her own moral superiority, Rosemary never lost an opportunity to remind Gypsy Pearl of it, but her innuendos were so subtle that only Gypsy Pearl took them in. They went right over Franchot's head, who was thinking what a good time they were all having.

Hip wasn't paying any attention. He was wanting a fix, and soon he got up and went into the toilet to give himself one. It was very weak stuff, he found; he had to take an extra jolt just to get himself straight. He'd see Cowboy about it when he and Gypsy Pearl went to Howard Street tonight. He hid his works behind the commode and joined the others in the living room.

Franchot was telling Rosemary about the plans he and Hip were making; she smiled, but her skepticism easily matched Gypsy Pearl's. She, also, had never known a junkie to quit stuff and stay off. In truth, though, Gypsy Pearl had known one, but he soon became just as addicted to wine, so she didn't really count him as staying off drugs.

Franchot turned to Rosemary later and, for Gypsy Pearl's benefit, asked, 'Girl, what's this stuff goin' 'round that you and me's gittin' married?'

Hip, feeling better since his fix, said playfully, 'Yeah, I

thought I was goin' to a weddin', accordin' to what Irene told me. What about it, chick? – you gon' hook m'big brother?'

Rosemary refused to look at Gypsy Pearl. She smiled nervously. 'Oh, I was just kiddin' Irene 'cause she teased me when she started goin' with Tal Murphy. I didn't mean for that loudmouth to put it on the radio. Lord, the things playin' can lead to!' she cried, but more in exasperation for the smile on Gypsy Pearl's face than for Irene's indiscretion.

After a quick unobserved glance at Gypsy Pearl, Franchot was content, and he changed the subject by suggesting that they watch television.

There were only two cans of beer left. Hip volunteered to go over to Two-Day Sheik's to get more; he had almost two hundred dollars. He had, in fact, intended to give Franchot at least fifty of it, as a token of his sincerity, but the longer it stayed in his pocket the more reluctant he became to part with it, except for stuff. To buy beer for them, then, would be a nice gesture. He bought a whole case.

They were watching 'The Ed Sullivan Show' when he returned. He passed the beer out, put twelve cans in the refrigerator, and went into the toilet for another fix. He sure as hell would find out from Cowboy what the hell was going on. Selling lemons wasn't cool at all.

Franchot sat on the sofa between the two women; Rosemary held possessively onto his hand giving it gentle squeezes every now and then, and every now and then looking out of the corner of her eye to see if Gypsy Pearl had dared a similar maneuver. She felt tired and wanted to go to bed and rest up for tomorrow's work at the factory, but she resolved not to budge; she'd stay all night before she'd leave Franchot to the wiles of that woman. Hip had junk in him, and there was no telling what that whore might entice Franchot to do once Hip went to sleep. Rosemary smiled to herself – yes, she'd stay all night, it wouldn't be the first time. Maybe if Gypsy Pearl saw that she'd keep her hands off him.

Gypsy Pearl laughed at Rosemary as much as at the television; especially when she saw the death-grip that Rosemary had taken on Franchot's hand. Did she think Gypsy Pearl was going to rape him or something? Oh, he was nice, of course, and she did like him, but she wasn't a home-wrecker. Besides, she was Hip's woman, and though she went with other men, it was only for his profit. She'd never had another man for kicks. But if Rosemary kept acting like a jealous bitch toward her, she wouldn't only try to take Franchot away from her, she would take him, dump him, and laugh like a maniac in Rosemary's face.

'The Ed Sullivan Show' ended. Hip stood slowly. 'You ready, baby?' he said to Gypsy Pearl. She looked at him for a moment with hatred. As if it mattered to him whether she was 'ready' to go out! She glanced at Franchot, then at Rosemary – who was gulping down the last of her beer to keep from hooting with joy – and then she smiled dutifully, and nodded.

'Wait a minute,' Franchot said rising. 'This is your welcome-home night, Lonnie. Ain't nobody askin' you for rent money, is they?' He turned the television off without taking his eyes from his brother's lazy smile.

'Hustlers ain't got no nights off, Shots. Every day and every night is takin' care of business. Besides, I gotta see a man about a burn.' He was the only one in the room who felt indifferent to Gypsy Pearl's going out – as long as he was obeyed. Franchot was angry about it, though he couldn't have explained why; Rosemary was happy; Gypsy Pearl was miserable and knew only that she wanted to stay here. Hip wasn't aware of any of them; all he was interested in was getting some good stuff from Cowboy, or getting his money back.

When they were alone Rosemary threw her arms around Franchot and kissed him in rapidly deepening kisses, as if he'd been away on a long journey. For the first time, he became aware of her jealousy. When she released his lips he asked, 'What was that for?'

'For auld lang syne,' she said, cuddling closer to him on the sofa.

He cupped her breast. 'Do you know what kisses like that lead to, woman?'

'Uh-huh. And I feel what they lead to, too,' she said, indicating his caressing hand.

'Want to show you, I give lessons, y'know.'

'Will it take all night?'

'Well, extended lessons do.'

'S'poze I wanna learn fast?'

'I got an easy-lesson course, too.'

'Which one is the best?'

'Depends on your cooperation, lady.'

'Well, I'm a slow learner, so maybe the extended lesson would be the best thing for me.'

'The customer's always right here,' and he lifted her from the sofa.

She giggled. 'You begin so quick!'

'Extended lessons need a longer warm-up period – Coffee breaks in between, too.'

'I don't like coffee,' she said, as he placed her gently on the bed in his room.

'Then don't take a break,' he said softly, turning out the light.

In the darkness they undressed, each acutely conscious of the sounds of the other, yet making as little noise as possible. Franchot watched her shadowy figure moving and smiled to himself: thanks to Gypsy Pearl he had reason to believe that tonight would be among the best he and Rosemary had spent together.

He climbed into the bed. She soon followed him and her smooth skin tingled with delight as his hand trailed slowly over it.

Each kiss carried them farther than the last to the goal they sought. Her hand gently rode over his broad back and shoulders, causing a thousand flesh-bumps to blossom on the surface of his skin. Their kisses continued and his fingers traversed the familiar forest just under the soft swell of her stomach. Her breath caught, she moaned, engulfing his ear with her sweet mouth. Her exciting scent hung in his nostrils; he savored the perfume of her body and took it into his with joy.

She opened to him as he moved into her warm valley that was so fertile and throbbing and pungently sweet. Her full thighs captured and held him, her hands, still for the moment, held his head while her lips devoured his. At every descending move of his body, a whispered encouragement, a moan, unintelligible music rose from her. She was as gentle as he was indurate. Her breathing became rapid and gasping, and she tightened her arms about him while his lips and tongue explored the recesses of her ears, her neck. His hands gripped the cotton resiliency of her buttocks.

Their rhythm increased, tightened. She cried his name as sensation overcame her, until, no longer able to hold back the violence within and between them, he burst in upon her, and she rose to meet his hot, lunging urgency.

A glow spread throughout her entire being. Her limbs shook, and she clung to him with tears of joy filling her eyes; as his rigidity relaxed within her, she sought to keep him there with perky contractions. He was willing, it seemed, to stay, but unable to meet the task.

Her tears were as much for the loss as from the pleasure.

Gypsy Pearl and Hip were greeted by a variety of looks as they left the building; curious, amused, admiring, and lustful. The men greatly enjoyed looking at her hips in the tight skirt she wore. Hip acknowledged the 'Glad to see you back, baby' greetings, but didn't stop to talk until a couple of junkies he knew asked him if he'd seen Cowboy: they'd been sold some of the weak dope, too.

On Howard Street they saw Jackie Brown staggering along a hundred feet ahead of them. He was heading for the neon lights of Mann's Manor, the M&M, and the Howard Bar, and he'd probably be thrown out of each of them before the night was over.

By the number of long black limousines that were parked on the M&M side of the street it was apparent that Father Divine had been around during the afternoon for a round of banqueting and speeches. When he visited Howard Street an air of mild, orderly bedlam pervaded everywhere. The street was sometimes entirely blocked by big, beautiful cars belonging to him and his followers. People had looks of pure joy on their faces; they came away from the meetings broker, but filled with righteousness and good food. The Streeters really admired Father Divine and called him a Master Player; he had, they said, a heavy game.

Jackie Brown missed the curb at the corner and fell in front of Mann's. He was struggling up and cursing when Hip and Gypsy Pearl reached him. Hip gave him a hand up, then asked if he'd seen Cowboy.

'Goddamn sidewalk!' Jackie cursed drunkenly. His beard looked like he hadn't shaved in a month; his face was so bloated that they couldn't tell if his eyes were open or shut. He licked the blood from his dirty, scraped hand with intense concentration. Everything about him was dirty, from his brown suit jacket and shiny, wrinkled powder-blue pants, to his torn laceless tennis shoes. He wore no shirt under the jacket and he smelled like a backed-up toilet.

Hip repeated, 'Man, I asked you if you seen Cowboy.' He wiped his hands on his handkerchief; they'd gotten damp from touching Jackie's clothes.

'I ain' seen a mothafuckin' soul, man. Gimme a quarter, willya?' He staggered and almost fell again. Hip jumped back; he wasn't going to touch the stinking mass again. Jackie had probably been lying in his vomit somewhere.

Jackie pried his eyes open for a better look at them. The eyeballs were scarlet, the meat around them puffed like a very old Chinaman's. Gypsy Pearl felt like crying at the sight of him. 'Give him a quarter and let's go, Hip,' she said.

With what might have been meant to be a smile but came across as a grimace, Jackie seconded her request: 'Yeah, Hip ol' buddy, gimme a quarter. I'll pay ya back soon's my ship come in.'

Hip turned away, pulling Gypsy Pearl with him. 'I ain't supportin' you, nigga,' he said. Gypsy Pearl looked back at Jackie; he was staggering across the street.

Inside Mann's Hip saw Tal Murphy standing at the bar talking to Irene Smith, who was seated. They were arguing, but Hip cut in anyway. 'You seen Cowboy tonight, Tal?' he asked.

Without taking his eyes from Irene's face Tal said, 'I seen him 'round a coupla hours ago, man, but I been tryin' t'talk some sense into this bitch here, so I don't know where he went.'

'Don'choo call *me* no bitch, Tal Murphy.' Irene shouted with tears streaming down her cheeks. 'I ain't none of your whores an' you ain't go' talk me into bein' one neither!' She tried to get up, but Tal pushed her back down onto the stool. Then he turned to Hip as calm as if he'd never been arguing.

'What's up, man? You the fourth cat who been in here lookin' for that stud. He sellin' lemons again?'

'Yeah,' Hip replied with a disgusted sneer. 'He puttin' out that weak shit like the panic was on or somethin'. Gotta do damn near a eighth before you even feel it.'

'You know you go' hafta damn near kill 'im before he even think about straightenin' you,' Tal warned.

'Yeah, well that's just what might happen,' Hip threatened. 'He gon gimme some more stuff, or my money back, or a piece of his black ass!' He turned to go.

'I hear you, baby,' Tal said. 'But you better be cool. I hear Slim McNair was 'round askin' about that trick you and your woman offed. If you press Cowboy he might drop a dime on you.'

'Yeah, but that chump gon' do somethin' for me, if I see 'im.'

Gypsy Pearl followed him out and down to the Howard Bar. Cowboy wasn't there, either. However, she picked up a trick, and was glad of the opportunity to get away from Hip for a while. Hip told her to meet him at the M&M. The john was nervous about Hip's presence until she told him that Hip was her brother. He was relieved as he ordered drinks for himself and her.

There was a full crowd in the M&M. The door was open and the music splashed out into the street along with billows of smoke and laughter. The dance floor was covered with women – some who could easily have been mistaken for men – clutching possessively at each other.

'Hip, *dah*ling! Come meet mother's new husband.' It was Lillie. Hip moved through the crowd excusing himself repeatedly.

'Dahling,' Lillie said as he came up to them. 'I want you to know that I thought you were simply *mah*velous Thursday night. Oh, child did you ever per*form!* Let mother feel your lovely muscles.'

Hip grinned shyly as Jorge morosely eyed Lillie's hand caressing Hip's arm. Lillie smiled approvingly at his begrudging face, then introduced him: 'This is mother's new *Fluck*, Hip – isn't he a dream?' Then he turned to Jorge: 'Dahling-sweet, this is Hip. His name is Jorge, Hip. It's pronounced: "*Whore-hey*".' Lillie giggled loudly as the two men smiled and nodded to each other. Jorge offered to buy him a drink, but Hip refused, asking Lillie if he'd seen Cowboy around.

'Oh, Mr Big Shot was around earlier, baby; about an hour ago.' He was gently squeezing Jorge's thigh and looking into the man's coal-black eyes. 'I think he's probably at Sue's; the game is there tonight, you know,' Lillie added.

Hip had completely forgotten about Sue's Sunday night games. Most of Howard Street's money crowd went there Sunday night. The crap games were expensive, as were the drinks and the women. To go to Sue's was a sign of affluence; one was really 'into something' if he could hang out there. It began to dawn on Hip why Cowboy was selling weak junk; he'd probably lost heavily last week, or was trying to build up a big bankroll for this week's play. Before leaving, Hip said to Lillie, 'If you see that mothafucka before I do, tell 'im I'm lookin' for 'im, dig?'

'I most certainly will, dahling,' Lillie answered.

Hip thanked him and steered his way through the dancers toward the door.

Too Loo came over to Lillie and Jorge, and said, 'Sister, *where* did you find this *dream*?' – indicating Jorge, whose bright face flashed a smile at the admiring Too Loo.

'While *dream*ing of course, dearie,' Lillie replied.

'Oh, Miss *It*, you're too *much*. Just look at his *gor*geous hair! Why don't you let him come up and see me sometime?' Too Loo leered lustfully.

'Now, Miss *Thing*,' Lillie retorted in mock indignation. 'You *know* better than that. Are you a *Communist*? Besides, it would interfere with my Spanish and his English lessons – among other things.' He turned to Jorge: 'And we *do* so want to communicate, don't we, lover?'

'We do everyt'ing,' Jorge said.

They all laughed and Jorge bought another round of drinks.

Nine

Sue's gambling room was in the basement, but she referred to it as the first floor. Hip entered the building and walked to the rear of the hall, to where he'd urinated a few nights earlier, then he made a U-turn to the left around a thin wall-to-ceiling partition where a door stood under the staircase, thick and locked from the inside.

He knocked, and after about a two-minute wait the door opened and Sue stood looking at him knowingly. 'Cowboy's downstairs,' she said flatly.

'How'd you know I was lookin' for him?' he asked, walking past her as she relocked the door.

'Junkies been lookin' for him all day. Two of 'em's down there now with blood in their eyes. Y'all start somethin' in my house and I'll have the cops on your asses quick. They already been here questionin' me about that man you and Gypsy Pearl robbed the other night – I ain't go' have y'all givin' my house a bad name, Hip. I mean it, too.'

He didn't answer. At the bottom of the stairs he parted the beaded curtains and stepped into a large rectangular room. It was lighted entirely by red bulbs, which reflected luxuriously and soothingly off the snowy walls and creamy ceiling. Every time he came to Sue's he marveled at the cleanliness of everything, at the richness of the surroundings and the soft, polished appearance here that contrasted so sharply with the upstairs part of the house, and Howard Street in general.

Men and women sat around covered card tables with a variety of smoking objects dangling from their lips and hands. The burnt tea-leaf odor of marijuana hung mixed with cigar and cigarette smoke. Sunday was blackjack night for the cardplayers, whose desire was to win or lose fast and spend the rest of the night balling. During the week, however, coon-can, skin, and tonk were the main games. Farther in the back, separated by a multicolored beaded curtain, was the crap room. Long sofas and plush armchairs were the only furniture in this room except for the large billiard table standing in the middle of it. It was lighted by a bright 150-watt bulb, and through the beaded curtain Hip could see men gathered around the table, intent on the galloping cubes.

At first he didn't see Cowboy among the twenty or so people congregated there and took another quick glance around the card room; but all he saw were a couple dancing to the hidden stereo, others talking together as they enjoyed the comfortable chairs along the walls, and six people seated at the ten-stool bar.

Sue stood directly behind him, trying to think of something which would frighten him enough to keep him from satisfying the obvious grudge he had against Cowboy while they were in here. Even Slim McNair couldn't help her if a murder occurred here. Her big, brown eyes, which always managed to look innocently surprised despite the horrors she'd seen on Howard Street, held Hip captive for a moment. He liked her nut-brown skin, which contrasted so pleasingly with the blond wig she wore. He liked her small breasts and thin waist, which flared out into wide, gentle hips and tapered down into shapely legs, formed by ballet lessons she'd had as a young girl. She hadn't taken the lessons long enough to overdevelop the muscles; they were just right.

He dug Sue.

She liked him, too, very much as a matter of fact, but he was a junkie and she didn't mess with them under any circumstances. 'He's in there,' she said, seeing him hesitate and look around. 'And I'm warnin' you, Hip – no trouble. I mean it.'

He knew she did. 'Okay, mamma – no trouble.' He smiled appreciatively as she moved in front of him and he watched the flow of her in her tight black toreadors.

As they stepped through the curtain one of the men at the table cursed: 'Som'bitch! Man, gimme 'notha pair dice, Joe. Can't make a fuckin' thing wid dese.' He threw the dice to Joe Magic, who was the houseman, and was given three brand-new pairs to choose from. It was Cowboy, slightly drunk.

He examined the dice carefully with a cigarette hanging from the corner of his mouth. His wide-brimmed white hat was cocked on the side of his head. He saw Hip but his expression didn't alter, and it seemed as though he hadn't taken his eyes from the dice.

The two junkies who'd asked Hip earlier about Cowboy were standing along the right wall with angry, impatient scowls. They exchanged nods with Hip – nods which said that they were on the same mission as he.

Around the table were concentrated the elite of Howard Street's fast life: Hammerhead Willie, Bill Grumsley, Fish-Man Floyd, Joe Magic, Red Shirt Charlie, and Cowboy, among others. These were the people who made the most of the vices of Howard Street; much of what they made found its way into the pockets of the big-time white gangsters and cops, lawyers and politicians. Even so, what they managed to keep for themselves made them rich, or, as Third Ward people said, 'nigger-rich.' The billiard table was loaded with bills, mostly those of fifty and one-hundred denominations.

Hammerhead Willie became agitated by Cowboy's long vetting of the dice and finally said, 'C'mon, man, ain' nothin' wrong wid dem craps. You sho cain't look no sevens on 'em!' He chewed nervously at an extremely long cigar and rubbed his hand over his long, sledgehammer-like pate.

'I'm losin' my money, jack,' Cowboy said, glaring at him, 'an' if I wann 'xamine dese dice 's my goddamn business.'

Fish-Man Floyd spoke softly: 'You ain't the only one losin' a taste, baby. If you figger to win some back you better start shootin'.' Most people listened when Fish-Man talked because it wasn't often and he meant what he said, whether it was a threat or a compliment.

But as Cowboy shook and prepared to throw the dice, Hip cut in: 'I come to see you about somethin' important, Cowboy.'

Cowboy stopped and fixed a penetrating stare on Hip. It had more hostility in it than the one Red Shirt Charlie had sent his way as he'd stepped into the gambling den. One of the other junkies took this opportunity to speak, too:

'What you go' do, Cowboy?' he asked. 'I don't like bein' burned, man.'

'I'ma shoot these dice,' Cowboy answered slow and deliberately. 'And if I win,' he went on, 'then I'ma see what you guys want so tough that you gotta mess wid me when I'm gamblin'.'

'I think you know why we here, man,' Hip said. 'In fact, I'm sure of, if you wanna know the truth.'

Cowboy licked his lips without replying and loosed the dice upon the green felt. They came up eight. 'Who got it?' he asked around the table.

Bill Grumsley was first to fade him.

'I think he 'bout due,' Red Shirt said, putting down two fifties.

'I ain't wid 'im,' Hammerhead covered, then, turning to Cowboy: 'Put down again,' he challenged.

Cowboy threw two hundred on the table. When the bets were settled all around he loosed the dice again. Six.

'Hundred on five an' ten,' Fish-Man offered. Hammerhead covered him.

Cowboy shot again. Nine. He picked them up gingerly, reciting:

'Preacher in the pulpit,
Preacher in the pulpit,
If ya wanna make an eight
make it fo' by fo' . . . Hahh, baby!'

The dice came five and three. Hammerhead wiped the sweat from his forehead and cursed. He and Fish-Man picked up their side bet while Cowboy picked up nine hundred dollars.

The junkie who'd spoken before walked to the table. 'Gimme my bread, Cowboy. I been waitin' long enough an' I wanna go git me some decent stuff.'

Cowboy looked at him indignantly. 'Man, is that what you wanna see me about? I thought y'all wanted to cop. I ain't sold you no bad stuff, what the hell you talkin' 'bout?'

Hip and the other two junkies stiffened simultaneously. It was plain that Cowboy didn't intend to return their money.

'Cowboy,' Hip said, and there was a deliberate threat in his voice, 'that stuff you sold me was damn near all milk sugar, man. I donno about nobody else, but you gimme my money or some good stuff – that's all to it.'

'S'poze I don't?' Cowboy looked at all three of them.

'Then we in for a little trouble,' Hip said. 'Speakin' for myself, I ain't never even come to you short. I pay with the full five bills, man, so I want five bills' worth of stuff.'

Sue cut in, 'Looka here, now, I don't want no fightin' in here – I done warned you, Hip. And, Cowboy, if you gon' argue with him, take it outta here.'

'Ain't nothin', Sue baby,' Cowboy answered.

The silent junkie suddenly came toward Cowboy menacingly, his face contorted and fists balled. 'Oh, it's somethin', nigga, and I ain't bullshittin' neither . . .'

Cowboy's hand dived under the sportshirt he was wearing and came out with a nickel-plated .22 revolver: 'Mothafucka, I said it ain't *nothin*'! You take one more step and your black ass is dead! Back off me!' he said to the other two. He stuffed his winnings into his pocket, eyeing them carefully. They froze as he backed out of the room. The women were staring wide-eyed, their mouths hanging open.

When he was gone Sue said to the players, 'Go on with the game, fellas.' Then, to the junkies: 'If y'all ain't spending no money, I think y'all's business here done gone.' And, to one of the women sitting and watching: 'Mommy, go get some drinks for the players. It's on the house, boys.'

Mommy, an amazon of a woman to whom Sue was a guardian, went to take the men's orders. She was very pretty but not very bright. The men who gave her their orders knew that she would probably bring them the wrong thing, but when she did, it was on the house. And, besides, most wanted to get her in bed, so they smiled at her mistakes indulgently.

Sue escorted the three junkies out as Red Shirt called for the dice.

'Bets on the table,' Joe Magic said. The game went on.

On the way out of the building Hip saw Gypsy Pearl coming

in with a trick – the same one she'd been with in the Howard Bar. He didn't acknowledge them, but went past them on his way to Mann's Manor to wait. The other two junkies walked toward Court Street . . .

Tal and Irene were still in animated conversation, Hip noted; he bought a soda and took it up into the gallery. He made a bet with himself that before another week had passed Irene would be turning tricks for Tal.

His mind turned to Cowboy. It really irked him to let Cowboy get away with burning him, but Tal had sounded a true note of caution – as had Sue – by reminding him that he was almost at Cowboy's mercy because of the robbery Thursday night; or Red Shirt's mercy; for that matter, anyone's mercy who had a grudge against him. But mostly Cowboy's, because he'd been there and could be a witness against him. The others could only cause him the discomfort of an arrest by means of hearsay. He didn't want to provoke Cowboy to the point of putting the man on him, but if he pursued the incident started at Sue's, Cowboy would have no qualms.

He'd been lucky enough to escape going to jail so far, and was mildly curious as to what it was like. Many of the Streeters talked about it, and, to hear them, one wouldn't think it was so bad; however, he wasn't anxious to find out firsthand.

He watched Tal and Irene. Tal seemed to have her under a spell now. Hip knew that he was a real talker, able to put his words in the most beautiful light and paint pictures that Irene's flimsy willpower could in no way stand up to. If she listened long enough, Tal would have her eating out of his hand.

There had to be a way of getting even with Cowboy without endangering his own freedom. Maybe he could set Cowboy up for a bust instead of the other way around . . . But he couldn't do that; he hated stoolies too much to be one himself.

Gypsy Pearl turned five tricks and was able to beat one out of thirty dollars before Hip decided to call it a night. It was close to two in the morning when she came in from the last trick. She hadn't been gone twenty minutes, and as she came up into the gallery Hip asked why she returned so quickly.

'He couldn't get a hard on,' she said shortly.

'Did he pay you?' he asked anxiously.

'Yeah, Hip, he paid me.' She didn't try to mask her contempt for Hip's concern about her getting the money.

He smiled and ordered her a drink and himself another soda.

'He was real nervous,' she offered. 'I think he was a fag tryin' to fool himself. Can I have cigarette money?' He gave it to her.

The band hadn't shown up tonight and she came back to get a quarter to play a record. 'I wanna hear Betty Carter's new record, Hip,' she answered his stingy 'What for?'

She wasn't very surprised when he refused her the quarter, and she sat patiently beside him. Someone else played the record she wanted to hear. Hip said, 'See? If you be cool, you can hear the damn thing for nothin'. I ain't got no money to waste on foolishness.'

After a while she asked, 'Did you see Cowboy?'

'That punk pulled a gun on me,' he replied angrily.

'What'd you do?'

He looked at her as if she'd asked the most stupid question imaginable: 'What you *think* I did?' he said sarcastically.

'Beat him up?' She wasn't really interested anymore.

'I left him the hell alone! That's what I did; and don't ask me no more stupid questions, woman.' A little while later he said, 'Let's g'on in, I'm tired.'

Ten

Things went pretty well for the Ritchwood brothers and Gypsy Pearl. Everyone seemed content, except perhaps Rosemary, but she hadn't voiced any objections yet.

Franchot found it amusing, and flattering, that Rosemary wanted to stay all night with him oftener than she usually had in the past. And he was happy when he came home from work to find Gypsy Pearl there cooking, cleaning, and even mending some of his clothes. He was also glad that neighbors had stopped dropping in, ostensibly to 'see good ol' Hip,' but in truth to gawk at Gypsy Pearl.

Rosemary would come downstairs as soon as she finished work; she'd help Gypsy Pearl with the dishes, and, if she came home early enough, with the food. And Gypsy Pearl secretly laughed at Rosemary's anxiety – but only after she herself had gotten over the slight shock and irritability she'd felt at seeing Rosemary leave Franchot's room in the mornings. Now she found it quite easy to laugh at Rosemary's jealousy. She was jealous of Rosemary, too.

Hip still hadn't broken his routine of sleeping till twelve noon; then he'd get up, sometimes telling Gypsy Pearl what time to meet him on Howard Street. Sometimes he came and went several times, if he wanted a fix and was near the house, and usually he took her with him after Franchot came from work. But most of her days were her own, as long as he knew where she was.

Franchot was getting anxious to see some signs of Hip living up to his promise to kick his narcotic habit. He didn't know very much about drugs or people addicted to them, but he'd heard enough about it to be pretty sure that a kicking addict couldn't have acted, looked, or gotten around the way Hip did.

A few days later he asked Gypsy Pearl if Hip was kicking;

she said she didn't know. So one night, as she and Hip were preparing to leave for Howard Street, he asked, 'When you gon' git yourself together, Lonnie? It's been almost two weeks and I ain't seen no sign of you kickin' that habit. And if you want that job you gotta be there by next Wednesday at the latest, or they gon' give it to the man they got workin' temporary. They only holdin' now because you my brother.'

'I'm weanin' myself off it, Shots,' Hip lied. 'Just be cool, bro. By next week I'll be workin' like a champ. It don't take but three days to kick, and I'm gittin' my fill of fast livin' before I straighten up for good. You can dig that.'

Gypsy Pearl was afraid to look at Franchot; she knew that if she did her eyes would tell on Hip. She fumbled around in her pocketbook to keep from screaming at Hip to stop lying.

Franchot wanted badly to believe him, but he couldn't really force himself to do so. In order to give Hip an out – to press him now would accomplish nothing – he asked, with an exaggerated show of ignorance, 'I thought it took longer to kick one of them habits.'

'Well, yeah,' Hip replied. 'It do – but that's what happens to guys who really strung out. Like, I mean, my habit ain't that bad, see? It won't take me long to kick.'

'Oh,' Franchot said with an air of satisfaction. He let the subject drop.

Once out of the apartment Gypsy Pearl turned to Hip. 'Why you tell Franchot that big lie, Hip? You shouldn't do that to your own brother, especially after he been so nice to us and all.'

They were standing on the stairs and he reached down and slapped her so hard that she had to grab the bannister to keep from tumbling all the way down. Hip said, 'Bitch, don't you *never* take sides with another man 'gainst me, you hear? *Never!*'

She made no answer. He raised his hand again. 'Yes, Hip,' she said very softly. The tears in her eyes were more from anger than the pain he'd caused her. She walked down the rest of the steps without even seeing them.

Back in the apartment Franchot sat in the living room trying to gauge his brother's sincerity. The more he thought about it the more skeptical he became. But he passed this off. He was willing to wait if his brother said he'd be ready by next week.

The next day it rained torrents and Franchot was forced to come home early. Gypsy Pearl was alone in the living room, looking out at the rain and nearly deserted street.

'Where's Lonnie?' he asked from the kitchen. He took off his wet jacket and hung it on the door of the toilet.

'Went to New York to buy dope.'

He looked at her gloomily for a moment, then sighed and went into his bedroom, closing the door softly behind him. He removed his wet work clothes slowly and dried himself with a towel. With the towel going over his body, his thoughts turned to the woman in his living room. It entered his mind to call her into the bedroom and, as his brother had suggested, throw her in bed and wail. But it was a thought that he had no intention of ever carrying out. He finished quickly and dressed.

She was still sitting in the same position when he entered the living room and sat down on the sofa. 'What he go to New York for when Cowboy right around the corner?' he asked.

'He said he ain't buying no more stuff from Cowboy behind Cowboy burnin' him and pullin' that gun on him at Sue's.' She nervously lit a cigarette.

Franchot said, 'I thought Cowboy gave him his money back?'

'He did, but Hip says he don't trust him no more, so he gon' git his stuff from New York from now on.'

He lit a smoke and let the conversation lag while he gathered his thoughts. He picked up an old *Ebony* magazine that was lying on the coffee table and thumbed through it without even seeing words or pictures. She went back to looking out of the window.

At length he asked, 'Do you really believe he tryin' to git off that dope?'

The earnestness of his gaze and the worry showing so plainly on his face almost made her tell him the truth. She felt her throat constrict as she answered, 'Yes, I believe it, Franchot.'

Her expression, the way she hastily pulled at her cigarette and went back to looking out of the window, told him that she was lying. He said nothing, hoping that she'd change her mind and tell him the truth. He wouldn't pressure her; she'd have to do it on her own. But as the minutes slipped by and she remained silent, he couldn't bring himself to feel any less sympathetic toward her for her loyalty to his brother, even though he tried. After all, he reasoned, she was his brother's woman, to protect him was her duty.

It was not that she didn't want to tell him the truth – and tell him something else too: that Hip was hinting at making the apartment a shooting gallery for junkies while he worked. If other junkies, who had no works or needed a place for a fix, came here, it would save Hip money on his own habit. He could use their dope and save his own. But she said nothing.

He watched her profile. Her long hair was pulled tightly back into a big braid that lay Indian-fashion across her shoulder; her nose, pert and shiny, was slightly tilted at the tip. Her soft jawline and slender neck tempted his lips; he wanted to feel the firm mellowness of her cheeks in his itching hands while her eyes looked up into his. He watched her fleshy lips and his grew hungry for the taste of them; he longed to have his arms take the place of the belt which held her quilted robe so snugly around her small waist.

He was looking at her in pure hunger when she turned and saw all of his thoughts exposed. Her own heart leaped with joy and fright simultaneously. Their eyes locked because he couldn't command his to turn away. He stood up and she didn't dare breathe as she watched the determined set of his features. Their thoughts tumbled with dual yeses, wild approvals of the chance a mere gesture would provide for them.

Franchot felt his knees loosely gathering the strength to support the two steps it took to reach her. He looked down at her, his dry tongue darting over his drier lips. She held her breath again, in anticipation, as he hoarsely asked, 'You want a beer?'

For a moment the incongruity left her mind totally blank.

She couldn't hold back a short uncontrollable giggle – it sounded as if it had come from another person altogether. Then, gaining quick control of herself, she smiled and said, 'Yes, Franchot, I sure would like a beer.'

He went into the kitchen feeling like a complete idiot, and she let herself revel in wave after wave of silent laughter. It left her feeling disjointed but vastly relieved.

He came back with two bottles of beer, and having forgotten to bring glasses, went back to get them.

They sat in relative silence, sipping their beer and every now and then making inconsequential remarks about the rain, his job, and his brother. All the while they talked, he gained in confidence; his brain seemed to open a little; his voice lost its strained traces, becoming quite pleasant as his nerves calmed. They lighted cigarettes. He told her of his ambition to buy some land one day and build his own home somewhere near the Atlantic Ocean. He relaxed even more, telling her other things: how he had a good chance of making foreman on his job next year, and eventually perhaps even forming his own construction company, which was his ultimate dream.

She listened, wondering if, in the end, Rosemary would be the one to share all this with him.

Suddenly he said: 'Is you and Lonnie thinkin' about gittin' married one day?'

She stared at him. Then she said calmly, 'I don't love him and I wouldn't marry without love – unless it was for money.'

'Well, if you don't love him, why—'

She cut him off. 'Because in this life a woman's gotta have a man to look out for her.' She'd answered this question so many times before that her reply was automatic. 'If I didn't have Hip ain't no tellin' how many times I wouldn'ta got paid by some drunk who couldn't come, or had my money took by Red Shirt Charlie or somebody like him.'

'What made you decide on my brother to be your protector?'

'Because he's the one who turned me out. And after I was turned out, he was the best fighter around Howard Street, and,' she added almost reluctantly, 'he was a man then and damn good-lookin' to boot.'

'Lonnie made you be a . . .' He hesitated.

'A whore. Don't be scared to say it.' Then boldly: 'I ain't 'shamed to be a whore so don't you be 'shamed to call me one. Be different if you was accusin' me of somethin' I wasn't.'

Franchot paused, then said: 'I didn't know he did stuff like that.'

'Well, he didn't *make* me be one. Like he didn't beat me or somethin' like that. It's just that his habit came down on him and we didn't have no money. He asked me to go out and git some dope for him and I did – the quickest way I knew how.'

'But he suggested it?'

'Yeah,' she said. 'Then he needed money for dope again, and I went out again and again. Shucks, I was whorin' for two whole months before I dug that I was a whore – bona fide, baby.' She laughed, then went on: 'I thought I loved him then; even thought he was gon' marry me. But I sure found out different. Do you know what? He really had some dope the first time he sent me out, and all the other times after that! He told me six months later.' Her smile was the wry one of a person who'd had a practical joke played on him and is bound to take it in stride.

'What you feel about him now? And why you stay with him?'

'I don't feel nothin' particular about him – sometime I don't like him very much, but usually I just don't feel nothin'. What else would I do if I didn't stay with him? He the same's any other man on Howard Street. I'd just have another pimp if I didn't have him.'

'You ever thought about quittin'?' Suddenly his voice had a sharp edge to it. 'You don't have to have a pimp, y'know? And you ain't gotta be a whore.' He wanted to smack her and kiss her at the same time.

'Yeah, I know all about it,' she said bitterly. 'I can just stop and some man gon' come and put me in a castle somewhere. Oh, hell, yeah!'

His voice softened. 'You talk like you done lost the knack for dreamin'. You shouldn't give up like that. Maybe you just ain't looked in the right places for that man.'

'I ain't dreamed in a mighty long time, Franchot,' she said untruthfully. 'My dreams escaped from me when I opened my legs to a man for money. Everybody in town know what I do for a livin', and I ain't seen one decent man who I want that wants me.'

He lowered his eyes, then quickly brought them up again to meet hers. His lips were dry again. She watched his darting tongue as she'd done before.

'I told you you wasn't lookin' in the right places – I want you, and I think I'm decent.' He couldn't rid himself of the lump which had formed stubbornly in his throat.

Her mouth hung open and she looked at him quizzically. He misunderstood and went on hastily to add: 'I mean . . . I don't just want you to . . . You know? I mean, I just want you for *you*, see? I like you for yourself. I don't care what you been before – I could easily fall in love with you, if you'd have me. See what I mean?'

She knew what he meant. She knew so well that she couldn't make any reply, so she began to cry. He was kneeling at her chair in a flash.

'Don't cry, ain't no sense carryin' on like this,' he cajoled tenderly, afraid to touch her. 'I sure as hell can't be the only man who'd want you. Woman, you gotta know that you beautiful. I know you know that. Any man'd want you.'

He took out his handkerchief and wiped her eyes clumsily, whispering soothing words and reveling in the scent of soap rising from her skin. She looked like a young girl being comforted by a parent who's just recently administered a spanking. The handkerchief was removed from her cheeks and replaced by his lips, which soon found her own lips, tentatively at first; then more forcefully, urgently.

He stood, pulling her to her feet to kiss again, deeply, lovingly. The thrill of it almost overwhelmed his senses. His arms held her tightly, trying to pull her even closer, to melt her entire length into his own.

They parted breathlessly, surveying the depths of each other's eyes. He couldn't stop himself from saying: 'I *do* love you, honey. I do, I do!' The words burst forth from him so wildly that he hardly recognized his own voice.

She tightened her arms around his neck, kissing the whole of his face with little moist enticing touches. 'Franchot. Oh, Franchot!' She repeated his name over and over.

Finally, with her cheek pressed closely to his, she said in a trembling voice, 'You don't have to say you love me. You don't have to say. If you want me to go to bed with you, you don't have to say you love me . . .'

'Shut up, honey,' he said tenderly. 'I said it and I meant it. I wouldn't say somethin' like that just to git you in bed. Please believe me.'

'I believe you, darlin'. Oh, my God, I believe you!' She began to cry again. 'I wanna go with you, Franchot, I really do. I wanted to the first time I ever saw you—'

He cut her off with another kiss and began leading her toward his bedroom. Suddenly they heard a key being inserted into the lock. Franchot immediately sat down on the sofa and picked up his now warm, flat beer. She walked into the kitchen just as Hip burst into the apartment.

He was furious and disheveled. The cut on his forehead had reopened and was pouring blood down into his eyes. Before anyone could ask what had happened to him he exploded: 'The dirty mothafuckas beat me for my money! I'm goin' back over there and shoot every cocksucka I see on Eighth Avenue!' He called to Franchot, 'Shots, loan me your gun. Them punks beat me. I ain't got no dope, man. I ain't got nothin'!'

His excitement was so great until they barely made out what he was talking about. He turned to Gypsy Pearl: 'Git your coat, woman, I need me a fix!'

Franchot came out of the living room calmly. 'I ain't givin' you no gun to go outta here and make a fool of yourself, Lonnie,' he said. 'And you ain't sendin' this woman out in this weather to git no dope neither. Where she gon' git it from? Ain't nothin' but a fool out there lookin' for a woman in the street today.' He had never seen his brother looking so wild-eyed or menacing as he did at this moment. He looked insane. His clothes were soaked through with rain and his own sweat; his skin could be seen through his shirt, and his pants were wrinkled and baggy.

When it got through to him what Franchot had said, he was taken aback. 'What the hell you mean she *ain't* goin' out? I said she goin' out. She gon' git the hell outta here and do *some*thin', man! You must be crazy or somethin'.' He turned to her: 'Bitch, I said git your coat, didn't I?'

She started toward the bedroom. Franchot shouted, 'Wait!' She stopped, looking from one to the other.

'She *my* woman, Shots,' Hip said while looking at her. 'And she gon' do like I say, or git damn near crucified!' Seeing that she still stood without getting her coat, he said, with a heavy threatening tone, 'Bitch, I ain't gon' tell you but one more goddamn time to *git your coat*!'

She went into their bedroom. When she emerged from the room with her coat on, a rather worn raincoat that must have been at least six or seven years old, all emotion seemed to have been drained out of her. Her expression was totally blank. She looked at Franchot without appearing to see him, looking beyond him.

Hip had her by the hand leading her toward the door. Franchot called out, 'I'll give you the money you need, Lonnie.'

Hip immediately released her hand, she rubbed at the pain his grip had caused her.

'Shots, baby,' Hip smiled happily, 'I wanna thank you. This is the last time you'll see me like this, man. Try to understand me, bro. I need your understandin'. I really do. I'm gon' straighten up and do right . . . It's just that them mothas in New York followed me and took every cent I had.'

Franchot tried to wave off his comments, but he persisted: 'I'ma little des'prit right now, Shots, but I'm straighten you out 'fore it's all over with. Just bear with me a little longer, bro, you'll see . . .' He reached greedily for the money. Franchot didn't even know how much he was giving him, he didn't care. It was dirt cheap to keep her from going out.

Hip stuffed the money in his pocket quickly – he'd seen a

twenty on top and didn't want to give Franchot a chance to change his mind. But even in his own anxiety he noticed that Franchot's, as far as Gypsy Pearl was concerned, was greater. He wondered passingly if they had been doing anything while he wasn't around. But he had some money now so it didn't matter if they had. He left the apartment, heading for Howard Street and Cowboy.

Franchot and Gypsy Pearl stood in the kitchen a long while after Hip left, looking at each other, saying nothing. Each knew it was impossible to take up where they'd left off before Hip had come. When at length Franchot spoke, he showed only his hurt and anger.

'Why was you goin' with him?' he almost shouted at her.

Her expressionless mask fell away, and just as angrily, she replied, 'Because I'm a whore, that's why – *his* whore!'

'After what happened between us in there' – he pointed at the living room – 'you still consider yourself his whore? After—'

The accusation in his tone seared her. 'After *what* happened?' she demanded. 'You talkin' about our agreement to climb into bed? Do my life change because you take me to bed? I been in a lotta beds, man. They don't change a doggone thing!'

He said, seething, 'Would you rather I paid you for it? Is that what you want?' He searched his pockets, forgetting already that he'd given his money away. 'I ain't got no money right now, Miss Professional Whore – how about credit? That's part of business, too.' His voice had risen to a yell.

She burst into tears and ran into her room, closing the door behind her.

Franchot went into his bedroom, got his raincoat and slammed out of the apartment.

Neither he nor Hip returned that night. He stayed upstairs with Rosemary.

Hip stayed at a rented room with a junkie girl with whom he'd taken off, after using her spike and giving her a share of his stuff.

Gypsy Pearl stayed awake, alone.

Eleven

Franchot went to work the next morning without going back to the apartment. Rosemary fixed him a lunch of cold cuts, lettuce, and tomato sandwiches. Outside, he looked up at his windows – Gypsy Pearl was there watching him. He turned away and walked toward the Kinney Street bus stop.

All morning long he worked listlessly, laying only about one hundred bricks. It didn't go unnoticed by the other workers, but it didn't matter either because he was far ahead of the rest of them and this gave them a chance to catch up with him. He was glad that, after seeing the mood he was in, no one bothered to talk to him.

Gypsy Pearl worked hard at cleaning the apartment; she couldn't seem to tire herself, nor could she really keep her mind off Franchot; but it helped to keep her hands busy. To stop would only make her sit and brood.

Around one in the afternoon Hip came in with two men and the girl he'd spent the night with. He'd realized yesterday that he had a useful tool against Franchot in Gypsy Pearl. He saw that his brother wanted her badly and wouldn't throw him out because he'd lose her, too. She was good insurance that he could use the apartment as a shooting gallery while Franchot was at work, and, if Franchot found out, he wouldn't be too quick to make a strong objection.

Hip felt, too, that as long as Gypsy Pearl used her body to pay their half of the rent, Franchot had no beef about him not getting a job. Indeed, he already had a job. She was his job. If Franchot didn't approve of his line of work, he was not overly fond of Franchot's, either; that made them even. Each of them was doing what he liked so there really shouldn't be any sweat about methods.

Gypsy Pearl called Hip into their bedroom and closed the door while the junkies he'd brought with him prepared the dope in the living room and admired 'Hip's pad.'

'What you bringin' them dopers up here for, Hip?' She dared to let anger creep into her voice. 'You know Franchot ain't gon' like that at all.'

'You oughta be glad, woman,' Hip said. 'I'm savin' you work. I ain't spent a dime, but I'm gittin' a fix; that means more money for me 'n' you. And what Franchot don't know sure ain't gon' hurt 'im.' His eyes narrowed then, searching her face: 'You ain't thinkin' about tellin' on me, is you?'

She only looked at him without answering. He asked again, 'I said you ain't plannin' to stooge, is you?'

'You shouldn't do this, Hip,' she replied evasively. 'Please don't cause him no trouble. If the cops run in here he'll be the one to git the blame because it's his apartment.'

Hip had already considered that. But what interested him more was the fact that she was begging for Franchot. He'd never known her to do that since she began whoring. She was obedient, even humble at times, but she'd never begged. He was glad of it, and more firmly convinced that something had happened between her and Franchot yesterday. Good. The profit would be all his.

Seeing that he still awaited an answer, she said at last, 'I gotta tell him. If I don't, some of the people around here will. But I won't tell if you promise you ain't gon bring 'em here no more. We doin' fine here, ain't no sense messin' it up.'

'You gon' tell on me, bitch?' His eyes riveted on her and his words came out with a hissing force. 'You must be forgittin' who the hell I am!' He smacked her, but it was a wild blow and she got her hand up in time to block the brunt of it. Hip cursed and started after her. Her legs hit the bed as she backed away and she fell back onto it.

Just then, one of the men called to him: 'Hey, Hip! Better come on, man. We ready to do up!'

Hip turned abruptly from her, threatening, 'I'll take care you later, bitch. I'ma straighten your red ass out good!' He went into the living room, smiling ardently at the heroin-filled eyedropper which the girl held out to him.

* * *

A half hour later the four junkies sat, still nodding and making incoherent conversation.

'Boss,' said one.

''Swhere i's at, baby,' said another.

'C'n see how the whole thing started,' the girl said.

'Dug that long time ago,' Hip put in.

'Yeah,' said the first.

'Yeah.'

'Yeah.'

'Y'all know where i's at,' Hip said before going into another nod.

'I's that other thing,' the girl said.

'Crazy,' said one.

'Boss-eyes,' said another. Then they all nodded again.

The girl, whose name was Anna Mae Poole, was lying all over Hip, in the affectionate attitude characteristic of many junkies after a good fix.

Gypsy Pearl stayed in the bedroom, torn between the desire to tell Franchot and the fear of what Hip would do to her if she did. It was almost impossible that one of the neighbors wouldn't tell him, or that the cops wouldn't find out soon enough from one or more of the very junkies for whom Hip provided a place to get off. But her resolution had faltered. Perhaps she had never really meant to do anything.

She finally got up and went into the kitchen to putter around. Maybe, she thought, it would work itself out somehow. Every now and then she cast an uneasy glance at the wall clock and into the living room. She knew all of them there.

Anna Mae had a white pimp named Brady Torrence, who tended bar at the Howard Bar. She was an extremely lazy whore and usually tricked only to make dope money. No matter what Brady did or said to her, she never made as much as he knew she could. He had made the fatal mistake of falling in love with her; she knew it and played on it to the hilt.

The only steady money she made was from tricks he lined up for her, mostly white men in the Italian neighborhood of Fourteenth Avenue. She always held out money on him, and seemed to enjoy the beatings he gave when he found out about it. Ever since they'd first started going together two years ago she'd been promising to buy him a Cadillac. He still drove his '50 Chevy.

Gypsy Pearl watched her climb all over Hip, kissing him, and, when she knew she was being watched, laying her hand on the front of his pants. Gypsy Pearl couldn't have cared less. There had been a time when she would have pulled out Anna Mae's burnished copper hair by the handfuls for it. Now she felt only contempt. Anna Mae was nothing but an indolent whore, trifling and sometimey – not worth the heels of a good pimp's long shoes.

Hip magnanimously pushed Anna Mae away and called Gypsy Pearl to come sit on the other side of him. Anna Mae tried to pout jealously, but because of the narcotic she couldn't look anything but stupidly content.

The two male junkies were named Tricky Dick and Dennis Warrent. They were an exception to the breed, since both drank large amounts of wine regularly, as well as using dope, and they could frequently be found drinking their full share with Jackie Brown and the other winos. Both laid claim to being jazz musicians. Dennis blew tenor sax at Mann's Manor and Tricky Dick was a would-be drummer who spent most of his musical career playing on a cardboard box with floor brushes in Caldwell Pen, where he was a regular feature six months out of any given year. Recently Dennis had gotten the manager of Mann's to give Tricky Dick a job; the manager was agreeable only because the other musicians chipped in two dollars apiece of their own money to pay him.

Dennis lifted his head from his chest, and with an obtuse smile languidly commented, 'That was some boss action, baby. I mean it swung, y'know?'

'Yeah, man,' Tricky Dick agreed. 'Tough, baby, real tough. I knew Cowboy'd see us straight after while. I wasn't even worried – he a awright cat.' It had been he who caused Cowboy to pull the gun in Sue's place.

'That might be, man,' Dennis said, 'but if that chump hadda took me through the changes I heard he took y'all through I'da offed him quick.'

'He had a gun, jack,' Hip defended. 'I damn sure ain't runnin' up against no gun.' He grabbed Gypsy Pearl roughly and pulled her to him, his manner changing to one of cheer and boasting: 'Hey, now y'all dig my woman, ain't she sayin' a taste?' He kissed her stiffened neck.

'Somethin' else, Hip. You got a lotta chick there,' Tricky Dick said, eyeing her covetously. 'She real tough. I know a lotta studs be in heaven if they could pull. She the best thing on Howard Street.'

While Hip smiled proudly, Dennis said, 'Gypsy Pearl awright, I mean, like, she nice people an' all – but, jack, ain't nothin' on Howard Street can touch Sue. That's the babe I'd like to git a shot at. She know where it's at, man . . .'

'But Sue ain't trickin',' Hip said.

'Shit!' Anna Mae put in. 'She *own* the damn whorehouse!'

'Yeah,' Hip answered. 'But she still don't trick.' He turned back to Dennis. 'I'm talkin' about whores, man – Who out there can touch my woman?'

'What about Big Louise?' Dennis retorted. 'I seen her turn more tricks than Gypsy Pearl.'

'That bitch ain't shit,' Tricky Dick said. 'She don't turn down no money from man or beast. If a trick ain't got five dollars she'll take two, or whatever he got. That ain't no whore, that's a dipsomaniac!'

'Nymphomaniac,' Anna Mae corrected.

'Yeah, well I know it's somethin' like that. She sure ain't too cool.'

'Y'all talkin' about crazy people – I'm talking about a stomp-down sophisticated thoroughbred whore like my woman.' Hip kissed her unresponsive lips.

Anna Mae, glaring at Gypsy Pearl, said, 'Shit, I can make just as much as her if I wanted to. The other night I beat a trick outta a hundred dollars and whipped it on my man.' She smiled triumphantly. No one said anything. 'Well, I *did*!' she said. 'And I gave Brady every penny, too.'

'Aw, bitch,' Tricky said sarcastically, 'you can't do nothin' with Gypsy Pearl an' you know it. You just color-struck, that's why you givin' your money to a white man – an' he still gotta

work, 'cause if he depended on you he'd damn near starve.'
It wasn't strange that his tone had become serious during the
course of his words, since he'd been wanting her to trick for
him, but had been rejected.

She puffed up with indignation: 'Well, the only reason she
make more than me is because she ain't no stuffer – she just
do drink! I can make—' Suddenly the impact of his statements
hit her. 'What you mean "color-struck," nigga? Don't you go
callin' me color-struck! You just mad because I won't have
your black ass.'

Tricky Dick, really angry now, said hotly, 'What the hell I
want with a garbagecan bitch like you? You been suckin' all
the come outta a cracka's prick for two years – what the hell
I want with you? You ain't shit!'

'I know I ain't – *but you is!* Why it bother you if you don't
have eyes yourself?'

'All I'm sayin' is you givin' money to crackas when you own
kind ain't got nothin'. If you had some scruples, bitch, you'd
hang your nappy head in shame.'

'One sure thing, you frustrated Max Roach, no matter who
I git: your black snake'll never crawl through this grass!' She
pulled up her skirt and patted her thighs to show him what
he'd never get.

He sat stunned for a moment, then his face contorted and he
started after her. 'Betcha my foot can crawl in your black ass,
though!' Before he could reach her Dennis had grabbed him
and sat him back on his seat. He calmed down considerably;
looking over at her he said, 'I wouldn't touch you with a dog's
prick, bitch – you probably all diseased up, anyhow.'

Gypsy Pearl was well sick of them all by now, and especially
of Hip, who was constantly toying with her hair, breasts, and
thighs. On top of that, Anna Mae was trying to get her goat.

'Hip, baby,' Anna Mae was saying, 'I didn't give you no
disease last night – and it was good, too, wasn't it?' She put
her hand on his arm and gave a gentle, meaningful squeeze.
When he shoved it away she became furious. 'You didn't do
that last night, did you, nigga?' she shouted. 'Last night you
told me I was ten times better than that bitch over there!'

'That was last night and I was jivin', woman,' he chided affably. 'Besides, you know a man'll say anything in bed—'

'You a damn liar, Hip Ritchwood!' she yelled and started to cry.

'Woman, stop all that noise!' Dennis said. 'You go' kill my high.'

'To tell the truth, Anna Mae,' Hip continued, 'if I had a choice between goin' to bed with you every night, or goin' with her just one night outta the year, I wouldn't even hesitate to pick that one night and that's the truth.'

Anna Mae had nothing to say. Gypsy Pearl looked again at the clock in the kitchen, which she could see from where she sat. With relief, she told Hip that Franchot would be home soon. He looked at her darkly, started to say something, but changed his mind.

To the three junkies he said, 'Y'all gotta split. My square brother'll be home from work soon and he'd have a baby if he saw y'all here gittin' high. I'll dig ya later.'

Almost before they were out of the apartment he turned to Gypsy Pearl and snarled, 'I got two good reasons to stomp you, bitch – gimme a bad one why I shouldn't.' She sat at the kitchen table silently smoking and didn't answer him. 'One,' he went on, 'you threatened to stooge on me to Franchot; and two, you tried to put me down in front of my friends, makin' them think Franchot run me. Tonight it'll be all over Howard Street that I'm scared of him.'

Still she said nothing. 'Answer me, woman!' he shouted, and at the same time punched her hard on the arm, so hard that she fell out of the chair and sprawled onto the floor.

'Leave me alone, Hip!' she cried.

'I'ma leave you alone awright!' He bent over her and hit her in the same spot again. This time she cried out in pain, scrambled to her feet, and ran for the bedroom. She tried to slam the door – not that it would have done much good, since it had no lock on it anyway – but he shoved with such force that she was thrown off her feet and landed on the bed.

He stood over her and punched her again on the now very tender spot on her arm. She cried out. The ugly smile on his face broadened. 'You gon' tell on me, huh? I'ma really give you somethin' to tell.'

She lifted her legs to try and ward off the blows and balled herself into a knot. Hip was very careful not to punch her in the face. He didn't want his meal ticket threatened. He began punching her thighs until they cramped. She tried to kick him, but she wouldn't scream for fear that someone in the building would hear her and tell Franchot. One of Hip's blows glanced her thigh, tangled in her skirt and sent it high around her waist. He looked down at her and stopped beating her. He reached down and tore the skirt away, then her blouse. His passion had taken a different turn. The sexual urge was too rare a phenomenon in him to let pass. He ripped away her brassiere and it bit into her shoulders before surrendering.

He didn't even bother to undress himself. She offered no resistance as he climbed onto her; she lay loosely not bothering to move, speak, watch. Her eyes remained tightly shut, though tears ran down the sides of her face, into her ears and hair. His body beat at hers savagely, in a manner she knew he would get no enjoyment from because he was too full of revenge. But they both knew that this pounding would be interminable, for a junkie's orgasm, if forthcoming at all, many times takes hours.

He was still on her forty-five minutes later when Franchot put his key in the lock and entered the apartment.

Hip heard him enter and smiled to himself as Gypsy Pearl tried to throw him off her. She couldn't budge him. The bedroom door was wide open.

Franchot looked quickly away and went into his room. His chest felt like it was about to explode.

The three ate dinner that night in silence. Before they were finished, Hip got up from the table, telling Gypsy Pearl that she didn't have to come to Howard Street tonight if she didn't want to. Hip was worried that Franchot would ask him about the money he'd given him yesterday, and he reasoned that if he left them alone together, Franchot wouldn't bother about it.

Franchot finished his meal wordlessly, and then went into

the living room, ostensibly to read the newspaper. Gypsy Pearl did the dishes slowly, and then brought a chair into the living room so that she could sit and look out the window. He looked up from his paper. She felt his eyes and turned to him.

'You wanna watch TV or somethin'?' he asked. 'I can take the paper into my room and read.' His voice was hoarse and weak in comparison to the steady gaze of his eyes.

'No, no,' she answered quickly. 'I just wanna look out the window.' She hoped that she sounded cooler than she felt.

He hid his face in the paper while she looked out the window, and at him in the reflection of the glass. The tension between them mounted.

Finally, simultaneously, their eyes met – and held fast. She knew that she had to speak, but all she could think to say was, 'I'm sorry, Franchot. I'm sorry.'

How glad he was! She had spoken first. But he wasn't ready to be weakened yet. Imperviously he said, 'Sorry for what? What you gotta be sorry for? You his whore, ain't you – made damn sure I seen it, too. Yesterday you beat me over the head with every word and today you threw it in my eyes. So what you so goddamn sorry for?'

'For everything,' she said meekly. 'For even livin'.'

He put the paper aside and turned on the television to a loud western. Rosemary came in a few minutes later.

Gypsy Pearl went to her room, where she lay on the bed and stared dry-eyed at the ceiling, listening to the television and Rosemary's occasional bursts of laughter.

Part Two

Baby, if you live,
your time will come . . .

Blues theme

Twelve

'You came to the wrong place, mister. Ain't nobody around here interested in demonstratin' for nothin' except more wine, more dope, and more johns for the whores.' Jackie Brown spoke caustically to the white civil rights worker who'd been hanging around the neighborhood for a week in the hope of organizing against two big Springfield Avenue department stores. Among the stores' hundreds of employees no blacks held positions higher than shipping clerk, though some had had college educations.

Jackie and the CR worker, who introduced himself as Harry Conrad, were sitting in Mann's Manor. Jackie had quickly convinced him that they both needed a midday drink. The day was warm and sun-filled; most of the Streeters were still in bed somewhere. Skeeter Green, the bartender, was the only other person in the bar.

Skeeter had opened the door to let some fresh air chase the smells of waste out of the place. The sunshine crawling slowly across the floor pointed out how badly it needed sweeping. He usually gave Jackie or one of the other winos a drink to do it for him, but he knew that it would take a bomb to dislodge Jackie from his seat at the present time, with Conrad buying the booze; so he quickly swept it himself and returned to his stool to listen to their conversation.

Conrad ordered two more drinks, then said, 'It certainly looks that way, Jackie.' His manner was almost apologetic. 'However, once the people in this section realize that what we're trying to accomplish is in their own best interests, I'm sure that we'll meet with much better success.' He was a tall man, with wavy black hair and deep-set blue eyes; handsome really, with a straight, sharp nose above a slit of a mouth that housed even, white teeth. There was a deep cleft in his chin and his face was so smooth that he appeared to have never touched a razor to it.

Jackie said, 'I'll let you in on a secret, buddy: it's gonna take another hundred years for the people around here to even realize what the hell you talkin' about, much less do somethin' about it. I'm a goddamn tramp, right? But I got this way by tryin' to do just what you're doin' now. You can't talk that freedom stuff to these hip people, man. They don't wanna hear – mainly because they don't wanna change their way of life. Too much effort. Workin' ain't no attraction for them. If you ain't got no money to give away then you might as well forget it.'

Harry looked at Jackie's bloated face with pity and mild repugnance – at the cracked and shriveled lips, the week-old beard, the lines of caked dirt shooting across Jackie's forehead. This was only Harry's second time in the field, actually working on his own among the city's poverty-stricken people, and neither his experience nor his CR training at headquarters had prepared him for the Jackie Browns, or for the squalor, violence, and apathy that he'd found on Howard Street. The blacks he'd known in school and at headquarters were nothing like these people.

Harry was typically white upper middle-class. He had a healthy respect for parents and family; he had a care for what his neighbors thought of him. He cared what happened to himself; he liked people generally and cared what happened to them also. He was idealistic and was glad to admit it. But it was only last year that he, at the age of twenty-two, had become aware of the plight of black people in America. Being white, when he thought of America and Americans he thought of white people. It bothered him tremendously that he'd never thought of blacks as Americans, too.

On taking stock of himself, he found that during his whole life, during every humanitarian impulse he'd ever had, he'd never consciously thought in any terms other than white American ones, unless, of course, the needy were charity-poster Asians and the like – the Help-a-Child sort of thing. It was as if he'd only last year discovered the existence of nonwhite Americans. Till then, his conscience had been nothing more than sympathy for a faraway misery; it had allowed him to preserve his prejudices and remain completely ignorant of the misery in his own backyard. Now he was stung with remorse.

When his serenity was disturbed by the pictures of policemen and dogs attacking women and children, he had to act. The sit-ins and pray-ins hit him like a religious revelation: the blacks were putting their faith in the white man's inherent goodness, in the white man's ability to see justice done. They were, indeed, putting their faith in him! It was a large order, but at least time was on his side, he felt. He was still young, still developing, still trying to change his attitude toward blacks, and he wanted to try to change theirs too.

But, as Jackie Brown had observed, he was getting nowhere fast on Howard Street. It would have been much easier to have people from the CR headquarters and its affiliates demonstrate, but CR leaders thought it best that the task force be the people directly involved in the neighborhood. Then none of the stores could claim that it was only 'outside agitators' who were responsible for the 'trouble.' Hope drawn from the CR people had been the only thing to sustain him since he had taken an active part in their movement. He needed now more than ever to cling to that hope.

Meanwhile, Jackie, with the whiskey in him, was feeling pretty good. His heart beat fast, because he wasn't used to good whiskey anymore, but his high was much warmer and fuller than the one he got from wine. The whiskey was harder to get down, but once there it settled like a ship sunk to the ocean's bottom.

With some difficulty he focused on Conrad and said, 'You one of them ofay liberals who's got high hopes, but if you stays on this street another week your hopes is gonna just zoom away. Now what you oughta do is go to one of them neighborhoods where the black men live halfway decent and organize them. At least they'll hold still long enough to hear what you gotta say.'

Conrad handed him the pack of cigarettes he'd just bought. 'I think you're wrong to feel like that, Jackie. The situation isn't as hopeless as you make it out to be. Quite frankly, I think you were defeated before you even started – your lack of tolerance is really your lack of confidence in yourself. I mean, look at yourself – no worthwhile person is going to give up on life the way you have. Perhaps "worthwhile" is a bad choice of words; I should say no intelligent, thinking person – and you said you went to college . . .'

'Yeah, that's right,' Jackie said defensively. 'I went to Rutgers on a basketball scholarship. I could've went to Princeton if I'd wanted to. You're lookin' at me now; but just because a man's clothes're poor don't mean his mind is, too.'

'I didn't mean to offend,' Conrad said.

'No harm. Jus' listen: the niggers around here are the most triflin' bunch you'll find anywhere, and if you set off the goddamn atomic bomb you wouldn't change a damn thing!' Jackie's words were thick with drunkenness, but his sudden fire startled Conrad.

'You're unduly harsh, Jackie. These people are no different than any others. All one needs to do is educate them, get them used to different things. They have to identify with what's best for them before they'll accept it. A person can go through his entire life doing the wrong things in the wrong manner; if he's not shown a better way he'll probably keep doing wrong, even if he's harmed in the process.'

Jackie gave him a contemptuous look and said, 'You been in them sociology and psychology books too long, man. That paper you're readin' ain't people, baby; it's another thing when you deal with flesh and blood – they got a frustratin' way of not actin' or reactin' like the book says they should. For instance, how can you explain some of these jumbled junkies around here who'll shoot up a friend's dope, eat up his food, wear out his clothes, sleep in his house and fuck his woman, and then, if that same friend takes an OD of stuff while he's with him, take everything he's got and leave him layin' there to die? A lot of 'em wouldn't take a friend to the hospital or phone for help. But if that friend survives, they'll flock around him like flies on a turd. Now they know this is dead wrong because they wouldn't want somebody to leave them like that. But they still do wrong, and y'know why? Because they *like* it! How you gonna explain that? And what about me – I know that what I'm doin' is wrong, too, but I still do it. You got an answer for that in them books?'

Conrad didn't answer right away; instead he ordered two more drinks. Skeeter the bartender was so interested in their conversation that he gave them the drinks on the house. He'd barely heard Jackie talk before today; in fact, he didn't know that Jackie could hold an intelligent conversation. He'd only heard him whine and beg for drinks. He pulled his stool toward the center of the bar, where they sat.

'It's still a matter of education, Jackie,' Conrad said. He felt his tongue getting in the way of his words and decided that one more drink would be his limit. 'I don't mean the three R's, but rather an education to give them a sense of correct values, moral, spiritual, and otherwise – a sense of fair play, if you will. These people must obviously be explained in terms of their environment. Their values are wrong, so naturally their application to the mainstream of this country's values will be wrong also. It's not so much that they like doing wrong, it's that they don't know any better.'

Jackie laughed. 'Mister, there's a law that sums up the whole attitude of this neighborhood toward your way of life. It's the hipster attitude, and even the little kids live by it. They write it on the sides of buildings, on fences and sidewalks – they even make up songs and poems about it. You ain't seen it yet?'

'If I did, I didn't notice. What is it?'

Jackie dramatically sipped his drink; focused his eyes on Conrad's, and said, 'You tell him, Skeeter.'

Without hesitation Skeeter recited, '"A man can't fool with the Golden Rule in a crowd that don't play fair."' He smiled at them brightly and settled back onto his stool.

Jackie took one of Conrad's cigarettes from the pack, and casually put the pack on the bar on the other side of himself, out of Conrad's reach. He felt that chances were good that the man would forget them. Skeeter watched the maneuver with amusement.

Conrad saw it, and thought it went well with the piece of Howard Street philosophy. Instead of saying anything about it, he innocently patted his pockets, got up, and went to the cigarette machine, giving Jackie a chance to put the others away.

'That's this neighborhood in a nutshell,' Jackie said.

'I can believe it,' Conrad answered. 'But I also believe it can be changed.' He straightened his tie in the machine's mirror.

It was hot and Conrad took off his suit jacket. His button-down white shirt was stained with sweat at the armpits. His hair, though, stayed immaculately in place. Jackie was forced to admire the naturalness of Conrad's wavy hair when he compared it to the conked, lifeless, greasy-looking marcel that Skeeter and so many of the Streeters wore. He looked upon hair-conking with scorn. It was always done by the most ardent admirers of the white people. They went to bed with rags around their heads, grease stained their pillows, and the women in bed with them had to remember to keep their hands away from their lovers' seven-dollar heads no matter what.

Conrad came back to his barstool, glad to get off his unsteady feet. He'd have to be going soon.

Jackie was thinking of another local rule: When you've got a fool on your hands, you're supposed to use him. With this in mind, he ordered another drink and reached for one of the new cigarettes. 'Man,' he said, 'what you're tryin' to do won't work around here; but all I can do is tell you. You stick around long enough and you'll dig it for yourself.'

'You could be right, but I have a job to do and I'm going to keep trying as long as I'm in the area,' Conrad said. He then ordered his final drink.

'If I had any money I'd bet you wouldn't last a month. I say that because you ain't really down—'

'Oh, come off it, Jackie,' he interrupted. 'Just because I'm white and not down on my luck doesn't mean – What are you laughing about?' he ended, showing irritation.

'Because you just tol' me what I mean better 'n I could tell you. I didn't mean bein' down on your luck. To be *down* is to be hip, with it – in other words, to know what's happenin', see?'

'Well, I misunderstood you. I thought—'

'That's what I'm talkin' about!' Jackie said vehemently.

'That's the whole thing with you comin' here. You done misunderstood it all! Dig, you can't understand this hole – you can't even understand the *talk* – unless you was born and raised here in it. This place has gotta be a part of you, and you part of it, and when it is, man, there ain't nothin' else. You gotta be indifferent to time passin', life stagnatin'. You gotta be able to say only two things that could mean a hundred things, good or bad. One of 'em is *mother-fucker*, and the other is *I don't wanna hear that shit*. And this is only a small part of what you gotta live for!'

Conrad said, 'You say that a person born and raised here doesn't have a chance in society at large. You expect me to believe that when I see Negroes almost every day who have come from this sort of environment and have raised themselves to positions of distinction?'

'Yeah. The ones in show business, y'mean,' Jackie said with heavy irony. 'Then there's them others who've convinced themselves they're white – we don't see them no more. An' the rest of us – we just ain't overcome yet. The whites claim they wanna give us a chance to be part of society now, but I don't think most of us believe it. Hell, more of us've been killed by whites than Jews by the Nazis. We gotta shut so much outta our minds, we shut out the things that might be good for us too. What're you gonna do about that? Is you gittin' the picture, man? You work for them civil rights folks, but it's sure pop they ain't taught you nothin' about soul folks, especially the Howard Street kind. You as square as they come. No insult meant, of course.'

Conrad was miffed, but he hid it with a smile. 'I may well be what you call a square, Jackie, but I know – I *dig*, if you like that better – I dig that people are just people no matter where they've been raised. No matter what they've been through they can be taught different. I'm sure that blacks weren't always in the position they occupy in this country; before slavery they had as much human dignity as anyone else, didn't they? Their actions here are more of a habit than their nature, isn't that right? So what they lost during slavery can be regained, can't it? Man is nothing but man, no matter what his color.'

'Just plain old folks, huh?' Jackie said sarcastically. He half felt that Conrad was right, but he didn't want to lose the argument.

'Yes, that's right. Plain old folks. You might be a cynical bum, but when it comes right down to it, you're plain old folks, too.'

'Shee-it!' Jackie hooted. 'Man, you really don't know where it's at, do you? I bet you believe in interracial marriage, too, huh?'

'I believe that's a personal problem between two people. If my sister wanted to marry you, that's her business, she's the one who'll have to live with you, not I.'

'Why do you take it for granted I wanna marry your sister?' Jackie asked.

'I don't. I merely was trying to illustrate my point.'

'By calling it a "problem"? Ha! And you might think you didn't take it for granted but you did; that's why you right away mentioned your sister. But don't feel bad, all the whites do it, bigot and liberal and in-between. Us darkies is used to you proposin' your sisters to us by now.' Jackie smiled triumphantly.

'First of all, Jackie, *all* marriages present problems; secondly: I don't *have* a sister; and thirdly: you condemn whites for stereotyping blacks, yet you feel perfectly free to stereotype whites. It seems to me that your logic is faulty.'

'I dig your first and second,' Jackie said. 'But I think I gotta right to the third. What've the whites ever been to the blacks but one big evil? You know what I think would solve your problem—?'

'It's not my problem, Jackie. It's yours too. It's everybody's – and I know what would solve it.'

'What?' Jackie asked.

'Simple human kindness, that's all,' Conrad replied.

For Jackie, the conversation had taken on the aspect of high comedy. He said, 'That's your idealism showing, man. That's the chump comin' outta you. Now, if you wanna be for real, you'd admit that it'd be a good idea to send all the blacks in America over to South Africa and bring all the Afrikaners to this country where so many of y'all feel the same way they do about white supremacy. Y'all could have a ball then because a lotta them Nazis is hiding there, y'know. You could then be supremely white, and all you'd have to worry about would be persecutin' the Jews and other religions. But there wouldn't be no more "Negro Problem"; no nightmares of big black pricks drivin' between "pure" white thighs, and no school integration. Tell the truth – wouldn't that solve it? Everybody would be happy except the rich bastards drainin' the wealth from South Africa before givin' it back to the blacks – did you know that a lotta them rich bastards live right here in Jersey? – and the Uncle Tom niggers. If we could start the swap right now, man, everything would work out just fine – and that's the truth.'

Conrad was apoplectic; but he calmed down when he realized that he was letting a wino get his goat. He said, 'You'll never get me to admit a senseless thing like that, Jackie – it's a stupid idea.'

'Why?' Jackie asked seriously.

'Because it isn't practical! Why should Negroes, whose parents, grandparents, and great-grandparents have given their lives to the building of this country, be forced to sever those roots to please supremacists – black and white? And especially now, when they're coming into their own economically and socially? This is as much a black man's country as it is a white man's. That's the *good ideal*; that's the one we're striving to reach. What you're advocating just isn't practical for anyone.'

'Especially for those sonofabitches who'd be forced to stop takin' the minerals outta Africa, right?' Jackie laughed and held up a dirty hand to stop Conrad's imminent outburst. 'Oh, I know it'll probably never happen – simply because it is a *good idea*. It's plain to see that both races would rather go on makin' each other miserable rather than separate and be happy with their own kind. And they're goin' to stay miserable, you can believe that! Even those who marry each other – them marriages could never be happy because the couples can't go one day without sayin': "My husband is a nigger," or "My wife is a cracker"; "He's white," "She's black." If they don't say it, somebody else will. Man, that bugs 'em in the end, ain't no two ways about it.'

Conrad now looked to Jackie like a funny caricature of himself. Jackie's eyes, constantly blinking, distorted everything he tried to focus on. He was facing the brilliant sunlight now streaming into the bar, and it bothered him so much that he got up and moved to the other side of Conrad. He took another drink, then said, 'Y'know, there is one thing that would bring about integration in this country – and real damned fast too. And that's if the black women would stop givin' cunt to white men. Wait a minute, let me finish! Black women have always been too easy for white men to get at; but if they – includin' the whores – keep their thighs closed to white men, you'd see a quick change in the whole country – and that's the truth!'

'We're seeing a change now without what you're talking about. Why don't you be serious, Jackie?'

'I'm stomp-down serious, man. The white man always wants what he can't have—'

'Not only white men – all men,' Conrad said.

'Right. But the white man is the greatest taker on the earth, so his ambition to git somethin' is stronger than every-body else's.'

'The longer you talk, the stupider you sound, Jackie.' Conrad was now becoming disgusted with him. Was this what he'd have to face among the lower-class blacks? How did you show Jackie that the whole white race didn't hate him if those who were sincere in their efforts to help him couldn't?

'You call it stupid if you wanna,' Jackie said. 'But if the white man ever finds that black women ain't available he's gonna do everything in his power to change that situation. Say, for instance, that every black bitch sneakin' around with a white man right now would tell him that they can't see each other no more because if she ain't good enough for him socially, then he ain't good enough for her sexually. Man, do you know them Southern politicians and crackers, and them rich Northerners would have fits? They'd not only change laws, they'd change attitudes, too! But I don't think it'd work – but only for one reason: the stinkin' bitches won't cooperate . . .'

As if to illustrate Jackie's point, Big Frieda, Bunny Scotia, and Big Louise came into the bar. Each eyed Conrad as a potential customer. Soon others began to straggle in and out, mostly junkies looking for Cowboy or Big-feet Roland. The dealers didn't usually show until about one o'clock in the afternoon, and from that time on would sell dope like they had licenses. If they happened to go to a movie downtown or to the Flick on Belmont Avenue, the junkies would pay or sneak into every movie looking for them.

Some left the bar very quickly after seeing Conrad, thinking he was a cop trying to pump Jackie about who was doing what on Howard Street. Jackie explained this to Conrad and asked, 'You think you can dig all this, huh?'

'I don't see the great difficulty involved in seeing that most of these people – including yourself, by the way – could do with a better shake than they've been getting. Psychotherapy would do wonders, along with understanding. Yes, I believe I could dig it. And I don't think it would be very hard if they – and you – would cooperate. You can't expect help without effort being made on your part, too, you know.'

'The longest day of your life, you couldn't dig it, mister,' Jackie said hotly. 'Do you know that if you gave any one of the people you see a hundred dollars, he wouldn't buy food if he was hungry? The whores'd give it to their pimps and the men'd go buy a suit and a pair of long shoes.'

'I know just giving them money wouldn't solve anything – by the way, what are long shoes?'

'Well, that's more of an expression than a shoe. Y'see, long shoes are success. They're the keen-toed design, right for kickin' a whore in the behind with when she comes up with short money or gits outta line. Some of the guys that got whores do kick 'em in the ass. The ordinary cat, though, is just satisfied to show off the shoes and quote the high price of 'em. It'd take too long to really run it down to you, man. Just say that long shoes means that the cat wearin' them is into somethin', or, if he ain't an outright pimp, he's doin' good, dig?'

Conrad nodded without speaking. Jackie went on: 'Like I was sayin' about the hundred bills: the suit and shoes would run about eighty bill, right? So he'd have twenty left, which his rent would take if he'd pay it all. But he wouldn't do that; he'd give the landlord maybe ten, then he'd bring the other ten to Howard Street and party with it. As for eatin' – he can always beg a sandwich somewhere. Anything that ain't showy don't impress him, see? He's got three main ambitions – and I happen to think that it's because he's in this country that he only has these main three – one is to drink and look sharp; two is to fuck as much as he can; and three is to have as much dope as he wants without workin' for the money to buy it with. In a word, his ambition is to ball. Now you gonna tell me that a people in a fucked-up position like this wouldn't be better off havin' to build a society of their own in South Africa instead of layin' around on their welfare-relief-collectin' behinds in this one waitin' for cats like you to do somethin' for 'em?'

Conrad's head was spinning. He was drunk and he hardly understood what Jackie was talking about. He ordered two more drinks and vowed to himself that this was his last. The spinning ceased and he saw the three prostitutes watching him. He smiled at them in a friendly but not a propositioning way.

Emma Dee came in and was immediately apprehensive, thinking he might be a spy for Slim McNair. He sometimes sent other cops around to ask questions about her. She hoped that Jackie hadn't heard of the fifty dollars she'd given to Red Shirt Charlie. Slim would beat her damn near to death and lock her up besides. He'd done it before. She walked to where the other women were seated. Big Louise was cursing Jackie for being so talkative and holding up a potential trick she could turn.

Hip came in with Slick Bill and Pinball. The three of them bought sodas and went up into the gallery. Harry Conrad was glad that it wasn't night, for he knew that night was dangerous for black men on Howard Street, let alone a white man. He had never stayed late and didn't intend to. Even white detectives had been mugged. And he never carried more than thirty dollars on him; but that was a good sting to a junkie, especially a sick one.

Jackie got up and went to the toilet as Dennis Warrent came slouching in out of the sunlight. His frog-eyes were bulging as they did when he'd had a good fix.

'Gimme a soda, Skeeter,' he said with a whining slur in his voice that also told of boss action. He saw his colleagues in the gallery. Jackie came out of the toilet in time to hear him call: 'Dig, y'all – Tricky Dick done took a OD up on Sue's roof.'

'Is he dead?' Slick Bill asked languidly.

'Stone cold in the market, baby,' Dennis replied just as dispassionately. Sipping his soda and lighting a smoke he added: 'I was with him.'

Pinball, who was as light-skinned as Conrad, and usually overcool about everything, asked eagerly, 'Well, who he cop from, man. Cowboy?'

'Naw,' Dennis answered. 'We copped off that stud from New Yawk who come over with that dynamite ever now and then . . . I forgit his name.'

'I know who you mean – Curtis Sheely,' Hip said.

'Yeah,' Dennis said, 'that's him.' He lazily scratched at his cheek – more to emphasize that the dope was good, and he was high, than because it itched. 'Baby, I'm telling y'all that it's boss.'

The others looked at each other. They'd just taken off an hour before. They looked at Dennis. He was bent, barely able, it seemed, to keep his head up. That's the kind of high they wanted. Pinball, his cool completely gone, said, 'What the hell are we waitin' for, man?'

'Damn real!' Slick Bill affirmed the meaning the question implied. 'Let's go cop before word gits around about Tricky Dick, otherwise won't be none left.' They all scrambled down from their seats and headed for the door.

As they passed, Slick Bill said to Dennis, 'Thanks for hippin' us, baby.' Then they were gone.

Dennis went over to their almost full glasses, filled his, drank what was left of theirs, and brought the empties back to Skeeter. Then he took a seat back near the men's room where his peace would be broken only intermittently, when his head would jerk up from his chest and he'd take a sip of his soda; it would last for another two hours at the least.

Jackie gave Conrad a see-what-I-mean look. But because he was drunk, Conrad misinterpreted it. 'G'wan and order, Jackie, think I'll have 'nother m'self. What t'hell.'

'Thanks, baby,' Jackie said pushing his glass to Skeeter. 'But I wanna know if you really dug that scene. Have I been tellin' the truth about what goes on? Did you see it? You watched the whole thing – did they give even a thought to the dead man? The first thing them cats thought about was where they could git the same junk to shoot in their arms.' He paused, then went on: 'White man, if you organize that, I'll give up drinkin', join the civil rights movement, and even the goddamn church!' He laughed loudly. 'That last part'd be goin' a little far, but I'd do it!' He began to laugh more, but it was cut off by a phlegm-filled nasty coughing fit.

Skeeter put the new drinks in front of them meditatively. Speaking to no one in particular, he said, 'Guess we'll have to git another drummer for the band tonight.' He called down to the women: 'Hey, Bunny, d'you know Fish Marsetti's number?' She nodded. He said, 'Tell 'im to be here tonight, okay?' She nodded again.

Jackie pointed to the women: 'See them whores, Harry . . .' It was the first time he'd used Conrad's first name. Conrad smiled at Jackie, saying he saw them.

'Not one of 'em batted a false eyelash at the news of Tricky Dick. They didn't feel nothin' because he didn't buy no pussy off 'em. That one, Emma Dee, she used to be his woman, too, before she started messin' 'round with a cop. She didn't even flinch at the news, did she? She don't give a sentimental fuck – not even for old time's sake. Now if you still don't believe you're in the wrong neighborhood at the wrong time, man, then you deaf, dumb, and blind. Go on up to them nigger neighborhoods where they wanna be white with black skin and see what you can do for them. Ain't nothin' you can do for us – Look at you, I got you drunk without even tryin'. You a hell of an example, white man!' An angry snap was in Jackie's voice as he looked at Conrad, who wasn't hearing him.

He was looking right past Jackie with a meaningless smile on his face.

'Don't you see, man ... ?' Jackie said. 'Goddammit, man, can't you understand? Let us the hell alone! Take the kids and teach them, but let us ball it out to the goddamn bitter end! We deserve that much!'

Conrad didn't understand, and he wasn't even trying now. That last drink had done it to him royally. And he'd been drunk only twice before in his life. He did know that he wanted to leave here, had to get out now. This wino and these people – who were they? They were out to destroy him.

And those carnivorous whores – they were trying to seduce him long-distance with their uninterested and uninteresting eyes. Their high-signs sickened him, whereas it used to amuse him. When he looked at them, all he could see was VD.

They wanted to give him clap and syphilis. He could see it eating away his nose, blinding him, rotting his balls off. They wanted him to carry it to some nice white girl. They wanted to destroy the whole white race through him! He smelled Jackie and the toilets. It all came crashing in upon his senses. He smelled the sweat and the stink of pork-grease-guzzling ni ... *niggers!* Why should he hesitate to say it? That's what they were – niggers! They all smelled like the pig that was so much of their systems. A man became what he ate ... niggers eat more pigs than anybody else, therefore niggers are pigs. It was a pure syllogism.

He trembled. He shouldn't think of them as niggers. Ever since he'd joined the CR group he'd honestly tried not to think of them as niggers. They were red-white-and-blue Americans, just like himself. Didn't they fight wars and pay taxes like everyone else? Like himself? But they couldn't be like him. He wanted to help build America, he wanted to obey the law and love his neighbors. These people hated everything, including themselves. They weren't like him. No. No. They weren't like anyone he'd known in his entire life. They were niggers, and he could see no way of getting around that fact – they wouldn't let him! They wanted to be niggers, just like Jackie had said: they wanted to ball and to be left alone.

Nigger! The word flashed across his mind so brightly that he almost fell off his stool, but Jackie grabbed him in time. He looked up to thank Jackie and saw the word stamped in big letters on Jackie's sweating forehead; it trailed down between the swollen eyes and snaked up into his flat, ugly nose. He looked at the women: it was slapped across their wide rumps. Undulating *g*'s dancing sexually between the other four letters, shaking their repulsive curlicues at him. *Nigger, niggers, niggers . . .*

Niggers were everywhere, on every corner of his sensibility. Niggers singing, dancing, boxing, laughing, drinking, fucking, running, shouting, whining, crying, praying, eating, shitting. Niggers in every shade, big, juicy-lipped niggers – and all of them staring at him, laughing at him! '*Dig us, Mister Charlie, white man! We is down, and, baby, let the good times roll!*' It was enough to give him nigger-itis. He had to get out of here before he got all niggered up – and that was worse than being all fucked up . . .

The word finally went away. He could even smile at Jackie and Skeeter putting cold towels on his forehead. He didn't remember coming into the toilet. Jackie said he fell out, was kidding him for not being able to hold his liquor. The toilet almost made him want to vomit again. He had to get out of here. He asked Skeeter for the tab.

He'd go home and sleep it off – couldn't go back to CR headquarters in his present condition – *Nigger!* It flashed on once more and he knew he hadn't passed out this time. If he felt this way when he woke up again he wasn't going back to CR headquarters at all.

He sent drinks and a forced smile down to the sitting hens and waved goodbye after solemnly shaking Jackie's and Skeeter's hands. When he staggered out into the piercing intensity of the sun's brightness his eyes smarted and began to water. His eyes hurt, but not as much as Jackie and the wriggly-*g* word had hurt his mind's eye – and his ego. He didn't wipe the water away. He let it develop into tears.

He'd forgotten to take his suit jacket with him . . .

When Conrad had gone Jackie turned to Skeeter with a wan

smile and held out both packs of cigarettes and a five-dollar bill which he'd managed to steal without even Skeeter seeing him take it. 'A man can't fool with the Golden Rule in a crowd that don't play fair,' he said.

'I hear you, baby,' Skeeter said. 'You sho 'nuff know where it's at. We can't fool around in their league and they ain't got no business in ours.' He pushed another drink to Jackie, on the house, then asked him to sweep the floor. 'Practice,' he said.

Thirteen

Irene Smith pleaded weakly: 'Please, Tal, I don't wanna do nothin' like that. Please . . .'

'Baby, listen,' he softly urged, 'we can make it together if you act right. It's for us, honey. You can do it for us.'

'Tal, please. I don't wanna be no whore. I just wanna be your woman . . .'

'And believe me, sugar, I want you for my woman – but all the way. You can dig that. Don't you see the possibilities for us to really tighten up? Baby, I wanna do things for us that ain't never been done before – but it takes bread, baby, bread! Then we can get away from here and live . . .'

They were lying on her bed; she in brassiere and panties, and he in his red silk shorts. He'd kept her from going to work today specifically to make his last attempt to turn her out. If he didn't succeed she'd have to find another man. He knew that the only thing keeping her from deciding to do as he asked was her fear of what Rosemary might say – or worse yet, might think and not say. There was no doubt that she wanted to do it; that was why she hadn't given him his walking papers when he'd first broached the subject last week. In fact, he sincerely believed that she'd known from the jump what he'd eventually ask her to do. It was an integral part of the Life, and she'd known the Life from childhood. She had surely known where he was at.

She hadn't had time to fool herself that she was in love with him. She only hesitated because she wanted to weigh the pros and cons of his argument. Besides, on her back with her legs gapped open was no infrequent position with her. She must have had at least fifty such thigh-spreadings since she was ten years old. But even if she did fancy herself in love, that was more reason to do as he asked. It was as simple as that.

She tried another circumvention: 'You wouldn't respect me

anymore, Tal. None of you pimps respect your whores, and I'd go crazy if that happened.'

He noticed that her attacks became weaker by the minute. He pressed the attack. 'Baby, I wouldn't only respect you, I'd worship you! Pimps respect their women – as long as the money's right. But, anyway, you'd be somethin' special. Right now I got more feelin' for you than I can ever remember havin' for any other woman; and we only been goin' together for two weeks. Honey, I'm as close to bein' in love as I ever been in my life – that's the God's honest truth.' He ran his hand along the plump curves of her body; the material of her panties *sssssss*'d as he trailed his palm across it to grip her buttocks.

'It's me and you all the way, Reenie. Coupla years and I'm plannin' to buy a house and settle down, I was thinkin' it'd be in Matawan or someplace where there's lotsa space and trees and flowers and stuff like that. Go' raise chickens and hogs and cows . . . I ain't picked the woman I want yet, but one thing I know: she gotta know the Life, she gotta be hip. That way she'll be ready to have a quiet life with me. I can't see makin' it with no square broad; they always want divorces and alimony. I can't see spendin' the rest of my life with no square on no terms. They say that whores make the best wives and I believe it 'cause I done seen it a whole lotta times. Made up my mind a long time ago that I ain't go' marry no woman 'less she done been a whore at one time. Whores know where it's at and what to do for a man. Ain't no jivin' around 'cause bein' happily married is what they always dreamed about when they was whores. They done been through everything and they's satisfied.'

He kissed her nut-brown shoulder, her neck and her thick cottony lips. She wasn't bad-looking, he thought. Not that it was important, but some johns wanted every whore to look like Gypsy Pearl. Irene would be able to make a nice piece of money for him. She was young, corpulent, and cuddly-like; she had very pretty legs, good, full breasts that made a man want to bury his face in them, and a behind that teased the front of every man's pants with its tantalizing rhythms.

He looked into her face and tried to kiss away the worry

and indecision he saw there. Her eyes frantically searched his, but she saw nothing that she could define; the small wrinkle between her eyes disappeared as his kiss took on more profound meaning and body. Suddenly her nostrils flared and she grabbed at his exploring hand, holding it in the place it touched so expertly. While she returned his kisses she thought.

Did he really mean what he so plainly implied about the house and marriage and settling down? If she could only be sure, there would be nothing in the world to stop her from trying to reach for his dream – it would be hers, too. He'd practically said that he wanted her to be the woman to share it with him: the whore-turned-wife. 'You and me all the way.' That's what he'd said. Yes. And the chickens, the hogs and the cows – it would all be so nice. She'd get up early in the morning and feed them – and him. And children ... he hadn't mentioned them, but surely there'd be children. They wouldn't have to be raised in a hot, crowded slum like she'd been. Her children and Tal's ... Oh, if he really meant it!

She loosened her grip on his wrist as his fingers began to search under her brassiere. But, God, she couldn't be a whore! Would she be a whore in order to be a wife? ... No! Would she be a whore in order to be his wife? ... He had a Cadillac and plenty of money – and his hand felt so wonderful! A home of her own ... Hogs, chickens, cows, trees, grass, flowers ... and children. Be his wife ... yes! Be his whore ... Lord God, yes!

'Oh, Tal!' she kissed hungrily at his lips, his eyes, his nose. 'I don't know, Tal, I don't—'

'You love me a little, don't you, baby?' he asked tenderly.

'Yes, Tal, yes, yes ...'

His hand was squeezing in between the tight panties and her burning skin. The hair parted, the pliant lips yielded. 'We can be happy, Reenie ... A whole lifetime together. Dig the scene, baby. Dig it – me and you. Can't you see it? Don't you wanna share my dream, baby?'

Her brassiere came off. He easily slipped her arms out of the straps. She was like a sleepwalker. More insistently he said, 'Me and you, Reenie . . . Our own home one day. *Dig it, baby.*'

'Tal!' she cried in total surrender. 'Tal, anything you say! Any—' Her words were cut short as his fingers touched the quick of her, roving blindly but knowingly deep into the dark sea of her body.

She clutched at him with her eyes tightly shut, 'For you, Tal. I'm doin' it for you!' she repeated over and over again, even when she could no longer see him and he was intimately kissing the place from which his fingers had departed. He pulled her to the edge of the bed.

The floor felt hard to his knees but he didn't mind. He was intent on what he was doing; knew that once a woman was hooked behind this action she would be on call forever. Her soft thighs rubbed easily against him as she bucked and twisted, now trying to get away, then trying to pull him into her. Her legs hung laxly, but every few moments her whole body would stiffen and quiver in rigid tension. 'Tal, Tal! Oh, honey . . . please, please, please,' she cried. He was driving her mad. It wasn't possible to go on – she would die. She covered her face with a pillow to muffle her screams. She stiffened again. It was too much. 'Tal!' she gasped as the room began to spin about her. And, softer this time: 'Tal!' There were spots before her eyes in all sorts of crazy colors. She became frightened and tried to push him away, but the pleasure engulfed her again; she allowed his lips to draw her back.

A flash of blinding light shot through her brain, pierced the fiery inner recesses of her being . . . 'Tal,' she cried again, but this time it was too weak to be heard. She went as limp as a rag doll, her legs slipped to the floor, and she could no longer move.

Tal got up smiling proudly at his handiwork. She was not the first that he'd rendered senseless by his skill; all of his girls dug it.

He lay down beside the spasmodic Irene; she was still whispering his name. She'd be a whore, he thought as he watched her. Either that or he'd break her damned neck.

*   *   *

Gypsy Pearl was picked up that night for prostitution by Danny Darden, an experienced vice cop, and a new detective he was showing the ropes to. When Hip had called Darden to the side, to try and make the usual deal, he was told that absolutely nothing could be done. The new man didn't know the score yet and would have to be weaned away from Police Academy ideals. Darden wasn't taking any chances that his partner would dare share in – or even overlook – a payoff.

'But, man, you gotta give my woman a break!' Hip exclaimed. 'You can talk to the guy. Look – I ain't got but twenty bills on me. I'll give it all to you and tomorrow I'll give you twenty more. C'mon, Danny, you know where it's at, man.'

'Yeah, but my partner don't, Hip. Y'know I ain't adverse to pickin' up a little money when I can, but I ain't takin' no unnecessary chances. Hell, for all I know he could be a plant. When they put a rookie on VS, he either knows somebody or he's tryin' to know about somebody. Sorry, Hip, no can do this time.'

Gypsy Pearl sat in the unmarked police car with the new man and nervously chain-smoked, watching Hip and Darden. They didn't seem to be making any headway; she usually was released by now and ready to turn another trick. She saw Hip gesturing and Darden shaking his head.

They were on Mercer Street, in the dark shadow of the big furniture building. She looked at her companion and gave herself a mental kick. She should have known better, would have known better if Hip hadn't insisted on her bringing in at least fifty dollars so he could buy a big piece of the New York pusher's dope.

Since Tricky Dick's overdose every junkie in town had been looking for the New Yorker. Howard Street stuff was so weak in comparison that many of the older junkies who got their stuff regularly from The Apple would scoff at those who didn't, claiming that the Howard Street junkies only had quinine and milk sugar habits rather than heroin habits.

Gypsy Pearl was becoming impatient and fidgeted nervously when the young cop beside her offered a smoke. She answered 'No' politely and took out one of her own; she did accept a light from him, though. Over the flame of his lighter she once again saw his sleepy-looking blue eyes that were somehow so innocent and boyish in their petulance; and the part he wore almost in the middle of his head was so out of date, so out of place with the overall look of him. This, and his fragile manner, had fooled her. He had propositioned her in the Howard Bar, nearly forcing his fifteen dollars into her hand. And in the room – the way his eagerness did an about-face so that he stalled . . . she should have known. But she'd shrugged off her growing suspicions, thinking he was just an inexperienced college boy from the engineering college on High Street, having relations with a prostitute for the first time. She'd intended to ease him with a soothing manner and a beautiful body: he was the type of customer she wanted to come again and she was going to make sure he'd want to. But when she was partially undressed a knock came at the door. She knew what it was even before he pulled his badge and announced that he was the police and she was under arrest. He let Darden into the room while she only smiled wryly at her generous thoughts of him: it was his first time with a whore – to arrest one.

The young cop had even wanted to arrest Sue, but Darden put a quick damper on that, explaining that it was a legal rooming establishment and the proprietor was not responsible for what people did in their rooms. He didn't explain, however, that Sue had protection and that he was going with Sue's ward, Mommy . . .

Hip had more than twenty dollars on him, but he wasn't about to get off more than that to Darden – he needed it to buy smack. He felt that the whole seventy-five dollars he had on him would satisfy Darden, but he wasn't about to test him; it was better that a whore go to jail than his habit go lacking. She'd probably get probation anyway, since this would be her first bust on record. She shouldn't have been so careless; it was her own fault.

Franchot! Hell, yes. Franchot would be glad to get her out of jail on bail and have Meyers squash the charge. He liked her so much, let him pay for the privilege like everybody else.

He looked at Darden's thin pockmarked face; he was sure

that the man only wanted more money. But he wasn't going to tempt him. If Darden took the money and, by some chance, she didn't trick anymore that night, he'd be up shit's creek without a paddle, in a leaky canoe.

Resignedly he said, 'Can't do nothin' for me, huh, Darden?' It was not a question but a statement, to which the cop answered negatively. Hip shrugged his shoulders. It was out of his hands now; he'd done the best he could. They walked to the car slowly.

Hip looked solemnly at Gypsy Pearl, 'Ain't nothin' happenin', baby.' She nodded vacantly without speaking. He went on to add quickly, patting her hand to comfort her, 'But don't you worry, girl. I'm goin' right now t'see Franchot – we gon' git Meyers and have you outta there in no time. Just be cool, hear?'

She nodded again with the same dazed expression. Then suddenly her hazel eyes widened in despair; she grabbed Hip's hand tightly. 'Don't tell Franchot, Hip,' she pleaded. 'If you can't do nothin', let me stay in jail till—'

'What you talkin' about, woman!' Hip said. He searched her face in close scrutiny, as if he were looking for something but dreaded finding it. Whatever he saw he lost before he could read any significance in it. With the power of dope dominating him, nuances didn't register deeply on his consciousness. Chagrined, he said, 'I ain't gon' let you stay in no jail, woman. Is you crazy?'

'Awright, Hip,' Darden cut in. 'You can talk at headquarters.' He climbed into the car, sandwiching Gypsy Pearl between himself and the other man, and shut the door.

As the car pulled away from the curb Hip shouted, 'Don't worry, baby, we'll have Meyers and a bondsman down there before you know it.'

She didn't look at him, but he was sure he saw tears welling in her eyes. The car turned right at Broome Street toward Springfield Avenue, then right again, heading downtown.

Hip watched until they were out of sight with a perplexed feeling nagging at him. He'd seen something in her tonight in that second before she'd turned her head away from him.

It hadn't been fear, at least not the scared kind. It was independent of him and he didn't like that at all. She was leaving him out of something that he felt was important for him to be involved in. Independence? An independent whore was unmanageable – a man couldn't tell her anything. But it hadn't been independence that he saw. He didn't know what it was, but he didn't like it.

He intended to go and tell Franchot, but changed his mind and went into the Howard Bar instead. Let the smart-aleck bitch cool her heels for a while; it would teach her not to look at him like she did tonight. He'd tell her about it, too, when she got out.

Two hours later he woke Franchot up. Rosemary was in the bed with him, but she didn't stir. They went into the kitchen and Franchot put on a pot of coffee as Hip sat at the table. Franchot almost dropped the percolator when Hip laconically said, 'The whore got busted tonight, Shots, and I ain't got no money for a lawyer and bail.'

Franchot was instantly wide awake and attentive, full of questions but not paying the least bit of attention to Hip's dull-voiced answers. Every object seemed to jump at Franchot in clear-cut dimensions – the table, chairs and the sink with a milk-stained glass sitting on it; the percolator, the checkerboard design of the floor's covering; the scabby crucifixed scar on his brother's forehead and the nicotine stains on his fingers; and Hip's skin, which was tinted a yellowish, sick color. He saw a cockroach go over the moulding up near the ceiling, appear again to reconnoiter his trail, then finally disappear. He heard Rosemary breathe in deeply, and the rustle of the covers as she turned in her sleep.

Though it was a struggle for Hip to keep his head up, he nevertheless noticed Franchot's anxiety. He waited for Franchot to speak, but his brother's quick, deft hands – and now, seemingly, his mind – concentrated on setting out the cups and spoons.

Hip broke the silence himself in an urging, baiting tone. 'Like I said, Shots: the bitch gon' have to go to jail, 'cause I ain't in no shape at all. The reason I woke you up was to find out if you could do somethin' for her. Like, I mean, I don't want you to git mixed up in our troubles . . . She can sure make the money to pay you back. You ain't gotta worry about gittin' paid or nothin' . . .' He trailed off and almost went into a nod.

Franchot poured himself a steaming cup of the coffee. Hip didn't want any and Franchot was glad of it, for he felt an acute desire to throw the brew in Hip's face. He hadn't trusted himself to speak before, but now, with an imperceptible quaver running under his voice, he said, 'I wanna help her. How much will it cost to get her out?'

'About four hundred altogether.'

'How much you got?'

'Me? I ain't got nothin', Shots.' He pulled out some money. 'Seven lousy dollars between me'n starvation.' His face was impassive; nothing in it indicated that he was lying, though Franchot suspected he was. The junkie whine neither rose nor fell in volume; it came out as easily as ice sliding downhill against ice.

Franchot silently sipped his coffee. The kitchen clock registered 1:15 A.M., and Hip went into a nod. When he jerked his head up fifteen minutes later he was surprised to see that Franchot had gotten dressed – he hadn't been aware that Franchot had even finished stirring his coffee. He marveled dispassionately at the New Yorker's good, good doogie.

'Lonnie, is you sure you ain't got no money?' Franchot asked, pulling an Orlon sweater over his head.

'Nary penny, except what I said, Shots.'

Franchot returned to his bedroom and a few minutes later emerged counting a stack of bills. Hip's eyes flashed greedily. He hadn't known that Franchot kept large amounts of money in the apartment. He filed the memory away for future use, in case he got sick and couldn't find any money elsewhere: apartments in the neighborhood were broken into with regularity; his brother's couldn't go untouched indefinitely. An easy enough explanation would be that some junkies probably thought he had some smack in the place and broke in to find it, but found the money instead. He'd make sure to take something else, too: a radio, toaster, and even the television, to avert suspicion that the money was the main reason for breaking in. He'd need help, but that was the easiest thing in the world to get. He'd keep cool about the money and slice two or three ways what they got for the loot . . .

Franchot was ready to leave and started for the door. Hip made no attempt to move. Franchot stopped, 'You comin' with me, Lonnie?' he asked.

'Naw. You can take care of it. Don't need both of us to hand Meyers the money.'

'She might want you there, y'know,' Franchot said acidly.

Hip was lighting a smoke; he stopped, took the cigarette from his mouth, looked at Franchot with a mocking glance, and said, 'Shit.' Then he settled more comfortably in the chair and took a deep drag on the cigarette without watching Franchot leave the apartment.

He sat for a long while after Franchot had gone, smoking and nodding, trying to get his thoughts in some kind of order; but the dope had been too good, he couldn't stop the heavenly peace from casting all other feelings and thoughts away upon the garbage heap of another time. And he didn't want to fight it away. Nothing in the sober world of reality was as good as this; only a fool couldn't dig it. His head dropping again; the cigarette fell from his fingers and burned a hole in his pants. He brushed lazily at the smoldering cloth, then examined it. The examination soon became hypnotic contemplation that threw him back into his comatose relaxation. He looked like a yogi concentrating on his navel, methodically searching for Om.

He was in this position when Rosemary came out of the bedroom to go to the toilet. She smiled and shook her head: 'Hey!' she called. His head snapped up. 'Where Franchot – in there?' She indicated the toilet.

'Went to bail my woman outta jail,' Hip answered, going on to explain the events of the night to her.

Rosemary was glad to hear them, but the warm glow of victory over a feared piece of competition didn't last, because Franchot, of all people, had gone to get it and fling it right back into her face. She went on to the toilet, then back to bed, but she was no longer sleepy in the least.

Hip poured himself a cup of the now lukewarm coffee and took it into the living room. He picked an armchair to sit in, stretched his long legs to their fullest length and crossed them at the ankles. He was through nodding now, so his thoughts were relatively lucid. They were certainly lucid enough to figure out that Franchot's concern for Gypsy Pearl was more than he'd bargained on. And she seemed to be up tight, too. Of course he'd expected Franchot to want to take her to bed, that was natural – in fact he really wanted it to happen so Franchot would be more deeply committed to his welfare, and through him, Gypsy Pearl's – and she could certainly make staying in bed one hell of a sweet encounter; like it was when they'd first got together. She'd have no trouble putting a cunt-collar on Franchot. But something wasn't cool in the way things seemed to be going. They acted funny, almost like . . . almost like they were in love! *Love?* Goddamn! To dig her action, yeah, crazy – but *love?* His brother and a five-and-dime prostitute! His square brother and his slick whore!

Hip's mind flashed back to the police car scene: the look on her face when he told her he was going to get Franchot to help. And the way she asked him not to . . . it was shame! She was ashamed! Not because she was a whore, and not because she was going to jail, but because she was a whore in love – in love with a lame who broke his back for a living.

He stubbed out his cigarette violently and burned his fingers in the process. That dirty bitch was ashamed to be his whore! Was trying to grab at the myth that whores and junkies straighten up at will. Well, baby, he'd show her something . . .

He calmed down, collecting his thoughts, trying to determine what course would be the most beneficial for him. He wondered if Franchot could be a big enough fool to want to marry her – to most lames that was the logical aim when they dug a chick; the inevitable square's conclusion when they loved a woman was to marry – then divorce or leave her and marry the next one they loved. They were never satisfied to dig her action and to let somebody else dig, too. No, they wanted it all to themselves; wanted to wallow in it until they'd had their fill – which didn't take too long, judging by the numerous married men he saw on the loose on Howard Street.

He hoped Franchot wasn't one of those who thought that whores made the best wives. That would be too much. Why should whores make better wives than, say, some dumb, religion-soaked bitch who was saving her dry little twat for Jesus? Squares like Franchot seldom asked themselves that question. They figured that because a whore knew so much more about men, they automatically knew how to make men happy, also. It was a lie, and just about anybody on Howard Street could verify it. The only difference was that a whore at least didn't mind letting a flesh-and-blood man dig some of her action. He lighted another smoke.

He didn't go for that stuff about whores making such good wives, but he had more respect for them than he had for a woman like Rosemary. She was the kind of broad he couldn't stand. She'd hem and haw and fight a man to make him think he was forcing her to go to bed with him, and all the while she intended to lose because she wanted it, too. That way she could salvage her moral standard from the trash heap it belonged on by blaming the man and making him feel like the worst kind of depraved animal. All women were whores and they were all the same to him. A bitch was nothing but a bitch no matter who she was; they spread their legs the same, wore cunt-rags the same when they had their periods, and sat on the toilet to do the same things; even though some might use golden douche bags, the same stuff came out of them.

Franchot was a goddamn fool. He didn't have to be in love with her; he might just pity her – and that was worse yet. Let a whore dig she's getting sympathy and the sympathizer is in trouble. She'll play it for all it's worth. Being sympathetic ends up being simple-thetic, and the profit would be all hers. And, no doubt about it, the bitch had a tough game going for her; she knew where it was at. In love? Franchot was a fool.

Meyers was usually to be found at the Dark Room on

Springfield Avenue near High Street. It was a small, expensive place that catered mostly to professional men. The Third Ward people couldn't afford it, and those who could, like Red Shirt, Cowboy, Fish-Man, and some others, weren't welcomed: they didn't have the right brand of sophistication. They seldom went there unless they were looking for Meyers, and the men who patronized the place didn't take their wives there. Tim Linden, the owner, allowed no whores to squat like vultures waiting for flesh-picking time, but, of course, there were exceptions. Gypsy Pearl was one of them, but Hip never let her go there unless he was really up tight for money.

Plush is the best way to describe the Dark Room. Meyers had an office on Park Place, but the Dark Room was his real office because it was here that he conducted most of his business, which mainly consisted of getting people off by payoffs to his downtown connections. Many people in the Third Ward didn't even know he had any other office, and, in fact, only knew his name to be Mr Meyers. But this was all they needed to know.

It took Franchot's eyes a moment to adjust themselves to the deep maroon lighting. There was no bar, only booths seating from two to six people. A silent buzzer summoned a waiter to take orders; the floor was covered with a thick red carpet, and women customers would remove their shoes because it was a delight to their feet, and their lovely little toes relished the luxury of it as much as their behinds liked the soft leather-cushioned seats. Conical red lamps hung on the walls above each booth and sent red lights up the walls to the ceiling and spilled it easily toward the red chandelier. Those seated in the booths could turn the light off if they wished. Stereo music gently permeated the entire place with cool jazz and pop songs; selectors were in each booth. Franchot could hear Miles Davis playing from his 'Sketches of Spain' album. It was the kind of place in which he'd like to spend an evening with Gypsy Pearl. Perhaps he'd dress up and do just that one day.

The lawyer sat in the last booth on the right with one of Tim Linden's exceptions. She was very black, smooth, and very beautiful. She seemed to belong to this kind of setting – slightly haughty with large, liquid almond eyes, short-cropped silky hair, and lips that were full and pouting. Her nose was much like Gypsy Pearl's.

Meyers was short and balding, with very strong hawklike features; thick horn-rimmed glasses gave him the appearance of his profession, though his *modus operandi* ignored its ethics. His Semitic ancestry was evident by the aquiline nose, big eyes, and the little droop in the center of his top lip that many Jews past forty develop.

He was busily talking to the girl, Joyce, when Franchot stopped beside the booth. She had been arrested recently, too, and he took his pay in trade. It was plain that Franchot's intrusion irritated him, but his voice didn't betray it when he cheerily asked, 'What can I do for you, my friend?'

'Friend of mine got locked up tonight,' Franchot replied. 'I want you to git her out as soon as possible – tonight if you can.' He expected Meyers to ask him to sit down, but Meyers didn't.

Dealing with the most intimate, and usually sordid, problems of blacks – petty gambling, cuttings, whoring, drunkenness, dope, and procurings – Meyers generally held them in contempt, especially since he found it so easy to use them. He didn't hate them for being black, but he couldn't respect them, either – mainly, as he said, for 'acting like niggers.' He had become jaded by his close dealings with the criminal and hustling element. Nevertheless he considered himself an authority on blacks in general. Often, among his colleagues, when the topic of discussion turned to race, he'd be heard to say, 'I know Negroes better than they know themselves,' which might have been true in the case of most of the blacks he dealt with, but was otherwise a presumption. He talked as if he knew more about the subject than all the black leaders combined; yet he never offered any solutions to their problems. Even if he'd had any, it was much more profitable for him to keep them in ignorance.

Still, in entirely different discussions, he'd refer to mankind as an insoluble enigma, asking pedantically: 'Who among us can comprehend the protean vacillation, the fickle mutability of man? I can tell you, my friends, mankind is an insoluble enigma!' This was the theme when the discussion happened to be communism or the Jews; but he *knew* those Negroes. If his colleagues noticed his lack of logic, they didn't seriously challenge it; it served their purposes too.

Franchot sensed Meyers' scorn, and knew it to be a fact when the lawyer glibly rejoined: '"She"? Pros charge, huh?' He automatically assumed Franchot to be a pimp, and there was a slight smirk on his thin lips. He saw Franchot look at the girl and said conspiratorially, 'Oh, she's all right. In fact, she's in the same predicament herself.'

'Can you do somethin' tonight?' Franchot asked.

'My fee is four-hundred and fifty – half now and the rest when the charges are dropped tomorrow.' Meyers patted Joyce's hand affectionately.

'I ain't got but four hundred,' Franchot said. 'I'll give it all to you now and we can call it square. It's all I got.'

Meyers grinned. 'It's set then.' He held out his hand for a handshake, but Franchot put the money into it without touching the hand.

Meyers stood and said to the girl, 'I'll probably be late, sugar. If I'm not back when the club closes go to your place and wait for me.' He bent and kissed those protuberant, pale lips of hers, which could easily have drowned his in flesh. Then he motioned Franchot to follow him and walked toward the exit with a stiff gait.

Try as she would, Rosemary couldn't go back to sleep. The living room light was still on, which indicated that Hip hadn't gone to bed, so she got up, put on Franchot's robe, and went to sit with him.

He was still in the armchair with his head thrown back against the rest. He was blowing a thick stream of smoke up toward the pearl-white ceiling as he continued to think about Franchot and Gypsy Pearl. He'd already decided that Franchot could have her body all he wanted, but she wasn't going to be anybody's woman but his until he was ready to let her go. He reasoned that, after all, she was his bread and butter – he didn't try to take Franchot's job, did he?

'Gimme a smoke, Hip,' Rosemary said, standing over him. He shook one out of the pack and indicated the matches which were lying on the coffee table. He had nothing to gain by being polite to Rosemary right now; she was just another broad who could light her own cigarettes.

She took a seat on the sofa and curled her legs up under her; she watched him as he continued to scan the ceiling. She wanted to talk about the threat to her love life, and he wanted to talk about the threat to his financial one, but both were afraid to admit that they had a situation they couldn't handle alone. An uncool dilemma was something that only squares fretted about. A down person didn't hang out problematic laundry like Blue Monday wash for everyone to dig: people peeped your hole card then, knew where you were at and saw that you weren't such-a-much after all.

Bothered by what she couldn't say, and in danger of saying it, Rosemary, in desperation, asked, 'Why do you use that dope, Hip? That stuff gon' kill you one day.' She was immediately sorry for intruding. She almost cringed as his gaze fell from the ceiling onto her with scathing anger. 'I didn't mean no harm,' she said apologetically. 'I just thought it'd be interestin' to know, that's all. You don't have to answer if you don't wanna . . .'

'I don't?' he replied caustically. 'Thanks for givin' me a choice.' His emaciated, tired face held a hypnotic spell over her; she could think of nothing except how hollow his cheeks were and the sunken darkness that surrounded his eyes. When she offered no further comment, he said, 'I use smack in order to live, Rosemary.' There was no hostility in his voice now.

She was relieved by his tone: 'Aaah, I don't believe that. You could do without that stuff if you really wanted to. Y'know, last week at our church, a detective from the Narcotics Squad at headquarters gave a lecture – I don't remember his name, Nastyrella or somethin' like that – anyway, he—'

'I know the chump you talkin' about,' Hip cut in: 'Nazifella.'

He lighted another cigarette without offering her one. 'What'd he have to say?'

'Well, he made it plain that people don't have to use dope, but they do it to escape responsibility and to escape from life, not to live, like you said. He said drug addicts were people who'd do anything—'

'Did he also tell you that they rob, rape, and kill when they got dope in 'em? Did he say they were maniacs?' His voice had a vicious grating in it. He looked as if he was about to jump up and attack her.

'He didn't say that, exactly – no,' she replied timidly.

'But ain't that the impression the people got listenin' to 'im?'

'I guess some did. But he said the most dangerous kind was them that needed a fix. He said they'd steal from their own family; take food right outta their kids' mouths. Name it, he said, and a dope fiend would do it.'

Hip said nothing for a long while. Then, with resignation, as if he'd been through this many times, he said, 'Y'know, I git so sick and tired of hearin' and readin' about what squares, mothafuckin' fools, say about junk. They so ignorant till it's a damn shame. Any tale that comes to their minds they connect with junkies. What the hell do they know? Do they use stuff? Do they know what a junkie goes through? – hell no! They read in the papers about some punk who got stoned on goofballs and did somethin', and right away they go screamin' for junkies' heads because of this lame, who wouldn't know dope from salt. Then some woman says a wild-eyed man raped her, and right away everybody assumes a junkie did it. A junkie with stuff in him don't bother nobody. You even got some dumb-assed doctors out there who tell the public that a guy can git a habit from smokin' pot – which is a fuckin' lie. But people believe that bull. I smoked reefer for five straight years before I even knew what heroin was. How come I didn't git no habit from it? I know a hundred people who smoke pot – how come they ain't got no habits?' He stopped talking long enough to snub out his cigarette and light another.

'You see this?' He held up the cigarette. 'Well, you'll git a habit quicker from smokin' this than you will from pot. The only reason pot ain't legal is because the big-money whiskey makers got the government to outlaw it because it was too much competition for them. A stud didn't have to buy whiskey when he could git high from stuff that grew, unattended, in his own backyard. The whole thing is a drag. They hyped the public against smokin' pot so they could kill 'em – at a profit – with cancerous cigarettes and liver-destroyin' liquor. But when they can make sellin' death legal, it's awright, dig? That means they's honorable, yeah. So fuckin' moral till they ain't shit! I know where they at.'

'But, Hip, they ain't got nothin' to do with you puttin' that stuff in you . . .'

'Oh, it ain't, huh? – that's what you think, woman. The outlook of the people in this country got everything to do with what they call "the drug problem."'

'Yeah, but why you have to use it, and why you seem to be blamin' people because you use it?'

'I ain't blamin' nobody. All I'm sayin' is that people oughta find out about somethin' before they go condemnin' it, that's all. It's just another case of ignorance bein' afraid of investigation. You wanna know why people use dope . . . I don't know. There's a lotta reasons, but unless a cat goes to a bug doctor and gits his head examined, they can only be guessed at. The one thing that'll make a junkie stop usin' is himself. Like they say: you can take the dope from the junkie, but you can't take the junkie from the dope.'

'Well, why *you* use it?' Rosemary persisted. 'Ain't you got no reason?'

'Sure, I got a million reasons. Take a look at the things that go on, like the way people act to each other, and you'll see plenty reasons. Every time I shoot up I'm sayin' to them: "Fuck you *and* your system, lames!"'

Rosemary asked for another cigarette. After taking a long drag, she said, 'I think your attitude is wrong, Hip. I mean, I can understand how somethin' that stands in the way of your goals can beat you down and all. But I think you gotta be strong; you gotta build up a physical and mental resistance, and a spiritual determination to go on as best you can, accepting things as they come.'

'Shit, *your* attitude's wrong, not mine. You talk that passive junk and you don't git nowhere, not against aggressive and exploitin' people. You gotta rebel and fight! That's what junkies is doin': fightin' against hypocrisy like yours. They see how y'all "good" citizens say one thing and do the exact opposite. Every time a junkie takes off he's rubbin' your face right in your own hypocritical shit. That's what y'all don't like about dope fiends – they take the freedom that y'all is scared to take. You keep on bein' passive and your behind'll be more familiar with shoe leather than your feet.'

'I ain't passive, but I do believe in Christian ethics and law and order. That's more than you can say. I think you use dope just to be down. You think it's hip, and that makes you one of the elite in a sea of squares. You oughta be tryin' to make this a better country to live in insteada tryin' to tear it up by the roots!'

Both their voices were tinged with bitterness and spite now, though neither was outright angry. Hip smiled maliciously at her and said, 'Sometimes I wish I could tear it up by the roots and start all over again. I betcha I could make it a hell of a better place and more human than what it is.'

'What would you do? – destroy everybody that don't use dope?' she asked derisively.

He ignored her remark. 'I ain't botherin' nobody. I ain't no cop and I ain't no soldier. I don't build no bombs and I don't fly no planes nowhere to drop none. I ain't no red-blooded American tryin' my damnedest to spill the red blood of other countries, and I ain't responsible for none of the mess in the world. I'm just a dope fiend. Why they persecute me? I ain't looking for nothin' but peace. Why they pick on me and call me one of the worst things in the world when they killin' people by the thousands – and gittin' ready to kill 'em by the millions? I ain't done nothin' to nobody. All I do is shoot good dope in my arm. Sure, I make an illegal dollar here and there and I don't follow no Christian ethic – but then, I don't claim none, neither. Y'all hypocrites can't say as much, can you?'

She thought for a moment before asking, in a softer tone now, 'Do all that really justify you, Hip? Is you s'pozed to just lay down because you can't change the world? That's a sorry excuse to be a nothin' dope fiend, if you ask me.'

'I ain't askin' you,' he snapped. 'I'ma dope fiend and love it. It kills me – lays me right out fine, baby.'

'It's gon' kill you for real in the long run. Look at what happened to that man yesterday: dead on somebody's roof. That stuff not only ain't good for you, it's dangerous!'

He laughed at her. 'Girl, it might not be good for me, but it's so damn good *to* me! When they found Tricky Dick on that roof it only proved that he was greedy and the dope was good. He blew his cool, that's all.'

His manner abruptly changed; he seemed to be talking to himself as he murmured, 'They sure is takin' a long time.'

She was confused. 'What you talkin' about, Hip?'

'Franchot and that whore,' he said. Then, staring at her fixedly, he added, 'Y'know, I think he tryin' to pull her. You dig what that means, don't you? If I blow her, you gon' blow him. You won't have no more man.'

'What about you?' she replied tartly. 'You won't have no woman, neither.'

'Don't need none as long as the dope don't stop. A woman can't do nothin' for me but show me where some dope is and gimme the bread to buy it with.'

'What you do for lovin'? Need a woman for that – unless you dig fags,' she mocked.

'Only woman I need is the White Lady that rides through my veins. That's the only bitch that can git under my skin; and can't no woman do it as good as she can, baby, I'm tellin' you. When that White Lady's ready, a flesh-and-blood chick can stick a pepperoni up her slit for all I care – I don't need her, and that's the truth.'

'Aw, Hip, you jivin'. You know ain't no dope can take the place of sex.'

'Hah! That's what you think, woman, but let me tell you one thing. When a cat mixes some heroin and cocaine together and shoots it, he gits a nut – a real nut, right in his pants if he ain't careful. That's what's called speedballin', and, believe me, baby, you ball with a lotta speed!' He closed his eyes as if he were remembering his last speedball.

'Well,' Rosemary said, slightly miffed at the insult to womanhood, 'if it do all that, why you got Gypsy Pearl?'

'I done already told you – for dope money. If she didn't make no money I wouldn't be messin' with her. A bitch ain't no good to me if she ain't got nothin'. I can do bad by myself.'

'You think that's right? You think prostitution is good, somethin' to be proud of?'

'Right? Good? Where you at, woman? – in the first century somewhere? If a woman wanna sell some and a man wanna buy it, what the hell is your phony morals gotta do with it? Yes, I not only think it's good and right, I know it is. A man is a natural pimp and a woman is a natural whore, anyway, regardless to what the law say. I dig natural law. Dig this . . . Why you think a man shows off his wife to his boss? Why you think them politicians play up the fact that they married? And why you think the dumb bastards in this country won't vote for a bachelor for president? Lemme hip you, girl – it's because he ain't got no whore to show. That's pimpin' Christian style, this showin' of wives! So if you git right down to the nitty gritty, the man *is* livin' off the woman. Just think: all this shit we go through for a crack hung up between some legs! That's where it's at, baby.'

'It still ain't like makin' a woman sell her body for money, though.'

'Shit, it's worse! – because it's hypocritical. The only reason the squares make laws against prostitution is because they full of secret envy for the pimps. Look at all the publicity and romantic worship that international playboys and broke royalty gits. The squares is jealous of them guys, but they can't do nothin' about it because the people love 'em. But me, they'll insult and even kill me, because I ain't a big enough pimp to tell 'em to kiss my behind. But I tell it to 'em anyway. As long as there's a woman out there willin' to give me the money she makes sellin' cunt, I'm gon' be smart enough to take it – and ain't gon' be no hypocrite about it, neither.'

'Hip, if we had leaders like you, this would be one of the most corrupt countries in the world.' Her hands were shaking as she lighted the cigarette he gave her.

'You think it ain't already? Is you stupid enough to think this morality stuff they preach is for real? Wow! Ain't nobody in this country got no business being dumb enough to believe that the leaders can rule without doin' all kinds of dirt – nobody can. This government ain't run morally and anybody who thinks so is a fool – anybody who says so is a damn liar.'

Rosemary had had enough. She got up and went into the kitchen. The clock registered four forty-five. She reheated the coffee while Hip sat in silence in the living room. When it was steaming she brought it in and poured for both of them. Hip accepted the fact that their former conversation was closed when she asked, 'Do you really think somethin's goin' on between them? You think he'll put me down for her if he can git her away from you?'

He knew she was really worried about the possibility of losing Franchot, but he couldn't resist getting in one last dig at her. 'Didn't I just run it down to you?' he said coolly. 'You's a whore, woman. You just ain't gittin' no money for doin' it. You ain't no more important to him than she is to me – can't you dig that? Damn right he gon' throw you over if he can git her, just like I'd git rid of her if I saw somethin' I dug better.'

They fell silent, sipping their coffees. She wasn't a bad-looking woman, he thought; and in thinking, the inevitable idea spread its possibilities through his mind. His next statement was automatic: 'Dig, Rosemary . . . I don't see no sense in us gittin' upset about them. Why don't we just switch? Like, I wouldn't mind diggin' things with you. You a pretty swingin' chick and you know where things at. If you put your mind to it, I bet you could make more money than she could anyway, y'know?'

She put her cup down so hard on the coffee table that it sloshed over and burned her hand, turning her anger into rage. 'Is you askin' me to be a whore, Hip Ritchwood? You dirty, rotten dog. And after all that junk you was just tellin' me – You wait till Franchot come back, he'll straighten—'

'Aw, lay down, bitch. What you gittin' all shook up about? Puttin' on like you so insulted or somethin'. You oughta be flattered. Who the hell is you, anyway? I don't see much difference in whorin' and free-fuckin' like you doin'. At least a whore is a businesswoman – bitches like you ain't nothin' but free samples of the product. Little Miss Tight-pussy is insulted – ain't that a bitch? I'm the one oughta be insulted!'

Rosemary jumped up, glaring. Her throat was too full of fury to speak; when she tried she only stammered. She wouldn't give him the privilege of seeing her cry. She stormed out of the room and slammed the bedroom door behind her. Hip was caught up in a breathtaking fit of laughter.

A few minutes later he got up, went past the so definitely closed door of Franchot's bedroom, got his works out, and let the White Lady have her way with him. She subdued his body's tremble and gave his weary soul rest. She sent him soaring like a celestial body. He was God, making the world in his own image, peopled by nothing but down souls bursting with all the happiness he could dispense to them. Not a worry anywhere in his world; not a wrinkle on one soul's brow. This was where it was at. This was where it had to be.

He was sorry that he could never bring this heaven back to the sorry world of so-called reality. If only he could have – everything would be groovy . . . people would dig . . .

He went into a tight nod, slumped bonelessly down into the chair on which he sat; and again, as God of the world, he slew the squares like Franchot; vilified the women like Rosemary, who didn't know where it was at. Who thought that whores were made by men when, in truth, they were made by nature – born – just like pimps: as natural as a moist pussy.

Fourteen

Franchot waited impatiently on the first floor of headquarters while Meyers and the bail bondsman, Solly Kaplan, went about the procedure of getting Gypsy Pearl released. He'd been chainsmoking for the last half hour as his tension had increased; two butts still smoldered in the heavy ash stand at his side while he lighted yet another. 'Just be cool, baby, be cool,' he said softly to himself. But he still couldn't keep from fidgeting on the big polished bench on which he sat. Finally he got up and paced the floor. The huge clock seemed to tick off the minutes abnormally slowly.

A beefy, red-faced cop sat behind a glass partition reading a book and chewing juicily on the stub of a cigar whose odor hung sourly in the air. He paid little attention to Franchot. Twice the phone had rung and he'd talked to a woman who claimed to be terrorized by a Peeping Tom. Both times he'd sent a squad car to investigate and they reported finding nothing but the woman, quite calm, desiring to have a policeman stay with her for protection.

Now as she called a third time, the cop, an old man who didn't wear any insignia that Franchot could see, was irritated and spoke gravely into the mouthpiece:

'Look, lady, I already sent a car to your house – twice. There's nobody in sight . . . No, I can't send a man to stay with you . . . Huh? You'll pay him? . . . Lady . . . Lady, I'm sorry, but I can't do it . . . Well, if he's not trying to get in, what's he doing? . . . Exposing himself, huh? . . . A Negro? There? Lady, if there was a Negro in that neighborhood at this time of the night he'd've been picked up . . .'

He put his hand over the mouthpiece and winked at Franchot, and, almost as if he were exonerating him from guilt, said, 'She's lying.' Then he removed his hand and spoke to the woman.

'Yeah, lady, okay ... Okay. I'll send them around again ...
No! No, one of them *can't* stay all night – it's against regulations
... I *know* you pay taxes, lady. Yes, you're entitled to protection
... Look, I pay taxes, too ... Take it easy, they'll look again
... Yes, ma'am, very carefully ... Please, lady, I *told* you – no!
... What? You like my voice? I'm flattered, lady, I really am.
Thanks ... No, I can't come, either ... You'll pay me, too,
huh? ... Sorry, lady, I can't do it.' A sudden flash came over
his already florid face. He rolled the cigar to the opposite side
of his mouth. 'Look, lady, I gotta hang up, they just brought a
murderer in ... Yeah, yeah, well, I can't tell them to hurry if
you don't let me hang up and let me call them ... Yeah, right
away ... For the last time – no! You just lock all the windows
and doors and wait.' He hung up.

Franchot was seated again. The cop scowled an imitation of
a smile at him and said, pointing at the phone, 'She just wants
to get laid.' Without waiting for comment he picked up his
book again.

The floor indicator above the elevator door began to
descend. Franchot's left eye jumped with a nervous tic; his
hands were cold, and he rubbed one across his hot, sweaty
forehead. He took out his last cigarette as the elevator reached
the ground floor.

Gypsy Pearl stepped out, followed by Meyers and Kaplan.
When she saw Franchot she stopped short, surprised. Meyers
almost bumped her. She blinked a timid smile at Franchot,
but her face plainly showed the embarrassment she felt.

Franchot's nervousness left him as he watched the three walk
over to the cop, and his features hardened. Their backs were
to him; she stood between the two men like a captured angel.
Her shapely legs and rounded buttocks, her thin waist and
the proud set of her shoulders and head, spoke their familiar
language to him, but he remained cold, almost indifferent.
And when she finally turned to face him, the chill from his
stare made her flinch.

He stood as they came toward him, but was afraid to speak;
he couldn't trust the fragility of his will. He turned to leave
and she followed.

Meyers offered them a lift back uptown but Franchot quickly refused, 'We'll take a cab,' he said curtly. He wanted to get her away from Meyers as fast as possible. He remembered the girl at the Dark Room each time Meyers looked at Gypsy Pearl.

'Well, make sure she's back here at nine o'clock this morning,' Meyers said, just as curtly.

'What for?' Franchot asked. 'I thought we was finished.'

'She's been booked. She'll have to go before a magistrate,' Meyers explained. 'But don't worry – it's just a formality. It'll be in his chambers, no one but him, her, and myself – and you, if you want.'

'She'll be there,' Franchot said. Then he and Gypsy Pearl walked the short distance to Broad Street where they could find a cab.

In the semidarkness of the taxi she stole furtive glances at him. Once he turned and caught her looking at him and she quickly became intent on the passing, almost empty streets.

The sky had just a flit of cool morning gray sliding in above the eastern rooftops. Every few yards or so they would see a man in work clothes, with lunch pail or paper or both, waiting at the bus stop, or another man walking toward one. Traffic was very sparse. She saw a bum lying in the door of a store, sleeping, and about two hundred feet further on, a cop walking toward him.

The cab was going up Market Street now, heading toward Springfield Avenue. Franchot broke their silence by asking her if she wanted a cigarette. She nodded.

When she bent forward to get the light he offered he watched the light of the flame on her face. His hands remained steady, but when the match was out he felt them trembling.

'Where's Hip?' she asked.

'Home waitin'. Sent me to git you.'

'Why didn't he come hisself?'

'I don't know – said we both didn't need to.'

'Seem like that's his job, since I'm s'pozed to be his woman.'

'I can go along with that,' he said sarcastically.

She wasn't as peeved as she sounded. In fact, she was happy

that Franchot was the one who came and got her. She turned again to look out at passing Newark.

They were on Springfield Avenue, having passed the Essex County Courthouse, with its big bronze statue of Abraham Lincoln, sitting with his high stovepipe hat at his side, surveying all downtown. Children would probably play on his lap this afternoon when the sun was bright and the day warm.

They stopped for a red light at the corner of High Street and Springfield Avenue, then continued on past the bank, the Dark Room, the big music store. The Lyric Bar went by, and the old Savoy Theater, which now belonged to Daddy Grace's followers, and the Essex Theater directly across from it: it still showed movies.

They passed West Street; next came Howard Street. As they turned in, she looked up at the enormous clock which hung above the corner entrance of the Howard Bar. She'd seen the clock ever since she was a young girl and it had always stood at one.

As the cab started along Howard, Franchot spoke again: 'You ain't his woman, you his slave.' His voice was flat, profoundly bitter. She could make no reply, no denial.

She saw Jackie Brown and another wino named Stanley White sitting in the doorway of the M&M Bar sharing some potato chips and a fifth of wine. The stopped clock and these bums, and her own life, made her reflect: Howard Streeters didn't really need time. Days swung into nights and back again, and nothing ever changed for them but the seasons. They did the same things day in and day out with little variation – hard drinking, fighting, tears, laughter; hard fucking, hating, and praying; hard, hard living, all passion, no love, not for each other and not for themselves.

The taxi turned down Mercer Street toward Broome. A few more blocks to go – and then what? She thought: Back to Howard Street when the sun goes down. Yes, Lord. They turned in Broome. Still she could say nothing. She was his brother's woman, whore, slave. Her will was not her own – was any Howard Streeter's? – it was no stronger than Hip's whim. He commanded and she obeyed. Yes, Lord.

They crossed Court Street. How dingy the whole neighborhood was in the fresh light of a new day. She could see the tenements all the way down to West Kinney. And then past Morton Street, where the school, a squat four-story brick building, was the one solid-looking structure. The janitor had already raised the flag above it. It stirred infrequently in the windless morning. On the corner was a small gathering of men – some on their way to work, others waiting for the bars to open.

Again she felt an impulse to tell Franchot about Hip's use of the apartment for the other junkies. Still she remained silent. They were now in their block, on Broome between Morton and Baldwin. The fire escapes on the front of the buildings looked as flimsy as spiders' webs; garbage was in the streets and would probably remain uncollected; yet even so, she liked it here. It was Franchot's neighborhood: it gave her a feeling of security.

Their building – 124 Broome Street – was on the corner of Baldwin, a narrow cobblestone still smelling of horse manure from the stables that had been there years ago. As they stopped, Gypsy Pearl looked up at the apartment's two windows; perhaps Hip would at least be watching for her. The blinds were drawn.

Franchot paid the cabbie and followed her into the hallway, next to the confectionery store; a light in the back showed it would be opening soon. As he went up the stairs behind her, he watched the swing of her hips and longed to touch them. He took his eyes from her and studied his own feet as they took each steel-encased step.

He had forgotten his keys and had to knock. Hip let them in. 'Thanks, Shots,' he said when they were inside. 'We won't forgit you, bro – and we gon' pay you back, too.' Then he looked Gypsy Pearl up and down: 'You awright, woman?' he asked.

'Fine, fine.' He grinned. 'Now go on to bed and git rested up. We goin' out tonight and git some of that money Shots done laid out for you.'

'Ain't no hurry, Lonnie,' Franchot protested. 'This woman oughta lay off for a while, man, she just got outta jail.'

'That ain't no big thing, man. This here is a whore and she s'pozed to whore. Gittin' busted is all part of the game – occupational hazard, y'know.' He turned to her: 'Go on to bed, woman.'

As she closed the door behind her, she heard Franchot protest again, but Hip cut him off, saying, 'Yeah, I know all that, Shots, but next time the dumb bitch won't be so careless.'

Gypsy Pearl sat down heavily on the bed.

Rosemary, with girlish petulance written on her features, leaned on one elbow in bed and watched Franchot slowly change from his street clothes to his work clothes. He saw her in the mirror, but he didn't feel like going through a hassle about whatever was bothering her, so he pretended not to notice her pouting.

When it was apparent that he wasn't going to say anything, she said, 'Hip's her man, why didn't you let him go git her?'

'What difference do it make who got her as long as she was got?' he replied, sitting on the bed to lace his brogans.

She sat up then and the sheet fell into her lap, revealing her nakedness. 'It makes a lotta difference,' she retorted. 'If something like that happened to me I'd want my man to come git me before I'd want some man I done just met to . . .' She hesitated: 'Unless you is her man already . . .'

Calmly he turned to look at her. 'Just what is you talkin' about, woman? You know damn well who woman she is.'

'I thought I did, but I ain't so sure now – you goin' around doin' her man's job and everything—'

'Listen, if you think I'm fool enough to give Lonnie that much money at one time while he usin' that dope, then you just outta your mind!' Anger sprang into him, mainly because she'd hit so close to his feelings and his guilt was pinched by it. But also, in that instant, came the further knowledge that he couldn't trust his brother – that he probably would never be able to trust him. And he realized that he'd known it all along.

Tears had welled in Rosemary's eyes. 'Hip told me that you

want her for your woman. And . . . and he asked me to be his whore. I told him I was gon' tell you.'

'Lonnie?' he asked numbly, stupidly, as if they'd been talking about someone else.

'No, not *Lonnie* – Booker T. Washington!' she snapped at him. 'And that ain't all he said. You should heard him talkin' crazy stuff, like a woman's a natural whore, and about dope. I believe something's wrong in his head, if you ask me. That ain't all I got to tell you, neither; him and that woman been lettin' dope fiends come in here while you workin', too. Next thing you know they'll be sellin' dope *and* her right here in your apartment.'

'How you know they was dope fiends, you seen 'em?'

'What other kinda people they know? No, I didn't see 'em, but I heard about it. You know ain't no secrets around here. They was seen. Ain't no tellin' what went on. They probably had a orgy or somethin'.'

'Shut up talkin' what you don't know, woman!' He believed her, but he wouldn't admit it to her or himself. 'Don't bring me none of these niggas' gossip about my brother. What's wrong with him havin' friends visit, so what? This ain't no jail, and they don't hafta be doin' wrong, y'know.'

'Well, was your precious, right-doin' brother wrong for askin' me to be a whore when I'm your woman?'

'What'd you tell him?' He was smiling now.

'I told him to go to hell!' she sniffed primly, and her long breasts swung like pendulums.

'Then you ain't got nothin' worry about. A woman ain't a whore unless she wanna be, so if you turn out don't come tellin' me somebody made you do it, hear?' He laughed and she soon joined him. He felt a strange mixture of pride and pity for her, knowing that she was only trying to protect herself; that she was afraid of losing him to Gypsy Pearl and fought in the only way she knew to keep him, even if it meant being catty and outright nasty and vicious. He also knew that she had good reason for her fear, and, though she mightn't be so bright, she would bring every device at her disposal to the fore in order to keep him. He felt a genuine tenderness for her as they smiled at each other. It was a threatening feeling that he didn't want to cope with right now – later perhaps, but not now. He was tired and he had to go to work. 'Git up and fix me some coffee and sandwiches, baby. I gotta be makin' it.' He kissed her and gave a gentle squeeze to one of her breasts.

As he sat at the table, the weight of the night's revelations seemed to wear him down, and the jolly note on which he'd left the bedroom a few minutes earlier had soured. He wanted Gypsy Pearl, there were no two ways about it; and if Rosemary had been in the least willing he'd have gladly switched with Hip. Even though there was something about Gypsy Pearl that puzzled him, something he couldn't understand. Yet Hip seemed to know every facet of her. And Rosemary, poor Rosemary. She wanted to save him, not only for herself, but from himself. She'd been so patient and loving. It had been three years now that she waited for she knew not what. She only wanted him, that was beyond doubt.

He stared at Hip's and Gypsy Pearl's closed door. He thought that he heard a sob, but he wasn't sure. He listened more closely but it didn't come again. If it had, what then? Was he really Sir Galahad, as his brother called him, looking for a distressing situation from which to save a damsel? Was it only that, or did he truly want Gypsy Pearl? Maybe he was just imagining things. He had so much to be suspicious about, it was no wonder he was bewildered. Of the four of them, only Rosemary was clear and understandable. If only Gypsy Pearl would let herself go, free herself, let him see her completely. Why hadn't she told him about the people who came to the apartment? He had come to believe that she would tell him if anything was wrong; now, he wasn't so sure. She had to come to terms with herself, she had to choose what she wanted. He would give her a little more time to collect her thoughts and discover her real desires. If it was him she wanted she'd make it known to him – and he'd know it.

Fifteen

Sunday was a radiant, lovely day, warm and happy in its brightness. People paraded around in their Sunday clothes; kids prepared to go to the movies. Sunday papers were being read and Sunday dinners cooked slowly with low fires. The big church on Belmont Avenue let its deep-toned bells ring out over the city, singing its song loudly into the placid clear blue sky. Radios spoke and shouted their gospels. People relaxed. At the Parental Detention Home Jimmy Johnson stole a knife from the kitchen and took it out into the recreation yard. He planned to escape today.

Mr Roundtree, the counselor, had taken a liking to Jimmy. He was a sports enthusiast and had been impressed with Jimmy's athletic ability and obvious leadership qualities. And Jimmy returned his liking. Mr Roundtree was the only adult in the home whom Jimmy could forgive, and he didn't want to hurt him. He'd taken the knife in case he had to scare him; if Mr Roundtree wouldn't try to stop him from going over the fence, everything would be all right.

Ever since he'd first walked into the Home Jimmy had been a leader, in the way most admired by the confined boys, whose ages ranged from eight to seventeen. He cursed the officials, smoked when he could get cigarettes, stole food from the kitchen, bragged about muggings and robberies – real and imagined – and about girls, felt other boys' behinds in the showers, and body-punched better than anyone there.

But Jimmy was afraid. At night in the privacy of his bed, he cried and cursed himself for being a punk. His homesickness was so bad that he'd stuff his mouth full of the sheet to keep from yelling. Then, when it was day again, he was his old self – brave and proud.

Though Butch and Brother didn't talk to him much, it didn't bother him, for he could always make them do what he wanted.

But when the news came about Sy, they avoided him altogether staying as far from him as their confinement would allow. To them, he was the cause of all their troubles. Wasn't he the one who suggested that they rape Sy's mother in the first place? Sy had jumped out of a window at Martland Medical Center. He was dead. They blamed him for this, too.

To make things worse, his mother, when she came to visit him, would cry and wring her hands the whole time. She kept asking him: 'Why you do it, son? Why you do it?' He couldn't stand that senseless question any longer – just as he couldn't have answered it had he tried – so the last time she'd visited him, he'd run back to his room and left her calling tearfully after him.

He couldn't stand this much longer; he'd bug out and everybody would call him a punk. He had to get out. They'd blame him for Sy as well as the crimes. He'd never get out of jail . . .

He didn't play basketball that afternoon in the yard; he watched as Mr Roundtree taught some of the younger boys the rudiments of the game. When the man's back was turned Jimmy suddenly broke for the fence, which wasn't much higher than ten feet. As if he had eyes in the back of his head, Mr Roundtree wheeled and caught him before he even reached the fence. But he wasn't expecting the knife, and Jimmy blindly plunged it into his stomach, then jumped the fence and ran wildly for the Third Ward.

Jimmy ran whole blocks before he realized that he still held the bloody knife in his hand, and he'd realized it then only because people seemed unusually eager to get out of his way. Once he'd gotten rid of it in a sewer, they paid little attention to him. He took every shortcut he could remember: through alleys, yards, empty lots, and through houses. Every now and then he'd hear a siren scream, and he'd hide until it faded in the distance. He avoided the busier streets as much as he could, but had to cross Central Avenue, Bergen Street, West Market. He finally made it to Belmont Avenue and had only a few more blocks to go. He headed for their hideout, the condemned house on Broome Street. They'd stashed a case of soda and some cookies and doughnuts there – he hoped desperately that no bum had found them. It would hold him for a few days, until the heat died down. Then he'd go down south to his aunt's, or, better still, try to get out of the country. He damn sure couldn't go home. His mother would probably want him to turn himself in. She was brainwashed and thought that nobody could escape the law, but he knew better.

At Prince Street, with about fifty yards between him and the safety he sought, a patrol car stopped. 'Hey, you!' one of the cops yelled. 'Halt! We wanna talk to you!' A boy running was always suspect if the cops had nothing more important on their minds.

Talk hell! Jimmy thought. He was tired but broke into a faster run. He'd already covered more than twenty blocks, and the excitement, the climbing over fences, the constant moving and ducking, had him breathing like a steam engine. His throat felt hot and swollen.

'Halt in the name of the law!' the cop shouted, then he jumped out of the car and gave chase while his partner turned the car around. A man tried to grab Jimmy and was given a vicious kick in the groin.

The cop was about fifty feet behind him and didn't stop to see if the man was all right, as Jimmy had hoped he would. The goddamn movies! Jimmy thought. In the movies the cop would've at least stopped to ask the man if he was all right – but this one kept hot on his trail.

'*Halt, kid I'm warnin' ya – halt!*'

Jimmy was ten feet from a hallway which he could use to escape through to the backyard that would take him down to Broome Street. He looked back and saw the cop kneeling and pointing at him.

As he went to step into the doorway, he heard a crack. His left shoulder was jolted forward as if he'd received a blow on the arm from one of the guys while playing 'Mine.' He fell inside, but scrambled hurriedly to his feet and stumbled toward the back.

Outside he ran straight into a low-hanging clothesline that seared him across the nose and eyes, temporarily blinding him.

He fell to his knees, and heard the cop's footsteps thundering in the hallway behind him. Jimmy jumped up and staggered to the fence, hoping the cop would think he'd made for the roof. He dropped to the other side of the fence and, once again, found himself getting up off his now very sore knees: he'd landed in the midst of a bunch of garbage cans. The noise was terrible; a few people came to their windows shouting and cursing his fleeing back. He hoped that no one recognized him – though it made little difference now. He didn't hear the cop coming after him, but he didn't slow down to listen, either. Only a few moments more and he'd be safe. He saw the boarded-up windows of the hideout and they looked like the gates of heaven.

He went to the cellar door and lifted it and quickly disappeared into its deep darkness. He let the door down easily and shot the bolt into place with a grateful sigh. He'd made it!

His security was short-lived: the cellar was inhabited by rats, some as large as kittens. One ran across his foot, and he couldn't keep from crying out. He'd always been afraid of them, ever since he'd been bitten by one when he was a baby. Upstairs – he had to get upstairs. Nothing but an occasional mouse there.

It was the usual four-story tenement building, abandoned now to make way for a new housing project that the city was putting up. The hideout was on the top floor in one of the front apartments from which the whole of the block between Morton and Baldwin streets could be viewed through the cracks in the boards on the windows. He and the other guys had often hidden up here and watched the cops or some other boys look in vain for them.

He went to look out immediately. There were only a few people lolling about, unaware that he was in the deepest kind of trouble. The confectionery store was open, and some of the kids he knew were doing the Slop to the raucous music.

No cops out there yet. But he knew they'd be searching for him sooner or later. His shoulder was burning something terrible; the bullet had hit him high in the meaty part of his arm and had come out in front. He could barely see the wound, because there was no light except the thin striations of sunrays piercing the gloom between the slits of the boards. He could have moved his shoulder to catch one of those needles of light, but the wound hurt so much that he didn't really want to see it.

In the kitchen, where a sink used to be, was a steel footlocker about three feet long. They'd used it to stash their loot because no rats or mice could get into it. He opened it and rummaged through it. The cookies and doughnuts were still there. Then his hand touched something strange and cold, and he jerked away, frightened; he remembered: here's where they'd put the gun that they'd stolen from old man Solomon's store. He pulled it out. He had a gun! Nobody was going to bother him now.

Sirens sounded somewhere near. He looked around for the case of soda; it was somewhere in this room. All that running had made him thirsty. Where was it? Sy had put it near the toilet. He couldn't see a foot in front of him as he walked carefully, his good arm extended. The other arm was burning and throbbing like a television commercial's version of a headache. He was sweating profusely, his shirt stuck to him. He tripped over something and the sudden movement shot pain up and down his left side and brought tears to his eyes. He'd tripped over the soda case.

He bent to fumble for a soda and his fingers touched something wet. Cautiously he raised them to his nose, then rubbed them with his thumb. He frowned. Was he losing too much blood? He ripped off a piece of his shirt and tied it tightly around his arm. Then he felt around for the bottle opener. He tried to hold the bottle in his left hand, but found it impossible: the arm had no strength and pained too much. He finally put the bottle between his knees and opened it that way. In one greedy swig he downed the whole bottle of the warm, sweet liquid.

The gun. It was a beautiful .38 caliber Smith and Wesson revolver. He stuck it in his belt, opened another soda, and took it into the front room with him.

Peeking through the boards again, he saw cops and cop cars

– it looked like a hundred of them. They were talking to some of the kids in the store. Heads were popped out of the windows of every building on the even-number side of the street from 116 near Morton to 124 on the corner of Baldwin Street.

A fat, red-faced man was looking over at the building Jimmy was hiding in; then he called the other cops to him and held a conference. Jimmy could almost hear him ordering the building surrounded. After the man finished talking they scattered in all directions. Jimmy saw Slim McNair and was tempted to take a shot at him, but he contented himself with cursing him and turned away from the window. There was nothing to do but wait now; when it got dark he'd try to get away.

He went back into the kitchen and carried the case of soda along with two boxes of doughnuts into the front room. The case could serve as a seat. Mice might run over him if he sat on the floor with the doughnuts.

Jimmy finished two more sodas and six doughnuts before he looked out through the boards again – more cops. He heard a noise. He whirled and moved stealthily to the kitchen door, pinched it open, and listened . . . voices downstairs. Fear welled in him. He closed the door and went back to look out of the window again, he prayed silently for darkness and shook so violently that the pain in his arm increased. 'They go' git me, they go' git me,' he said weakly.

The electric chair! . . . He'd killed Mr Roundtree and they were going to send him to the chair. He was convinced of this. Rape and robbery and murder – that was electric chair stuff. He sat down on the case and immediately got up to look outside again.

This scene – he felt sure that he'd lived through it before. The cops, the deserted, dark building; a dream maybe? . . . No. But he'd never had this happen to him before. No cops had ever chased him to this extent before. They wanted to kill him. He had killed somebody. Then it dawned on him – the movies! He'd seen it in the movies; a James Cagney picture. Yeah. He was like James Cagney, trapped inside and surrounded by cops. Jimmy felt a sudden exhilaration and smiled.

But James Cagney hadn't been shot in the arm like him – *he was wounded!* Now he felt the arm; the bleeding had almost completely stopped and it was numb – until he touched it, then hot needles, thousands of them, pricked his whole left side. He almost cried out in pain.

James Cagney had let them take him to the chair, too. But Jimmy wasn't going to let them get him. He wouldn't give up and die like a roasted pig . . . Hell, no.

Again he went to the window; then back to the door. He had to stop going back and forth. He had to do something, but, dammit, what? Lord, please hurry and make it dark. He grimaced back anxious, frustrated tears. He didn't realize that a soft moaning was issuing from the back of his throat, but he caught himself saying: 'Momma, they go' kill me!' Abruptly he cursed himself for being a punk. His face became rigid, his shoulders straightened in determination. James Cagney hadn't cried when they had him trapped. He wouldn't cry, either.

Opening the door, he stepped out into the hall. He looked up at the skylight, but it was boarded up, too. He looked over the bannister: they were searching on the second floor.

A head popped out on the ground floor, did a double take, and a voice yelled, 'There he is! He's on the top floor! He's up there!' The head disappeared but the same voice yelled: 'Hey, Riley, tell the captain he's on the top floor!'

Jimmy didn't move. The head came back into view. 'C'mon down, kid,' it said. 'Nobody's gonna hurt ya.'

James Cagney smiled, pulled the gun from his belt, and fired. The bullet hit the floor beside the cop and sent up a little cloud of dust. The cop jumped back yelling at the top of his lungs: 'He's got a gun! Tell the captain he's got a gun!' Then, in a lower tone to someone nearby: 'That little bastard almost shot me! You men watch out.'

Jimmy went back inside the apartment and back again to the window. He saw the red-faced man talking animatedly to five others. That must be the captain, Jimmy thought. Above the store he saw Gypsy Pearl looking down on them, her long hair hanging loosely over her shoulders.

'Stinkin' whore bitch!' he spat. If it had been her, like Butch wished, instead of Sy's mother, he wouldn't be in all this trouble now. He considered taking a shot at her. Now he wanted a cigarette. He went into the kitchen and inched the door open. They wouldn't be too quick to run in on him now that they knew he had a gun. A man with a gun is God, and they knew it. That captain was getting their strategy together, but he was ready for them. Hurry up, night!

The skylight was boarded up! The significance of the fact hit him like a physical blow. How was he going to get out, even in the dark? He couldn't get it open without them hearing him, without them taking shots at him. All they had to do was shoot straight up and they had him. He was trapped.

He was trapped!

He bumped his arm against the doorjamb and almost sank to his knees as the pain engulfed him. He couldn't get past them; he couldn't get out – but he had to, he just *had* to! He was crying again from pain and fear. Sweat was pouring from him, his head was a waterfall of perspiration. His arm throbbed. The gun slipped from his hand; he felt too weak to hold it any longer.

'*He's still up there!*' a voice yelled from below. Jimmy didn't know what to do, and he didn't care. He sank to the floor near the door, leaving it slightly ajar in case anyone tried to sneak up on him.

A few minutes – perhaps an hour, he didn't know – passed before he heard voices again. He jumped up, gun ready, breathing in gasps. He had to hold his breath to hear them. 'The captain says it's awright for 'im to try,' some said below.

Try what? Jimmy's mind questioned. Footsteps! Somebody was coming! A volunteer – they were sending a volunteer on a suicide mission to get him or be killed trying. He was going to shoot it out with one of their crack shots! Maybe they wanted him to waste his bullets, then they'd close in. They thought they were so slick, goddamn cops. He was wise to them and their tricks.

He waited, listening to the approaching steps. Whoever was coming was making sure he'd be heard. Jimmy pointed the gun at the head of the stairs, ready. His hand trembled. This was it – the nitty gritty. James Cagney waited with a face full of determination. He wanted a smoke real bad now.

He heard a familiar voice calling his name. He couldn't pinpoint it. Again it came: 'Jimmy, Jimmy, it's me, baby.' Who the hell was 'me'? A man's voice . . . Jackie Brown! It was that goddamn bum, Jackie Brown!

'What the hell you want?' Jimmy shouted at him.

'I wanna talk to you, Jimmy.'

'Well I don't wanna talk to you! You git outta here and leave me alone, Jackie. I got a gun and I'll kill you!'

Jackie kept coming. 'Jimmy, at least let me talk to you,' he said. And by this time he was standing on the landing. He saw the gun pointing at him, but seemed to pay it no attention.

Jimmy lowered it. 'You got smokes?' he asked impulsively.

'Smokes?' Jackie's distorted face made a smile. 'Sure, baby, sure. I got some. You can have 'em all; just let me talk to you.' He reached into his pocket for them.

'Just stay right there!' Jimmy said dramatically. 'I got you sighted. Try somethin' and I'll blow your head off.' He observed that Jackie needed a haircut very badly, and his overall appearance – this wasn't the Jackie Brown he'd known.

'Jimmy, Jimmy,' Jackie said soothingly. 'You know I wouldn't do anything to you. You know that. Let me come in and we'll have a smoke and talk this thing over.'

'We can talk from here. Throw over the smoke and say what you gotta say.'

'This ain't no way to talk, Jimmy. Let me come in. I won't try to take you down or anything, I promise.' Jackie's voice, so normally slurred and croaking, was strong now; clear, with words that were less carelessly enunciated than was his usual habit.

Jimmy noted this also, though he didn't attach any particular significance to it. The last thing he would have thought was that Jackie had not taken a drink since hearing about his plight, and was, in his way, trying to impress him. 'What the hell your promises mean to me, bum-wino?'

'Jimmy, you gotta trust me. They got the place surrounded. You can't get away; let me come in—'

'Throw the smoke!' Jimmy repeated.

'Listen. I'll smoke with you, but I ain't throwin' nothin' if you ain't gonna trust me,' Jackie said defiantly and took a small step toward the apartment. 'What say, partner, can I come in?'

Jimmy had the gun pointed right in the middle of Jackie's chest. He didn't speak, so Jackie came on.

'Awright, c'mon,' Jimmy said. 'But don't try none of that hero stuff on me, Jackie. This ain't the movies, you hear? They give you a gun?'

'You know better than that, baby. Here.' He pulled a crumpled package of cigarettes from his pocket and held them up. 'This is the only thing I got on me – and there ain't too many of them left.' He smiled crookedly.

Jimmy backed away to let him come in, warning, 'I'm tellin' you in front, Jackie: Try somethin' slick and you a dead ass.'

They smoked their first cigarettes in silence, about fifteen feet apart. Jimmy stood near the door, casting an occasional nervous glance at the head of the stairs so they couldn't sneak up on him. Jackie sat on the footlocker.

Presently Jackie broke the silence: 'They gave me fifteen minutes to try and talk you into givin' yourself up, sport. How 'bout we do it in ten?'

'Fuck you, man! Is you sick?' Jimmy said violently. 'I ain't lettin' them send me to no electric chair. I'm havin' trial and sentence right here, so you can forget it.'

'You can't get away, Jimmy; they're all around the place! Act like you got some sense, baby—'

'Act like *you* got some, *baby*!' Jimmy made a sudden move to emphasize his words and shut his eyes with the pain. When he could see again, Jackie was moving toward him. 'Back up, goddammit!' he shouted. 'Git off me!'

Jackie did so quickly. Then: 'What's the matter, Jimmy? You sick?'

'Naw, I ain't sick – I'm wounded. They got me in the arm.' He sounded proud.

'You need a doctor—'

'Lay off! I don't need nothin' but to git away. And soon's it's dark I'm makin' it, too.'

They fell silent again. Jackie nervously G.I.ed his cigarette, remembering, it seemed, better times, for he smiled.

'Jimmy,' he said presently, 'listen to me, please. This ain't the end of the road for you. You got your whole life ahead of you yet. Don't throw it away; you don't have to throw it away. I'm not sayin' you won't go to jail, but you sure ain't gotta go to the chair. You can start over, baby, you're young, you got a good chance.'

Jimmy looked at him contemptuously. 'You a fine one to talk about throwin' life away. Look at you! A bum! I used to look up to you – ain't that a bitch? I used to look up to *you*!'

'I know,' Jackie said softly. 'I know I disappointed you and a lot of other people, too. But don't use that as an excuse to throw your own life away. Give yourself a better break than I did, Jimmy. Please.'

'I'm givin' myself a break. I'm goin' out like a champ; the way a down stud s'pozed to.'

'No good, Jimmy. That ain't where it's at. What you think is down is nothin' but bein' foolish.'

'Ain't nobody go' say I went out like a punk. Ain't nobody go' say I wasn't cool. No cop-outs. You ain't go' make me cop-out – forgit it, man!'

Jackie offered him another cigarette. 'It's no good, Jimmy. Sure, you might impress some stupid people by what you're plannin' to do, but you'll die and they'll call you a fool and forget about you in a month. I wanted to impress people, too. I used to think it was the hippest thing in the world to smoke pot, talk slick, and have everybody say I was down. Ain't nothin' in that bag, Jimmy, believe me, I know. Do you want to know the real reason I left school? I was kicked out. I thought my ball-playin' was secondary to my personality, and that even if I couldn't hold a ball I could get by for myself alone.'

Jimmy squirmed uncomfortably, listening but wary. Jackie went on: 'I was in the toilet at college showin' everybody what a cool cat I was. Six of us, smokin' pot. Somebody smelled it and called a prof who took our names. Me, bein' raised in the so-called hip atmosphere of this neighborhood, I figured it was best if only one of us took the weight to save the rest from punishment – what I didn't know was that if I'd kept my noble, big mouth shut none of us would've been punished. But, since they had a pigeon – me – they used it. Brave, hip, take-the-weight me!'

He was deep in thought as he lighted another cigarette. He gave Jimmy another, though he hadn't yet finished the last. 'I know now that I wasn't bein' brave or hip: I was only tryin' to impress people, be a martyr. All of us around here wanna be a Jesus and take somebody's guilt on ourselves. It's part religious trainin' and part wantin' to be a "thoroughbred." Well, it don't happen that way, Jimmy. In the real world it's every man for himself. Self-preservation is for real among people who got somethin'. I should've kept my mouth shut. And when nobody took any notice of what I'd done for them, I finally said to hell with the world – but I still didn't look out for number one the way I should've, I existed on pride, poor pride. You're lookin' at the result of it, Jimmy. Don't be like me, don't be like *us*. Take my word: bein' classified as a hip thoroughbred by poor, doin'-bad niggers is not worth throwin' your life away for. Yeah, they'll call you boss people, but they won't do a damn thing for you but forget you as soon as possible. Once in a while your name'll pop up in conversation and they'll talk about you with lovin' reverence; then you'll be forgotten until the next time they can spare a thought for you. That's all you'll get, Jimmy.'

Jimmy looked at him sullenly. This was almost the jive the bum in headquarters had said to him. All the bums seemed to know everything about life except how to live it, he thought. Winos knew all about what was wrong with the world. Knew how to separate the sugar from the shit, yet they wallowed in the shit like it was the sugar. What qualified them to know so much? If they knew so much why weren't they rich?

'Awright,' Jimmy said in an accusing tone. 'So you got kicked outta school, but that wasn't what made you a bum. You still had a good job at the Boys' Club, but you blew that too. I remember you tellin' me about that fair-play business, and all the while you wasn't nothin'. You ain't nothin' but a whole buncha words and they ain't nothin', neither. What the hell can you tell me?' He turned away from Jackie angrily, remembered his situation, and faced him again.

Jackie said: 'I'm still tellin' you that it ain't no good to try and impress people unless you got somethin' real to impress them with. Don't do it just for the hell of it. You think any of those guys I took the weight for would help me out now? None of 'em ever even spoke to me after that. Don't try to do anything for people, Jimmy. Don't live or die for them, because they don't give a damn for you! Understand – *they don't give a damn!* Look out for number one, that's all.'

It was plain to Jackie that he wasn't getting through. The boy was hurt, afraid, and thoroughly disillusioned with him, especially with him. The eyes that had at one time placed him on a level with God now reflected only contempt for him. There appeared to be nothing that could change that.

They talked – or rather Jackie talked – about basketball and how he planned to straighten himself out soon and move to another town, maybe all the way out to California. He put forth the idea that perhaps Jimmy, when he got out of jail, could come live with him. They could both make a new start.

It was no good. Jimmy didn't want to hear him and couldn't believe in him any longer. The fifteen minutes that the police had given him was just about up. The only thing to do was to get the gun from the boy. Because of the distance between them and the darkness, Jackie didn't know how he'd manage it. Yet he couldn't let this young fool get himself killed. It was almost his fault that Jimmy had come to this.

'Another smoke?' he asked. Their time as surely up by now.

'Yeah,' Jimmy replied. A noise came from the hall; Jimmy jumped and hurt his arm again. Moaning, he grabbed at it.

Now! Jackie's mind screamed. 'Here, catch!' he said and threw the pack with a high arch. Jimmy had to stop it with his gunhand. As he raised it, Jackie jumped at him. He'd thought that he had moved fast, temporarily forgetting that his athletic reflexes were long since shot.

The loud report of the gun seemed to shake the very foundations of the building. Jimmy's face was as full of surprise as Jackie's. He'd never meant to pull the trigger, never meant to shoot Jackie. It had happened automatically.

In the following seconds they stared wide-eyed at each other, mouths open. One was holding the smoking gun and the other his bleeding chest, which seeped blood generously through his splayed fingers.

'You shot me, Jimmy!' Jackie gasped unbelievingly. 'You shot me!' He swayed drunkenly for a moment, staggered a few steps backward, and then fell forward on his face, dead.

Jimmy's body became a jerking heap as sobs took control of him. He stared down at the body. 'You shouldn'a tried nothin', you shouldn'a tried nothin'. I told you, Jackie! I told you, I told you . . .'

A shout from outside pulled him back from the edge of hysteria: '*Hey, Brown! You okay up there?*' When there came no reply the voice shouted again. This time Jimmy went to the bannister, looked over it and yelled in a croaked voice:

'I killed him! I shot him dead! If you don't go away and leave me alone I'll kill you too!' He was screaming now: 'Leave me alone! Leave me alone!'

He ran back into the apartment and tripped over Jackie's body. A low groan emanated from the back of his throat. Pain, pain . . . it seemed that his every nerve was being scraped with a file . . . his arm, his side, his head. Everything he even looked at hurt, but to shut his eyes was as painful. Out of blind rage he kicked the body away from him, then slumped down beside it, staring, moaning, 'Momma . . . Momma. Help me, Momma . . .'

It was getting darker. He knew they'd make their move soon. He checked his gun: three bullets left. Sy had shot a cat with it when they first got it, leaving five, and he'd used two. But the cops didn't know how many bullets he had – or guns, for that matter.

He still lay on the floor, but calm now, waiting and ever on the alert. His hand was sticky from the blood covering his left side. A small, drying puddle of it was on the floor next to him. The hot irons of pain still clung to him. He was dizzy and light-headed and had fainted several times, but only for seconds each time. The blood on the floor frightened him because it looked like so much – a gallon at least.

A crash somewhere downstairs made him jump. Someone cursed – probably stepped through a rotten place in the floor, he thought. Every sound they made down there reverberated agonizingly through his head. They were on the floor below him, but he had nowhere to go. He yearned to tear those boards from the skylight and be free. But he only had one arm. Four flights up and no place to go, no place to hide.

It was so hot and close in here. So hard to breathe. He could feel where the blood was soaked through his pants and made them stick to him in places. Carefully, as if he were afraid of disturbing the dead man, he got up. Feeling that he was on the verge of passing out again, he shook his head, and shooting stars raced maddeningly around him.

Then, when his head cleared, everything seemed to move about as if in a slow-motion dream. He wondered what his mother would say when she heard about this. She was probably sitting in some damned church; that's where she usually spent all day Sunday. Her and the rest of that fat-assed holy crowd she hung around with ran from church to church. She was praying and shouting and singing while he sat here in all kinds of trouble.

He smiled briefly. Dee Dee, that new chick he'd pulled: she would be impressed. Jackie was wrong. Didn't know what the hell he was talking about. That's why he was a bum.

If only he had somebody to talk to. He felt so alone, like he was the only person in the world, despite the cops downstairs and the noise of the crowd which had gathered outside. He'd never felt so alone in all his life. Why didn't they do something? He couldn't stand this quiet, this being alone in the dark with a dead man.

He gave a little cry of pain and discovered that he hugged

himself. He put the gun on the floor; it was as if a great weight had been taken from him.

Somebody was on the stairs! Coming up to his landing! He jumped up and almost lost his balance as a dizzy spell hit him. He got himself together quickly and picked up the gun. *They were closing in!* He dropped the gun and when he bent to pick it up he couldn't find it. The moan began in his throat. Where was it! Where was the goddamn gun! His hand rubbed wildly over the rough floor, hit the gun, and sent it skidding up against Jackie's body. Jimmy finally retrieved it.

When he looked out of the door it was just in time to see a figure dart across his line of vision, then another. He began to cry, but not out of fear now. His heart beat frantically and the pulse in his temple leaped. He backed away from the door with his knees feeling as if they were about to collapse. The blood ran from his wound but he didn't notice. He got down behind the footlocker and lifted its lid to give him greater cover. Now James Cagney was ready. Let the bastards come.

A cop kicked the door open and fired blindly into the room's darkness. Jimmy fired at the flash. He heard a grunt and the thudding of a body.

'Come on, you cocksuckas!' he shouted at the top of his now feeble lungs. 'I'll kill you all!' No more tears now for anything; he wiped them away. James Cagney laughed and fired at another figure that silhouetted itself in the doorway a second too long. This time his shot was answered by a scream: 'Yow! My leg! I'm hit in the leg!'

'Kill ya, goddammit!' Jimmy shouted. 'Kill ya all! C'mon!'

Three shots rang off the footlocker. He laughed at them, just like James Cagney. Another figure was trying to pull the first one out of the way.

Jimmy had forgotten everything except that he was James Cagney shooting it out with the cops. There was no sense of danger now; no fear. He forgot to be afraid. He was free. He forgot the amount of ammunition he had; why he was even here. It didn't matter, this was glory. He was Cagney – he was better than Cagney. He was what Cagney only pretended to be! He was real. He forgot about Butch and Sy and Brother.

He forgot about Sy's mother and his own. He forgot Dee Dee and Jackie Brown – that bum was dead two years already.

He'd also forgotten about the back bedroom window, and when the impact of a bullet smashed into the back of his neck he was more surprised than Jackie had been.

His head snapped violently; he was almost thrown over onto his left side. The room became sunshine-bright for an instant and then plunged into darkness. His reflex made his finger jerk the trigger, which sent his last shot zooming into the baseboard of an obscure corner of the room. He tried to scream, but could hear no sound except the re-echo of the booming thud of the bullet that had hit him. His face was against the floor and he smelled the rotted, warped wood.

Someone's feet were in front of him, the person was bending down. He rolled his eyes up to see who it was but couldn't.

'You ain't dead yet, little nigger?' Slim McNair said, his eyes pouring hatred all over Jimmy.

Jimmy tried to speak, to curse, but the blood gurgled in his throat and choked him and spilled over his lips. He kept hearing an extremely loud noise that reminded him of the ocean. It was his own breathing. He saw Slim put the gun close to his face; he smelled the burnt powder; his mind screamed: *'He go' shoot me again!'*

He didn't hear the report, just saw the infinitely short flash of light and felt the tremendous rush of hot stream engulf his head and spread immediately over his whole body. There was just the hint of pain ... then darkness. He actually sees the darkness coming toward him, rolling over him in the swelling motion of waves ... he feels himself lifted by it and he rides on a calm, soothing sea ... It seems that very far off, farther than the horizon, a pinpoint of red is coming toward him ... its speed is such that it looms upon him before his senses can realize how close it is ... it grew so! It shakes him until he feels like his limbs are torn from his body ... then it passes and the darkness comes again with its smooth quietude. It is a warm, comfortable bed in winter's cold ... He snuggles under its cover with grateful relish.

Slim McNair went to the door and called out: 'C'mon in. I got the little punk.'

Sixteen

It was Friday, almost a week since the deaths of Jackie and Jimmy, and Hip hadn't been home since Tuesday.

He hadn't been near the job Franchot had held for him either, and it was given to someone else. Franchot found that he was more relieved than disappointed at this confirmation of his suspicions. But his relief was tinged with guilt: he'd come little by little to suspect that he'd only offered the job to Hip so that he could see more of Gypsy Pearl; he couldn't remember having had any intention of asking Hip to move back into the apartment until he'd met her. In fact, he'd just about given up on Hip; but one look at her and he'd generously asked his brother to come home. It was all pretty obvious.

Several times during those days of Hip's absence Franchot had been tempted to ask Gypsy Pearl why she hadn't mentioned the people who'd come to the apartment. He knew for sure now that they were junkies; people who knew them had told him so – he even knew their names. But he didn't put the question; he was afraid she might lie. Finally he managed to convince himself that if anything wrong had gone on, she would have told him. So, if it was true that junkies had been there, the shooting gallery part was untrue. It had therefore not been important enough for her to bother him with it.

Rosemary was on the scene whenever Franchot was home – openly suspicious and possessive, and increasingly irritating to Franchot. Gypsy Pearl, however, seemed quite unconcerned about her; she was just happy to be there, to stay in the apartment every night, not to have to go out and hustle. She missed Hip – it was impossible not to, he'd become such a fixture in her life – but at the same time it was a relief not to have to put up with him.

None of them went to Howard Street, but Irene Smith – the street's newest whore – had told Rosemary that Hip was there every night with Anna Mae Poole. As much as she wanted to gloat aloud over this infidelity to Gypsy Pearl, Rosemary kept it to herself: if Franchot knew that Hip had another woman, it might be all the encouragement he needed to take up with her himself. Not that Hip would necessarily put Gypsy Pearl down on account of Anna Mae – many pimps had more than one whore, and Hip was as greedy as any – but Franchot might see it differently. Rosemary loved him and was determined to fight for him.

During the first nights of Hip's absence, fighting for Franchot meant giving him and Gypsy Pearl no opportunity to be alone together. By Friday her pride was telling her to be a brave lover or none at all. This was right, it was good. She would pit her attractiveness against any other woman's. She had to risk it sometime; and her nerves wouldn't be able to stand their strained threesome much longer.

So Rosemary stayed upstairs in her own apartment Friday night, to the surprise of Franchot and Gypsy Pearl, who'd come to regard her as an ever-present jailer and nuisance. They ate dinner, expecting her to come barging in at any moment. They washed the dishes, expecting her, and they sat together in the living room, expecting. It was eight-thirty and she hadn't come.

Gypsy Pearl decided to take a bath, and Franchot began reading a book he'd bought a month ago. She joined him in about an hour and he asked if she wanted to watch television.

'No, not particularly,' she answered. 'What's that you readin'?'

'Oh, just a novel I can't seem to finish for the life of me. Thought I might wade through it tonight, but now that I got it, I know I can't. Too deep for me – all that psychological stuff, y'know.' He stood and stretched, then let out a loud grunt as a sharp pain caught him in the back. He placed both hands at the small of his back like an old man with rheumatism.

'What's the matter?' she asked worriedly.

'Aw, it ain't nothin'. A little pain in my back. Probably strained it on the job. Been botherin' me lately.' An idea came to him: 'I think maybe I oughta go around to that place on Howard Street and git me a massage. Them back plasters sure don't do no good ...' He left the statement hanging and cursed himself for being so obvious. She knew as well as he that few, if any, blacks went there. Even though it was in the heart of the black-belt, it catered to whites. He couldn't remember ever seeing a black man go inside unless it was to deliver something.

She saw through his subterfuge, and without even a knowing smile, said, 'Ain't no sense spendin' money for somethin' I can do for free, Franchot.'

'You can massage?'

'I sure can. Take off your shirt and I'll show you.'

He removed his shirt while she went to get the rubbing alcohol from the medicine cabinet above the kitchen sink. He lay face down on the sofa, and when she came in and saw the broad expanse of his brown, well-muscled back her hands became prickly in anticipation.

The tension between them rose fast as she sat down beside him, opened the tall bottle, and spread the cold fluid as evenly as she could over his back. It was not so much from the cold that flesh-pimples rose so rapidly on his skin, but from her touch.

All week long they had hardly spoken, except perfunctorily. Jimmy Johnson and Jackie Brown had provided their chief topic of conversation, mainly because they were afraid to talk about what really concerned them: Hip's disappearance and its apparent connotations.

They didn't talk now. She gently rubbed his back and could almost hear him purring. 'Ah, that's good,' he murmured.

Her hands, soft and skilful, moved slowly up and down, up and down. She smiled, contentedly, secretly, at his averted head resting on the blue silken cushion. Forgotten were Hip and Rosemary; her arrest and release; Jackie and Jimmy. Everything but themselves at this moment was forgotten.

'Hmmmm! Girl, you sure got some educated fingers,' he muttered.

'Your back is a good teacher,' she whispered.

He felt himself becoming heated, growing large under her caressing hands. He knew that if this kept up much longer he'd turn over, grab her and . . .

But he didn't turn over. He lay there instead and suffocated in pleasure. The guys on the job really had something when they bragged about their wives doing this wonder to their backs. He wasn't angry at her anymore; wasn't even a little resentful. His feeling for her swelled within him. She must have felt it, too. It certainly must be communicating itself to her via her fingers, hands, arms. His back was burning now with her passion-filled touch.

Without really meaning to, he suddenly turned onto his back and looked up into her face. His was full of the naked want of her. Innocently, she asked, 'What's wrong, Franchot?' as if she hadn't known.

'You ain't his slave, you ain't his woman – no more! I don't care about nothin'. You just ain't!' His voice was very hoarse. He grabbed her by the shoulders and pulled her down to him.

A jumble of disturbing thoughts raced through her mind as their kiss lingered. She was not as caught up in the moment as she'd anticipated. She was thinking that he was here with her only because she hadn't been honest with him, she had obtained him under false pretenses. His feelings were so plain while hers weren't as yet defined clearly. For if hers had been she would have told him the truth about Hip and the junkies he'd brought to the apartment again on Tuesday afternoon. Why couldn't she tell? Why? Why? What sort of perverse loyalty to Hip was this? Some wit had said that the loyalty of a whore was a virtue that virgins, in their ignorance, never attained. But what sort of loyalty was this that destroyed her chances to love a man she really wanted to love!

She was also afraid. Not for herself so much as for Franchot. She knew Hip well and remembered Red Shirt Charlie. Hip was capable of provoking a fight with Franchot – and both were the type who'd rather die than have something they considered theirs taken away from them. If she said yes to Franchot a fight would be almost inevitable.

210 | Nathan C. Heard

The kiss was fulfilling; but her mind was so cluttered. This was where she wanted to be; where she belonged, with this man if she must belong to someone. Oh, she felt it down to her toes!

When they finally broke the kiss she was trembling and out of breath, quivering and melted inside. She laid her head on his chest and he felt her wet tears.

'I love you, Franchot. God, I love . . . love you!' She kissed his chest.

He buried his face in her hair. A hint of roses was there and he took the scent into his depths. Then he lifted her head and kissed her eyes, her cheeks, her full, moist lips, and her beautiful, symmetrical nose. Her hair fell around his face.

His hands roamed the soft knolls of her body until the tension exploded around them and from them. His hand found her soul and she parted her robe and her body. His fingers came ever inward to the center of her sensitivity, to the yielding, succulent, sweet marshland of her being.

Her voice whispered soft yeses, affirming his right to her. This was so real, so real; but she was fearful of opening her eyes for fear that she'd find herself in the embrace of a Howard Street trick. Even now she couldn't entirely forget who she was, couldn't lose herself in love.

This was the time to decide, the moment to give all to and for love; now was the *now* to become a woman, full-grown and complete.

Someone knocked at the kitchen door. They jumped apart, disheveled, eyes misted and smoldering in passion. They couldn't pretend that no one was home because the kitchen light was burning brightly and the door was half glass. She straightened herself while Franchot, mumbling, put on his shirt and went to answer the door.

It was Rosemary. Franchot decided then and there that something would have to be done about her. She was a nice woman and all that, but he wanted Gypsy Pearl, and come hell or high water, Gypsy Pearl was the one he was going to have.

'Rosemary,' he said sternly, 'I don't know what you think you doin', but I want you to stop it right here and now.'

'What you talkin' about, honey? I ain't done nothin',' she said with open-faced innocence. 'What's that smell? – alcohol?' she asked, sniffing the air.

He told her that he'd rubbed his legs with it, and was instantly sorry that he'd felt the need to lie. 'Dammit, don't play stupid with me,' he said, getting back to the cause of his irritation. 'You been sneakin' around tryin' to catch me and this woman doin' somethin' and I'm gittin' mighty tired of it!'

Alone with him, Rosemary might have been cowed. But there was Gypsy Pearl, not only the woman with whom he'd betrayed her, but a witness to her response now. She was aware of the subservient positions whores assumed with their men, and to prove that she was a woman of independence, a cut better than Gypsy Pearl, she hotly retorted, 'Who you talkin' about sneakin'? Don't you call me no sneak! If you don't want me to come down here when you and this, this *person* is alone, then, dammit, say so!'

'Did I say that? All I said was—'

'Well, that's what you meant!' she interrupted. 'You don't have to pretend – and if you think I don't know what's goin' on between y'all, then, mister, you got another think comin'!'

Franchot looked dumbfounded, trying to speak, but her outburst, so unfamiliar, caused him to sputter only.

'Go right ahead and lie!' Rosemary continued. 'Tell me to my face that ain't goin' on between y'all. Go ahead, I dare you, Franchot Ritchwood!' Then she wheeled to Gypsy Pearl. 'Is you gon' deny it, you half-white bitch?' Abruptly she lowered her voice, fighting to keep control of herself. 'One of y'all, *please*, just have the nerve to tell me to my face that ain't nothin' goin' on. I'll believe it, I swear I'll believe it if y'all feel the need to keep lyin' about it.'

Both looked at her but neither spoke. Franchot was truly concerned, and showed it; but Gypsy Pearl had an amused half-smile.

'Well, thanks for the truth. Thank God for the truth,' Rosemary said, giving Gypsy Pearl a brutally cutting glare. 'Whores *can* tell the truth, too – even when they's fuckin' a whole family, can't they? But they can't be nothin' but whores in shape, form, or fashion! When they gits tired of one member they just slide in bed with the other, as nice as you please. I bet if their daddy was alive he'd be next on your list, wouldn't he, whore?' She was crying now and caught her breath to say more, but Franchot intervened.

'You wrong, Rosemary. You done said just about enough. Now hush it up or git outta here.'

'That's what you'd like me to do, ain't it? Well, nigga, you got your wish!' She started for the door, turned, and said, 'When that tramp gits tired'a you – and, believe me, she *gon'* git tired – and your sense come back from wherever it done took a vacation, just come upstairs. I damn sure ain't comin' to you no more!'

'Wait a minute!' Franchot shouted. She stopped. 'You listen to me, woman. You ain't got no reason to act like this.' He didn't want to hurt her, but he couldn't bring himself to lie outright. He wished Gypsy Pearl would say something. Finally he blurted out, 'I want you to apologize, Rosemary. You ain't got no claims on me and I ain't got none on you, so quit actin' like a cheated wife.'

'Is *that* what you wanted me to wait for? I'd drop dead before the words got outta my mouth. You'd better be glad I ain't your wife, 'cause if I was, you and her'd be dead niggas by now – not for what you doin', but for thinkin' I'm damn fool enough to believe you ain't doin' nothin'.' She was disgusted, shaking with rage and outrage and an utter sense of defeat.

Franchot was trying to make himself angry and not wholly succeeding. He knew one thing for sure: Rosemary was not going to be easily pacified. 'You know how I feel about you, Rosemary, but if you keep runnin' off at the mouth I'ma put you outta here.'

'*Put me out!*' she exclaimed. 'You ain't said nothin', man, like, I'm *gone!*' She stalked out, slamming the door behind her with such violence that the glasses on the sink rattled.

They listened to her running footsteps on the stairs. He went to the door, opened it, and shouted after her, 'When you ready, I'll accept your apology!' Her apartment door banged shut.

He closed the door, and he and Gypsy Pearl stood looking at each other for a long time, not speaking, not moving.

Franchot smiled nervously, guiltily. She did not smile back. She was thinking that it all had been too much; she wasn't used to this sort of thing, and she was exhausted. She'd never before been responsible for hurting anyone as Rosemary had been hurt.

If she and Franchot were to have each other, it wouldn't be now. She was grateful that he knew it too.

Seventeen

Friday night, and Howard Street was celebrating as usual. It seemed that everyone had decided to spend their paychecks and hustling money in the M&M. The joint was jumping, fags, lesbians, squares, and all. Outside, the night was mild and the soft summer wind smelled remarkably sweet.

Hip sauntered out of Mann's Manor with Anna Mae Poole hanging on his arm. They started over to the M&M to join the gay set. He was feeling particularly good because word had come from Martland Medical Center that the man he and Gypsy Pearl had robbed was going to be all right, though he had lost a lung. Hip was as happy as if someone had offered him a speedball.

Anna Mae, still Brady Torrence's woman officially, had been giving Brady good money, but Hip took a nice piece from her himself. He suspected that she gave it to him to alleviate the guilt that Tricky Dick had made her feel for giving money to a white man. But he didn't care what the reason was, and cared less for her feelings – he got it and everything was crazy. Any time she could get away from Brady, and especially when he went up into the white neighborhoods to line up weekend tricks for her, she sought out Hip. To swing out with him showed that she was still a 'soul-sister' and dug her own kind.

'Oh, *sister, do* it! *Shake* that thing, baby. Shake it where it *hurts!*' Lillie was shrilling when they entered. His shrieks and hand-clapping were to encourage Too Loo, who danced in the middle of the room, whirling and shaking that thing to the jukebox's exciting sounds of Dizzy Gillespie's 'Manteca.' Both fags were interpretive dancers by profession, and Too Loo was almost as good as Miss Curtis, the queen of interpretive dancers, who was so beautifully womanlike that he modeled female clothes and appeared in fashion magazines.

Hip and Anna Mae had to wait until a couple headed for Sue's before they could get seats at the bar. It was so crowded that the back room had been opened up. Fat Mose, the bartender, had to call his wife, Angel Pope, to come help him handle the business.

Sadie Tucker was in the back, looking very sick. Back there, too, were Bill Grumsley, Big Frieda, Bunny Scotia, Red Shirt Charlie and his crowd of big-timers. Emma Dee, looking mad at the world; Dennis Warrent hanging near the jukebox; Stanley White, still crying drunkenly over the loss of his drinking partner Jackie Brown. Big-feet Roland was with Snag and Sweet Possum; Fish-Man Floyd was with Boosting Margaret; Moochie, the meanest butch-broad around, was having an argument with Sis Domingoe over Cotton Alice. Gorgeous, stacked Mommy sat looking lovely and stupid while Joe Magic tried his level best to get her drunk enough to say yes to his insistent pleading; Tal Murphy sat out front with Irene Smith.

Emma Dee was mad at the world because Mommy, angry at Sue for refusing to let her have a room with Danny Darden, had told Emma Dee about Sue and Slim McNair. Emma Dee was furious at Pop – her name for Slim – and had given Red Shirt every cent she'd made tonight. This was the best way to hurt Slim, but she still wasn't satisfied. She didn't want to merely hurt him, she wanted to destroy him.

The music ended and Too Loo, executing a smooth pirouette, fell dramatically into a graceful heap on the floor. He smiled demurely at the loud applause, got up and brushed the dirt from his slacks.

'Miss *One!*' Lillie exclaimed enthusiastically. 'Chile, I'm here to say that you're simply *de-vine!* Oh, too, too much! You per*formed*, dahling; Miss Curtis couldn't have done better. Mother's *proud* of you!' He turned to Jorge, who was still clapping, and said in mock jealousy: 'Sweetie, don't clap *blisters* on your hands. How on *earth* do you expect to squeeze mother the way she likes it if you have *bli*sters!'

Hip was having a ball. He hardly thought about anything except having a good time; least of all had he given much thought to Gypsy Pearl, Franchot, or the job he hadn't gone to get. The only sour note had come last Tuesday, when he'd had to smack Gypsy Pearl again for remarking about the junkies he'd brought to the apartment. He promised himself that next time he brought her to Howard Street he'd make her spend the entire night tricking Sadie Tucker style: standing on the corner waiting for slow-driven cars with white faces peering through the windshields looking for a woman. He wouldn't even let her sit in one of the bars for a rest; he'd keep her out on the street until everything closed for the night. Then he'd take her to Red Tower, buy her a hamburger and a cup of coffee, and send her home walking. A man had to show a bitch who was boss. As loose in the head as Mommy was, he thought, even she seemed to be wrapped tighter than Gypsy Pearl. At least she didn't question her man's every action . . .

The whiskey flowed, the music swung, the money flew fast across the bar. The butch-broads danced with their women and the fags had their men and it was 'let the good times roll.' Cowboy came in with Slick Billy-A and Baby Lawrence. In a rare gesture of goodwill Cowboy ran the bar, and everyone raised their glasses to toast him.

Lillie was getting stoned out of his head on Canadian Club and Jorge plied him with more in order to get him drunk enough to pass out, because he wanted to try Too Loo for the night. The dance had aroused his interest in Too Loo's sexual ability.

Between records Lillie stood up and called for attention. 'I'm going to propose a *per*sonal toast to the generous Cowboy, everyone.' Then he recited:

'Here's to the bull with the great *long* rod,
That *rav*ishing bull, who stuck the cow so *hard*.
Now, if it weren't for that bull with the great *long* rod
– Where in hell would you get your beef, *by God?*

He winked lustfully at Jorge while the crowd laughed and applauded. But Cowboy didn't treat again. He'd only done it the first time because he, Slick Billy-A, and Baby Lawrence had offed the New York dope dealer. They'd taken his money and his dope and sent his pulverized body to Penn Station in a cab. Cowboy felt good about it. He hadn't liked the idea of the man taking his trade away from him. Somebody with good dope hurt his business, and a man couldn't stand for that kind of stuff.

Suddenly, Hip noticed a subtle shift in the crowd's mood. People began looking around in anticipation. It only took him a moment to realize what it was: it was time for a loud-talk session. And no amount of balling could prevent at least one from occurring; in fact, a session constituted much of the concept of a good time. 'Talk loud and draw a crowd' was the motto of the supercool characters. The louder one talked the more the onlookers thought one was saying.

The eyes of the crowd were centering on Tal and Irene. He was posturing like a rooster, rising to the occasion, but she sat in ignorance. She hadn't yet received her indoctrination into the hip life, and Tal knew it was time, knew what was expected of him as Pimp. His reputation depended upon his performance. The whole phenomenon had a double meaning for pimps and whores: an exhibition of freedom and virility for the man, and proof for the woman, through the subjugation of her will to his, that she belonged to someone.

When he felt the moment was right, Tal rose, took a long cigar from his breast pocket, and told Irene to light it for him.

She looked at him half amused, thinking that he was kidding her because he'd spoken loud enough for everyone in the place to hear, and everyone who knew her was aware that she got violently sick on smoke. She couldn't stay one straight hour in a bar because of the smoke, and if she didn't get some fresh air into her lungs she'd have a vomiting fit.

She shook her head at Tal and started to speak, but he grabbed her jaws with one hand, gaping her mouth open like that of a fish, and stuck the cigar into it.

'Bitch, I said light my cigar!' he said forcefully. The bar became immediately silent, the jukebox was stopped; conversations ceased, ready for the night's real fun.

'Tal,' she mumbled around the protuberance, knowing now that he was serious. 'Please, honey, you know I can't take smoke.'

'Okay,' he said, releasing her jaws. 'If you don't wanna light my cigar, then tell everybody what I did to you last night.'

'Tal!' she cried in alarm.

'G'on, tell 'em, I said! Tell 'em how it felt, how you cried when I put all this in your fat behind.' He patted the front of his pants.

'Oooooh!' Too Loo shrilled, 'it should've been *me* driving *that* Cadillac, chile!' The laughter in the place was spontaneous but short. It didn't break the tension.

Tal was smiling maliciously. 'You ain't go' tell, huh? That's two orders from the Black House you done disobeyed. A good whore don't do that, bitch. You need a lesson.' He smacked her softly, just enough to prime his anger. She began to cry.

'You just ain't go' say nothin', is you? Well, since you don't wanna talk, you must wanna puff—' he struck a match and put it to the cigar – 'so puff!' She only held the cigar loosely in her mouth. Tears were streaming down her face. 'Goddammit, woman, I said puff!' he said, his voice rising. He was succeeding in his attempt to get angry.

Fat Mose watched uncomfortably. Though he'd seen this ritual many times before, he found it increasingly hard to take. Irene looked truly pitiful. Few, however, looked upon her with pity, and the Code didn't allow anyone to interfere.

Irene tried to puff. Pop-eyed, she retched and held her stomach.

'If anything come out, bitch, I'ma rub your face in it,' Tal warned. 'Puff harder – I wanna good light.'

The cigar had become soggy with her tears and the mucus from her nose. 'Harder!' Tal ordered. 'Inhale it!' He was really in his glory now. He looked over at the other pimps to gauge the success of his performance.

One of the butches, half in real pity for Irene and partly in an attempt to cement a future opportunity, stepped up to breach the custom of noninterference. In a husky voice she said, 'Whyn't you cool it an' let the babe be, man? Ain't you showed your ass enough?'

He turned to her in a rage. 'You mind your mothafuckin' business, bitch!' he bellowed, and put his hand in his pocket to indicate that he had a knife or gun.

Ordinarily he couldn't have gotten away with this behavior among the butch-broads, but it was a cardinal sin to butt in someone's business, especially a dispute between lovers. The butch turned away without another word. Tal turned back to Irene. 'Puff!' he said sharply.

When she did, the cigar along with her insides shot out like a cannon, splattering Tal from chest to feet. He yelled, 'My suit! Bitch, you done fucked up my clothes!' He slapped her so hard that she flew off the stool and tumbled hard onto the floor.

Derisive laughter broke out. It was a poor pimp whose loud-talk backfired on him; he wasn't so hot after all. As the respect he'd been building collapsed, Tal became nearly insane with anger and cursed Irene with the nastiest words he could think of. He kicked her several times as she hugged the floor. She was too sick to care.

Fat Mose leaped across the bar, scattering bottles and glasses in every direction. He grabbed Tal roughly, lifting him completely off his feet like a toy, and flung him into the arms of the crowd. Then he called Angel Pope and had her take Irene to the ladies' room. Anna Mae Poole went with them.

The show was over. Everyone had been well entertained, and they had something to talk about for another few hours. Tal would go home and change, then he and Irene would make up in some other bar. That was the way it usually went.

Hip's back was to the door, but he knew that something was going on behind him, for the crowd had suddenly grown quiet again. He turned and faced Brady Torrence.

Seeing the look on Brady's face, Hip looked past him and casually took a swig of his soda. He was glad that Anna Mae wasn't with him at the moment. After letting his glance again touch lightly on Brady, Hip turned back to the bar. All of his senses were alert. He could feel Brady's angry gaze on the back of his neck.

Brady wasn't about to let Hip ignore him. After a moment, he walked over and tapped him on the shoulder. 'Tell me somethin', man,' he said, his voice like gravel. 'I hear you been swingin' with my woman.'

Hip turned to him with a smile, sizing him up. Brady was short and powerfully built. A receding hairline shot highways along both sides of his head to meet at the bald circle in back; a reddish brown moustache matched his hair color. Massive shoulders sloped down into well-formed, muscular and hairy arms and hamlike hands. His fighting ability was common knowledge on the street; he'd had to dump quite a few guys to establish his position there. Yet, because he was white, he wasn't respected as a black man who'd only accomplished half as much as he. Like a black man among whites, he was discriminated against, though not to the same degree, and his reaction was similar: he took what they threw at him, grumbled sometimes, but bore it.

Hip finally deigned to answer him – and it resulted in a cop-out. 'Man, I don't even know what you talkin' about. I ain't been swingin' with your chick. I ain't done nothin' but buy her a few drinks.' Then, to save some face, he said, 'Ah didn' mean no hahm, mistuh white folks, suh. Ahm trooly sorry.'

The crowd accepted it with a mild rumble and Hip, relieved, smiled sardonically.

Brady was taken off guard: he'd expected a fight, especially from Hip, who was such a good fighter. But he didn't really want to back Hip into a corner where only a fight would settle things, so he let the mock apology and the cause of it pass with a warning: 'Awright, I'll go for that, Hip. But I'm tellin' you just this once to stay away from her. Cool?'

'Cool, suh,' Hip said.

Just then, Anna Mae came out of the ladies' room with Angel and Irene. She saw Brady as she started over to Hip. She stopped, astonished; her knees almost gave out, then she stood stock-still with guilt written all over her.

'Beat me home,' Brady said in an ordinary tone, but everyone knew by its searing undertones what would happen to her tonight.

Without a word Anna Mae headed straight for the door, amid the crowd's tittering, cackling laughter. Brady's eyes shot daggers into her fast-receding back. He didn't follow until she was out of the door.

'Oh, Miss *Thing*!' Lillie called to Too Loo. 'Where *is* that chile *go*ing in such haste?'

Too Loo replied, 'I don't know, Miss *It*, but she *cer*tainly had to leave from where she *was*!'

'*Dah*ling, I'm telling you that it's just too *too* much!'

'Oh, it *is*, sister dear, it *is*.' Too Loo sneaked a wink at Jorge.

Emma Dee had sat through all the happenings of the evening without cracking a smile. The only thing on her mind as she downed drink after drink was that lying, dirty, two-timing fat bastard, Slim McNair. She was mad enough to eat the whiskey glass. Bunny Scotia had come to sit with her, seeing the morose mood she was in, and had tried to cheer her up. But it was in vain, for Emma Dee's sullenness soon turned into a crying drunk.

'Bunny,' she sobbed, 'he done beat me and put me in jail and, and all the time makin' it with Sue behind my back.'

Bunny listened patiently. There was no other way to help.

'I ain't gon' stand for it,' Emma Dee said, 'I jus' ain't! I'll kill him first. He was probably givin' that bitch my money, too, and Lawd knows she don't need it, do she, Bunny?' Without waiting for an answer she continued, 'I'm gon' git even, you hear? I'm gon' straighten that nigga out for fair! Bunny, you know I wouldn't mind him havin' another whore if he'd let me know about it, but she ain't no whore and he was sneaking behind my back.'

An idea came to her. She got up without saying anything further and started to leave just as one of her regulars approached her. 'Not now, baby,' she said politely. 'I got some important business to take care of.' She walked away without bothering to listen to his protests.

Bunny wasn't exactly happy herself. Big Frieda had given Bill Grumsley some money and was claiming his attention as was a whore's due. Bunny knew she'd have to get a trick soon. She approached the one Emma Dee had left standing in the middle of the floor, but he didn't want her. Too fat, he'd said.

Everyone else in the place seemed to be occupied, so she decided to go to the Howard Bar and pick up something there; couldn't have Big Frieda outdoing her with Bill. She passed close to them on her way out and was treated to a triumphant look from her rival, who quipped: 'It ain't a battle of pussies after all, is it, bitch?' Bunny stopped, looked at Bill. He only gave her an indifferent smile. Then he turned away and she went out.

Hip was wondering if he should go home and have it out with Franchot. He knew that even squares like Franchot had a limit beyond which they couldn't be pushed. But damned if he was going to work on some rich bastard's job, slaving for just enough to live on. That wasn't his idea of good living. Why the hell couldn't Franchot start a construction business of his own? They could be partners then. He could see it now: *Ritchwood & Ritchwood*, or *Ritchwood Brothers Construction Firm*. Now that would be cool. They could give Gypsy Pearl a secretary's job – that way they wouldn't have to pay for one. And she could trick on the side. They'd be rolling in money. The men who worked for them would probably spend half their pay with her, and he and Franchot would split 60/40, because, after all, she was his woman ... But Franchot was such a lame that he'd probably turn down the money she made. That would be all right with Hip, too.

Maybe he should just stay away from Franchot, though he was his brother and all that. He and Gypsy Pearl could go back to their old room ... if he didn't want a job that was his business. *Didn't nobody own him.* If he wanted a swinging life instead of squaring up, who was to say he couldn't have it? Not a damned soul! He didn't owe anybody anything. And if they moved out they wouldn't have to pay Franchot.

It might be better to go back tomorrow while Franchot was at work. But it would have to be in the morning, because Franchot worked half-days on Saturdays.

He walked over to Cowboy, 'Gimme two things, man,' he said.

Cowboy nodded. 'Wait for me outside. You know I'm in shape, don't you?'

Puzzled, Hip asked, 'What you mean?'

'I got the same thing that cat from the Apple had.'

Hip brightened, 'You is! Well, swingin', baby. Hurry up. I'll wait across – better make that three, man. I'll be across the street.'

Before leaving, Cowboy asked Fat Mose, 'Any game tonight, jack? I'm feelin' pretty lucky.'

Fat Mose, who usually ran crap games on Friday night, shook his head. 'I'm havin' one tomorrow afternoon – same place,' he said.

'Shit, man. I feel lucky tonight. I was go' put somethin' on your back – you musta sensed it.' Cowboy laughed.

'You ain't never been able to do nothin' with me and you know it, sucka,' Fat Mose replied with a good-natured jeer. And it was true. No one could remember him having lost badly in one of his own games; and they were as honestly run as Sue's.

'Yeah, well we'll see about that tomorrow, chump,' Cowboy said, before leaving to meet Hip . . .

Emma Dee, in the phone booth at the Howard Bar, looked anxiously around before dialing. Neither the M&M nor Mann's Manor provided the privacy she needed for the kind of call she was making. The Howard Bar was almost empty right now; the crowd would inevitably drift into it later. Competition was no worry to the owners of the three bars, because the Streeters were very democratic with their money. They'd spend just as much in one bar as another.

'Police Headquarters' said a gruff voice on the other end of Emma Dee's line.

She spoke softly into the mouthpiece: 'I wanna talk to somebody about a cop who's livin' off the earnin's of a prostitute . . . That's right, a *po*-lice officer of the law . . . Yeah, I'll hold it.'

*   *   *

Three hours later, Lieutenant Tom O'Brien sat in an unmarked patrol car with two uniformed officers and Emma Dee. They were parked on Mercer Street near West. She and O'Brien were in front, and the other two in back.

She was a godsend to O'Brien. This was the chance he'd been waiting for, and he'd break Slim McNair down to his socks and have him thrown off the force. Everything that an officer of the law was supposed to be, Slim wasn't. He had a nasty attitude not only toward suspects irrespective of guilt or innocence, but toward his colleagues as well.

O'Brien believed that Slim had deliberately murdered Jimmy Johnson. The long silence between shots, the powder burns on the boy's face, were too unusual; especially when the first shot that hit the boy must have rendered him helpless. But this, like many of Slim's antics and the circumstances surrounding them, couldn't be positively proved against him. O'Brien wanted only positive proof against Slim; he didn't want Slim to slip through his fingers and thereby give him a chance to yell about racial discrimination if he went after him again. If only half of what Emma Dee told him was true it would be more than enough to fry Slim's badge right off his flabby chest.

O'Brien's plan was simple: he gave her one hundred dollars in marked money. She in turn would give it to Slim, and when he took it, it would be just too bad for him.

She said that Slim always met her in the alley beside the Divine barber shop, usually around one in the morning, after her peak trade was over. There was little question about him showing up, because it was Friday and Friday was always her best night.

At twelve-thirty they all left the car and walked completely around the block so as not to be seen on Howard Street. She took them to the alley and showed them where they could observe without being seen themselves. She and Slim never went farther into the alley than the other side of the thin door which shut out the street.

O'Brien had one of his men station himself across the street in the shadows of the alley next to the Howard Bar. He was to move in when Slim and Emma Dee entered to make the transaction, and prevent any attempt to escape.

Emma Dee followed her usual pattern. Slim's orders were to wait in the doorway of the tailor shop for him from 12:45 till 1:30. If he didn't show up by then she was free to leave, but she had better not leave a minute earlier than she was supposed to. It was almost exactly one when she stepped into the doorway of the shop and lighted a cigarette. She was late but she knew for a certainty that he hadn't come yet. It was the first time since she'd known him that she'd been late, and she hoped it would be the last.

Slim came at 1:15 and followed her into the alley. Before they were two steps inside he demanded, as usual, 'How much you make tonight?'

'I did good tonight, Pop. A hundred on the head,' she said cheerily.

'That's my girl,' he said. 'No more holdin' back on me, huh? Puttin' your black ass in jail the last time did some good.' He reached greedily for the money. 'Where'd you get all this new money from?' he asked, taking out his lighter for a closer look at it and a suspicious one at her.

She didn't answer. She couldn't, because she hadn't been prepared for questions. What the hell were they waiting for? she wondered.

'I said where'd you get this new money, bitch?' He grabbed her, but just then two flashlight beams hit them with almost physical force. The door of the alley flew open behind them. Slim jumped, reaching for his gun.

'Freeze, McNair! This is Lieutenant O'Brien. Don't you move!'

The flashbeams came closer and Slim put up his hands automatically. The lights blinded him, he couldn't see Emma Dee, but the mixture of surprise and hatred in his face made her turn away from him.

'Lead the way out, Feeney,' O'Brien said, sandwiching Slim between himself and the man he'd spoken to. The light from a streetlamp flooded the alley and O'Brien had the third man pat Slim down and take his gun and a knife he had on him.

'All right, mister pimp, mister juvenile killer, you're under arrest,' O'Brien said. 'It's been a long time coming but it's here to stay. Get going!'

Emma Dee stood on the sidewalk watching in sober fear at the horror she'd brought to her man. She was sorry now and wanted to take it all back. She hadn't really meant to hurt him this bad. 'Wait!' she called out. She walked over to them and stood in front of Slim, who looked down at his manacled hands in stupefaction. She started to speak, to tell him how sorry she was, that she hadn't meant this, that she would testify for him in court, deny everything. But before she could get a word out of her mouth, he coughed up as much phlegm as he could and spat it into her face.

She screamed and raked the right side of his face deeply with her nails. 'You mothafucka you! Your ass gon' git put *under* the jailhouse! I'm gon' testify on you like I was in church!' One of the officers pulled her away as she was still cursing, 'You bastard, you black bastard!'

O'Brien ordered Slim taken to the car and told her, 'You'll have to come along with us, miss.'

'I'll be glad to!' she said, emphatically nodding her head and wiping her face off with a dainty lace handkerchief at the same time. She threw it into the gutter and followed him down the street.

The street had suddenly become filled with people. They spilled out of the bars and houses jeering Slim and – for the first time that anybody could remember – cheering the police. Shouts and comments came from everywhere.

'Ahm sho 'nuff glad they got that dicklicker, man!'

'Hey, Slim! That's what you git for workin' for white folks 'gainst us. Haw, haw, haw!'

'Yeah, they cain't use yo' black behind no mo'! Yaaaaah!'

'My daddy used to say the most prejudiced white man in the world was a nigga with authority. We ain't gotta worry 'bout Uncle Tom Slim no mo'. Hey, Slim! How it feel to be on the receivin' end, you punk mothafucka?'

All up and down the block the people chanted: '*Slim, Slim, Slimy Slim!*' knowing that he hated the name and delighted to be able to use it with impunity. They reveled as they watched him flinch from each 'Slim!' Those closest to him saw the tears in his eyes and laughed all the more and chanted all the louder: 'Slim!'

Eighteen

About nine the next morning, when Franchot was out working, Hip came home. He brought two junkies with him and Gypsy Pearl felt as if her anger would burst her throat; she became so choked up that she couldn't utter a word for a few minutes. She took it out on the clothes she was washing, rubbing with a vigor that could ruin some of the delicate pieces.

One of the junkies, named Little Satch, had recently gotten out of the hospital, having gone there with yellow jaundice contracted from a dirty needle. It had been he who had told Hip about the man at Martland Medical Center.

The other was EJ, a punchy ex-fighter who'd thrown away a really good chance for the middleweight boxing title. He was a lefty who'd switched to a right-handed style and had developed one of the best left hooks in the business. Now all his fighting was with other junkies over who would be first to take off. He'd just come back to the Hill after partying big in New York for a few weeks, where he'd dropped eight hundred dollars. Broke in New York was the same as broke in Newark – but Newark was home.

Hip had met Little Satch and EJ as he was coming through Howard Street this morning on his way to the apartment. They had been seeking a spike and were willing to share their stuff with the person who'd loan them one. Like most junkies, Hip, even though he had dope and in fact had only recently taken off, couldn't pass up the chance for a free fix. So he brought them home with him.

Gypsy Pearl was determined to tell Franchot this time. He only took Hip's nonsense because of her, but now that she'd declared her love for him, surely she owed no loyalty to Hip. Now Franchot could claim her for himself with a completely clear conscience. Rosemary hadn't come to the apartment since her argument with him, and Hip had broken all his promises.

Hip breezed in with Little Satch and EJ, went into the toilet to get his works, and came out looking at her in defiance. 'I don't wanna hear nothin' outta you, hear?' he threatened.

'I didn't say nothin', Hip,' she replied, wanting to curse him, to tell them all to get out. But her anger turned in upon herself because she knew she was incapable of saying anything.

He barked, 'Well, don't. Nary a word,' and walked into the living room. EJ, following Hip, spoke to her. She didn't answer.

She'd done many things for Hip, because he'd wanted them done. Things that she was ashamed of and things that any woman would be proud to do for her man. She'd saved him from numerous arrests; gone hungry so that he could eat and have dope. She'd sold her body and a goodly portion of her soul for him. Stolen clothes for him; sold drugs when he had more than he needed and wanted money. Anything a woman could do for a man she'd done for him. She used to know why she'd done them, but she didn't know any longer, it had all become so mixed, so meaningless.

Franchot had to save her. She couldn't be a whore, a prisoner of Howard Street, all her life. Franchot had to save her. He had to make her tell Hip, once and for all, to go to hell.

She stood in the doorway of the living room watching the three junkies making their preparations. The ritual was interrupted momentarily by an argument between EJ and Little Satch about who would be first – Hip had only loaned the spike, so he was automatically last – and Little Satch, mainly because he was afraid of EJ, finally consented to be second.

Gypsy Pearl watched as EJ tied his belt around his arm while Hip opened the glassine bag, dumped its contents into a bottle cap, added a few drops of water and a tiny ball of cotton after holding a flame under the cap until the dope dissolved, and then stuck the needle into the cotton and drew the liquid into the eyedropper. He handed it to EJ and turned back to dumping another of the bags into the cap. Little Satch had argued successfully against dumping all three bags in at once so that EJ or Hip couldn't get more stuff than he.

EJ was too nervous to hit himself; he had trouble finding

a vein. Little Satch took the spike from him, found a vein, and thumped the needle into it with his middle finger, as if he were flicking away a cigarette. He was so nervous himself that he almost missed the thump. EJ pressed the rubber tip of the dropper and the dope slid slowly into his arm. Immediately his face seemed to fill out, grew calm, like a heavy-lidded mask; his mouth went slack as if he couldn't hold his lips together.

He backed the dope: shooting in slowly, then letting the dropper fill only to shoot it back again. He did this about five times before Little Satch began complaining that he wanted to get high, too. EJ backed the dope a few more times before snatching the needle out of his arm and handing it to Little Satch, who paid him no more attention and began his own fix.

He was very light-skinned, so much so that his veins, or what could be seen of them, showed moldy green through his skin. He'd been using the same veins so long and regularly that his arms were striped with scar tissue. He plunged the needle into his right arm several times and in several different places without drawing blood up into the dropper. Then he took the belt and tied it around his left arm, pulling it tight enough to stop the circulation, desperately trying to make the elusive veins come to the surface. He put the end of the belt into his mouth and rubbed the arm frantically, stuck the needle in again and again. Soon he was sweating. He cursed the arm as if it were a separate entity, as if it were the arm's fault that he couldn't get the needle into a vein. At last he got a hit, and he breathed a sigh of relief as the drug ejaculated into a vein and through his system. It took complete control of him.

Hip connected easily. He was secure and happy because his own stuff was safe in his pocket and he wouldn't have to share it with anyone.

Gypsy Pearl curled her top lip in disgust as she watched him join the others in a nod. Yet, as often as she had witnessed this scene, she was still awed at the serenity junkies achieved with a fix. She remembered that once she'd been tempted to try it herself. She'd bought a bag from Cowboy and hidden it to use sometime when Hip wasn't around. If he'd even suspected she was going to try it, he'd have beaten her – ostensibly to protect her from it, but actually because if she began, there would be less money for his own habit – this she knew. It had taken her a long while to get up her nerve, and finally, when she'd been about to get the bag out and begin the preparations, Hip had appeared—

He interrupted her now. 'Woman, stop standin' there lookin' silly. You seen me git off before!' She hadn't realized she'd been staring. Then, in his dope-whine, he said placidly: 'C'mere, momma.' To the others he said, 'Hey, y'all, looka my sweet chick. Ain't she pretty?'

The same old thing, she thought as she went to him. Whenever he got high he had to let everyone know that he was one up on them because he had Gypsy Pearl, the best whore on Howard Street. Why couldn't she hate him?

He sat up straight and patted her behind, then his knees. She only hesitated a second before plumping herself into his lap. As soon as she was settled, he went into another nod, holding on to her hand like a child who's afraid of getting lost.

—Hip had walked in on her before she'd had a chance to get Cowboy's bag out of hiding. She'd been so nerved up, so edgy, and so startled by his arrival, that she'd looked at him almost as if she'd never seen him before, as if she'd never really noticed before what dope had done to his face, his body, his life. When he left the room again, she took Cowboy's stuff and flushed it down the toilet. She'd never been tempted again.

Looking at him now, she saw that death mask again. He was Hip. He was down. He was with it. He was nothing. He'd traded his manhood for a junkie's dream. Yet she couldn't be sorry for him; he'd never wanted anything out of life in the first place. She looked at EJ and Little Satch. 'None of 'em want a damn thing!'

'What you say, baby?' Hip asked, lifting his head.

She realized she'd spoken aloud. 'I didn't say nothin',' she answered. 'Just hummin' to myself.'

'Oh,' he said and shut his eyes again.

She was the first one to jump when the door came crashing

in. It took the others a few seconds to recognize the narcotics officers with Detective Nazifella leading them.

'The man! The *po*-lice!' Little Satch shouted. Suddenly there was a mad scramble in the room. Gypsy Pearl screamed as she was dumped from Hip's lap onto the floor. He put something into her hand. 'Shove it!' he hissed. 'Quick, shove it!' The cops were busy trying to stop EJ from getting out the window, shut up Little Satch, and deal with Hip's demands for a search warrant. Without even thinking about it she pushed her hand up under her dress, moved the crotch of her panties aside and, holding four bags between her index and middle fingers, placed them expertly within the soft fissure of her body. It took less than five seconds and the cops had not seen her do it. It was not the first time she'd done it to save Hip from a bust. She could, if the dope was found on her, be charged with possession and be faced with a fifteen-year sentence – but that wasn't a whore's worry; it was automatic to try to save her man at all costs.

The largest of the detectives had grabbed EJ by the legs and was pulling him back into the room while another had him by the belt. EJ kicked back so hard that the three of them ended on the floor. The big man pulled his blackjack. EJ grabbed his arm and they struggled, rolling over the other cop and knocking over the coffee table.

Little Satch, screaming like a crazed person, only stopped when Nazifella slapped him across the face and pulled his gun, ordering Hip and him to sit on the sofa.

EJ was getting the best of the big cop, pummeling him so hard with right hands to the body that the man dropped his blackjack.

'Get him!' Nazifella yelled with a smile. EJ was on his feet now. Both men charged him with force that took them toward the window. The glass smashed and cut deeply into EJ's arm. He yelled and seemed to go crazy. With a great reserve of strength he flung them both away and blood from his arm splattered around the room. He punched out with his good arm and caught the smaller cop on the jaw. The man went down, but grabbed EJ's legs while EJ tried to beat him off. The cop, realizing finally what was happening, pulled with all his might and snatched EJ's legs from under him while the big cop threw punches at EJ's head. Now both cops had their blackjacks. They rained blows on his head like trip-hammers until he struggled no more. Then they threw him on the sofa with the others.

Hip said again to Nazifella, 'Is y'all got a search warrant, man?'

Nazifella stood over him and looked down disdainfully. 'Yeah, Hippy-dip, we got one.' He landed his big fist squarely in Hip's face, knocking his head against the backrest. 'Did ya read it good?' Nazifella asked.

Hip was coming forward like a fighter off the ropes. The cop backed a step, brought his gun up and had it level with Hip's eyes. Seeing the gaping black hole, Hip stopped, frozen with his right hand cocked in midair.

'Don't stop, nigger,' Nazifella snapped. 'Keep comin' so I can blow you a new asshole!' But Hip melted back down into the sofa, muttering under his breath.

Seeing that everything was under control, Nazifella said, 'Awright, now that our little fun is over, let's get down to cases. Where is it?'

'Where what?' Hip asked.

'Come off it!' Nazifella said shortly. 'Where's the stuff? Who's got it?'

Silence.

Nazifella promised to let everyone go but the person who had the dope. 'I just want one of you,' he said. Then looking at Little Satch: 'We've been tailin' you ever since you left the hospital, boy. We know—'

'I didn't do it, Mister Nazifella, I swear! I didn't do it!' Little Satch cried. His eyes were wide and sweat dripped from the tip of his nose.

'You didn't do what?' Nazifella asked with a comic raise of his bushy eyebrows. 'Are you going to say you didn't break into that drug cabinet at the hospital after you were released? Because if you are, I'll personally break your neck right here and goddamn now! So tell me, what was it you didn't do?'

Little Satch said no more. 'Awright,' Nazifella continued,

'I'm giving one of you a chance to save the rest – the last chance.' He was still met with silence.

EJ was conscious again and glaring hatefully at the two cops he'd fought with. He took out his handkerchief and futilely tried to stem the flow of blood.

All Gypsy Pearl could think about was Franchot. What would he say! What would he think of her now? He had every right to hate her. It would be her own fault if he did. She looked very worried. The dope between her vulvic lips felt like a hot iron, she was so conscious of it. She thought that if she had to get up it would surely fall out.

'Okay, have it your way,' Nazifella said. 'You're all under arrest.' He pointed to Little Satch with the gun. 'Search him,' he ordered.

Little Satch ducked. 'Please, Mister Nazifella, don't point that pistol at me – it might go off!'

'If we don't find that dope, it just might at that!' Nazifella came back tersely.

They made Little Satch strip in front of Gypsy Pearl, even made him bend forward and spread his buttocks. She turned her head more out of embarrassment for him than modesty for herself.

Nazifella misinterpreted her motive and said, 'What's a whore with your reputation so goddamn bashful about?'

She made no reply to him and kept her head averted while each of them was stripped in turn and searched. The only thing they found were some pills and capsules that Little Satch had taken from the hospital.

This wasn't what Nazifella wanted. He knew that there was some heroin involved in this gathering and he was determined to find it. He turned to Gypsy Pearl. 'Looks like it's you, Miss Twatseller.' He walked over to the phone and called for the paddy wagon and a detail to search the premises. Then, to the other detectives: 'Keep your eyes on her until we turn her over to a matron. Make sure her hands stay in sight at all times.' He said to her: 'We're gonna give you the bucket test, little girl.'

She knew what that meant for she'd had it before when she was picked up with Hip and suspected of having dope: they'd taken her to a matron who'd given her a bucket to urinate in. Many women addicts hid their stuff inside their bodies, and in addition to the bucket test, were made to spread their buttocks and vulvas for matrons to look into.

Nazifella held up the eyedropper. 'This belongs to you, Hippy, and if any drugs are found in this apartment they belong to you also.'

'What you talkin' about, man?' Hip exclaimed. 'If you don't find nothin' on me, you ain't puttin' nothin' on me. This ain't my house, I don't know what's in it.'

Gypsy Pearl turned astonished eyes on him. He was willing to let Franchot go to jail; technically, anything found in the apartment belonged to the one in whose name it was rented, and Franchot could be charged with possession of narcotics.

Hip gave her a terribly threatening look, and she returned it, but she said nothing, though she was tempted to take the dope and give it to the cops. She resolved instead that she was not going to let Franchot take the blame for Hip. No harm would come to him for Hip. She wouldn't allow it. Even if she had to take the possession herself. If Hip tried to put it on Franchot she'd break every rule by which she'd been taught to live and put the blame where it belonged – on Hip . . . and herself. She knew that a good whore never put her man in jail, but this was going too far. Nothing mattered except Franchot's innocence. And hadn't she declared her love for him? Didn't this almost make her Franchot's woman?

Nazifella had guessed that she had the heroin on her, and he also saw the looks that had passed between them. He was hoping she'd give it up so he could charge Hip with the possession, for he knew that she didn't use dope. He'd always had an acute contempt for drug addicts, not because they used drugs, but because of their readiness to sacrifice all human values and human beings for a worthless habit. To him, junkies represented the supreme failure of mankind; all the dignity to which mankind aspired was subverted by the craving of junkies. They hid behind the skirts of their women: their mothers, sisters, wives, or girlfriends. He hated them for this, too. He felt that a man who wasn't strong enough to face the world stripped bare of the superficial strength obtained from drugs and alcohol was not a man at all. He had been on the narcotics squad too long and he'd seen too much. He knew that some of his judgments were much too harsh, that sometimes society created conditions conducive to things like drug addiction and alcoholism; and many times he'd resolved to change his attitudes. But then he'd run across a junkie like Hip, who had only one standard – self-preservation – and he'd be thrown back from his decision to change. It hurt him, too, because in dealing with junkies he was many times forced to adopt their methods and standards. This made him no better than they in a sense, made him as principleless as they – and made him hate them all the more for it.

Like now. He knew that the woman didn't use drugs, but if he found it on her she would have to be charged nevertheless, and the real culprits would go scot-free, except for Little Satch. The eyedropper would be charged to Hip, of course, but if the woman didn't speak up he'd be in the clear of a possession charge, for he certainly would never raise a hand to help her by admitting that it was his, and neither would the others.

When the wagon finally came the men were put into it and a weeping Gypsy Pearl was taken to the detective's car. Hip thought she was crying because she was afraid. It didn't occur to him that she wept for Franchot; what was about to happen to his apartment she felt was her fault for not telling him the truth. For being loyal to something and someone who had consistently proven to be unworthy of it. And because she couldn't do otherwise. She wept all the way downtown.

Franchot returned home at about two o'clock and found the apartment in chaos. From the moment he'd entered his block he had been bombarded with accounts of the big raid, replete with personal gems of knowledge from his neighbors, speculating about what they didn't know. People were glad to have something to talk about, and the atmosphere of the block was almost festive. Franchot entered the apartment and closed the door in the faces of a dozen people.

Every room looked like a hurricane had paid a recent visit

to it. Chairs had been left overturned; dresser drawers spilled their contents onto the floor; cupboards were emptied, their utensils scattered all about. Cushions had been strewn about in deliberate malice. In the bedrooms the mattresses had been left half on and half off the beds; his clothes were every which way; suitcases had been left opened, jars left uncapped with their contents spilled or spilling. Surprisingly, very little, except for the lock on the door, had been broken, but in view of the mess, that was not much comfort.

He got a bottle of beer from the refrigerator, picked up an overturned chair, and sat down in the midst of the desolation, fighting to keep himself calm.

There was no longer any doubt that Rosemary had been right when she'd told him what had been going on in the apartment while he was at work. He felt as though Gypsy Pearl had betrayed him, even though he'd never asked her anything about it. She should have told him of her own volition, if she loved him – if she loved him! Did she? He couldn't be sure. He knew only that he still loved her. Even as he sat here hating everything she stood for, he loved her to desperation. If only she weren't so under the influence of his brother, so dominated by her whorishness, she could be as good a woman as any man could want. She was what he wanted, in any case.

All she needed was to be treated like a woman instead of a whore; to be guided away from Howard Street and the life, or nonlife, it offered. She could be rescued. Her condition was not her fault but his brother's – perhaps even indirectly his own, since it was he who had driven Lonnie to Howard Street. She was not bad or stupid, she was only afraid.

Franchot got up and paced back and forth through the debris, absently setting objects upright as they came into his path, lost in thought. Then he swallowed down the rest of his beer, hunted for his emergency padlock, managed to secure it to the battered hardware on the door, and went to see Meyers.

Franchot hadn't known that she'd taken the weight for the

possession, and when he got to headquarters with Meyers and found out he exploded angrily at her.

'What the hell's the matter with you, woman? Is you crazy or somethin'? You don't hafta take his weight, the police know you don't use no dope and just protectin' him. Tell 'em the truth!'

All she did was cry and shake her head. She didn't even tell him that she wasn't doing it for Hip, but for him.

'For God's sake, why not?' Franchot demanded.

'I can't do it, Franchot. I just can't!' she cried. They sat on a bench on the fourth floor. She threw her arms around him and buried her face in the crook of his neck.

Meyers said calmly, 'Do you want to go to jail, Miss Dupree?'

Without raising her head, she shook it vigorously.

'Well, you will, if you don't tell the truth,' he said. 'I've been warned against trying to get you off and I'm not going to risk my career, especially when there's no need to do so. You would do well to follow my advice as your attorney. These police officers know you're lying, Miss Dupree, and if you continue to, they're going to prosecute you as vigorously as they would the most vicious dope dealer. They will make an example of you and there's nothing I can do about it. Whatever you value most you'd better choose – freedom or prison.' Meyers had already guessed what was going on in her mind and the predicament with which she was faced. He decided to wait and see how things developed before further advising her and Franchot.

Franchot lifted her head and handed her a handkerchief. The lawyer's last sentence stayed foremost in his mind, but he didn't think of her decision in terms of freedom or prison; he thought in terms infinitely more important to him: Which did she want most, his brother and all that he offered, or himself? She had to decide now.

'I'm gon' think about it, Mister Meyers,' she said at last. 'But I – I just can't send Hip to jail – I think I'd rather go myself than send somebody else.'

'No!' Franchot said sharply. 'Ain't no thinkin' to do. You

gotta decide now!' He was angry enough to choke a decision from her.

They fell silent and the minutes ticked by slowly. Meyers called Franchot aside and explained what he thought made her reluctant to decide what she wanted to do, and how, if she did admit that the dope was Hip's, and Hip denied it, the weight might wind up falling on the one in whose apartment it was found. It was hard, he said, to convince a jury that a person living with a drug addict and a prostitute could do so in innocence. Franchot listened closely to him, nodding his head every now and then as he got the fuller picture.

He went back to sit beside her, not thoroughly convinced, however, that anyone would think he had something to do with dope and prostitution. But he said nothing to her.

Finally he got up again and went into the detectives' room. The germ of an idea grew in his mind. If she wasn't forced to decide, everything he'd dreamed of would be lost.

Nazifella came over to him. 'Are you gettin' through to her?' he asked.

'No sir,' Franchot replied. 'That's what I came in here for. I want you to arrest me.'

'What!' The cop looked puzzled. 'Arrest you? What for?'

'Because the dope was in my house. I wanna take my own weight. She can go free and I can make bail. My lawyer's here.'

'Look, Ritchwood, we know about you, you're clean. A decent man. We don't want to hook you with something you didn't do. We know whose dope it was, it only remains for the woman to tell the—'

'Yes, sir,' Franchot interrupted impatiently. 'But I don't want her to go to jail for him, and that looks like what she plans to do. I gotta make her see what she's doin', sir. She ain't gon' say it's his so let's see if she'll say it's mine. I'm askin' you to arrest me. It was in my house.' His face was set in determination.

Hip was brought in just then with a detective trailing him. When he saw Franchot his face lighted. 'Shots, baby! You come to bail me?'

Franchot said nothing and Hip was made to sit down on a bench along the left wall of the large office.

Meyers brought Gypsy Pearl into the room. She sat at a desk while Nazifella whispered Franchot's proposal to the lawyer. Meyers then told her about it.

'No! No, he's lyin'! It ain't his! He's lyin'!' She'd jumped to her feet.

'Well, tell 'em whose it is!' Franchot yelled at her. 'Tell 'em the truth!'

'Shots!' Hip said in surprise. 'You don't want her to tell on me, do you? They'll put me in jail, man. She already up tight, baby, ain't no sense in us goin' to jail when she can go. And especially you, man. You ain't done nothin'.'

Franchot glared at him. 'I ain't goin' for nothin', Lonnie. I'm goin' for somethin'. For bein' a fool, for one thing – but you wouldn't understand. Neither of y'all would.' His glance took in both Hip and Gypsy Pearl.

In a choked voice, she said, 'It was found on me. I'm the one who got the possession—'

'Shut up, goddammit!' Franchot snapped. 'It's his! But since you don't wanna admit the truth, I'm takin' it. Anything found in my house belongs to me – that's the law, ain't it, Mister Meyers?' Without waiting for a reply he said to Nazifella, 'Gimme some statements, sir, I'm ready to sign and you git all this junk over with.'

'Would you sign for the spike they got me charged with, Shots? I mean, since you determined to put yourself in jail anyway, ain't no sense in both of us goin', is it?'

Franchot looked at him, started to say something, changed his mind and said, 'Yeah, Lonnie, I'll take that, too.' Then with heavy sarcasm, 'It sure ain't no sense.'

'Franchot,' Gypsy Pearl began, 'you don't have to sacrifice yourself—'

'Shut up, bitch!' Hip shouted at her.

'That's right,' Franchot taunted, 'You just shut right up like he say. You just do everything he say. This here is more than a sacrifice to me, it's a revelation. You done chose what you want most.' He turned to Nazifella. 'Unless they done somethin' else, sir, I guess you can cut 'em loose. I'm ready.'

Both Nazifella and Meyers had sized up the situation, and even Hip had a vague notion of what Franchot was trying to do. With growing amazement he'd begun to realize the extent of his brother's feelings for Gypsy Pearl, conceding at last that it was more than a desire to get her into bed. Franchot was trying to force her to choose between them. For her, no choice at all would be a choice for Hip.

Hip began to think hard, sizing up the present and future possibilities of this situation. If he offered to take the weight for Franchot before she made a choice, chances were that she'd still be his woman after this was over, and Franchot would still be in his corner. He knew that Franchot wouldn't want a woman who couldn't make up her mind whether she wanted to save him or another man from jail, or sacrifice herself and their chance at happiness by going to jail herself when she didn't have to. With Franchot most things had to be 100 percent or nothing.

Still, he thought, it was a hell of a thing to go to jail; something for a man to think about. Why couldn't Franchot be satisfied with her cunt and not her soul? Why couldn't he understand that she was a whore? Why did squares like him always want to put aprons on bitches like her? She was born for man's use, and any way a man chose to use her was cool and nobody's business but his and hers. The bitch understood that, that's why it was so hard for her to make a decision. She had dreamed for a little while and thought she'd like to be a housewife; that was all right, it was normal. All whores did that now and then, it was expected. But it wasn't for real. It wasn't where it was at. Nevertheless, some chump like Franchot inevitably filled a whore's brain with the useless hope that he was different. That he could marry her and take her away and nobody would ever know about her past – forgetting that he'd know; he would always know. And he would never forget.

Hip realized that the burden was now on him, for she seemed prepared to stand here forever, torn between what she was and what she thought she wanted to be. If he said the word he could have her until another pimp came along. Somebody had to go to jail, and Franchot had the most to lose by going. He himself had very little to lose. The dope would be there when he got out, and so would the whores – beyond a doubt. Besides, he would probably need Franchot again someday. A decision to take the weight would be a sound investment in his future.

Meyers realized that nothing would be accomplished by allowing the woman more time to make up her mind, and he was getting a little impatient with standing around. He had an idea that could clear this whole mess up and nodded to Nazifella to bring Hip outside.

Pulling Hip to one side, Meyers asked, 'Do you have a record?'

'No, and I don't relish gittin' one neither,' Hip said defensively.

Meyers winked at him. 'I believe I can get you probation if you'll listen to me. Everyone knows your brother is innocent. You can get him off the hook. I don't know how close you are but, as a human being, I shouldn't think you'd want a thing like this on your conscience. Now, if you'll confess, I promise to do my damnedest to get you off with probation. And I think you've heard about my ability to get people off. What about it? We can get this mess cleared up quickly.'

Standing near the door Gypsy Pearl overheard them. Her heart soared. If only Hip would do that, it would all be solved. She wouldn't have to send anyone to jail, or go herself. If only he would!

Hip was looking through the door at Franchot while he pondered Meyers' proposal. Franchot kept his face averted. Hip turned to Meyers. 'You really think I can cop probation, Mister Meyers?' he asked.

'I really think so, Ritchwood.'

Hip hesitated, swallowed rather obviously, and walked back into the detectives' room. He hurried to speak before he could change his mind, 'Awright, Mister Nazifella, it was my dope and works.' He felt like crying.

'Will you sign a statement to that effect?' Nazifella asked.

'Yeah,' Hip replied softly. 'Yeah, I'll sign.' He looked at Franchot. 'Will you come see me, Shots?'

Franchot knew he'd lost what he most wanted. Hip had won after all. A smile just barely lifted the corners of his tightly compressed mouth as he looked first at Gypsy Pearl, whose relief and happiness tried to reach out to him, and then at his brother. Finally, he said, 'I don't know what I'ma do, Lonnie, except maybe some heavy thinkin' . . .'

'Shots, baby. I know you gon' find it hard to believe, but this time, when I git out, I'm gon' git myself together. I really mean it this time, bro. I hope God strike me dead right this very minute, if I don't. I'm gon' square up and git a job. I'm through with dope, Shots. I mean it, bro.'

Franchot's expression didn't alter. 'We'll see, Lonnie,' he said flatly. Then he turned and walked toward the door. Nazifella told Gypsy Pearl that she could go too.

She and Meyers caught up with Franchot in the elevator. The lawyer asked, 'Are you going to bail him?'

Franchot didn't look at him as he answered, 'No.'

'Well, then I'll just run along. Oh, by the way, I told him that I'd try to get him probation if he confessed. You are going to retain me, aren't you?'

Franchot looked at him this time. 'No,' he answered again. Meyers nodded and left them alone.

After signing a statement, Hip was put into a cell with Little Satch. EJ had been taken to the hospital.

'Man, you's a fool!' Little Satch exclaimed when Hip told him what had happened. 'Betcha I wouldn't take no weight when I didn't hafta.'

'Shit, I ain't worried,' Hip said confidently. 'I'm probably gittin' probation, anyway. That's what my lawyer said.' He lighted a cigarette. 'Guess who I'm pullin' then?' he added.

'Gimme a smoke. Who?'

'Anna Mae Poole,' Hip said handing him a cigarette. 'Take her right away from that cracker. Yeah, man. Then I'm gon' really stretch out tough. Between her and Gypsy Pearl I'ma have me a Cadillac in no time. Talk about into somethin'! Man, I'll be outta sight.'

'Anna Mae ain't nothin', man. I don't see what you want with her. She triflin'.'

'Oh, she can make a nice taste,' Hip said. 'She just need somebody to put a foot in her behind every once in a while. Somebody with a lotta drive – like me.' He was smiling enthusiastically, as if he were in his Cadillac already.

Little Satch, suddenly irritated, said, 'I don't see what you grinnin' about – we in jail! I know that bitch I got ain't go' lay with me through the bit. Somebody go' pull her, sure as you born.'

'That ain't nothin', man,' Hip said. 'You know the name of the game: Cop and Blow. You lose on this end, but you gain on another. Ain't nothin' to cry about.'

'Yeah. But when you blow ain't no sense shoutin' hallelujah about it, neither. How can you grin when you lose?'

'I wear the same grin when I win, baby – you know where that's at.'

Little Satch took a long drag on the cigarette and let the smoke out slowly through his nostrils, 'Yeah, well I guess you right there. Hey, dig – you think your chick go' lay with you if you git a bit?'

'Don't make no difference if she do or don't. I'll cop her back when I git out. She ain't goin' nowhere.'

'You sure don't wanna blow that, man. That bitch is a gold mine!'

'If I blow, man that's the name of the game. I ain't gon' worry about it. Six months from now I'll be makin' so much that I won't even look back. You dig that?'

'I'm with it,' Little Satch said. He put his sweater under his thin buttocks and leaned back against the wall to catch a nap. Both of them knew that they were going to be sick in a few hours and each was secretly glad that he had someone to share it with.

Somewhere in the cellblock someone was singing a rock'n'roll love song. Little Satch opened his eyes and said in disgust, 'I wonder why every time these dumb mothafuckas git locked up they go to howlin' teenage love songs?'

'Be cool, baby,' Hip said. 'That's just their way of cryin'.'

* * *

In a taxi going back uptown, Gypsy Pearl let her tears of relief flow freely but silently while Franchot sat stiffly at her side.

They had covered half the distance uptown when he turned suddenly to her and said, 'I think you better pack your things and leave. I'll – If you want I'll help you find another place.'

She could hardly believe she'd heard him right. She looked at him in astonishment. 'Franchot! Why? I thought you loved me. I thought maybe now we—'

'I thought you cared somethin' about me, too; about the future we could'a had together. But you threw every thing away back there in headquarters. You still Lonnie's slave, so ain't nothin' for us. Y'see, I don't want no wife who gotta hesitate to decide if I'm worth more than another man and the corrupt way of life he lives.'

'Franchot, you don't understand,' she pleaded. 'It wasn't that way. I—'

'I understand enough to know I been dreamin' foolish dreams. I hope Rosemary got more forgiveness for me than I got for you. I'm sorry, I'm truly sorry, but the fact is that you ain't never gon' be Pearl Dupree, or Pearl anything. You gon' always be Gypsy Pearl, and Gypsy Pearl ain't gon' never abandon Howard Street. She ain't gon' even want to for real. So if we was to try to make it, I don't think it'd be too long before you went back. If there wasn't a Rosemary I guess I'd try, but . . . I don't want the hassle. I'm sorry.'

She felt an icy chill running through her as she softly said, 'You could be wrong, Franchot. I love you and I'd try, I would do anything for you.'

Except choose me! he thought.

They were going up Springfield Avenue, each deep in thought and uncommunicative. Franchot thought about Rosemary and hoped that he could make up for the pain he'd caused her.

Gypsy Pearl began to fully realize that he'd meant what he had said, that there was no forgiveness for her, and, strangely enough, with the realization came resolution and acceptance of his decision. She couldn't do otherwise. He had his values and she had hers. She had tried to measure up to his, and through trying, even though failing, she could understand them. She couldn't live his life, but she could appreciate it, perhaps even more than he himself.

As they passed the old Savoy Theater, a crowd was gathering for a Daddy Grace meeting. They were dressed in gay colors and had happy smiles on their faces. Her eyes were dry and clear; she even managed a smile as she turned to Franchot and placidly said, 'Tell him to let me out at Howard Street, please.'

He nodded, looking out his window.

'And, Franchot?' she said. The cab turned into Howard Street.

This time he looked at her, 'Yes?' They halted in front of Mann's Manor.

'Sometime, when you feel like partyin', I'll give you a reduced rate.' She blew him a kiss, got out of the cab, and walked beautifully into the bar.

Payback Press

Non-Fiction

FIGHT THE POWER
Chuck D isbn 0 86241 720 1 - £12.99 hbk
THE NEW BEATS
S. H. Fernando Jnr. isbn 0 86241 524 4 - £9.99 pbk
BORN FI' DEAD
Laurie Gunst isbn 0 86241 547 0 - £9.99 pbk
BLUES PEOPLE
LeRoi Jones isbn 0 86241 529 2 - £7.99 pbk
BENEATH THE UNDERDOG
Charles Mingus isbn 0 86241 545 4 - £8.99 pbk
BLACK FIRE
Nelson Peery isbn 0 86241 546 2 - £9.99 pbk
BLACK TALK
Ben Sidran isbn 0 86241 537 3 - £8.99 pbk
PIMP
Iceberg Slim isbn 0 86241 593 4 - £5.99 pbk
THE NAKED SOUL OF ICEBERG SLIM
Iceberg Slim isbn 0 86241 633 7 - £5.99 pbk
SPACE IS THE PLACE
John F. Szwed isbn 0 86241 722 8 - £12.99 pbk
SWEET SWEETBACK'S BAADASSSSS SONG
Melvin Van Peebles isbn 0 86241 653 1 - £14.99 hbk (includes CD)

Fiction

BLACK
Clarence Cooper Jnr. isbn 0 86241 689 2 - £6.99 pbk
THE FARM
Clarence Cooper Jnr. isbn 0 86241 600 0 - £5.99 pbk
THE SCENE
Clarence Cooper Jnr. isbn 0 86241 634 5 - £6.99 pbk
WEED & THE SYNDICATE
Clarence Cooper Jnr. isbn 0 86241 718 X - £6.99 pbk
HOWARD STREET
Nathan Heard isbn 0 86241 764 3 - £6.99 pbk
THE HARLEM CYCLE VOLUME 1
Chester Himes isbn 0 86241 596 9 - £7.99 pbk
THE HARLEM CYCLE VOLUME 2
Chester Himes isbn 0 86241 631 0 - £7.99 pbk
THE HARLEM CYCLE VOLUME 3
Chester Himes isbn 0 86241 692 2 - £7.99 pbk

THE LONELY CRUSADE
Chester Himes isbn 0 86241 745 7 - £7.99 pbk

NOT WITHOUT LAUGHTER
Langston Hughes isbn 0 86241 768 6 - £6.99 pbk

ONE PEOPLE
Guy Kennaway - isbn 0 86241 719 8 - £8.99 pbk

UNDER AFRICAN SKIES
Ed. by Charles Larson isbn 0 86241 766 X - £8.99 pbk

INDABA, MY CHILDREN
Credo Mutwa isbn 0 86241 758 9 - £9.99 pbk

PORTRAIT OF A YOUNG MAN DROWNING
Charles Perry - isbn 0 86241 602 7 - £6.99 pbk

GIVEADAMN BROWN
Robert Deane Pharr isbn 0 86241 691 4 - £6.99 pbk

THE NIGGER FACTORY
Gil Scott–Heron isbn 0 86241 527 6 - £5.99 pbk

THE VULTURE
Gil Scott–Heron isbn 0 86241 528 4 - £5.99 pbk

CORNER BOY
Herbert Simmons isbn 0 86241 601 9 - £5.99 pbk

MAN WALKING ON EGGSHELLS
Herbert Simmons isbn 0 86241 635 3 - £6.99 pbk

DEATH WISH
Iceberg Slim isbn 0 86241 710 4 - £5.99 pbk

AIRTIGHT WILLIE AND ME
Iceberg Slim isbn 0 86241 696 5 - £5.99 pbk

LONG WHITE CON
Iceberg Slim isbn 0 86241 694 9 - £5.99 pbk

MAMA BLACK WIDOW
Iceberg Slim isbn 0 86241 632 9 - £5.99 pbk

TRICK BABY
Iceberg Slim isbn 0 86241 594 2 - £5.99 pbk

DOOM FOX
Iceberg Slim isbn 0 86241 762 7 - £5.99 pbk

THE JONES MEN
Vern Smith isbn 0 86241 711 2 - £5.99 pbk

PANTHER
Melvin Van Peebles isbn 0 86241 574 8 - £7.99 pbk

ONE FOR NEW YORK
John A. Williams isbn 0 86241 648 5 - £6.99 pbk

SPOOKS, SPIES AND PRIVATE EYES
Ed. by Paula L. Woods isbn 0 86241 608 6 - £7.99 pbk

Poetry

THE FIRE PEOPLE
Ed. by Lemn Sissay isbn 0 86241 739 2 - £8.99 pbk

Call us for a free **Payback Sampler** which gives you more information on all the titles listed. The sampler also contains extracts from our most recent publications together with information about the authors.

Our books are available from all good stores or can be ordered directly from us:

PAYBACK PRESS, 14 HIGH STREET, EDINBURGH, EH1 1TE
tel # 0131 557 5111, fax # 0131 557 5211
EMAIL info@canongate.co.uk
WEBSITE http://www.canongate.co.uk

All forms of payment are accepted and p&p is free to any address in the UK.